Kiss Me Deadly
By Shannon Stacey

When Khail lays his fatal touch on his next victim and she doesn't die, he's faced with a human immune to his deadly power who has seen him shift form—and he's able to have physical contact with a woman for the first time in centuries.

Falling for a shapeshifting messenger of Death wasn't on Bridget Sawyer's agenda, but things are about to get even more complicated. The Unkind is determined to claim her.

Warning, this title contains the following: explicit sex, graphic language, and non-sexual violence.

King of Prey
By Mandy M. Roth

In a place where realms combine and portals open passages to the unknown, a prophecy speaks of fertility being restored to his people through the taking of King Kabril's mate.

The prophecy neglects to mention she lacks something vital to his kind—wings. Kabril, King of the Buteos Regalis has no interest in taking a human mate. His kind believes humans are dirty, vile creatures who rely on machines to lift them into the air. The last place he wants to go in search of his mate is Earth, but he's left no choice.

Never did he expect to find love on a planet with one moon, people who lack wings and a stubborn vixen who makes his heart soar. When he does, he fears the truth about who and what he truly is will steal it away. Little does he know his enemies fully intend on doing the taking.

WARNING: This book contains hot, explicit sex and violence explained with contemporary, graphic language.

Firebird
By Jaycee Clark

Legend has it firebirds bring both good fortune and destruction, Reen has become an expert at both...

Reen is an expert at destruction and annihilation. She's a Hunter, an elite, one of their best assassins, she's also a legendary firebird—a creature of lore. Saker, a member of the Falcon order, is her soul mate from a bloody past she desperately tries to forget, but one that haunts her every moment. The two are thrown together in a desperate search for missing women.

The Collector is a man who loves the hunt, preying on the unusual, on the special—all to keep these women for his own use. The Collector favors shifters, the rarer the better. He traps them, keeps them, and turns them into his own private collectables.

Saker doesn't want Reen to be a part of this dangerous mission, but she has other plans. Unfortunately, so does The Collector...

Warning, this title contains the following: explicit sex, graphic language, and violence.

Caged Desire
By Sydney Somers

He's trapped…she's suspicious—to earn his freedom all he has to do is win her trust.

Locked in a cage for almost fifty years, Logan has had nothing but time to plot his revenge on those who wrongfully condemned him to spend eternity in the deepest regions of a South American rainforest. But with one look at the alluring vampire who holds his freedom in her hands, revenge becomes the farthest thing from his mind.

Eve Blake is puzzled by the wooden crate delivered to her door. Even stranger is the large golden eagle inside. It doesn't take her long to realize the majestic creature is far more than he appears. Finding a man in the cage previously containing the feathered animal gives Eve every reason to suspect the shifter was locked away for a reason.

Can she trust him when he promises not to harm her if she releases him? Or will her decision cost both of them more than they bargained for?

Warning, this title contains the following: explicit sex, graphic language, and violence.

Seize the Hunter
By Michelle M. Pillow

Fate is giving her the one man she'd never want for her very own.

Princess Ari of the planet Falconia knows it's her time to marry and has picked out several suitable men in her mind—none of which are Falcoan Army Commander, Rurik of the Fifth. The man tormented her as a child, causing her untold humiliations. But there is really no need to worry about such a match. Shifters cannot rule and Rurik is a natural born falcon shifter.

Trusting destiny, Ari sips from the Marriage Chalice, sealing her future. But things don't go as planned. It would seem fate is giving her to the man she despises. How can she find happiness with the one man she could never want for her very own?

Warning, this title contains the following: hot, explicit sex and violence explained with contemporary, graphic language.

Talons

A Samhain Publishing, Ltd. publication.

Samhain Publishing, Ltd.
2932 Ross Clark Circle, #384
Dothan, AL 36301
www.samhainpublishing.com

Editing by Angie James
Cover by Anne Cain

First Samhain Publishing, Ltd. electronic publication: October 2006
First Samhain Publishing, Ltd. print publication: January 2007

Contents

Kiss Me Deadly

Shannon Stacey

Dedication

For Mandy, Michelle, Jaycee and Sydney for sharing this flight with me, and for Angie, for air traffic controlling.

Chapter One

It was a simple thing for Khail to make his way into the dwelling of the woman.

A door propped open, a moment of distraction, and he was in—death on the faintest whisper of wings. Concealment was effortless. Mortals were patently oblivious to the many dangers surrounding them.

Khail waited in the deepest shadows of the bedroom without so much as a twitch until the woman slept and then—with an ancient spell no more than a fleeting thought passing through his mind—he shifted into the shape of a man. Hair as black as the raven's wing flowed over his shoulders much as it had when he trod the steppes of his Russian homeland hundreds of years before.

He walked softly on bare feet to stand beside the woman's bed. Hers would be a painless death and her loved ones would be told it was a freak incident. A thrown blood clot. An unexplained coronary event. And they would know she passed away in her sleep peacefully, with no pain.

The death of this woman and the grief of her family would be more drops added to the eternal, bottomless well of his punishment.

Khail began to chant, his lips moving but the sound resounding only in his mind. As the chant came to an end and sorrow flooded his senses, Khail pressed his naked fingers to the human woman's lips, stopping her breath. Stopping her heart.

And then she screamed.

Bridget Sawyer came awake in a hurry, barely realizing the scream of terror had come from her own throat.

In the split second between nightmare and wakefulness, she imagined a naked man touching her lips, talking to her without making a sound. She scrambled to her hands and knees on the bed, kicking free of the covers. Backing up to the headboard, she reached over and turned on the bedside lamp. Then, over her own ragged breaths, she heard the flapping of wings.

A freakin' bird. There was a damn bird in her house.

A very big bird, she thought, as it came to rest on her dresser. It regarded her without blinking. It was kind of creepy, perched there like a statue. And scary, as well. With that beak and those talons, it could do some serious damage if it got spooked and decided to attack.

Though it was ridiculous to care if the bird saw her naked, she inched her hand slowly down the bed and retrieved her robe from the foot. Trying not to make any sudden moves, she slipped it on. After knotting the red satin sash, she turned her thoughts to shooing the bird out of her house.

The bird fluffed its feathers, turning its head this way and that as if scoping out the nearest exit. That was fine with her. But then it resumed staring at her with beady little eyes.

It had to have been hiding for hours. Before it got fully dark she'd propped the door open to carry in firewood. Though it was spring, the nights could get chilly in the White Mountains and she liked the crackle of burning logs in the fireplace. The bird must have gotten in at that point. But that was an awfully long time for a winged critter to be so still she didn't even know it was in the house. How could she not have known a bird *that* big was hiding in her bedroom?

Taking her pillow with her, as it seemed slightly better protection than the paperback on her nightstand, Bridget started making her way toward her bedroom door. She never turned her back on the big—hell, it was *massive*—bird, and it never stopped unblinkingly tracking her progress.

Bridget considered her options. If she went and opened the front door and then tried to shoo it out, they could spend hours going around in circles from room to room. It made more sense to herd the thing into the front room and close the bedroom door. Then she could work on getting it outside.

"Okay," she said out loud, and the bird twitched at the sound of her voice. "Here's how this is going to go. I'm going to wave my pillow at you, and you're going to fly yourself the hell out of my bedroom. *Capische*?"

The bird cocked its head to the side, looking for all the world as if it were considering her words. Then it took flight and Bridget tried to hide her five-foot-six body behind the queen-sized pillow, stumbling backwards and ready to dive under her bed if need be. The bird had to tilt to fit its wingspan through the doorway and she sucked in a breath when she realized the true size of him. That was one damn big bird. Much bigger than any bird she'd ever seen in these woods.

When it had settled on the back of her couch, its talons clutching but not quite punching through the soft, battered leather, she scrambled through the doorway herself, pulling the door closed behind her. In the soft glow from the light over the kitchen sink, she watched it. It watched her right back, seemingly content to let her do whatever she was doing. She sidled a few feet to the left and pulled the bathroom door closed as well.

So that left her and the giant black bird alone in the single large room that functioned as living room, dining room, kitchen and office in her tiny cabin. Time for stage two.

Bridget walked toward her front door, intent upon propping it open so she could shoo the bird in that direction if he didn't go willingly. When she was a few feet from the door, however, the bird—a very large raven she realized, as improbable as that seemed—flew between her and the objective. Its harsh calls and flapping wings backed her up so quickly she almost tripped and fell on her ass. Not until she was more than halfway back to her bedroom did it settle. This time it perched on the back of a kitchen chair. The damn thing even seemed to shake its head at her.

Curiouser and curiouser, she thought, feeling very much like Alice fallen down the rabbit hole.

Bridget drew in a deep breath, then blew it out, her aggravation increasing by the second. She always had difficulty falling asleep, and now that she was fully awake she'd have to start the process all over again.

Twice more she tried moving around the room, but each time she neared the front door, the raven chased her back. Bridget was beginning to feel uneasy. The consistency of its actions and the eerie way it looked at her gave her the impression it was actually intelligent. She wasn't up to dealing with a bird capable of critical thinking.

It was definitely time for a Plan B. For the first time she wished she hadn't hidden herself so far away from civilization. The only people she could really call for help would be the police or fire departments— assuming anybody was available. It was after midnight. It would take somebody at least a half-hour to reach the cabin, and the long, winding dirt path that passed as her driveway could be treacherous in the dark, especially now in the spring. She wasn't going to ask that of anybody just because she had a bird in her house.

Another option was retreat. She could return to her bedroom, close the door and deal with the problem in the morning. But Bridget knew herself well enough to know she'd never go to sleep with a raven loose in the house. She'd be listening for it, waiting for the rustle of wings. Wondering if it would damage anything. It had to go now.

"Look, buddy," she said quietly. "I want to go back to bed. You need to go fly around outside and do whatever it is birds like you do at this time of night. So I'm going to open that door and you're going to fly through it, okay?"

Hey, talking to it had worked getting it out of the bedroom. Now, though, it only stared at her without so much as twitching. Hoping they'd come to some kind of understanding, Bridget started once again for the door. The raven reneged on the deal, however, and took flight, once again trying to drive her back.

This time she was ready for it. Holding the two corners of one end of the pillow, she swung it like a plank, knocking the damn bird clear across the room. She felt a spasm of guilt—but it wouldn't let her open the door, dammit—as it tumbled through the air.

Then things got a little crazy. Bridget's vision blurred and a split second later a very large, very naked man bounced off her pine paneling and hit the floor with a thud.

Oh shit. That did *not* just happen. There was no such as thing as...whatever the hell that was. Like a werewolf, only a bird. A werebird?

He lifted his head and blinked at her with those same dark eyes.

Ohshitohshitohshit. What the hell was going on? She had to be dreaming. But on the off chance she wasn't, Bridget dropped the pillow and ran for the door.

"No," the man called in a husky, cracking voice. "Do not...open the...door."

Yeah, sure buddy. Like she was going to listen to a naked man who'd just been a bird flying around her house. Bridget turned the knob and yanked open the door.

The shadows of the cabin's deep porch erupted in a whirlwind of black wings and hoarse raven calls. *Oh my God.* There had to be hundreds of them. Her mind blanked, instinct took over and she slammed the door closed. Just in time, judging by the thuds against the heavy wood.

What the fuck is going on here?

She'd landed in a horror novel. Shit like this did *not* happen. Bridget whirled, relieved to find the naked man still on the floor. God, he was tall. And writhing in pain, clutching his head. She thought about conking him a good one with a frying pan, knocking him unconscious long enough to tie him up, but then she heard a sound that made her blood run cold.

Tap. Tap. Tap. Hard beaks on glass. Still running on instinct, Bridget ran from window to window, closing the interior storm shutters and sliding the latches closed. She had to pass by the man on the floor to get to her bedroom, but he made no move toward her and she didn't dawdle on her way by.

She slammed the last shutter closed just in time to catch the glass as the window gave. The man in the front room screamed once, a short and angry cry, and then the small cabin was encased in silence.

The only sounds were the short, ragged breaths Bridget forced in and out of her lungs.

What the hell was going on? And why the hell hadn't she installed a phone jack in her bedroom? Every person on the planet had a phone on the bedside table but her. Brilliant.

Still panting, she took stock. She was stuck in her bedroom. No weapon, no phone. A huge raven had just turned into a tall, naked man in her living room.

She still couldn't believe it. The images replayed over and over in her mind. And yes, the bird had turned into a man in mid-air. So either something terrifyingly supernatural was going on, or she'd suffered a total psychotic break.

Oh, and let's not forget there was also a crazy flock of what looked to be were-ravens on her front porch. And none of them wanted her to leave her house.

Oh...shit. What if he opened the door and let them in? She had to find some way to defend herself and get back out there.

Wasting no time, she lifted the curtain rod from its brackets and slid the drapes off the end. The wrought-iron rod with its faux-spearhead tip wasn't the most rugged of weapons, but she wasn't sure she had the strength to bludgeon the man with the wooden closet rod.

When her breathing was as calm as it was going to get and the feeling of impending coronary doom had eased, Bridget tiptoed into the front room, her decorative spear at the ready.

The intruder was on his feet, which wasn't so good. But he was still alone, which was. The light spilling out from her bedroom lamp combined with the low-wattage bulb she always left on over the sink to bathe the room in dim, spotty light.

He was tall—at least six feet—and definitely built. Bronzed muscles, but not too bulky. Thick, black hair flowed just past his shoulders and she could just make out a closely-cropped mustache and goatee. His most distinguishing characteristic, that she could see, was a dick that would be the perfect "after" picture for enlargement spam. If she wasn't scared half to death, she'd probably be impressed. Actually, she was sort of impressed anyway.

"What are you?" she demanded, her fingernails biting into her palms as she practically strangled the curtain rod in her hands.

"I am—" He clutched his head and groaned, then dropped to his knees. He stayed down for about thirty seconds, then he struggled back to his feet. "We...are the Unkind."

What the hell was that about? Maybe he'd suffered a concussion when she slapped him into the wall. And the Unkind? She'd definitely fallen into a horror novel. Or a sci-fi movie.

Maybe they were some kind of devil-worshipping cult that had sold its soul to Satan for the power to shapeshift. Was she the sacrifice? Her legs felt like jelly, and she prayed she could stay on her feet.

She glanced toward the phone, inconveniently hanging right next to the door on the kitchen wall. Another brilliant move on her part. She needed to keep him talking. Maybe he'd start moving and she could inconspicuously get to the phone. Then she'd only have to fend them off the half-hour to an hour it would take help to arrive.

"So you said 'we'. Are all of those birds men, too?" *And do they all look like you? Because...damn.*

"We are the Unkind."

She took a deep, calming breath. The guy seemed willing to talk, such as it was. "Yeah. An unkindness of ravens. I get that. What I don't get is why you're all flying around the northern New Hampshire woods at this time of night. You guys aren't even indigenous to..."

Okay, sure Bridget. Like ravens who morphed into tall, well-endowed men were indigenous to anywhere.

"You are not dead," he said simply.

Her breath caught in her throat as her heart started pounding again. Dead? She was supposed to be dead? Her stomach rolled, and even though it was in the opposite direction of the phone, she took a couple of involuntary steps backward toward her bedroom.

If an entire flock of naked men wanted her dead, she could only fend them off for so long with a curtain rod.

"Why?" he demanded.

The question baffled her for a moment. The situation—this conversation—was totally surreal. Now that the initial terror was over, she didn't appear to be in mortal danger. But this man talking about her being dead kept the adrenaline pumping through her body.

"Why am I not dead? Look, werebird guy, you've got me scared shitless and I'd really like it if you went away, but you haven't done anything yet that would kill me." And it was fine with her if it stayed that way.

"My touch should have killed you."

She remembered the end of what she'd thought was a dream—the man's fingertips on her lips, his mouth forming silent words—and shuddered. She considered another retreat to her bedroom, but she wasn't sure that would accomplish anything. If she stayed and talked, she might convince him to leave peacefully, and take his feathered friends with him.

"I'm not sure what whacked-out chat rooms you've been visiting, pal, but why do you think touching my mouth would kill me?"

She thought of poison, then, and squashed an urge to lick her lips nervously. Instead she dragged the sleeve of her robe across them.

"That is the curse," the man stated.

They were getting nowhere. He wasn't exactly a brilliant conversationalist and she still had no idea what was actually going on here. But he wasn't moving at all, and she had no hope of getting by him to the phone. She really didn't know what to do.

While she wasn't the least bit sleepy anymore, her mind was still trying to catch up to the fact a six-foot-something man with a raging erection—it was difficult not to notice—who previously had been a bird was standing in her cabin in the middle of the night.

But he'd made no further moves toward her. Neither his facial expression nor body language struck her as menacing. Though she was still incredibly freaked out, she no longer felt directly threatened.

"So, what do we do now?" Bridget asked when the silence stretched on.

"I want to touch you again."

Khail watched the woman flinch at his words. He knew it was the wrong thing to say, but he couldn't hold it back.

It had been three hundred and sixty-one years since he'd touched a woman with any result other than her death.

The woman must die.

Khail shook his head, trying to ignore the collective voice of the Unkind. It was better when he looked at her—the drone of their voices faded away somewhat. His thoughts were his own.

The woman managed to look both fierce and vulnerable, standing there in her shiny red robe with her flimsy metal weapon. Her hair was nearly as dark as his own and fell straight to a little below her shoulders. Her skin was pale, and her eyes big and dark in her face.

The robe gaped slightly above the belt, giving him glimpses of the smooth tops of her breasts. Her long, shapely legs were barely covered by the short length.

Yes, he wanted to touch her. He *ached* to touch her again. He wanted to touch her lips, her face. He wanted to run his hands through her hair and down over her back. And maybe he could. He had touched her and she hadn't died.

The stirrings of humanity he'd thought long erased from his soul nearly drowned out the angry buzzing of the collective's thoughts.

"My name is Khail," he offered. The Unkind rallied at this claim of individuality—a high-pitched screech reverberating through his mind— but subsided when he looked into her eyes.

"Kale? Like the cabbage?" The woman was frowning, but her knuckles were no longer white as she clutched her weapon.

"My true name is Mikhail Pavlovich Barsukov, but I am called Khail. Who are you?"

"You came to kill me with your supervillain death-touch and you don't even know who I am?"

He didn't quite understand what a supervillain death-touch meant, but her meaning was clear. "We are the balance between good and natural death and evil and unnatural death. We are random. We are unexplained...unexpected."

"So...why me? Why did you choose me to die?"

There was an ageless sorrow in her eyes that called to him, but he had no answer for her. "We are random."

He noticed then that as her gaze flicked down to the aching rise of his cock, her jaw would tighten and her fingers would tense on the metal rod she held. He could do nothing about his physical state—just the *thought* of touching her made him hard. So he went to her rocking chair and lifted a thin throw blanket to wrap around his waist. He tucked the end in, and then flicked the switch for the light fixtures— he'd been watching the mortals' technological progress for centuries. Perhaps full light would help put her at ease.

Instead, when she got her first fully-lit look at his face, she sucked in a sharp breath. "Oh my God. It's *you.*"

The metal rod slipped from her fingers as she turned and fled into her bedroom, slamming the door behind her.

Khail stared after her, stunned by her reaction to his face.

It's you. What did she mean by that? She couldn't know him. He came from a place she had never been—where no mortal had been. And yet recognition had clearly dawned in her eyes.

Open the door, Mikhail, the voices murmured in his head.

He turned toward it, then stopped. If he opened the door to the Unkind, the woman would die.

She has been chosen. It is her time to die.

No.

Shrieks of anger echoed through his mind, almost obliterating his own thoughts. *She is special,* he forced through.

She is chosen.

But not for you.

Khail had no idea where that thought had come from, but it felt right. The woman had survived his deadly magic. She had stood strong with only a puny piece of metal with which to defend herself. And he felt that she was meant to be his.

The warrior he had been grew within the cursed shell of a man he had become. The voices ebbed and flowed in his head—angry, hissed threats—but he tried to concentrate on blocking them out. And he vowed silently to keep the woman safe. He would not let the Unkind have her.

Chapter Two

Bridget leaned against the closed door and switched on the overhead light. There was no lock on the knob, and she had no furniture light enough to move yet heavy enough to keep him out.

She tried to control her breathing well enough to hear what was going on in the living room. It seemed quiet out there, but he'd been naked. Even a large man could step silently in bare feet.

When he had initially covered himself she had breathed a sigh of relief, only to choke on it when she got her first really good look at his face. It *wasn't* the face of a stranger. In fact, it was a face she knew intimately. Not knowing what else to do, she'd run.

Now, somewhat satisfied he wasn't going to change his mind about being a nice guy and burst through the door, Bridget went to the line of books—a dark fantasy series for young adults—on the shelf above her dresser. She chose one at random and flipped through the book until she found a sketch.

The words were another's—the author an old man with a youthful imagination—but the illustrations were her own. The black pencil sketches were stark, but suited the series and they, along with prints she sold via the 'net, allowed her to work from her solitary haven in the woods.

The man who called himself Khail wasn't in every illustration, but he was in many. Bridget had captured her current visitor right down to the weary agelessness of his eyes. Somehow, the character she'd been drawing for the best-selling series for several years was standing in her living room.

But what did it all mean? Bridget sank onto the edge of her bed, staring down at her drawing. She could accept that death had come for her. Considering her life to this point, it wasn't even that much of a surprise. After suffering at the hands of foster "fathers" and the ex-husband in her past, the real surprise was how painless it would have been. She would expect death at the hands of a man to be accompanied by shouting and screaming and pain. A lot of pain, as it almost had once before.

She could even accept that death had come for her as a bird who shapeshifted into a man. Granted, that one was a little harder to comprehend, but since she'd seen it with her own eyes and she wasn't dreaming, it was hard to deny.

What she couldn't readily accept was Khail's image in her artwork. The mystery of how that came to be—the *why* of it—disturbed her. But what upset her even more was the possibility she and death had been intertwined for a long time. It really shot holes in the whole "random" thing, too.

She leapt off the bed when a knock on the door sounded. Dropping the book, she kicked it under the bed as the knob turned and Khail appeared.

"What is your name?" he asked, filling her doorway.

There seemed to be no point in not telling him. "Bridget. Bridget Sawyer."

"I don't know what to do now."

He looked like a little boy who'd just lost his puppy, and Bridget sighed. A flock of death birds had caused her to barricade herself inside her cabin with a stranger wearing a blanket like a bath towel, and yet her strongest emotion was sympathy for the intruder. Maybe she'd gone totally bat-shit crazy, and this was all just a hallucination.

"You could leave," she said mildly, though she guessed that wasn't an option for him or he'd have already left. And there was a little piece of her not ready for him to go quite yet. That, she couldn't even begin to understand.

His appearance in her cabin had turned her life upside down, but his presence in the chaos he had created brought her comfort. He'd brought death to her door, and yet she still felt if she stepped into his arms he would hold her and keep her safe. The contradiction made her head spin.

"If I open the door, they will come for you," Khail responded. "Our voice is like an angry buzzing in my head. But it is not so loud when I am with you, so I came in here to think."

An angry buzzing explained why he kept clutching his head. So why exactly was he resisting those voices in his head? Was there some underlying bond between the two of them, as suggested by his presence in her illustrations, that he felt as well?

"I'd rather not discuss this in my bedroom," Bridget said quietly, not so accepting of his presence that she wanted him where she slept. "Let's go in the other room. I'll make coffee and we can talk about this like...whatever we are. Insane people."

He started to turn, but then he stopped and laid his palm against her cheek. She flinched. She couldn't help it, despite all the years of head-shrinking she'd undergone before deciding a solitary life in the woods was all the therapy she needed.

"You are so beautiful," Khail whispered, his thumb tracing the arc of her cheekbone.

His words—the gentle caress of his touch—stirred something deep inside of Bridget. Something she would rather had stayed deep and unstirred. "You're only saying that because I'm still breathing."

It was thrown out there as a joke—a throwaway line to lighten the sexual tension suddenly sucking the oxygen out of the cabin—but she had to admit she was fishing just a little. She'd been called many things in her life, but she couldn't remember a man ever calling her beautiful.

Then a thought struck her and Bridget slapped at his hand. "You saw me naked!"

Khail smiled. It was slow and awkward, as if he hadn't smiled in a long time and was trying to remember how it was done, but Bridget's stomach flip-flopped. *He* was beautiful.

"I tried not to stare overly much," Khail said, but there was a gleam in his eyes that told her he was full of crap. "But it was like a starving man trying not to ogle a leg of lamb."

His contrite, yet mischievous, expression made her laugh, and she slapped a hand over her mouth. The sound was incredibly foreign to the little cabin. What did she ever have to laugh at, here in her self-imposed solitude? And how could she even think of laughing *now*, under these conditions?

"Don't hide your laughter, Bridget." He pulled her hand away from her mouth and his thumb lingered over the pulse point of her wrist.

Bridget was out of her ever-loving mind. She had to be. She pressed her thighs together in a wasted effort to suffocate the yearnings growing between them. And she tried to ignore the physical knot of lust making her lower back ache. All this despite the fact that if his plan had worked, she'd be dead right now.

But she wasn't dead. And neither were the desires she'd spent so many years trying to unsuccessfully quell by her own hand.

"What's going to happen to me?" she asked, hating the telltale quiver in her voice.

"I don't know. Somehow you are immune to us, and that cannot be ignored. But I won't let them have you, Bridget. I will fight them in my mind and I will fight them with my bare hands if need be. But I will not give you over to them."

How had he gone so quickly from trying to kill her to being willing to die for her? "But why not, Khail? I don't understand why you're doing this."

"Nor do I. But I know you're beautiful and your smile makes me feel uncursed and I want to hear you say my name over and over again."

"I'm afraid," she whispered.

"There is much to fear," Khail admitted. "But not from me. Do not fear me."

And she didn't, Bridget realized. She was very afraid of what lay beyond the cabin, but she didn't fear Khail. That shocked her, so she tried again to dispel the heightening awareness between them. "We can't stay in here forever. Eventually we'll run out of food and I'm a total bitch when I'm hungry."

"I know hunger," he replied in a quiet voice, and the look on his face told Bridget he wasn't thinking about his stomach.

God help her, but she wanted this man. There was a part of her brain still railing against the events of the night. But a larger part acknowledged she was supposed to be dead already and she might still turn out that way very soon, so why not?

She was drawn to this man. She couldn't deny that. The pull toward him she felt was like that of the moon on the ocean. And why deny herself this pleasure? She had been denied too much in her life, and if she was going to die anyway, she should grasp this opportunity for a little pleasure before it was too late.

So...*why not?* Bridget unknotted the sash and let the robe slide from her body.

Khail's eyes widened as he sucked in a deep breath. He murmured something. It was in a language Bridget didn't understand, but the awe with which he looked at her needed no translation.

He dropped the blanket so it pooled at his feet, and his fully-erect cock twitched. Bridget expected to find herself flat on her back in the blink of an eye, but Khail didn't move.

His hands were tightly fisted and the muscles of his jaw clenched and unclenched. She would have been frightened if not for the raw desire she saw on his face. He wasn't angry. He was—as he'd said— hungry. "Knowing what you know, you would lie with me?"

"Crazy, huh? I must be out of my mind." There was no doubt about that, actually. But if she was going to be murdered by a flock of birds, she saw no harm in sex with this beautiful stranger first.

"I would answer that, but my words would be suspect as I want nothing but to bury my cock deep in you and hear you cry out my name in pleasure."

Judging by the moistness between her thighs and her taut, aching nipples, Bridget's body agreed that was a good plan. "It *is* crazy. I've had a lot of pain in my life. But my body wants you. And the look on your face makes me feel as beautiful as you tell me I am. Nothing makes sense anymore, but there is one thing I'm sure of—right here and now I want you to make love to me."

Now, she thought. *Now his control will break and he'll throw himself on top of me.* Then the fantasy would end and the reality would be a disappointment, as had always been the case for her.

Khail stepped closer until he could take her hands in his own. He pressed a kiss to one palm and then the other. Bridget's body trembled as a desire she hadn't felt so strongly in years—if ever—blossomed in her very core. He ran his hands up the outside of her arms. Trailed his fingertips down the inside, back to her hands. Again he stroked up, this time to glide across her shoulders.

"Your skin is so soft," he whispered as he cradled the back of her neck before plunging his fingers through her hair.

When a small whimper of pleasure escaped Bridget's throat, Khail groaned and pulled her body hard up against his own. She gasped as her breasts were crushed against his chest, and the rigid length of his cock pressed against her stomach.

Khail ran his hands down her back, his fingertips digging not quite painfully into her muscles. When he grabbed her ass and pushed her pelvis against his thigh, they both groaned.

"Please, Khail," Bridget almost sobbed.

"I've not had my fill of touching you yet, *moya kisa.*"

"How 'bout you touch me with your cock now and you can touch me with your hands again later, okay?" The words coming out of her own mouth shocked her, and she almost giggled at her boldness.

He chuckled, capturing her wrists with his hands. "How is it that you are more impatient than I?"

"It's been a long time since I've been touched by a man."

"For me it has been almost four centuries."

Bridget peered up at him, smiling sweetly. "It's been almost four centuries since you've been touched by a man?"

Khail laughed, and in the next second Bridget was flying through the air, only to land in the center of her bed. "A man? Move over, *moya kisa*, and I will show you that Mikhail Pavlovich Barsukov is a great lover of women."

When he covered her body with his own, Bridget thought she would stop breathing. He really *was* beautiful—all that hard muscle and dark golden skin. Despite the circumstances of his arrival, she was very glad he was there. She brought her legs up and crossed her ankles over his ass, urging him to enter her, but he only smiled and shook his head.

"Patience. I will see to your needs when I am finished touching you."

"See to my needs?" She giggled—she couldn't help it. "You're such a polite gentleman, Khail."

He drew back, sitting back on his calves, still straddling her. Crossing his arms over his chest, he glared down at her—although the intimidation factor was lessened by the upturn of his lips at the corners.

"Polite? I am a Cossack, *moya kisa.* A fierce warrior. On horseback, there is none feared more than I. So, woman, you will lay there while I touch you. Then, when I am ready, I will fuck you until you cannot walk."

Heat rushed through her veins before pooling at the juncture of her thighs. Bridget gazed at his face—the fierce warrior's countenance marred by tender eyes and slightly smiling lips.

And touch her he did. She lost all track of time as his hands roamed freely over her body. Gently—almost reverently—he explored her flesh. She should have felt self-conscious—she always had in the past—but he looked at her with such naked lust and adoration, she felt like a goddess. He cupped her breasts in his hands and shuddered, as though the sensation of touching her brought him as much pleasure as the act of being touched brought her.

Then his fingertips captured her nipples and Bridget tensed, waiting for the painful tweak. When Khail was still for a few seconds, she opened her eyes to find him gazing down into her face. He smiled and gently rubbed a thumb over each nipple. He bent his head, swirling his tongue over the tip of each breast in turn. His gaze was tender when he looked down at her again.

"I won't hurt you, Bridget. Never would I find my own pleasure in your own pain."

Bridget fell just a little bit in love with him right then. That he not only sensed her hesitation, but had taken the time to reassure her, made her eyes well with tears.

"I...I couldn't help it." She didn't want to go down that road. She didn't want her *what the hell, I'm gonna die anyway* one night stand spoiled by her painful sexual history. And now would come the false understanding—the godawful pity.

"I, Mikhail Pavlovich Barsukov," he said in a farcical, booming voice, "will show you how the great Cossacks tame even the most skittish of steeds!"

She laughed, and the past disappeared like a popped bubble. "You fuck your steeds until they can't walk?"

He snorted in his attempt not to laugh. "I meant the gentle touches, wench."

"So touch me gently some more, great Cossack," she said, and laughed again.

When his fingers slid down over her stomach and his palm cupped her mound, Bridget's amusement fled and she groaned. He pressed the heel of his hand against her swollen clit, applying a little pressure, and she moaned, her hips arching off the bed.

He ran a finger through her moist heat and slid it into her. Bridget whimpered, her hands clawing at the bedspread. This...*this* was what sex was supposed to be all about, and she opened herself to it—and to him. Lifting her hips, she parted her knees further, giving him full access to her most intimate part.

"You are like the finest of silks," Khail murmured, never breaking eye contact with her. She felt as if she were drowning in his dark, passionate gaze, her body loving these new depths of pleasure and hungering for more.

Bridget threaded her fingers through his thick hair and pulled his face down to hers. As his lips met hers, he slipped another finger inside of her and gently brushed his thumb over her clit. She whimpered into his kiss, her hips pushing against his hand.

"Come for me, *moya kisa*," he whispered hoarsely against her lips.

"I..." She didn't want to tell him she'd never come for a man before. The only orgasms she had came by her own hand.

"Come for me, beautiful Bridget." His soft urgings and the hardness of his knuckles had her panting. *Oh God. So close...*

"Get yourself nice and wet for me and then...*then* I will fuck you. Come, *moya kisa.*"

And she did. She screamed out once—in surprise as well as pleasure—as her muscles spasmed, her cunt clenching his fingers.

She'd barely caught her breath before Khail shifted. He grinned down at her, slowly sucking her juices from his fingers. Her body tightened in response.

"Are you ready for me now?" he asked, his voice husky and low.

She had to swallow hard before she could speak. "Does that mean you've had your fill of touching me?"

"Never. But I can't wait much longer, and if I don't get inside of you, I'll come all over myself like a virgin."

She smiled. "I'm ready for you."

He moved to lay between her thighs, but stopped. "Is my weight too much for you? Do you prefer me on my back?"

She saw the tenderness in his eyes—the truth of his question—and gave up a little more of her heart. He didn't care if he was too heavy for her. He cared if he frightened her.

"I trust you," she whispered—words she'd never before said to anybody. And she meant them, she realized. Somehow she knew she could give herself to this man and he would cherish her.

He entered her slowly, carefully, and Bridget lifted her hips to welcome the exquisite stretching sensation. She panicked briefly, sure she couldn't take all of him, but Khail stopped. He rocked his hips, pulling back and then slowly sliding forward. The friction felt wonderful and her body welcomed him deeper with each gentle stroke. Finally he filled her and was still, but for the cock pulsing inside of her.

She gazed up at Khail. Sweat beaded at his hairline and his arms trembled as he held his weight above her. The man had been celibate for almost four hundred years and he still had the capacity for restraint?

"I'm not fragile, Khail. I won't break."

"I want you to...find pleasure with me," he said through gritted teeth.

"And I will if you move—" She rocked her hips up. "—just...like...that."

And he did. Bridget wrapped her legs around his waist, urging him on. Her hands couldn't get enough of him. She ran them through his hair and over the smooth muscles of his back. They settled on his ass and she scraped her fingernails over the taut muscles that flexed with every thrust.

Khail shifted, lifting her hips until her feet rested on his shoulders. He plunged into her, the depth of his thrust nearly taking her breath away. When he reached down and used his thumb to put subtle pressure on her clit, Bridget came. Her head thrashed and she dug her nails into his flesh as her muscles spasmed and the waves of pleasure ripped through her body.

She'd barely returned to Earth when Khail let her legs drop so he could lean forward and kiss her. His clipped mustache and goatee tickled her upper lip and chin, but she parted her lips to let his tongue slide over hers. She sighed against his mouth, perfectly content to kiss this man for hours.

But he lifted his head to gaze down at her with those bottomless dark eyes. She smiled, trailing her fingertips lightly up his back just to watch him shudder.

"You are beautiful when you come, *moya kisa.*" He grinned, making her heart flutter in response. "Do it again."

"I can't just—" She yelped when he grabbed her ankle and crossed one leg over the other, turning her sideways without withdrawing. He pressed her knees together and began moving with slow, even strokes.

"Oh, my...*Khail*," she cried. The new angle—the new pressure—had her clutching the bedspread. There was no way she could have another orgasm so soon. No way.

Keeping his right hand on her knees, Khail put his left next to her head and leaned over her. A whimper escaped her throat as he quickened his pace, but not nearly enough.

"Yes, I am yours, Bridget." He leaned slightly to the right and took his hand from her knees to cup her face. He turned it gently, not enough to pull her neck, but enough to see her. "Open your eyes. I want to see your face when you come for me."

His strokes quickened and she knew his orgasm was near.

Suddenly he reared up and uncrossed her legs so she was flat on her back again. He reached over her head and grasped the top of the mattress, using the muscles in his arms and back to drive his cock deep into her.

Bridget cried his name again as the orgasm overtook her, even more intensely than the last.

"Mine," Khail growled into her neck as he thrust into her harder and faster.

He roared her name as his hips bucked and he spilled himself into her. Aftershocks wracked her body with each thrust, until they were both spent, panting and slickened with sweat.

Khail collapsed on top of her, then immediately rolled to his back, taking her with him. In her languid state, she was perfectly content to rest there, her head on his chest.

But in the seconds after the greatest orgasm of her life, the rapid pounding of Khail's heart was nearly drowned out by the thumps of winged bodies throwing themselves against the wooden shutters.

Chapter Three

She must die.

Khail sat, once again wrapped in the blanket, at Bridget's kitchen table, waiting anxiously for her to get out of the shower. They had made love there, but then she shoved him out so she could actually get clean. No sooner had the bathroom door closed behind him than the Unkind wormed their way back into his head.

During the night, while he made love to Bridget and then held her in his arms, it was as if the Unkind couldn't infiltrate his mind. For the first time in centuries his thoughts were his own and he'd felt almost human. They'd thumped against the windows for a short time, outraged at his intimacy with the chosen one, but they hadn't gotten into his head.

She must die. Bring the woman out.

He pressed his fingers to his temples and tried to conjure an image of Bridget as she came under the steaming water, her cunt squeezing his fingers. The buzzing abated slightly, but he knew they were out there. Watching. Waiting.

He didn't know how to defeat them. He shared a collective consciousness with them, but knew of no fatal weakness in the supernatural flock.

You cannot destroy us, Mikhail. You are one of us.

And he would destroy himself along with them if it would keep Bridget safe. But he had no weapon, no magic, at his disposal.

Kill the woman, the Unkind demanded.

I trust you, Bridget had whispered.

Khail clung to that voice in his mind. It was a gift she hadn't given lightly, he knew. And he would never betray her.

You betray the Unkind.

Yes. I do. Khail was no stranger to battle. This would be the first, however, he couldn't win with a good horse and his scimitar.

When Bridget finally emerged, clad once again in the red robe, with her towel-dried hair hanging free, Khail breathed a sigh of relief.

Something about her unburied the humanity he'd thought lost deep inside of himself. When he held her, he was a man again—a man with an identity and cleansed of the blood on his hands. A man not cursed by the Unkind.

He watched Bridget pour herself an oversized mug of coffee, and he thanked her when she refilled his water glass. The slight jerkiness to her movements let him know some of the afterglow of their intimacy was fading and their reality was creeping back.

"Why do you have those wooden shields on your windows?" he asked when she had seated herself across from him. He'd seen them on the outside of many homes—his own, so long ago, had had them in lieu of glass—but he'd never seen them on the inside before.

"They're emergency storm shutters. I try to use the exterior ones because they protect the glass, but up here a blizzard can come up out of nowhere. If it's very sudden or the middle of the night, I don't want to have to go outside. Especially since I live alone. They also come in handy if your house is attacked by a flock of pissed off, murderous werebirds."

He winced at her flippant use of that word, but laughed despite it. No doubt she understood the gravity of the situation—humor was simply her coping mechanism.

"My turn," she said, and he braced himself for the inevitable question. Could he face her if she knew how he'd come to be cursed? He could see the ghost of past violence in her eyes. Would she turn away from his past? "If you're an almost four hundred year old Cossack, how do you speak English so well?"

He almost laughed out loud in relief at her painless question. "I've been practically invisible among the humans for centuries. Watching. Listening. I speak many languages and know many things. Why do you choose to live such a lonely existence in such a remote place?"

Almost immediately, Khail regretted carelessly tacking the question onto the end of his answer. Bridget's fingers tightened on her coffee mug and her gaze shifted away from his.

"It's not as remote as it seems. Well, it is from the front, but there are homes and camps not too far away over the hill to the back. That's how I was able to get electricity and phone run to the cabin, though they cost me a small fortune."

She hadn't answered his true question, and they both knew it.

"How are we going to get out of this?" she asked after too long a silence.

To Khail, it spoke volumes that she'd rather talk about the threat of death hovering over them than her past. Perhaps she was only giving voice to her fears, but he got the distinct impression she was changing the subject. And he let her.

"We...*they* don't know why you didn't die. Their anger makes them determined to solve the puzzle of *why*? I can feel it."

"I take it this doesn't happen often?"

Khail shook his head. "Not in my collective memory of the Unkind."

"If I'm immune, then I should just be able to walk outside, right? Let them touch me."

"Perhaps their mere touch will not kill you. But the touch of hundreds—maybe thousands—of razor-sharp beaks and talons would most certainly hurt you."

Bridget shuddered, and Khail resisted the urge to go to her. If he took her in his arms now he would make love to her again. They needed to focus and perhaps come up with some solution to their problem, unlikely as that seemed.

"But," she said, turning her coffee cup around and around in her hands, "if they stalk me and then tear me to shreds, that's not random.

Although my being chosen was, it didn't work and they should go randomly end somebody else's life."

"I cannot be sure anymore that my finding you *was* random. I believe it was meant to be."

Her gaze shifted away from his in an almost guilty way, he thought. "If our coming together was meant to be, why won't they go away?"

"I'm sorry, *moya kisa*. I don't know the answers."

"What does that mean—*moya kisa*?"

He felt like a boy trying to kiss a girl for the first time—bashful and hot around the neck. "It means...my little cat, or my kitten. It's a term of endearment, I guess you would call it."

Bridget laughed then, and he was pleased to see some color return to her cheeks. "What is so funny?"

"That's a pretty ironic endearment coming from a guy who's also a bird, don't you think?"

He chuckled, but shrugged his shoulders. "It is what my father called my mother."

"Tell me how you came to be cursed."

Khail's heart tightened in his chest. He didn't want to talk about it. The pain of that day throbbed always like a sore tooth, and just the thought of reliving the events aloud made the pain flare.

And he dreaded her reaction to what he had done. She was not a woman to forgive violence easily.

"Tell me, Khail. Please."

The soft caring in her eyes was his undoing. Already he could deny this woman nothing, even at the risk of driving her away from himself. He rose from his chair to pace the room. Even though well-lit, the cabin, with its covered windows, seemed to close in on him. He desperately wanted out, but he couldn't leave without Bridget, so he would stay. To stay, he must talk.

"In the year 1645, I was away from home often. I was either fighting or training to fight. One day I came home to find my wife and my little girl murdered."

Khail heard Bridget's sharp intake of breath, but he didn't turn. While that part of his story was the most personally painful, it was not the worst of it.

"In the village they told me who had done it—a drunkard who I had taunted for his poor horsemanship. True, it was the gravest of insults among our men, but his honor was not worth the lives of my family. I hunted him like a wild antelope. I ran him to ground in a church—he had begged sanctuary in a holy place. I slaughtered him. And when his wife tried to shield him with her own body, I cut her down, as well."

He heard Bridget rise from her chair. From the corner of his eye he saw the hand pressed to her mouth in horror, the tear running down her cheek. She was moving slowly toward her bedroom.

"And as that innocent blood I spilled in a blind rage soaked into that holy ground, so I was cursed."

He turned to her then, and the fear in her eyes made the gorge rise in his throat. "Bridget, I would never hurt you."

"You're no different from...all of them," she said, and then a hoarse sob broke free from her throat and she fled to her bedroom, slamming the door behind her.

We cannot be denied.

Khail wanted to raise his face to the ceiling and scream out his rage and heartache and uncertainty. But it would serve no purpose but further frightening Bridget, and he would do anything to prevent that.

She is ours. The Unkind will take her.

No, she is mine, Khail thought fiercely, his hands curled into tight fists.

We will not be denied.

You will, because I will not let you have her.

You are cursed and you both belong to us. The woman will die.

౮ఠ౪

Bridget sobbed into her pillow until the tears ran dry, and still she didn't move. Men...rage...violence. It was the story of her life, and even here in the haven she'd built for herself she couldn't escape it.

She had cried also for Khail. He had committed violence and caused pain, but he had received much, as well. Closing her eyes, she tried to picture a happy, uncursed Khail with a wife and a daughter. But all she could see was him, blood-soaked with his face contorted in rage.

Bridget had been adopted as an infant, orphaned again at five, then sent into a foster system that dealt her abuse, humiliation and pain—both mental and physical. She'd escaped the system and gotten married far too young to the first man who wanted her. Her husband had abused her for ten years before he put her in intensive care and himself in prison. Yes, she knew the color of blood and the taste of fear and rage.

Khail had seen both sides. She knew his past—and the Unkind—weighed heavily on him. He'd slept restlessly, even after the hideous birds had stopped throwing themselves at the windows. He had tossed and turned, and sometimes violently shook his head as if to dislodge the memories and the voices filling his dreams.

He would quiet when she touched him. She caressed his cheek and murmured soft nothings until his brow smoothed and he breathed deeply again. But when she fell asleep and moved away, it wasn't long before his thrashings woke her again.

Khail was a man haunted. Haunted by what had been done to him and by what he himself had done. That would change a man irrevocably.

Bridget rolled to her back and stared up at the ceiling. Almost four hundred years ago he had committed an act of violence that turned her stomach. But now...well, she believed he still had it in him.

He was a warrior, with a warrior's intensity and passion. She had no doubt if the ravens came, Khail would slaughter them in her defense if he could.

But he was also the man who had made love to her so sweetly. A man who had the care to be attuned to the subtle nuances of her body—so concerned the ghosts of her past would destroy the pleasure he wanted her to feel.

He wasn't like the other men she had known, and Bridget sorely regretted telling him he was. She wished she could take back the words she had flung at him in her shock. How it must have cut him to have the first person he could share his curse with turn away in horror.

Her anger shifted to the Unkind. What kind of punishment offered no chance of redemption? What good was a man serving penance eternally with no hope of forgiveness?

Angry, sad and confused, but feeling slightly more composed, Bridget stalked to the bedroom door and flung it open. Khail sat in the rocking chair, his head in his hands. Her heart ached for him, but she couldn't bring herself to touch him quite yet.

"How the hell is three and a half centuries of killing people punishment for killing somebody?" she demanded, not caring that her voice was too loud in the small cabin.

"We don't take lives without feeling the loss. We feel the grief of the loved ones. Each victim of the Unkind is like a lead weight hung upon my soul."

"They all seem eager enough to see me die," Bridget reminded him, thinking they'd be sorely disappointed by the lack of grief in her loved ones. She didn't have any.

"It is fear. We...*they* do not understand you, but you have defied the natural order of things and that frightens them."

"Is there no mercy?" Not that she'd ever been shown any. "Your wife and daughter were murdered, for heaven's sake."

"And if I had arrived at that moment and struck him down, then I would not be cursed. It was the hunting of him that started my soul on the road to damnation. It took me nearly a week to find him and then, in a rage, I cut him down in front of sacred relics while he begged for his life."

Bridget closed her eyes. *No, please,* the little girl inside of her begged. *Please don't hurt me anymore.* The voice grew older. *You're hurting me. Please stop. Please...*

"You should know," Khail said, dragging Bridget out of the past, "that I don't regret killing the man who murdered my loved ones. But I regret killing his wife. Every single day of the last three hundred and sixty-one years I have mourned her death as keenly as I have the deaths of my wife and my sweet Ekaterina. She is the cross I bear, and every life I have taken since is a weight added until the regret crushes my very soul. My crime is my penance for all eternity. *That* is my curse."

Bridget watched the tears shimmering in his eyes, but they didn't fall. Her own, though, flowed freely over her cheeks. This man came from a place she wanted nothing to do with—a place of violence and bloodshed and death. And yet she still wanted to pull him into her arms and stroke his hair until the sadness left his eyes.

Khail took a deep breath and blinked away the unshed tears. "I don't know what brought me to you, Bridget. I don't know if it was an accident or a part of some divine plan. But for the first time in my life I feel peace. I can't help but believe I was meant to find you. If you turn your back on me, I will be lost. The man who manages to live inside of me will be lost and I will be nothing."

Bridget thought of his presence in her illustrations. While she couldn't even begin to guess why, one thing seemed pretty clear. She and Khail crossing paths was no accident. But why did she have to be destined for a death-delivering, shapeshifting, cursed Cossack? Just once life could have given her the joy without the pain.

She should tell Khail about the sketches. But she guessed he wouldn't know any more about their meaning than she did, and right now he looked emotionally wrecked enough.

Suddenly his face turned pale and he sat once again at her small kitchen table. His fingers gripped the edge as if he were struggling to remain upright.

"Is it getting worse? The buzzing?"

"Yes. The drone is getting louder...more persistent. They are gathering strength and as their determination grows, more of their collective thoughts make it through to me. The Unkind is determined to have you. But I am just as determined to keep you."

Bridget set about making fresh coffee just to give her hands something to do. While her mind was exhausted, her body was wondering where the hell its morning walk had gone to.

Her cabin was the first thing in Bridget's life to be totally hers. It represented safety, security and home. Every item in it was hand chosen with great care. So much care, in fact, that she considered the small log home almost an extension of herself. But right now all she wanted to do was leave it.

The walls were closing in on her. She couldn't throw open the shutters and raise the window to breathe in the fresh, mountain air. She wanted the sun, not the dim artificial lighting from the few lamps they kept on. She feared she would lose her mind soon if she didn't get out.

"Why are they just throwing their bird selves against the windows?" she asked after a few minutes of tense silence. "If they're so determined to have me, why not change into men and beat the door down?"

"We have to be in the dwelling of the chosen one in order to change. It would be too tempting otherwise to simply try to live as men."

Bridget was quiet for a moment, considering his words. The time was coming when a plan—no matter how bizarre—would have to be hatched. Being a prisoner in her own home sucked.

"How about this?" she asked casually. "We crack the shutters and let a bird get in. He changes into a man and we have a conversation. Either he'll remain one with the flock and we'll negotiate or he'll somehow reclaim his individuality like you and I'll have *two* naked guys stuck in my house with me."

His expression was nothing short of horrified. "You would let the Unkind into your home? Voluntarily? Are you *mad*, woman?"

"If you have a better plan, spit it out because we have to *do* something. My sanity's going to run out long before the food does."

"I think that's a bad plan. A very bad plan."

She wondered if he was that afraid of his flock or if he just didn't want another naked guy hanging around, stealing his thunder.

"Okay...how about fire? We could make big torches and wave them around to keep the birds at bay until we get in my truck. Then we can at the very least drive to someplace more spacious and less remote to hide."

"They would create an air current that would extinguish the flames as soon as you stepped out. There's no place you can hide from them. Plus, if I walk out your door I'll shift into bird form. Will you believe it's me if I tap on your window with my beak?"

"Maybe I could put a necklace on you," Bridget teased, imagining a big raven in her pearls.

Khail didn't smile. "We won't make it to your truck."

"I have to *do* something!"

"What if it's only me?" The question came quietly and the anguish in his eyes cut her to the quick. "What if, for some reason, you're only immune to *my* touch? If you let another in and he succeeds where I have failed, my mind will break, *moya kisa*. My body will not die, but my soul will be dead forever. I *cannot* lose you."

The intensity of his words backed Bridget up a few steps. Where did this bond come from? How could he be so powerfully attached to her in such a short time?

She knew, somehow, fate had brought them together. His presence in her sketches, her immunity to his deadly touch, suggested it was all part of some great master plan. And perhaps the immediate depths of his feelings for her were a part of his fierce warrior nature.

But her own heart refused to be so freely or quickly given, despite her already being closer to him than she had any other person in her life. And why, if fate meant for them to be together, was fate making it so damn hard?

"Another plan," she said, changing the subject—too abruptly judging by the flash of pain in his eyes. "I'll call somebody. I'll call the fire department and tell them a flock of crazy birds is keeping me from leaving my house. Maybe they can spray them with the fire hose or something."

"They can't see them."

"*What?*" Bridget threw up her hands in disgust. "Are you shittin' me? The creepy werebirds with the supervillain touch of death are fucking *invisible*, too?"

"I don't know why you can see us when nobody else can."

She couldn't do it any more. There was no way out, but she couldn't be trapped like this for another single second.

"Fine! I give up." She ran toward the door, ready to get it over with, but Khail grabbed her arm before she could reach the knob. "I can't win, Khail. And I have to leave this house. I've been a prisoner before, and I won't be one again. I won't. I *can't!*"

She fought him, kicking at him and trying to twist her wrists free. He held fast, absorbing the abuse and hauling her up against his body. His arms tightened around her, holding her close until her rage gave way to sobs.

⁎⁎⁎

Khail still tasted the acrid fear of her near death on his tongue.

He'd nearly missed her. The triumphant shrieking of the Unkind as she moved ever closer to their grasp had almost driven him to his knees, but then his fingers had closed around her wrist and he'd jerked her away from the door. They almost got her. The bastards had nearly taken her from him.

Why do you defy us, Mikhail? Why do you betray the Unkind?

Leave her alone.

We will wait. Our patience is eternal.

He stroked Bridget's hair while she cried, easily absorbing the blows when she occasionally hammered at his chest with her fists. Holding her kept him from beating his own fists against the wall.

He couldn't protect her from this. He didn't know how. With no horse under him or scimitar in his hand, he was no better than an old woman. And he was going to fail her as surely as he'd failed his wife and daughter.

Pain permeated his senses. He wanted this woman to be his forever. Not because she kept the Unkind at bay. Not because she was the first to survive his touch. But because he already loved her.

Bridget slipped away from him, but she didn't move in the direction of the door so he let her go. Instead she went to the sink to splash cold water over her face. She shuddered a couple of times as she pulled herself together.

Mikhail.

Rage welled up inside of him, but the stronger his anger became, the louder the Unkind grew.

Mikhail...die... You must be punished. The woman must die. We are...coming.

The droning became more persistent and Khail instinctively moved toward Bridget as she turned from the sink. He reached out for her, but she pushed him away.

"Please, *moya kisa*. They are so loud in my head."

"Oh, boo-fucking-hoo. Why don't you just leave me alone—go shit on somebody's windshield or something."

He watched—stunned by her anger—as she walked away. He forced himself to let her go despite his need for her. Her emotional upheaval was understandable, and yet her words still pierced him like a pike through his gut.

She was about halfway to her bedroom when they heard the scraping sound. He turned, trying to identify the source just as Bridget shouted, "The fireplace!"

Khail moved toward the counter, intent on grabbing a knife from the block, but Bridget was moving toward the hearth. "No!"

She got there before he could stop her. Black feathers dusted her cheek as a raven, covered in soot and slightly bedraggled, flew past her. The flapping of its wings didn't cover the scurrying sound of another making its way through the pipe.

"Bridget, go in the bathroom," Khail yelled as the raven flew toward him. "Go now!"

He whipped the blanket from around his waist and swung it like a net. The bird didn't have time to react and Khail caught it, gathering the blanket corners together like a hobo's sack. He slid the ends under the heavy table leg. It wouldn't hold if the raven shifted, but it bought him the seconds he needed to get to Bridget who, of course, hadn't listened.

He watched her as she pulled a heavy, metal grate across the opening, and realized while he was capturing one of the Unkind, Bridget had quickly pulled paper and wood from a box next to the hearth and laid the makings of a fire. As the scraping sounds in the chimney grew closer, he watched her slide the top of the grate onto three pins which held it fast with quick turns of the heads. Then she pulled a long match from a tin box and struck it against the stone. Flame flared to life, and she poked it through the grate and set it to the crumpled paper.

The reaction of the Unkind was immediate and dropped Khail to the floor. He clutched his head, shaking it as if he could dislodge the agonizing screams of outrage. Behind him he heard another male screaming along with them, but he was powerless to move.

Bridget, he shouted in his own mind, but the words never left his throat.

Bridget knew the instant the bird had fully retreated from the chimney pipe because the smoke already burning her eyes started drafting properly. If the birds were smart enough to block her chimney, she'd be screwed—and even if they didn't it would get mighty hot keeping a fire going day and night—but she'd cross those bridges when she came to them.

Now she had to deal with the two men writhing on the floor of her cabin. After grabbing a large—but manageable—chunk of wood from the box, she stepped over a now-naked Khail.

Oh God, she couldn't believe what she had said to him. It was cruel, but she'd been so overwhelmed at that moment. She would have to make it up to him somehow.

But for now, the bigger concern—the naked blond guy covered in soot thrashing under her blanket.

Their physical torment already seemed to be easing, and Bridget's fingers tightened on the log. She could knock him over the head, but she was afraid she'd kill him. A dead raven couldn't negotiate. Then again, she probably *couldn't* kill him—they were immortal, so the only result would be that eventually her arm would get tired.

When the man started to rise, Bridget froze. She had no idea what the hell to do now. Even though she'd suggested this very idea, she hadn't really thought it through all that well. Thankfully, she heard Khail getting to his feet as well. At least she wasn't alone.

"What's your name?" she asked the new naked guy—who wasn't nearly as impressive nude as Khail—and she was pleasantly surprised by the steadiness of her voice. She must be getting used to this horror novel crap, after all.

"We are the Unkind."

"So I've heard. But what is *your* name?"

"We are the Unkind. You must die."

Creep. Bridget jumped a little at Khail's touch and she almost dropped the makeshift weapon she had no idea what to do with. He was silent, and she assumed the two men were either communicating telepathically or simply sizing each other up. She guessed the latter.

"I told you to hide in the bathroom," he said to her in a low voice.

"I was busy. And why the bathroom?"

"So you would have water if I was taken and you had to remain in there."

"You must die," the blond said. "We are the Unkind."

Bridget was pretty sick of hearing that. And she was about to tell him so when he made a sudden break for the door.

Chapter Four

The guy should have remembered the blanket, Bridget thought. By the time he slipped, recovered and started running again, Khail had time to react. She watched him tackle the intruder as though he were a linebacker instead of a Cossack. Just in case, though, she hurried to the door, wielding the log like a baseball bat. She couldn't let him get to the door or to the shutters.

"She must die, Mikhail," the blond said through gritted teeth as he tried to get his fingers to Khail's throat.

"You are not taking her from me, Hermann."

Bridget wondered if they all knew each other's names or if their mental link simply coughed up whatever information they needed. She watched them wrestling on the floor, and her fear ebbed slightly while she pondered how ridiculous two naked men looked rolling around trying to thumb each other's eyes out.

The small table overturned as each man fought for control. Khail managed to throw a punch to the jaw, snapping the blond's head back. But then Hermann managed to get his hands around Khail's throat and Bridget's fear returned. She moved forward, hoping she could hit the intruder with the log hard enough to stun him without missing and hitting Khail instead.

Then suddenly they stopped. With no visible communication, they just moved apart and sat staring at one another, panting. Exertion and hostility had both of them flushed a deep scarlet, and bruises were already blossoming on Khail's throat to match the ones on his adversary's jaw.

"We will talk," Hermann said, but his voice retained the slightly flat quality that told her he was still one with the flock.

"Do me a favor—fix the table and sit in the chairs." Both men did as she asked, though the items that had been on the table remained scattered across the floor. "Now scoot yourselves in. That's good."

Now, at least, she could pretend they had pants on, which would make any negotiations slightly less unnerving. Khail nude she could handle, but Hermann was another matter entirely.

"Why are you not dead?" he asked bluntly.

"I don't know. I've already gone through all this with Khail, and with your mental mojo, you should know that. I don't know why I didn't die. I don't know why I can see you. And I don't know why you still want me dead."

"You have upset the balance."

"I thought it was all about being random. You randomly tried to end my life, and I randomly didn't die. Why can't you let it go at that?"

Hermann looked decidedly perplexed, which Bridget took as a good sign. If *they* weren't one hundred percent sure of what was going on, perhaps they could be swayed.

"Why do *you* think I didn't die?" she asked, curious as to whether or not they had their own theory.

By now she'd set the log down and moved close enough to rest her hands on the table and lean forward. She realized her mistake a second too late.

Hermann exploded out of the chair, catching her on the way by. They hit the floor, her head thankfully bouncing off his arm rather than the hardwood floor.

His fingertips brushed her mouth and she realized his lips were moving. She had a quick flash of Khail doing that very same thing.

Oh shit. He was trying to kill her. She jerked her face away just as a growling mass of muscle collided with them. This time her head did smack the floor as Hermann was torn away from her.

A knee—she had no idea whose—caught her in the side and she rolled away. She scrambled for the log she'd carelessly dropped once the men were seated. Finally she found the chunk of wood. She pushed herself up, but her free hand slipped in spilled coffee and she went down again.

Black wings slapped her in the face and she realized with horror the men had shifted. Fear kept her frozen for a few terrifying seconds. Obviously she wasn't as accustomed to this supernatural shit as she'd thought. The two ravens circled in the air like seasoned air combat veterans—feinting, testing one another.

Bridget gained her feet, but stood helplessly as they began dive-bombing one another. She lifted the log, then lowered it again when she realized she couldn't tell which one was Khail.

The ravens tangled amidst a flurry of wings and talons. They both shrieked and blood droplets hit the floor before they broke apart, each retreating to an opposite corner of the room.

Twice more they went at each other, and Bridget grew more terrified with every pass—with every spilled drop of blood. Which one was Khail?

An idea came to her, and she ran to the door and hit the switches for the full overhead lights. In the sudden glare she could see both ravens were tiring, both of them wounded.

She watched intently and finally spotted what she was looking for. As one of the ravens flapped his giant wings, a fine, almost invisible dusting of soot sifted to the floor. She eased forward, waiting for her moment. When the Hermann bird dipped as if about to swoop up under Khail, she swung like Babe Ruth and the raven sailed toward the far wall.

He shifted before the collision, and even though she was expecting it this time, the visual impact still stunned her. Khail shifted at almost the same moment, and she was dismayed to see him sink onto the couch, his chest heaving and blood running down the side of his face. There were numerous—hopefully superficial—slashes on his arms and chest.

He would have to wait. Hermann was crumpled on the floor in front of the fireplace. Bridget ran to the kitchen and yanked open the third drawer from the fridge—the dreaded junk drawer. It took only seconds to find the bag of zip ties. She grabbed a few and headed back.

Hermann was already stirring, so she acted fast. One zip tie drawn tightly around each wrist, then another connecting those two. She had no hopes they would hold him if he shifted, but he wouldn't be grabbing at her again anytime soon.

In the meantime she was relieved Khail got to his feet and went to the sink to wash some of the blood away and refresh himself. He managed to give her a shaky smile on his way back. "I will live, *moya kisa.*"

She wanted to throw herself in his arms, but Hermann was fully awake and glaring at her with undisguised hostility. It took a great deal of willpower not to give him a cheap shot in the ribs. "What the hell was that about?"

He blinked. "You must die. Mikhail has betrayed the Unkind."

It struck her, then, what had happened. "You think he botched it on purpose, don't you? You decided he was what...so overcome by my snoring and bedhead that he mis-chanted so I could live? So you were sent in to do it properly."

His silence confirmed her theory, so she turned to Khail. "Did he get enough of it done? To be able to tell, I mean?"

"No, you were able to escape his touch before he was finished with the words."

So the Unkind had no idea if Khail's touch had misfired or if he'd done it deliberately. And they also still had no idea if it was only Khail's touch to which she was immune.

"Maybe I should let him try again," she mused aloud.

"You *are* insane," Khail muttered.

"At least we would know for sure."

"The risk is too great. I would rather we never know than risk losing you."

Bridget sighed. Even in a high stress situation he managed to be utterly romantic. And it worked, damn him.

"Then we may as well figure out how to get him out of here," she said, "because this accomplishes nothing. We can't prove you didn't not kill me on purpose, and they won't be satisfied until they try again. We're not going to let them, so he may as well go."

"The Unkind will come," Hermann said smugly.

She gazed down at him, noting he hadn't even tried to test the strength of the zip ties. Not that she trusted him. He'd already gotten the better of her once—twice if she counted his entrance through the chimney—and he had a slightly mean look to him.

"How did you come to be cursed?" she asked. As long as he was talking, she might as well indulge her curiosity.

There. It was only a flicker, but for a second she'd seen a glimpse of humanity and emotion—remorse. "I beat my wife to death in a jealous rage. She was innocent."

Bridget took a step backward, her blood suddenly so cold it was as if she'd been submerged in ice water. He was a wife beater. The tremors began so deep in her muscles she hadn't a prayer of hiding them. Her hand shook as she unconsciously raised it to rub the spot at the back of her skull—the site of the fracture that, along with six other broken bones and a ruptured spleen, had almost killed her.

He's dead. The son of a bitch who had vowed to love and cherish her until death they did part had died alone in prison, in the cage her testimony had provided for him.

She looked Hermann in the eye. "I want you out of my home."

"Shall he leave by the front door?" Khail asked pointedly.

For a fleeting moment, Bridget didn't care. The whole damn flock could fly in and pluck out her eyeballs as long as this abusive, murdering piece of shit left her cabin.

She took a deep breath, trying to separate the past from the present. She wanted Hermann gone, but how the hell were they supposed to get him back outside without opening the door or a window? The prospect of simply shoving him into the bedroom and somehow securing the door didn't appeal, either. Being barricaded inside a three-room cabin was bad enough. She didn't want to lose a room. Besides, in his human form he could open the storm shutters for his feathered friends.

"You're going out the same way you came in," she finally announced.

Both men looked at the fireplace and shuddered. The fire was almost out—it had been clumsily built in haste, after all—but small flames still licked at the kindling.

"I suggest you climb out the pipe faster than you climbed in," she added. "And if you're communicating with the flock right now, hatching a plan, you can stop. Any bird in that pipe but you on your way out is going to get barbecued. *Capische?*"

"We will come for you," Hermann said in that flat voice she was really coming to despise.

"And I'll kick your ass again," she promised.

෪෬

Khail almost sagged to the floor in relief when they were alone once again. Getting Hermann to shift, then shoving him into the fireplace was quite a chore, but hearing him scrambling up the pipe to keep his tail feathers from getting scorched made it almost worth the effort. As soon as Hermann was free of the chimney, Bridget built a small fire and then pulled Khail over to the couch.

He put his arm around her and she snuggled up to his side and sighed. Khail kissed the part in her hair. "I am sorry, *moya kisa.*"

He felt her take a deep breath. "It's not your fault, really. You are what you are and what happened, happened. I really, really hate the phrase 'it is what it is', but...it is."

"I don't know—"

"I don't want to talk about it anymore," Bridget interrupted. She pulled away from his side, and when he made to protest, she actually smiled at him. Parting her knees, she moved to sit astride him. His cock rose immediately, seeking the heaven between her thighs. "I'd rather see if we can make your naked ass squeak on my leather couch."

For a moment she begged with her eyes—*please just let me pretend for a few minutes that everything is okay.* Finally, he relaxed his face with a slow smile.

"My ass will not squeak," he said in the booming "Cossack" voice that made her laugh. "And no squeaking could be heard over you bellowing my name anyway."

"Prove it," she replied, a naughty gleam having chased the desperation from her eyes.

He growled and started tugging at the belt of her robe. "You're a saucy wench, Bridget Sawyer."

The red satin knot gave him fits and he'd have ripped the damn thing off her body if he didn't like the way it looked on her so much. He gave up on the knot after a few more tries since the little minx was enjoying his frustration too much to help.

Instead Khail slid his hands inside the robe, gliding them over the tops of her breasts. He skimmed over her collarbone, her shoulders, pushing the red satin back as he went. The contrast of pale skin framed by scarlet fascinated him, and he slid the satin over her nipples, teasing her with the slippery fabric.

Bridget squirmed on his lap, and when the heat of her moist cunt brushed the length of his cock, Khail groaned. He wanted to bury himself in her, explode into her, filling his woman with his seed. Bending his head forward, he drew one strawberry nipple between his lips, sucking gently before turning his attention to the other.

Her fingers tangled in his hair and she arched her back, thrusting her breasts toward him. His muscles trembled ever so slightly as his aching cock strained toward the heat between her thighs. He cupped her breasts, his tongue teasing first one peak and then the other until she whimpered.

When Bridget reached down between their bodies and took him in her hand, Khail's sac tightened in anticipation and a fine sheen of sweat broke out on his brow. Her touch was tentative at first, hesitant, and excited him all the more for it.

"You have the touch of an angel, *moya kisa*," he whispered hoarsely.

"Mmmm...but would an angel do this?"

Bridget slid backwards off his lap, settling between his thighs. Her lips parted and there wasn't enough willpower in the world to keep his hips from lifting, the head of his cock meeting her halfway.

His whole body jerked when her lips closed over him, and he put his hands over his head, digging his fingernails into the leather to prevent himself from grasping her hair and fucking her mouth frantically like a sex-starved youth.

But he didn't want to frighten her or make her feel like she wasn't in control, so he gritted his teeth and let her do all the work.

Her tongue flicked over the tip of his cock, lapping at the drop of moisture there like the kitten he called her. He managed not to explode, but when she swallowed his length again and cupped his balls in one hand, he had to slide his own hands behind his neck and interlock his fingers to keep from holding her head while he pumped into her mouth.

"You are killing me here," he groaned.

She chuckled around his flesh and the vibration shot straight through him. His hands broke free of his willpower, but at the last second he stuck them under her arms and hauled her back onto his lap.

She grinned at him, then licked her lips. Tucking her knees against his hips, she raised herself up and grasped his cock once again.

Khail hissed in a breath through his teeth as Bridget lowered herself onto him. She was wet and ready for him, and he groaned aloud when he sank fully into her.

Her breasts were tantalizingly close to his face and he caught one nipple between his lips. He nipped at it—gently, tentatively—and when Bridget moaned and threw her head back, he nipped a little harder. Then he moved to her other breast to torment it in kind. She started rocking, creating a delicious friction that hummed through his body.

"Oh...Khail..." She moaned, and the flush of her cheeks and the husky way she said his name put him on the brink.

He reached down and pressed his thumb to her clit. Her hips bucked, her cunt squeezing his cock, as he made gentle circles around the nub. Her muscles tensed and she cried out—cried his name—and then Khail followed her over, pounding up into her as her body clenched, milking him dry.

Bridget collapsed against his chest as tremors wracked them both, and he curled his arms around her, her head tucked under his chin. It took a few seconds to realize the heaving of her chest was not panting. She was crying silently.

He tipped her chin up so he could see her face, and his heart ached to see the tears streaming down her face. "Did I hurt you? Did I frighten you? I am sorry, Bridget. I—"

She shook her head, but all he could see was the trembling of her lower lip as she tried to get the words out. "I...I wish you were my husband."

Sorrow at a loss they had yet to suffer and rage at the gods and the Unkind filled him, and he pulled her close again. He squeezed her tightly, as if he could physically bond her to him so nobody could ever take her away from him. He would never have enough of this woman. *Never.*

His own eyes burned as his fierce, sweet little kitten sobbed into his chest. "Being your husband would be the greatest honor and joy of my life. Perhaps..."

But he let the words trail away. There was nothing he could say to ease her pain—nor his own. As she had said, *it is what it is.* To live with false hope would only hurt her more when the inevitable came.

Assuming she lived. He pressed a kiss to her hair. Because no matter what vows he made, if the Unkind found a way in en masse, there was nothing he could do to save her. He would fight to the death, but he would lose, and then they would have her.

"I am afraid," he admitted, the words so foreign to him he was surprised he could speak them aloud. "I will bleed for you, *moya kisa.* I will gladly die for you. But I am so afraid I cannot save you."

"There's something I have to tell you," Bridget whispered, and the hair rose on the back of his neck.

Chapter Five

Khail's words shook Bridget in a way even seeing him shapeshift hadn't. If her fierce warrior feared all was lost, she would find it very hard to keep it alive herself.

She thought of her sketches—of the published illustrations. After Khail's confession, she had forgotten them, and then they'd been distracted by Hermann's arrival. Perhaps subconsciously she feared the drawings would change everything—but for the better or for the worst she couldn't say. She knew, however, the time had come to share them.

"I need to show you something, actually." She pulled out of Khail's embrace, and her heart skipped a beat when she saw the intensity in his eyes. "I know I should have shown you earlier, but I...I was scared."

He followed her nude into the bedroom and then waited silently while she fished under the bed for the book she'd kicked under there. She flipped the book open to the first illustration featuring his likeness, then handed it to him. His expression changed from puzzlement to wonder to horror, and her own stomach clenched in response.

"What is this?" he asked hoarsely. "Where did you get this?"

"I'm an illustrator. I drew an early sketch from that series and offered it for sale on the Internet. A publisher saw it and thought it would be perfect for a series they'd recently bought. I've been doing the illustrations for the books for several years."

"Do you know what this is?"

"I know it's you. I don't know how, but you've been living in my subconscious for years, apparently. And in my dreams."

Perhaps she had sensed his bloody past, causing her to cast him in the role her muse had chosen for him. And maybe this had been fate's way of preparing her, making sure she would recognize her soul mate when he appeared. For she could no longer deny that's exactly what Khail was.

"This is the Beyond, *moya kisa*. It is the place of the gods and of the Unkind."

Bridget shuddered, colder than she'd ever been in her life. While years of sketching her one true love may be romantic, she did *not* want to be fated to this place of death. "Why is it in my head, Khail? How do I draw this?"

"I don't know," he admitted. "Have you ever cheated death? Not merely by waking from a coma or resuscitation, but have you ever walked Beyond and returned? Have you ever been declared legally dead?"

Even in the intensive care unit, her heart had never stopped beating. Not until her knuckles began to throb did Bridget realize how tightly her hands were clenched together in her lap. *No, it can't be that. Please let it be anything but that.* "No."

"There must be something, Bridget," Khail persisted, his hand covering hers. "You are an aberration, and we must know why. If there's any way I can save you, it lies in your drawings. It lies within you."

She jerked away from his touch, tears stinging her eyes. "I don't like to talk about it."

Horror burned like acid in her stomach. Shame, confusion, anger and so many other emotions she thought she'd laid to rest besieged her. She shuddered, clutching his fingers so hard it had to be painful for him.

He settled back on his heels, never looking away from her face. "So there is something. Tell me, love."

Bridget took a deep, steadying breath, then let it all out in a rush. "I'm the child of a domestic murder-suicide. My father shot my mother when she was eight months pregnant with me, then shot himself. She was clinically...they did a Cesarean..."

That was all she could get out, but judging by Khail's expression, it was enough.

He closed his eyes and dropped his head. "You were born of a dead mother."

"Yes." Tears spilled over her cheeks and she had to swallow hard past the lump in her throat. She'd never told anybody but her former therapist about the circumstances of her birth. Even her husband hadn't known.

Being taken warm and alive from her mother's lifeless body had not seemed to her to be the miracle the tattered newspaper articles claimed it to be. Rather it seemed nothing but a tangible starting point for the dark pain and loss that would be her life.

"Physically, spiritually, you were still one with your mother when she died," Khail said. "Your soul was carried by hers into the Beyond, until you were delivered and your body called it back. The gods were kind and let it return. That act was a gift. A gift no others but the gods themselves can take back."

She digested that for a moment, trying to grasp the concept of her life as a gift when she'd always considered it a curse. "And that hasn't happened before?"

"Technology has changed things, but still very, very few have actually walked in the Beyond. The chances of the Unkind randomly choosing one of those people are...well, you are the first in my own time as cursed."

"Does that mean I won't die?"

With his eyes closed, Khail opened his mind to the Unkind. *She is Untouchable.*

Impossible. There has not been an Untouchable one in many centuries. You would employ lies now in your betrayal.

Her soul has walked Beyond. Concentrating, he imagined Bridget's sketches, transmitting the mental images to the collective. *She was born of a dead mother.*

The buzzing receded, surged, then receded again. A consultation with the gods Beyond, perhaps?

It is decided you speak the truth, Mikhail. The woman is Untouchable.

Then leave this place. Khail braced himself.

You will come and suffer your punishment, Mikhail. You are of the Unkind.

And if I don't?

There was a sharp hissing sound, and Khail winced at its vibration through his mind. Maybe he could bargain for time—just a little more time in which to love Bridget enough to get her through a lifetime. *Her* lifetime. He could never get enough of her to last him through his own endless existence.

Mikhail, you will come and accept your fate. Your betrayal must be accounted for. If you do not come willingly, we will drive you mad. So mad you might hurt the woman.

I will never hurt her.

An unholy shrieking speared his brain, lingering for so many seconds before fading it actually left a phantom pain, an echo of their anger. *You cannot close yourself to us, Mikhail. We can hurt you. How many days...even hours...can you stand the pain before you do what you must to end it? Come to us, Mikhail. You are of the Unkind.*

When Khail finally opened his eyes and reached up to stroke her cheek, Bridget exhaled in relief. He had looked so pained she was afraid he might leave her. It was a ridiculous fear, she knew—her father's shame was not her own. But she knew it logically, not necessarily emotionally.

"You will die someday, but not at the hands of the Unkind. You will probably be a very old woman when your time comes."

There was a sadness in his eyes that didn't quite jive with what she considered welcome news. "What? Why are you looking at me like that?"

Before he even opened his mouth, it hit her. With the threat of imminent death lifted from her shoulders, the underlying reality hit home. There was no happy ending for them here.

The supernatural ravens camped outside the cabin weren't going to simply fly off to their next victim, leaving her and Khail to live happily ever after. She'd fallen in love with an almost four hundred year old winged shifter of death—one who couldn't even leave this cabin in the form of a man. Had she really thought they could play at being normal people?

"It's time for me to leave you, *moya kisa*."

Bridget's throat closed and she had to fight to get air in and out of her lungs. It was too soon. Too sudden. She wasn't ready. "No...no..."

It was all she could get out. Everything else bottlenecked in her throat. She had just allowed herself to love this man. She wanted more time. She wanted *always*.

"They will torture us as long as I stay, Bridget. Though the touch of the Unkind won't kill you, they *can* hurt you. And they will try to use me to hurt you because I must be punished for my betrayal. I can't let that happen."

She shook her head until she could speak again. "What betrayal? It's not your fault I didn't die."

"My betrayal was in falling in love with you, *moya kisa*."

Her heart ached in her chest, and she clutched his hands. "Just stay in here, then. Just stay in here where they can't get to you."

"You know that's not possible. As long as I'm in here, you can't go out there. You can't live that way. They would hurt you and then take me anyway. And I can't stand their voices in my head any longer. I'm afraid I'll go mad. I have to go."

He turned and left her bedroom, and Bridget cried out. This couldn't be happening. "Not yet! Don't go yet! Please, Khail, don't leave me."

At the front door he turned to face her. "It will only prolong the pain if I stay. Within minutes this will all be behind you, Bridget. You'll be free, and I want that for you."

"Just a little more time," she pleaded.

"It won't be enough. There isn't enough time in all eternity for us to prepare to let go." He pulled her into his arms and kissed her, a brutal kiss from the depths of his soul. Bridget wrapped her arms around his neck, unwilling to let it end, but he pushed her away. "There is one thing I'd have you never forget, *moya kisa*. For the rest of your life remember that you have been loved as truly and as fiercely as a man can love a woman."

Then Khail opened the door and Bridget grabbed for him, but he shifted. Tail feathers tickled the tips of her fingers before the world exploded in a tornado of black wings and razor-sharp beaks and talons.

"No!" she screamed, waving her hands and trying to drive them away from her already falling raven. She stumbled down the steps of the porch as they dragged him through the dirt.

The flock ignored her, as if killing her had never been their objective at all. She tried to crawl to him, ignoring the cuts she received as she shoved birds out of the way.

There was blood. So much blood. The flock was tearing Khail's flesh from his bones, and the gore rose in Bridget's throat. They were going to kill him.

"Stop!" she cried as black bodies swarmed in a violent frenzy, obscuring her view. "He's been punished enough. He has *suffered* enough!"

A raven flapped in her face, determined to drive her back onto the porch. She grabbed at it, trying to rip its feathers from its body. "Fuck you! He's mine. He is *mine*!"

The bird finally retreated, and she screamed as a bloody pulp was lifted into the air in front of her, impaled on the talons of a particularly large raven.

As quickly as the Unkind had come, they were gone. The air was still, the woods silent, and the sky a clear and brilliant blue.

Bridget sobbed until she gagged, a cluster of bloody feathers clenched in her fist. She lay uncaring in the dirt, her tears making tiny mud puddles.

A bird—an average, everyday bird—called out cheerfully, and Bridget screamed. It was a raw, primal scream ripped from the very depths of her soul.

"Why? *Why* did you give my life back to me? To watch me suffer? To get off on my pain? This is a gift? Well, I don't want it. Do you hear me? I don't want your fucking gift!"

She rolled up to her knees, her tear-stained face turned to the sky. "Take it back. Take *me* back if you can't give him to me."

There was no response. Only the happy chirping of tiny, benign forest birds. Bridget covered her ears and sobbed some more.

80C3

The next three days passed in a brutal fog of tears and rage. Bridget had nothing with which to distract herself from her emotions. She didn't own a television and she didn't have the concentration for reading. Nor did she have the heart to work. The thought of sketching Khail's face and the hellish place that owned his soul was beyond her ability to cope.

Several times she had picked up her pencils, only to find her mind flooded with images of Khail not as the antagonist of the series, but as her lover. As the man who had stolen her heart. As the wounded bird ripped apart by his own Unkind.

It occurred to her she would have to force herself to draw again. Her livelihood depended upon it. But she didn't believe she would ever be able to illustrate for that series again.

She showered. She put food in her mouth and chewed and swallowed. Made coffee, drank it, and then made more. She even brushed her hair. But her heart was in none of it. She just didn't care any more.

Bridget would survive. She knew that. Horrors were overcome, strength was renewed, contentment was found. But she was so damn tired of simply surviving the cycle. Contentment didn't do it for her anymore. She wanted to be happy.

She'd laughed once. Torturing herself with memories of their lovemaking, she'd thought of the loud and fierce Cossack voice he'd used to amuse her. It had made her laugh again to think of it, but her amusement had soon faded to more tears.

On the fourth morning, Bridget got out of bed determined to take a walk. She wasn't nearly ready to put the pain of her loss behind her—she didn't think she'd ever be able to this time—but she needed to reconnect with the life she'd made for herself. The life that had been enough for her before Khail flew through her door.

Bridget embraced the chill of the spring morning, letting it revive her senses and bring color to her cheeks. She was too worn out and weak from lack of sleep to match her usual brisk pace, but she wandered down the path that doubled as a sorry excuse for a driveway on her bimonthly trips into town.

Trying her best to block out the happy twittering of the birds, she concentrated instead on the solitary beauty that had first drawn her to this place. Flowers were blooming. Lush green leaves had returned to the deciduous trees. She wished Khail could see it.

She was almost to the brook when she saw a flash of movement through the trees and around the bend. She froze—it was too tall to be an animal and moving too fast. It was a man.

He came around the bend, stopping when he realized she was standing there. Convinced her mind was playing cruel tricks on her, Bridget simply stood there, waiting, as he started walking again. He looked the same—right down to his lack of clothing—but he was smiling when he reached her. He cupped his palm to her face and then—with his warm hand against her cool cheek, she knew he was real.

And he was in the form of a man. He had said they couldn't do that—that they were only men inside the dwelling of the chosen ones. Yet here he stood, in the middle of her driveway. It just wasn't possible.

"Khail?" Her voice was little more than a whisper, so afraid was she he was merely a mirage conjured by her tortured mind.

"I have served my penance, *moya kisa*. The gods have gifted my life back to me."

Gifted, as she had been. She who was now immune to the random death meted out by the Unkind.

"What does that mean?" Life had taught her not to give hope wings, but it swelled nonetheless.

"It means I can gorge myself on roast mutton and try one of those Caramel Macchiato things and make love to you day and night for the rest of our lives. It took time for my body to grow accustomed to being mortal again—an excruciating process—but I am here now, and I'm no longer of the Unkind."

"They lifted the curse? So you're like me now? Immune to them?" She hardly dared believe it, and she felt a need to have the specifics. *This* was truly a gift worth keeping.

"I have done my penance and the gods deemed me worthy of the gift—and they heard your pleas as well. Sometimes things are not as random as they appear. I was always meant to find you, and I am free to grow old with you, *moya kisa*. I am forgiven."

He barely got the words out before she was in his arms. She clung to him, reveling in the strength of his arms as they held her close to his chest. His *naked* chest.

"We need to buy you some clothes." She giggled. "Eventually."

Khail tipped her chin up and kissed her—a soft, warm welcome home kiss that washed the pain and sadness of their lives away like a cleansing spring rain. "I love you, Bridget Sawyer."

"And I love you. As truly and as fiercely as a woman can love a man."

He lifted her right off her feet and swung her around, hugging her almost too tightly. She laughed, and he laughed with her, their shared joy ringing through the woods.

She closed her eyes and nuzzled her face against his neck. "Thank you," she whispered.

From far away came the faint answering call of a single raven.

About the Author

Shannon Stacey married her Prince Charming in 1993, and is the proud mother of a future Nobel Prize for Science-winning bookworm and an adrenaline junkie with a flair for drama. She lives in New England, where her two favorite activities are trying to stay warm and writing stories of happily ever after.

You can contact Shannon or sign up for her newsletter through her website: www.shannonstacey.com.

King of Prey

Mandy M. Roth

Dedication

To Jaycee, you've had a hell of a year and through it all you've still managed to find humor and love in all around you. You're an amazing mother, friend and author. Anytime you need a late night "lay it on the line" session, my door is always open. Villains got nothing on us, babes. Besides, if all else fails we can find our way "over yonder". I still have no idea what that means. Seriously though, you've been with me every step of the way and for that I'll never be able to thank you enough.

To Michelle, you never flinch when I rope you into another project. You smile and step up to the plate. I hope we never stop getting into trouble together because the bailing one another out is way too much fun to stop now.

To Shannon, you've officially entered paranormal territory. Welcome to the club, hon. A word to the wise, screen your calls. When you see my number, clear your schedule. I can gab with the best of 'em.

To Sydney, may we never lose our writing jitters and always be shocked to be here, doing what we love.

To Angie, we've made it through another project without the need of heavy narcotics. I'm sure my shaking hands and stuttering will subside soon. Sorry for any hair loss I might have caused you. All joking aside, thanks for your insight, edits and shoulder to cry on. They are all much appreciated.

Prologue

Accipitridae Realm

"King Kabril, you cannot stand idly by while your people cry out for you to lead. Our race will not survive unless you take a wife. The mating magik that governs our lands will not grant unions the blessing of children if the leader himself refuses to sire offspring. You know the laws, the way of the land and the demands you must meet as king. The time has come, my lord. This can wait no longer. The people of Accipitridae need you to act now."

Though Sachin's words were the truth, they were not what Kabril wanted to hear. No. He much rather preferred hearing all was well and that none of the people under his rule were upset. Of course, those moments were few and far between as of late. Sighing, Kabril leaned back on his throne and stared into the reflective mixture Sachin held in the bowl. He ran his fingers over the scrolled armrest and glanced down at the carved hawks. A slow smile caused by pride moved over his face. Pride in his people, their traditions and their beliefs, even though those very beliefs were the cause of the unrest.

The people of his kingdom assumed their issues with conceiving were due to his reluctance to accept what they deemed to be destiny. Kabril wasn't a staunch believer, as he should be, but it came from being the one forced to accept a wife he did not want. As their ruler, it was his sworn duty to do what was best for the kingdom, regardless how much it pained him.

"My lord," Sachin pressed, his reluctance to let the subject rest putting Kabril's already taxed nerves on edge.

Taking a deep, calming breath, Kabril reminded himself of how proud he was, and should always be, of his people's customs and beliefs. Although he was less than pleased with the Oracle—whom they held in such high esteem—choosing a bride for him. According to the prophecies, the Oracle would select a woman fit to lead his people and he was honor bound to obey. It was also said the union would produce children, something their kind sorely lacked. Once heavily populated, his lands were no longer bursting with the sounds of children singing and playing. In truth, Kabril could scarcely recall when it was the sounds indicative of children stopped but he knew it had been far too long.

War had claimed the lives of many of his people. Still others, while immortal to a degree, possessed the ability to pass on to the afterlife should they so choose. There came a time in many people's lives when they were ready to move on. It mattered not what the cause was, their population was low, as was morale. Riches only did so much to calm the people. They wanted families.

"Cursed Magaious," he spat, not caring if he took one of the Epopisdeus' names in vain.

Sachin clapped acrimoniously. "Bringing down the wrath of the bird gods will surely ease your burden, my lord. For if you curse one, they all rise to strike."

"You push me too far, old friend." Kabril smoothed his fingertips along the wood of his throne, ignoring the internal nudge to free his temper.

"You do not push yourself far enough."

Giving Sachin a daring look, Kabril let loose another curse upon the gods. He once again selected the god he knew Sachin honored weekly in hopes of provoking his friend. He was in the mood for a fight and Sachin was always a worthy adversary. The two often sparred until matins. Depending upon the day, Sachin would either continue the match or lay his sword down to go honor the gods. Kabril had long since given up his prayers to higher powers. "A pox on Magaious and those who follow him blindly."

Sachin merely tipped his head a little and released an exasperated sigh. "Remind me again which of us is older? You seem to be acting like a fledgling, my lord."

Arguing with Sachin would get him nowhere since it was clear Sachin was not going to take his bait. Kabril drummed his fingers on his armrests, trying to devise a plan for avoiding marriage.

Especially to a human female.

Why was it the Oracle seemed to favor reopening the portal to Earth? The prophecy only stated his need to find his mate. It never said she was an Earthling. It wasn't as if an Earth woman was fit to be queen of his people. Their species was substandard to say the least. They lacked the means to be anything but human.

Kabril shuddered. The mere thought of not being able to shift forms into that of a hawk and soar the skies nearly caused him to lose the meal he'd eaten to break his fast.

The very idea of relying on machinery to lift me into the sky. How repulsive.

Not only that, but humans were foul as well. Their entire world was polluted, overpopulated and riddled with disease. The only thing Earth had less of than Accipitridae was war. His breed, the *Buteos Regalis*, had been at war with the *Falco Peregrinus* for centuries. Longer than even Kabril could recall the reason why and he was nearing his four-hundredth cycle, though he had only held the throne for one hundred and fifty of those cycles.

What was will always be.

Glancing around the Great Hall, Kabril realized it had not changed much in that time frame. Open saucers with floating wicks hung from the ceiling on chains of gold. The oil within them burned at a steady pace and on occasion he would catch glimpses of a servant scuttling about to refill them.

No. Nothing was easy. It never was. He needed to relax, take time from the demands of the throne even if just for a day and then return to it all. His schedule stopped allowing for rest periods some time ago and seemed to be brimful from morn until night.

Kabril sorely missed the days of roaming about freely, shifting shapes and soaring anywhere his heart desired. He preferred the Tocallie Mountains in the Northern Region of Accipitridae because of their isolation and beauty. Waterfalls cut through the large, foliage-covered terrain creating a serene and secluded paradise. He'd often heard Earth possessed such places of beauty and wonder but had never seen them with his own eyes so he was skeptical.

The Tocallie Mountains were favored by him for another reason—it was one of the largest portals to and from Earth. A place where, over the years, many of the humans' flying machines entered from a spot on Earth they called the Bermuda Triangle. Though rumor had it that other spots fed into the Tocallie portal too. Additional portals throughout his kingdom served as gateways from other regions of Earth but none were as active as Tocallie. As much as he disliked the humans and their flying machines, he did like to learn. Physics and medicine were two of his favorite areas of study—neither of which a king had any use for. Still, that didn't stop Kabril from seeking out new sources for learning.

Sachin cleared his throat, drawing Kabril from his thoughts. "My lord."

"What did I miss this time?"

A chortle broke free from Sachin. "Did the 'my lord' give it away?"

"Yes." Kabril cast a speculative glance at his long-time friend.

"Good." Never one to refrain from disagreeing with Kabril, Sachin was a breath of fresh air in a sea of followers. "I was saying you should visit your soon-to-be-bride and win her trust."

"Win her trust?" he echoed, afraid his hearing had gone awry.

Sachin's lips trembled. It was easy to see his personal guard and trusted friend found great amusement at Kabril's response. Sachin ran his hand over his black goatee and shook his head. "King Kabril, you must get to know the human, make her love you."

Shocked, Kabril jolted, almost falling off his throne. "Surely, you jest. Get to know *it*? Make *it* love me?"

"Perhaps we should begin with you not referring to your future wife as 'it'." Sachin turned his head and Kabril knew it was to hide his smile. The moment his friend was composed, Sachin touched the dagger on his side. It was a nervous habit Sachin had always had. The man took great solace in the knowledge his weapons were close. His silver gaze landed on Kabril. "Tell me you were not planning on abducting your future wife."

"I was actually planning on sending you to fetch her. I've no desire to visit Earth." The very idea made his stomach turn. Sachin couldn't really expect him to travel to a realm full of heathens. No king would. At best he would linger near the Tocallie portal while he sent one of his other guards through with orders to procure books and other learning tools.

"I am sorry but I will not go unless you accompany me, *my lord.*"

"Do you dare to defy me?"

Sachin leaned down and grinned. "Kabril, do not make me knock your pampered arse from that chair. You can and will go with me to find your bride. You can and will get to know her. Befriend her even. You can and will get her to love you. If I can still tolerate you after all of these centuries, I am sure she will at least be somewhat fond of you."

"Sachin?" he asked, his mouth agape. "Cease your blathering."

"Do not *Sachin* me, *my lord.* And I will not cease my anything. I have known you all of my three hundred and ninety-five cycles. I am permitted to uncover your veiled eyes when called for." He assumed a posture of superiority and shook slightly. It took Kabril a moment to realize Sachin was laughing.

Unable to stop himself, Kabril joined him, laughing from the gut. It felt good to release some of the tension he'd had locked away. In truth, Sachin knew him well. He knew that being direct worked to a certain degree. He also had a knack for taking an opposing view on a matter only to get Kabril to argue the point—all the while agreeing with Kabril. "Very well. It may be best for me to learn a *few* Earth customs."

"Actually," Sachin said, "I have something better in mind. May I suggest you alert the Advisors you will be on Earth for many moons? Perhaps Iorgos should be contacted to sit in while you are gone?"

"You wish me to call one of my brothers home to rule while I am on Earth for many moons? Now I know you jest. It is clear you suffer from the pull of the moons, Sachin. Mayhap you should seek the council of an old crone." Since four moons orbited their planet, one so large it was seen even in waking hours, it was always safe to blame them for madness.

Shaking his head, Sachin chuckled. "No, my lord. I do not jest and I have not been afflicted by the moons. There is much work to be done."

"Work?"

Sachin grinned mischievously. "Ah, the king must learn to speak as humans do, without drawing attention to himself. He must also learn the Earthly art of wooing a woman."

Kabril cringed. Nothing called "wooing" could be good.

Chapter One

Earth, two weeks later...

Rayna Vogel stared at the old home, reminiscent of baroque styling, and smiled. It had been a long time since she'd seen the sculptures adorning the corners. Layers of dirt and webs had blanketed them to the point she'd long since forgotten how beautiful they were. While visiting her grandmother's house when she was little, Rayna would wander down the street just so she could catch a glimpse of the unique home. Over the years, its ownership changed hands many times and Rayna tried her best to welcome each family. She'd been out of town for business when the newest one moved in.

She held the dish full of chicken divan and prepared to head up the steps to meet her newest neighbors. Never a social butterfly, Rayna had to force herself to get out, stay in contact with people and avoid spending time with only the animals she photographed. Animals were so much easier to deal with than people. They didn't expect her to hold long, drawn-out conversations or to return their phone calls. It was great. She loved her job.

"Can I help you?" a deep, slightly accented voice came from behind her.

Startled, Rayna tossed the dish in the air and narrowly missed dropping it onto the ground. A strong hand gripped her shoulder, and a yelp almost escaped her. Composing herself, Rayna turned and came face-to-face with a tall man with raven hair, a dark goatee and a body deserving of a magazine cover. His silver gaze, while certainly something she'd never seen before, was captivating and put her at ease. "Umm?"

"Umm?" There was no mistaking the mocking tone of his voice. He put a hand in his pocket and glanced at the dish. His nose wrinkled and for a minute, Rayna thought for sure he'd be sick. "What, may I ask, is in there?"

"It's a chicken dish," she blurted out. "I brought it to welcome you to the neighborhood. I live just down the road a bit. I'm not the greatest cook in the world but I'm not so bad—"

"Chicken?" He gasped, his eyes widening and the blood draining from his face as he reached for the dish. "You brought us chicken? To eat? A bird? For food? For us?"

Puzzled, Rayna took a step back and tried to understand what the problem could be. She came up blank. "Are you a vegetarian?"

"Sachin, how much longer must we endure this gods-forsaken realm? And why must we be—"

The silver-eyed man before her seized hold of the dish and stood at attention. "Kabril, good of you to join us. I was just greeting our neighbor." He stared at her with a question on his face. "I do apologize but I didn't quite catch your name."

"Rayna," she said, eyeing the manner in which Sachin held the dish. He looked as if he thought it would bite him. Unnerved, she glanced over her shoulder to find an equally tall man with the same jet-black hair and striking good looks. This one had eyes of gold, reflecting the mid-afternoon sun back at her. He also lacked a goatee, though he had the start of a five o'clock shadow. Her knees felt weak and her pulse sped as she stared at the man. His gaze raked over her, slow at first, like she was being judged.

"Kabril." Sachin took a step closer to her and cleared his throat. "Kabril," he said, this time more forceful than before.

Rayna never took her gaze from the man on the porch. The lightweight, white shirt he wore was unbuttoned a bit, revealing his tawny chest, and the sleeves were cuffed to mid-arm. She licked her lower lip, desperately trying to push thoughts of tasting his skin from her mind. For a split second, Rayna could have sworn she heard Sachin address Kabril as my lord but she was too swept up in the man's presence to pay much heed to how he was being addressed.

He shook his head. "W-what?"

Sachin let out a low chuckle. "Kabril, this is our neighbor Rayna."

"Rayna." Kabril's accent matched Sachin's, neither of which Rayna could place. He clenched his hands, causing the muscles in his arms to flex.

She moaned and instantly wanted it back.

Kabril's golden gaze flashed to Sachin and his brow lifted inquisitively. "Tell me she is the one."

The one?

Sachin shifted awkwardly and smiled. "The one who brought us dinner? Why, yes. She is. I'll take this inside now."

Rayna reached for the dish. "No. I mean, it's okay. You don't have to pretend to want it. I get you're not a fan of chicken. Sorry about that. I just wanted to welcome you and your—" she glanced at Kabril, "—friend to the neighborhood."

Sachin held firm to the dish. "Ah, yes. Thank you. We are here to open a new practice for Kabril. He's an avian vet, you know. I'm just his assistant."

Her eyes lit. "You work with birds? I photograph wildlife for a living."

"I know," Sachin said so softly she almost missed it.

Kabril closed the distance between them, his walk that of a refined gentleman but with a tinge of roughness. "I choose this one. She is most pleasing to the eye and..." his gaze slid lower, "...will birth fine sons."

"Huh?" While it wasn't the most intelligent response she'd ever had, it seemed fitting at the moment. The more she thought about his statement the funnier it became. Laughter bubbled up from her as she put her hand out to greet him. "Cute. Anyway, nice to meet you, Dr. Kabril. I'm sure you get this a lot but if you have a chance, I'd love for you to stop by my place and have a look at Henry."

"Henry?" he asked, a jealous note evident.

"Well, maybe Henrietta. I'm not sure if the red-tailed hawk is a boy or a girl. I just know he hurt his wing. He won't let me near him to check how bad, but he seems okay with the idea of me putting food close by." A knot formed in her stomach. "Please don't ask me to go into detail on how I feed him. I called a friend of mine who owns a pet store. He drops off mice for me to put out."

Sachin snickered. "You care for an injured hawk?"

She nodded.

"I shall see to your Henry and then we will leave this gods-forsaken—"

"Kabril," Sachin said with a warning.

"I have selected," Kabril said, as if it summed up everything.

Sachin tapped his fingers on the dish. "Yes, but the choice is not yours to make, Kabril."

A defeated look passed over Kabril's handsome face. "You mean she is not the one."

"Not the what?" Rayna glanced back and forth between the men. Whatever inside information they were sharing with nothing more than odd looks wasn't something they were letting her in on.

Sachin shook his head before going into the house.

Kabril put his arm out to her and smiled. It looked forced but she didn't question him. "Rayna, I would very much like to see to Henry's condition. Lead the way."

She slid her arm into his. The action was very unlike her but she couldn't deny how good touching him felt. There was certainly something about the man that made her trust him. Her instincts were good, having never led her astray before so Rayna didn't hesitate to go with them. "Thank you."

"The pleasure is all mine, I assure you." The confident smile Kabril cast in her direction warmed her through her toes. "Tell me more of your Henry."

"My Henry?" she mused. "I like the sound of that. Although, I don't own him. He's a free spirit. A wild, beautiful creature I want nothing more than to see back in good health."

"I sense the truth in your words," he said.

The comment was odd to say the least. She kicked a loose stone on the side of the one-lane road as they walked towards the place she now called home. Kabril tugged gently on her arm and used his free hand to point towards the sky. "Look there. Do you see it?"

She looked up and spotted a large bird in the air. The late spring breeze tickled her skin but she ignored the cold as she realized what she was staring up at. "Is that another red-tail hawk?"

"Yes." He drew her closer to him. Heat seemed to radiate from his powerful body. "I believe your Henry is truly a Henry."

Shocked, she shook her head and continued keeping her gaze skyward. "No. That can't be him. He was hurt. I saw him trying to fly but failing."

Kabril chuckled. "That is a female flying above. She's calling for the male. It involves a courtship of sorts."

"So," she grinned, "Henry has a chick?"

"A chick? As in a fledgling?" The serious tone of his voice made her laugh.

"I mean as in a hot woman. A girl. A sexy significant other. A wife. A ball and chain. A..."

As Kabril slid his hand over hers, she stopped spouting off and enjoyed his touch. His golden gaze fixed on her. "A ball and chain? Is that really a description one uses for their mate here?"

"Uh, mate?" Rayna steered him to the side of her house. "Funny, I think your term is stranger than mine."

Kabril drew in the human female's sweet scent. His loins burned with the need to find solace in her divine body. Her dark hair was pulled into some sort of a twist, leaving long strands of it free and cascading over her slender shoulders. She stared up at him through eyes so blue they nearly stole his breath. When Sachin had told him of the beautiful women to be found on Earth he'd dismissed him. As he pulled Rayna closer to him, he knew he owed his old friend an apology. Not only was she beautiful, she sparked a primal urge in Kabril that no wench had prior.

The pants, or jeans as Sachin had referred to them, dug at his erection painfully. He wanted to be home, in his realm, in his clothing—discarded of course—bedding Rayna until she cried his name out in ecstasy.

He smiled as the thought of taking her, pleasing her every way imaginable left his blood pumping. Sachin's words of wisdom beat in his head. He couldn't steal her away to his realm. Well, he could but according to Sachin doing such a thing would leave a human female clipping his wings while he slept or unmanning him. Neither was an option.

Perhaps I could chain her until she submits?

The idea had merit.

"Do you see him?" Rayna asked, jerking Kabril from his erotic thoughts momentarily.

It was hard to keep from glancing at her wrists, imagining them bound above her head as he licked his way down her body. He had little doubt he could have her moaning in delight before the sun went down. Her long legs would easily wrap about his body, holding him to her as he pumped in and out. Kabril swallowed hard, his eyelids fluttering and his breathing erratic.

"Hello, Dr. Kabril?"

He jerked, his gaze darting to her lush breasts. "What? Oh, yes. Please call me Kabril."

She pointed to an oversized tree and winked. "Henry's up there. He's not currently perched on my chest."

Clearing his throat, he tried and failed to keep a blush from staining his cheeks. He was a king. Kings were not embarrassed to be caught admiring a glorious pair of breasts. And, oh what a pair they were. He forced his gaze towards the bird, slightly caught off guard by his randy behavior. "You must be Henry."

I can heal you, little bird. Do not fear me. He pushed with his mind to the hawk currently staring down at him. *Is that fine by you?*

The bird nodded in agreement and flapped its good wing. Rayna drew in a deep breath and clutched his arm. "Kabril, look. It's like he understands."

"Yes," he said, savoring her tender touch.

The smile that lit her face moved him. "Do you mind if I grab my camera? I'd love to have pictures of you treating Henry."

It was best she be away while he first worked with the bird since his ways would differ greatly from those of the human bird doctors. Besides, having Rayna away from him, even for just a bit, might help to alleviate his rock hard cock. His dick twitched at the thought of sinking into Rayna's body and he knew clearing his mind of her was hopeless. "That would be nice."

Chapter Two

Earth, three months later...

Rayna Vogel walked carefully along the narrow path. The waterfalls around her continued to draw her attention and it was only a matter of time before she either killed herself trying to see their beauty or got the picture she desperately wanted. Hopefully, the second of the scenarios prevailed.

Her boot slid on the loose gravel and Rayna lost her footing. Her heart felt as if it leapt to her throat and blocked the scream wanting to come. A strong hand caught hold of her, plucking her from the air with an ease and strength normal men didn't seem to possess. As she stared into a set of unnaturally golden eyes, she couldn't help but smile. A nervous giggle sounded from her and her cheeks heated out of embarrassment.

"Careful, I would very much like you to remain in one piece," Kabril said, his voice so deep and so sexy that Rayna had to bite back a sigh. She still had yet to place his accent. It wasn't thick but it did tinge his voice ever so. She'd often tried to get exactly where he was from out of him but Kabril liked his secrets and she didn't mind letting him have them.

He set her on her feet and visually inspected her. "Are you hurt?"

"Just my pride." She tipped a bit, losing her balance and seized hold of his forearm. The man didn't seem to have an ounce of fat on him. She squeezed and visions of having Kabril's powerful body above her, sliding in and out of her filled Rayna's head.

She couldn't tear her gaze from his square face and piercing eyes. When she'd first met Dr. Kabril Kingston he'd seemed a bit on the cold side, almost regal in his mannerisms. He also seemed prone to odd displays of chauvinistic behavior, all of which his assistant explained away as being part of Kabril's unusual sense of humor. Now that Rayna knew Kabril, she realized he was one of the warmest men she'd ever met. Not to mention gifted. He'd managed to get Henry up and flying in no time at all. He definitely had a magik touch. He had a way about him, one that made her feel safe and cared for.

He glanced over the edge. "I am dangerously close to making you wear a safety harness, Rayna. You, unfortunately," he puffed out a long breath, "do not have wings."

"There is a better than average chance I'd wring my neck with the harness so it's best you not."

Laughing, he held her close to him. "I have no doubt you would. You are so very different than most women I know."

"Hey, is that a knock on how clumsy I am?" She grinned, enjoying his teasing more than she should. His warm hands seemed to push heat through her body as he held her close. Rayna shifted awkwardly in an attempt to stop the moisture Kabril was more than capable of producing between her legs. One glance from him and Rayna's body reacted.

"No. Not clumsy. More like absentminded," he whispered, the bass in his voice moving over her, causing her to sigh.

She drew a deep breath in, savoring a mix of lavender, sage and cedar—the scent of Kabril. It took everything in her not to touch him in a way she shouldn't. Not to stroke his massive chest. Lusting after a man she considered a friend was wrong. They'd never actually set friendship boundaries though. Still, it was wrong. She'd been closer to Kabril in the last few months than she ever had been with anyone else.

"I'm not absentminded. Am I?"

"Rayna, you dropped this," Sachin said as he joined them. He held the lens cap to her camera in one hand and a rather large smile upon his handsome face. The man never moved far from Kabril's side. At first, she'd assumed they were brothers. They even argued as siblings would. She had little doubt Kabril was the older of two. Sachin also tended to goad Kabril whenever possible, as a younger brother often would. She'd been shocked to learn they were not related but rather close friends.

Chuckling, Kabril touched her cheek lightly. "No, Rayna. You are not absentminded in the *least.*"

She gave him a fake snarl and pushed past him, mindful of the steep ledge. "And you're not the least bit arrogant. Are we going back to camp or are you two going to start exchanging weird looks when you don't think I'm watching you?"

No sooner did the words come out her mouth then Kabril and Sachin did exactly that. They glanced at one another. Sachin's expression was one of amusement. Kabril's held something else. Something Rayna couldn't pinpoint. It was too cute not to comment.

"See, that's exactly what you do to me. You always make me feel like I'm missing out on an inside joke. It makes me crazy." Lunging forward, she ruffled Kabril's chin-length black hair. His smile warmed her heart. "There. That's more like it. I hate it when you look like the weight of the world is on your shoulders. You dragged me down here because you wanted to document your studies. As much as I'm loving this vacation, I like to see you happy more."

Kabril caught her hand and drew it to his lips. He took her by surprise, planting a kiss on the back of her hand tenderly. Before Rayna could remark, Kabril had drawn her into his arms. A slow, racy smile moved over his face. "Hello."

She swallowed hard. Her pussy responded with a spasm and she had to focus on something, anything other than Kabril or risk begging him to fuck her against the rocky wall. "We should get back to camp. It'll be getting dark soon and I still want to take a bath."

Kabril perked up. "A bath?" He exchanged another long look with Sachin and nodded. "By all means, camp it is then."

"You are so weird," she said, laughing softly as she fell in line behind him. Rayna's gaze landed upon his luscious ass and she closed her eyes. If gawking at the waterfalls didn't get her killed, Kabril's tight butt just might.

ഇൽങ

Kabril stood quietly, watching from the shadows as Rayna bathed by the river's edge, silently wishing she were his chosen one—his mate. Sachin continued to assure him they were close to finding the human female and to just be patient. Being around Rayna was making that incredibly difficult. Especially when thoughts of fucking her and no other continued to haunt his every moment.

He was pleasantly surprised that Sachin didn't argue when Kabril mentioned bringing Rayna somewhere they could have easy access to Accipitridae while still being somewhere justifiable. It wasn't as though Kabril could convince Rayna to hover thousands of feet in the air on the chance he be called home. He would have some major explaining to do, not to mention she lacked wings vital to pulling that off.

He'd fallen behind in his duties as king but didn't want to be separated from Rayna just yet. This way, he could sneak off to his realm and handle royal matters while still managing to make it back to be with her.

Perhaps if I take her home, the prophecy will assume one human female is as good as the next?

No. It would never work and he knew it. Still, it didn't hurt to dream.

He knew it was wrong to look upon Rayna bathing without her knowledge but had rationalized it out several nights after arriving at the campsite. All of his kind possessed varying degrees of magiks. It was no surprise one of Kabril's strongest gifts was that of being able to control other animals. After all, he was a leader by birth. The jungle wasn't exactly safe to wander about alone. Bathing in the river was even less safe. So long as he was near, he could mentally will the other animals away from his mate.

My mate. If only that were true. I would happily accept the human before me.

The words played about in his head. Never did he think they would sound so perfect. Then again, he hadn't planned on finding

Rayna. He'd expected something else and would no doubt get it whenever he found the mate Sachin swore was close. He'd get something other than the beautiful, loving woman before him. Rayna was divine. Everything he wanted in a wife and so very much more. Within the first week of meeting her, he'd all but forgotten she wasn't like him. Wasn't a *Buteos Regalis*. It didn't matter. Nothing but claiming her and making her his wife did.

If only I could.

His loins burned with the need to possess her. Thoughts of bedding Rayna plagued his dreams and remained a constant in his waking hours. The woman's scent alone was enough to drive a man insane. Roses and sandalwood. Even now Kabril could still smell her lingering scent on him. His cock dug painfully at its confines and he swallowed hard, hoping his erection would go down on its own. Seeing her naked wasn't helping matters.

Rayna wore her long, silky, light-brown hair pulled into a loose bun at the top of her head, as she always did when she bathed late at night. His preternatural eyes could see perfectly in any light and it was easy to make out the blonde highlights in her sun-kissed hair. The tiniest of freckles graced her nose and tanned shoulders whenever she'd been in the sun too long. The caramel look the sun's rays left her with was intoxicating. Kabril wanted to lick every inch of her, see if she tasted as delicious as she looked.

Glancing over her shoulder, Rayna stared in his direction. Kabril knew the darkened shadows covered him and didn't bother to move. He let his gaze rake over her slowly, taking in the sight of her breasts. Her nipples were dark and puckered as if waiting for him to take them into his mouth. Reaching down, he undid his pants and slipped his hand in, fisting his rigid cock. He needed release or he'd risk the beast side of him taking over and possibly claiming Rayna—not bothering to wait for this mate Sachin swore was near.

Three months ago, Kabril seriously considered simply plucking Rayna from Earth, taking her to his home and demanding she submit to him. Sachin had been right. The ways of old would not have worked with an Earth woman. Especially not one as headstrong as Rayna. No, she would have removed vital parts of his anatomy. Though, dying by her hand would be acceptable.

He stroked his cock, staring at the small swell of her lower abdomen and imagining his tongue there, licking, tracing its way to the juncture of her thighs. Kabril knew Rayna had only a small thatch of well-maintained hair upon her mound because he spent many a night assuming the form of an Earth-sized hawk and watching her. It was not exactly comfortable to take on the form of a creature so much smaller than his normal shifted form but he did it all the same. At six-foot-six in human form, Kabril was even bigger shifted, quite a difference from the size of an Earth hawk. Also a significant difference between Rayna and himself in normal form.

Rayna seemed so tiny to him, so petite, that at times he worried if he would harm her should he sink his cock into her and claim her for all time. Sachin assured him all would be well when the time came, should his actual mate prove to be Rayna's size, but Kabril couldn't think past her. *She* was who he wanted in his bed, carrying his sons and ruling by his side for all eternity. Thoughts of hurting her didn't sit well with him. Since Sachin had a tendency to wander from Accipitridae to Earth, when he assumed Kabril wasn't paying attention, and bed human women, Kabril trusted his judgment on the matter.

Kabril watched her closely as he continued to stroke his cock. Every muscle in his body was tight, hungry for Rayna. Her gaze remained locked on his area. Could she see him? No. That was foolish. She was but human and lacked the extraordinary vision of the shifter races. Still, her gaze remained. As he ran his hand down the length of his shaft, Rayna touched her stomach, the same place he'd envisioned licking. As her fingers trailed their way to the apex of her thighs, Kabril's breathing grew shallow. Would she touch herself as well? Better yet, would she think of him while doing it?

That's it, ta'konima—*my love. Touch yourself. Show me how you wish me to touch you.*

Rayna cupped a breast with one hand and let the other hand slide between her legs to the place Kabril desired to be. As she parted her slit, he had to fight off his orgasm. He should last longer than he did while masturbating. It was almost embarrassing how quickly even the thought of Rayna could make him come. Holding the base of his cock firmly, Kabril managed to narrowly avoid spilling his seed. The sight of Rayna fingering herself, rubbing her clit while she stared in his direction was too much. He palmed himself and stroked as fast and as furious as he wanted to take her. He wanted to pummel his cock into her silken depths until both their bodies were spent and his seed planted in her.

Rayna rocked against her hand, riding it to the point it glistened with her cream. The scent of her arousal permeated the air, filling Kabril not only with lust but with the carnal knowledge that he would take her and soon. It was no longer a choice. Between his obsession with her and the news coming from Accipitridae of the *Falco Peregrinus*' repeated attempts to take power, Kabril had to return for good—and soon. Leaving without his mate wasn't an option.

She's not my mate. He reminded himself. *But if I have any input in my affairs, she will be my queen.*

It mattered not what the people thought of him should he return home without his chosen bride. All that mattered was that he could not survive without Rayna in his life.

Rayna shook her hips slightly as she arched her neck. From the tiny whimpers to the way her body twitched, he knew she was coming. Stroking his cock faster, he didn't fight it when his body wanted release. Instead, he came with her, sending come jetting from his body into the brush before him, all the while keeping his gaze locked firmly on Rayna as pleasure ripped through her body.

Something rustled across from him, on the other side of Rayna, and Kabril fought with his still erect cock to get it back into the confines of his pants. Rayna apparently heard the noise as well, which was strange considering how faint it was. She dressed quickly, pulling her T-shirt on and slipping into her shorts. The knowledge she wore no undergarments would consume him the remainder of the night. Visions of her coming by her own hand would grip him for centuries.

Chapter Three

Rayna glanced in the opposite direction of camp and did her best to focus in the darkness. If it weren't for the light of the moon, it would have been pitch black. The jungle had been eerily silent while she bathed, right up until she'd given in to the urge to touch herself. Spending her days and her nights near Kabril was proving to be too much for her. Back home, she could at least get away from the lure of him because he had his practice and she had work. Since he was an avian veterinarian and her passion was photographing birds, it seemed fitting they spend time together. She had to remind herself that while she enjoyed taking pictures of birds, any animal would do. She'd spent months in various remote corners of the Earth, chasing down that perfect picture of whatever animal it was she'd been sent to shoot.

After being charged by two very angry tigers, Rayna had decided to avoid anything bigger than her for a while. In fact, it was Kabril's idea she take some time from her normal work and aid him with his research. He'd even tried to pay her much more than she'd ever dream of charging. Rayna wouldn't hear of taking his money. She lived in her great-grandmother's home, left to her in a will. It was long paid for and she had no family to take care of. Her safaris paid well and her tiny town had little in the way of shopping to tempt her with. While she wasn't rich, she was comfortable.

Looking around at the beauty of the tropics, Rayna knew she'd made the right decision in coming on the trip. The environment was soothing and she couldn't imagine being away from Kabril for the month he had planned to be away. That, more than anything, had prompted her to accept his invitation. She'd grown accustomed to seeing him daily, hearing his laugh and simply knowing he was close. Sachin lived in Kabril's guesthouse and was someone she would have missed as well. His odd sense of humor complimented Kabril's, making him a welcomed addition. He also seemed to watch over Kabril. It was out of the ordinary but Rayna never questioned it.

The sound of a twig snapping and leaves rustling grabbed Rayna's attention. Nothing seemed off yet her inner alarms were going off. She squinted in hopes it would help her see whatever was there. Thoughts of jaguars and other jungle predators filled her head, making her jerk back as fear crept over her.

She stepped onto the shore and dressed as quickly as she could. Her shorts clung to her wet body as did her shirt. As Rayna bent down to grab her boots something splashed in the water. No part of her wanted to dwell on what wildlife called the river home. Still, the urge to glance over at the water bordered on overwhelming. It appeared still and what little moonlight made its way through the canopy of trees managed to reflect off the water's surface.

Something splashed again, this time sounding much closer than the last. The hair on the back of her neck stood on end and the urge to flee was great. Never one to back down from a challenge, Rayna hesitated, sure her mind was playing tricks on her. Taking a deep, calming breath, she nodded.

It's probably a frog or something.

Rayna turned to head back to camp and ran face first into what felt like a truck. A really warm, muscular, fantastic smelling truck.

"Ouch."

"Rayna?" Kabril asked, the sound of his voice making her feel safe.

Relief swept through her and she tossed her arms around his neck. He stood tall, taking her with him. She dangled for a moment and went to release him. Kabril didn't allow it. He wrapped his large arms around her and held her off the ground.

His golden gaze locked on her. "Rayna?"

Her mind wanted her to tell him she was fine and to put her down. Her body had something altogether different planned. She swallowed hard and did her best to pull herself together before she did something stupid like beg him to fuck her.

"Umm, Kabril," she whispered, running her hand through the back of his hair. "You're going to hurt yourself. Put me down."

"You are naught but chest high and scarce weigh more than a feather," he said, his speech suddenly sounding so very different than normal. Thoughts of castles, knights and men of power filled her head.

Rayna rolled her eyes playfully and snorted. "The 'I could have fallen out of the pages of a medieval romance novel' vibe you got going is cute. Put me down now." She pushed lightly on his upper chest but Kabril didn't release her. "Please...my lord."

"No," he said quickly, still holding her. "To you, I am always Kabril."

Confused but willing to play along, Rayna nodded. "So you're saying I can't give you cute lil' pet names like pookie bear and honey bunches?"

"Bear?" He licked his lower lip and she had to fight back the moan that wanted to come. "Not the animal I hoped for but if you wish. Though, I might take to calling you mine."

The idea of belonging to him left Rayna shivering in anticipation. She could only imagine what it would be like to have Kabril sliding in and out of her body, taking and giving pleasure until they could no longer move. Her erect nipples poked through the wet material of her shirt as she wiggled to get down. They scraped against his muscular chest and pleasure shot through her, leaving Rayna hissing as if she'd been burned. Kabril slid a hand lower and cupped her ass. Her breath hitched as heat flared through her body.

His warm breath skated over her cheek and he chuckled. "Something wrong?"

"Yes...erm...no." She bit her inner cheek, trying and failing to rid herself of the heat he caused. "I think I'm on fire."

Kabril dragged her against him, causing her to rub along him just right. "On fire?" he asked, sounding all too keen on hearing more.

Denial was futile. She nodded and Kabril lifted her chin, forcing her to face him. Capturing her mouth with his, Kabril left her legs quivering and her holding tight to him for fear she'd fall during his sensual assault. Rayna fed from the sweetness of Kabril's mouth. The kiss was intoxicating, as she knew it would be.

Kabril dominated their kiss, circling his tongue around hers and leading every step of the way. "Rayna," he murmured, continuing his glorious invasion. He held her cheek with one hand and her body with the other. The sheer power in his arms was not lost on her.

"Kabril," she said breathlessly. "Please."

Please put me down was what she was going to say. It wasn't what came out. Good thing considering being put down was the last thing she truly wanted to have happen. He slid his hand under her wet shirt and Rayna didn't stop him. Instead, she ate at his mouth, kissing him with the hunger of a crazed woman. For three months she'd longed to have him do this to her and wasn't about to stop it now. She didn't have the willpower to make him stop, even if she wanted to.

The next thing she knew, she had her legs wrapped around his waist and her arms around his neck as he worked his hands further under her shirt. He tweaked her nipples, rolling them between his forefingers and his thumbs with a precision she didn't want to question. The idea of him bedding other women sickened her.

"Rayna," he murmured, kissing her neck and cupping her breasts. He nipped playfully at her shoulders and let out a manly chuckle as she rubbed against him.

Rayna wanted more. She needed to feel him inside her. There were too many articles of clothing between them. She tugged at his open shirt, running her hands over the planes of his chest. His muscles rippled under the weight of her touch and Rayna lost the ability to control her breathing. She shifted her hips, rubbing her body against his, striking his long, thick cock just right. Release was near. She arched in wild response, pushing her clit against his clothed erection. His lips greeted hers at the same moment her orgasm struck. Kabril drank her moans down, smothering them with his kisses. She wanted more.

Kabril jerked his hands out from under her shirt and she unwrapped her legs from his waist. He didn't put her down. Instead, Kabril kept her close, his breathing choppy and his movements stiff.

"Why did you stop?" she asked, feeling rejected.

"Because I refuse to take you on the ground like a savage."

"I wouldn't mind." Shocked by her own words, Rayna felt her cheeks staining with a blush.

"Kabril?" Sachin appeared from the shadows, silencing any further confessions that might have fallen from her lips. His silver eyes were narrow and he seemed focused on something behind them.

Rayna was a tad surprised Sachin didn't comment on the fact she was being held off the ground by Kabril. He seemed fixated on something else. Her brow furrowed. "Sachin, what's wrong?"

His gaze met Kabril's. "We are not alone."

Kabril tightened his hold on her to the point she could scarcely draw in air. "K-a-b-r-i-l."

He released her quickly, causing her to stumble. Sachin was there in an instant, steadying her. Kabril growled and gave her a slight tug, pulling her away from Sachin. The men stared at one another for what felt like eternity. Testosterone coated the air. Scared of a possible wild animal stalking them, Rayna batted them both in the arm. They were acting like idiots so she didn't mind stooping to scolding them. "Guys? What happened to we are not alone? Huh? I don't want to be the main course for a jaguar. Pull it together here."

No sooner did the words leave her lips than tension seemed to fill the air. Suddenly, the sounds of the jungle all but halted. Her breath hitched and she took a small step towards Kabril. As silly as it sounded, he made her feel safe regardless what she might have to face.

"How many?" He glanced towards Sachin.

Sachin's gaze never left the surrounding area. He shook his head slightly. "I do not know. Take Rayna to safety. I shall see to—"

Kabril scoffed. "We are in unfamiliar territory, old friend. I will not leave you to your own devices. Not when it is clear we are outnumbered."

Rayna stared at Kabril, noting his speech was different once again, as was Sachin's. "Guys?"

"Worry not, *ta'konima*," Kabril whispered, putting his body before hers.

She arched a brow, wondering what the hell it was he'd just called her. From the sound of the sharp intake of breath Sachin took, she had a funny feeling it meant something significant. Her luck, he'd just insulted her in the worst way and she was oblivious.

He crouched a bit, taking her with him. Sachin followed suit. Kabril motioned with his head towards the far left of the river. "They are coming in from that way as well."

Sachin nodded, appearing to have already caught on to the fact they were being surrounded. Rayna was still lost. "Wait? Jaguars are now hunting us in a pack. I thought they weren't ones to travel in groups. I thought—"

Her words were cut short by the sudden sound of something swooshing overhead. Kabril tossed his body over hers, taking her down and pressing her to the ground. He shouted something to Sachin but the noise level reached proportions that drowned him out. As quickly as Kabril's weight had landed on her, it was ripped off. Rayna sat up fast, pushing to her feet. The sound that could only be described as hundreds of birds flapping their wings ended. The strangest part of it all was that Sachin and Kabril were missing, leaving her alone on the edge of the river.

"Kabril?" She turned in a slow circle, doing her best to pierce the darkness with nothing more than her eyes. "Sachin?"

Fear gripped her.

"Kab-ril?" she asked, her voice cracking under the weight of her nerves. "This isn't funny. You two have the strangest sense of humor. Kabril?"

Nothing.

Rayna wasn't sure how much time passed but she knew it was a significant amount. Something rustled in the brush to her left and she froze. "Kabril?"

A single feather drifted down before her face, nearly causing her to scream. Calming herself, Rayna plucked it from the air. The bird it belonged to had to be huge. The feather was over a foot long and had something dark, warm and wet on it. She brought it closer to her face and gasped when she realized it was blood.

She turned quickly and ran head first into something. Strong arms grabbed her shoulders and she gave in to the urge to scream a half a second before she brought her knee up, hard and fast.

"Rayna." Kabril deflected her knee with his upper thigh right before she would have made contact with his groin.

Her eyes widened as she realized it was him. "What? Where? Kabril?"

A soft smile slid over his handsome face, easing some of the tension in her body. "I am here and you are safe."

"What about Sachin?"

"Here," Sachin said, appearing behind her, causing her to push her body against Kabril's.

Rayna pressed her forehead to Kabril's chest. "You two need to hum or something when you walk. You scared the hell out of me. And where did you two go?" She glanced around. "Are the jaguars still close? I think they attacked a bird." She held the bloody feather up for Kabril to see. "Poor thing."

His gaze hardened. "Discard that immediately, Rayna."

Stunned by the directness in his voice, Rayna simply stared at him.

He ripped the feather from her hand and tossed it aside. "Return to camp this instant."

She blinked, sure she'd heard him wrong. He couldn't be issuing orders to her like he was her master. "Excuse me?"

He pointed towards the campsite. "Go!"

Sachin moved up next to her and cleared his throat. "Kabril."

"What if the bird's not dead, Kabril?" she asked, deciding to seize the moment. "Shouldn't we look for it? You could help it. It's what you do, right?"

Kabril's nostrils flared and his entire body went rigid. "I gave you an order. Do not disobey me on this."

Rayna took a giant step back. Anger consumed her, leaving her throat constricted as she fought to keep from crying out with rage. Something on Kabril's face changed as a sigh tore free of him. He made a move to come to her but she put her hand up, stopping him. "Don't. I'll do what you *command*. I'll go back to camp but know that I'm doing it to keep from choking you, not because you ordered me to."

"Rayna, no." Kabril made another move to come to her, this time finding Sachin stepping in his path. "I did not mean to—"

She folded her arms over her chest and gave him a droll look. "Didn't mean to what? Open mouth, insert foot? I'm sorry I asked about the bird. I assumed since you're an avian vet and all that you'd care. Guess I was wrong." She glared at him. "About a lot of things."

Sachin glanced over his shoulder at her. "Rayna, forgive him. The, umm, jaguars," he nudged Kabril, "yeah, jaguars, left him worried about how safe you were. He isn't acting like himself right now. He worries about you. We both do."

"Yet you don't bark orders at me like I'm a dog." She gave Kabril a cross look. He cringed under the weight of her stare. "Don't you think I was worried about you two? Huh? For all I knew, you two were being mauled to death twenty feet from me. You don't see me ordering him around, do you?" Rayna didn't wait for an answer. Instead, she turned to head back to camp, mumbling on the way, "Thinks he's king of the jungle. Asshole."

Kabril winced at the sound of Rayna cursing him as she headed towards camp. The camp wasn't exactly an ideal place to send her to alone but leaving her near him and the scene of the Falco's attack was far worse. Kabril was likely to lose his temper and shift—something Rayna didn't need to witness. Besides, if a Falco happened to escape them, it would come directly for Kabril since he was king. A Falco would have no interest in a human.

Ah, there was a point I too thought I would never have an interest in a human either. Now look. I am at the mercy of one.

Sachin coughed slightly and shook. It took Kabril a second to realize he was being laughed at—again. He punched out quickly, catching Sachin's right cheek. "I do not find this amusing."

His chest tightened at the thought of Rayna falling into the enemy's hands. He couldn't believe his enemy had tracked him down on Earth and attacked.

Rubbing his jaw, Sachin nodded. "I know. Still, you did not have to take your anger out on Rayna. She was unaware the feather belonged to the Falco. Her heart is big. Her concern for you is even bigger. Did you not sense the fear in her voice when she called your name?"

Kabril had sensed her fear. It had eaten at him as he flew high in the air above her, killing the enemy and disposing of them downriver. It had pained Kabril greatly, not being able to shout out, let Rayna know he was near. The last thing he wanted to do was have her find out what he truly was during a battle. She wouldn't understand.

Sachin patted Kabril's shoulder. "Go. Fly for a bit and clear your mind. I shall guard Rayna."

Still muttering curses, Rayna headed for her tent. Something shuffled to her side and she glanced in that direction. A man with long blond hair was there, glaring at her through eyes of burnt umber. He wore a loincloth of all things. Her mind tried to rationalize why he was there and where he'd come from but she came up empty.

"So you are the human their king is so fond of," he said, his voice deep.

Confused, Rayna shook her head and took a tiny step back. A wry grin spread over the stranger's face. "Running is pointless. Come quietly and I shall make your death as painless as possible."

My death?

The man moved closer and something deep within Rayna snapped. She bent down quickly, seized hold of one of the retaining wall rocks for the fire and pitched it at him. A scream tore free of her as she did. The man sidestepped the rock with ease, looking amused by her efforts to keep him at bay. The dirt she'd accidentally cast with the rock rained down upon him. His laughter faded instantly as some of the dirt made its way into the wound on his side.

He lunged at her. Rayna tucked and rolled away from the fire pit, kicking with one leg as he approached. She scored a direct gut hit. Pain radiated up her leg. The man was solid muscle. He snaked an arm around her waist and the next thing she knew, she was being lifted off the ground.

High off the ground.

As the campsite below seemed to shrink, her stomach dropped and fear held her screams. She knew she should call out. Do something. Anything to alert Kabril and Sachin of what was happening but she could scarcely wrap her mind around it let alone warn others.

ഇരുന്ന

"Calm down," Sachin said, keeping a safe distance from Kabril.

"Calm down?" he echoed, wanting to kill something, anything. "The woman I wish to rule by my side for all eternity runs off into the jungle rather than spend another moment with me and you tell me to calm down?"

"We will find her, my lord."

Kabril froze. "Why is it you are not correcting me—telling me how we will find my mate soon and that Rayna can never rule by my side?"

Sachin whistled as he averted his gaze. A sinking feeling came over Kabril as he clenched his fists. He knew Sachin well enough to know his old friend was up to his antics again. "Why is it I think you have been trifling with me from the moment we came to Earth?"

"Perhaps," Sachin kept his gaze directed anywhere but at Kabril, "it is because I have been trifling with you."

"What?" he bellowed.

Sachin stiffened. "I know you, Kabril. You would have resisted your pull to her had you known the truth. It is part of your stubborn nature, *my lord.*"

"The truth?" Kabril arched a brow in question, not liking the added my lord. "What truth?"

Sachin held his secrets close. Growling, Kabril stared at his long time friend. "This conversation is far from over. Now we hunt for Rayna. Once I have her safely within my sights, you will tell me all you have been keeping from me."

"As you wish, my lord." Sachin bent his head and yanked his shirt off, shifting into partial hawk form as he did. Large brown and white feathers rippled over his shoulders as a set of wings emerged from his upper back. Sachin, like Kabril and most other strong warriors, could shift portions of his body on command without pain and for indefinite periods of time. They could also do full shifts if need be.

Kabril did the same, shifting enough to be able to fly. As his wings sprouted forth from his shoulder blades, Kabril took a deep breath, enjoying the rare treat. While on Earth, he had to use caution not to be discovered. Shifting was a luxury. He flexed his wings, each spanning close to ten feet and took one last look around the campsite.

He shouldn't care that Rayna walked out on him but he couldn't help himself. Even if she wasn't the woman the prophecy spoke of, he'd come to care for her. The jungle was no place to wander alone. Especially not with an enemy attack having just been thwarted. As Kabril went to lift off the ground, he noticed something near the doused fire pit. One of the retaining wall rocks was missing.

He glanced around the area and found it off to the side of the site. There was something else there. A single bloodied feather. Not the one he'd forced Rayna to drop—a new one.

Suddenly, it felt as if he'd been struck in the midriff, the air swooshed from his lungs and his knees weakened. He was unable to believe they'd missed a Falco warrior, even with the proof lying right before him. Kabril clawed at the ground, shaking his head in denial as his body contorted in pain—partially shifting, then un-shifting, at an alarming rate. Vaguely, he heard someone crying out. It took a moment for him to register the fact that it was him and that he was calling for his mate—his Rayna.

Chapter Four

Kabril held tight to one of his Advisor's throats. The urge to choke the life from the man was great. "Speak out against my decision again and I will kill you with my bare hands."

Iorgos, his brother and soon-to-be the next target of his rage, touched his shoulder tentatively. "Kabril, unhand him. He speaks only the truth. To invade *Falco Peregrinus* with no preparation, to rescue, what—a human female who is not even your chosen one is beyond foolish. It is deadly."

Swinging his fist, Kabril caught his brother's jaw and sent him hurtling into the thick castle wall. "They have *my Rayna*! I am king here. When I order an attack, it is to be carried out. No questions asked."

Iorgos stared up, his blue gaze icy. "You have not been king here for many moons."

"Think you to overthrow me, little brother?" Kabril asked, his voice bristling with anger.

"Why should I not?" Iorgos was always the one to butt heads with Kabril. Second to the youngest, he was a long way from actually seeing the throne for himself but had the leadership skills Kabril needed in his absence. "You abandon your people on a quest to retrieve the one the Oracle foretold coming yet you are gone for many moons before returning with tales of another female. You then wish for our men to rush to their deaths to save a pathetic, vile human. Seems to me, big brother, overthrowing is the least I could do for you. The female's life is not worth even one of our own, let alone hundreds upon hundreds."

Sachin stepped forward and delivered a swift kick to Iorgos' side. "Speak no ill of your future queen! Rayna is a wonderful, loving human who has done as the Oracle predicted and won the heart of our king."

A chorus of gasps followed Sachin's statement. The Advisors began whispering amongst themselves while Kabril stared at his long-time friend. Sachin's words began to sink in and Kabril felt his resolve crumble. He'd not been in his right state of mind from the moment Rayna went missing and suddenly, Sachin's hints hit Kabril with the force of a hundred men. "She is my...my...my true mate?"

Nodding, Sachin lowered his gaze but stood proud. "On the day you first laid eyes upon her, my lord, you whispered how sweet she was and that you would give all to have her be the one. I knew better than to tell you she was your mate because of how stubborn you can be. You did as I'd hoped you would do. You made her like you, won her trust and, I believe, her heart."

"But I lost her." The words fell from his lips in more of a sigh than anything else.

Sachin glanced at the table full of Advisors. "Our queen has been taken by our enemy. All of you are aware of the prophecy. Should our lands once more know the sound of children, we must act quickly. Our king wishes to strike with our combined power. Dare you deny him this?"

ഇറ

Rayna sat, her knees tucked under her chin and her gaze planted firmly on the back of her abductor. The man, or whatever he was, leaned over, dipping his hand into clear water and using it to rinse his wounds. Each time he brought the water to his open flesh, he hissed, leaving Rayna little doubt how much pain he was in. He'd favored his side for awhile. She noticed right away how filthy the wound was, caked in dirt and blood.

She slid her foot back and forth on the river's edge, still unsure where she was. The area, while dense in foliage, trees and flowers, wasn't the same as where she'd been. It also wasn't as humid.

The man glanced over his shoulder. "We are in the Tocallie Mountains. In the Accipitridae realm."

She opened her mouth to comment but he cut her off. "And no, this is not Earth."

Not Earth? Accipitridae realm?

Closing her eyes, Rayna tried and failed to process all that had happened. Men who grew wings and flew in the air didn't exist. Other realms didn't exist. None of this could be real. She pinched her arm, trying to wake herself up, but realized it was a living nightmare.

"W-who are you?"

The man continued to cleanse his wounds. "An enemy of your king."

"My king?" she asked, not following.

A sardonic grin spread over his face. "I suppose you would not view Kabril as your king. Humans have no respect for anyone other than themselves. Not that I advocate showing allegiance to the likes of a *Buteos Regalis*, especially that one in particular but it is better than answering to no one. Our leader may have his faults yet we, for the most part, stand behind his decisions." He didn't sound so sure of himself.

Rayna wondered if the man truly believed in what his king did or if he merely wanted her to think he did. Either way, she had no intention of dying by his hands. "Is threatening to kill an unarmed woman considered a fault?"

His gaze lowered slightly as if he were ashamed. He stiffened, suddenly looking composed. "We have more values than the *Buteos Regalis.*"

A Buteos Regalis?

Her mind raced and what she landed on did little in the way of clearing up matters. "Royal hawks?"

The question forming on the man's face alarmed her. One of them needed to have a clear idea of what was going on and it sure the hell wasn't her. "Either you are a skilled liar or you truly do not know."

"Know what?"

"Who and what we are," he said, his voice even.

Suddenly, the idea of knowing everything terrified her more than her current state of ignorance. Blood-tinged water slid down the man's bare torso and into the top of the loincloth he wore. Rayna glanced around, trying to see if anything would work to bind his wounds.

"If your goal is to escape, you should understand the portal back to your world is at an elevation you will plummet to your death. Should you attempt to cross it without one of us there to hold you it will not end in your favor."

"I was looking for something to help stop your bleeding," she said, not bothering to hide her annoyance with the man.

"Oh." He appeared puzzled and then something in his expression seemed to soften. "I am Lazar of the *Falco Peregrinus*."

She clutched her knees to her chest tighter. "As in a falcon?"

The corners of his mouth twitched slightly. "Yes. As in a falcon. And your name is?"

"Rayna," she said, unsure why she gave him any details without fully understanding what was going on.

"I am sorry to be the one to tell you of all you did not know." Lazar went to one knee and looked out from sympathetic eyes. For an abductor, he wasn't as fearsome as he'd first seemed. Setting aside the fact he had wings that sprouted from his upper back and then disappeared within seconds, he wasn't so bad.

She steadied her breathing and avoided making any sudden moves. "Does it hurt?"

Lazar lifted a brow and glanced at his wounds. "I have been hurt worse."

"I meant your wings. When they come out and go back in, does it hurt?"

A slow, steady grin spread over his face. "If I go too long between shifting my skin itches and I long to feel the air against me as I soar in the skies above. But no, the shift itself is painless."

"Why," Rayna focused on the ground, "did you call Kabril a king? He's a doctor and he doesn't have wings."

The sick feeling in the pit of her stomach returned and she was positive she didn't want to hear Lazar's answer. He cleared his throat and she met his gaze. "How is it you could spend so much time with him, yet know so little?"

I'm wondering the same thing.

She shrugged.

"Maybe you are not the one he seeks. I assumed when I witnessed the two of you conducting the starts of coupling, I thought you were she. The human it is said he is destined to mate with."

Rayna ran her hand through the grass next to her, wanting desperately to be home. Her bottom lip trembled as the thought of Kabril taking another woman to his bed beat at her mind. The implication of what Lazar was saying wasn't lost on her. "Kabril is like you? He can," she ripped a handful of grass from the ground and clutched it to her, "grow wings too?"

The pity in Lazar's eyes only served to cut deeper into her heart. None of what was happening was a dream. It was as real as the grass she held and the air she breathed. It also meant Kabril had lied to her. Gained her trust and used her.

"My orders were to seize the human female, alive or dead, and return to the castle at once." He looked to the sky. "I do not think it wise to follow these now."

"W-why?"

"Because it is clear his omissions have hurt you enough. I wish not to see my king inflict more pain upon you for simply falling prey to our enemy. As I have said, our king is not without fault. There is a time to follow blindly. This is not one of them."

Inflict more pain?

Rayna gasped. "They want to hurt me? Why?"

His refusal to answer left Rayna wondering how much to the story there was. Lazar was clearly hiding something. What? She wasn't sure.

Lazar touched his wounds with reluctant fingers and she knew he was in a good deal of pain. "We should rest. Others will come in search of you."

"Others?" Rayna moved towards him quickly, no longer caring that he had the ability to sprout wings.

Lazar chuckled. "I will allow no harm to come to you, Rayna."

She eyed his wounds, the one on his side in particular and snorted. "No offense but I don't think you're—"

"The soil from Earth has something ours lacks. Something in your soil inhibits our ability to heal quickly. Under normal circumstances, my wounds would be nothing more than faint scars by now."

She vividly recalled the dirt hitting him after she threw the rock. "I'm sorry."

Lazar patted her hand. "You were attempting to protect yourself. You have nothing to be sorry for. I," he sighed, "on the other hand, do. As soon as I am able, I will return you to your realm. It would be wise if you were to disappear for a while there. The Falco wish greatly to possess you. They believe King Kabril will lay down his sword and barter for your safe return."

Envisioning Kabril wielding a sword wasn't as hard as it should have been. All the times she'd referred to his behavior as regal and his speech as implacable haunted her. As much as she wanted to argue the point that Kabril wasn't the king Lazar spoke of, in her heart she knew Lazar spoke the truth.

She picked a purplish-colored leaf from a plant near her and dipped it into the crystal clear water. "This isn't poisonous, is it?"

Lazar shook his head and chuckled. "No. The flowers the plant will get late in the season are harvested and used in medicine. Was your goal to poison me?"

Rayna knew he was joking. She took the leaf and pressed it to his open wound as gently as she could. He hissed but let her continue, pulling leaves, wetting them and putting them over his open wound.

He caught her hand in his and stared at her, their faces dangerously close. "You tend to me when, by rights, you should be vexed by all I have brought upon you."

"Without you, I'll plummet to my death, remember?" She smiled, trying to make light of a situation she wanted nothing more than to crumble and cry in. Falling to pieces would accomplish nothing. She wanted to go home. Lazar could get her there. Something about him seemed genuine and she needed someone to trust.

His smile faded as his gaze flashed towards the sky. "Run!"

Confused by his sudden change, Rayna simply stared at him. "What?"

Dark shadows eclipsed the sun. In an instant Rayna was yanked to her feet by her hair. She cried out and tried to break free, only to find herself being thrust towards a hulk of a man. Dark brown, almost black wings spanned out at least twelve feet in each direction. The menacing stare he leveled on her shook Rayna to the core.

"Humbert," Lazar said, his voice strained. "No."

The brute holding her glowered in the direction Lazar's voice had come from. "Is this the human?" His lip curled. "Disgusting creatures."

"No. I took the wrong one. She was near their king but is..."

Humbert's lecherous gaze slid over her, making her skin crawl before moving back towards Lazar. "You have always been weak where females are concerned." He spat as he glared at Lazar. "The king anticipated as much from you, Lazar. He sent you to test your allegiance."

"But I seized the wrong—"

"It matters not. She will not be permitted to leave now that she's seen our realm. And you, Lazar, you shall be handled accordingly." The man untied one side of his loincloth and fear coursed through her veins.

Lazar moved quickly, attacking the man nearest him. In an instant, the man was sinking in the water, his throat sliced open. Lazar's fingers were bloodied. She looked closer and realized his fingernails were now long, dagger-like. She had little doubt they were the weapon Lazar used to kill the man, even in his weakened state. He held his wounded side and staggered. "Humbert, I will not...will not..."

He swayed and went to one knee, dashing Rayna's hopes of being spared from Humbert. She tried to rush past Humbert but he extended his wings, blocking her path. He stuck his chin out defiantly. "Going somewhere?"

Without thought, Rayna kicked him square between the legs. Humbert doubled over, clutching himself as a choked gasp broke free of him. Her gaze snapped to Lazar. Beads of sweat broke on Lazar's brow and he swayed a bit, touching the ground with one hand to steady himself. Rayna rushed to his side. "Are you okay?"

He nodded a second before his eyes rolled to the back of his head and he tipped forward, splashing into the water. Rayna didn't hesitate. She dove in after him. The icy water shocked her system but she didn't stop. She continued onward, reaching for him through the clear, cold water.

༄ᴑ◌ᴈ

Kabril grabbed hold of his chest and felt as if someone had hit him with a block of ice, stealing his breath. His arms cramped and he lost his focus for just a second, but long enough to jar him from flight. His wings folded in, cradling his body as he fought and failed to draw in air. Something seized him from behind, lifting him and ceasing his decent.

"Kabril!" Sachin's voice pushed through the pain, clearing Kabril's head.

The icy feeling vanished almost as quickly as it had arrived. The innate knowledge something was wrong with his mate settled over him. His iron will surged forth. "Rayna!"

"What vexes you, my lord?" Sachin asked.

"Rayna's hurt. The situation is grave."

"Is she...?" Sachin swallowed thickly. "Is she still alive?"

As much as Kabril wanted to believe she was safe and all would be well, his gut told him differently. He pushed off Sachin and flew in the direction his mate's distress signal had come from. "I do not know."

The Tocallie Mountains spanned a great distance and were easy to get lost in. Nothing could keep him from Rayna now that he'd connected with her on another level. Sachin tried to change course, heading in the logical direction—towards the closest portal but Kabril remained steady, following the pull of his mate. A clearing appeared and he spotted a Falco warrior near the edge of a spring. Red tinged what should have been crystal clear water. A knot formed in his throat as his heart hammered furiously.

Rayna.

A strangled cry ripped free of him as he began his rapid decent. Kabril broke through the surface of the icy water, already knowing how cold it was. The velocity at which he hit the water left him shooting past his target. Rayna's long hair danced in the water, lifting and swaying with a sickening silence as her limp body headed downwards. A Falco warrior was near her, his body lifeless as well. Kabril recognized him immediately as one of the men he'd fought with. Torn between rage and concern for Rayna, he thrust his anger down and seized hold of his mate. Her body was as cold as the water she was submerged in.

Holding her close, Kabril kicked, using his powerful body to take her quickly to the surface. He drew in a deep breath the moment he emerged but Rayna did nothing. Her body remained listless. Every fiber of his being called out to the Epopisdeus, begging them for forgiveness and to spare the life of the one he loved.

Love?

The scope of his feelings hit him, causing unshed tears to fill his eyes and his chest to tighten at the thought of losing her. Someone pried Rayna from his cold hands before someone else yanked him free of the water. Kabril knew his men were close, trying to help but he needed to be near Rayna.

"N-no!"

His teeth chattered as he reached for his mate. The moment he touched her cheek, a sob fell from his lips. "Magaious, I beg of you, take my life in place of hers."

A circle of gasps sounded around him but Kabril ignored them. It mattered not what his men thought, only that Rayna survived. He would rather die knowing she lived on than to go a single day without her by his side.

Sachin stood silently watching his long-time friend hold firm to the woman he'd grown to love. It pained Sachin, knowing he'd withheld the truth of who Rayna was from Kabril. He directed his gaze skyward and closed his eyes as Kabril openly prayed to the Epopisdeus he'd shunned so long ago. Sachin joined in, silently calling upon the bird gods to intervene.

He glanced to the side and found Humbert being lifted away, his wings, hands and ankles bound. Curses spat forth from his foul mouth and Sachin vowed to cut the man's tongue from his head before the night was out.

His men lifted a second Falco warrior from the depths of the frigid water, not bothering to tie him. They followed behind Humbert and the others in the direction of the castle. Sachin didn't need to instruct his men to put the two in the dungeon. It went without saying. He did have to give a rather stern look at the remaining guards, fearing they'd take it upon themselves to kill the Falcos instead of allowing the king the pleasure.

Sachin eyed his friend and went to turn his back to give Kabril a private moment for mourning Rayna when a bright light shone down upon them. At first, it bordered on blinding before dimming enough to allow Sachin to make out Kabril's and Rayna's outlines.

The sound of Rayna coughing was music to his ears. It was as if the heavens opened and harps played. Afraid his imagination and wishful thinking had run away with him, Sachin watched his old friend carefully. The moment Kabril tipped his head back and let out a fierce growl of triumph, Sachin drew his sword and held it high.

"Praise Magaious!"

Kabril rocked Rayna, holding her so tight Sachin wondered if his friend would hamper her already labored breathing. He moved to Kabril's side quickly. "I can carry her while you regain your strength, my lord."

Rayna's blue eyes drifted shut and her head lolled back. Kabril kept hold of her. "No."

"Kabril," he whispered, putting his hand on his friend's shoulder. "You are in no condition to fly with her in your arms. You could drop her. Is that what you truly want?"

The weight of the decision showed in Kabril's eyes a second before he handed Rayna to Sachin. The trust given to him was not misplaced. Sachin inclined his head before securing Rayna and taking flight. Kabril flew close to him, no doubt monitoring Sachin's care of his mate.

Chapter Five

Rayna's head felt heavy and her body laden with lead. She groaned as she opened one eye to peer out into the darkened room. Light filtered in through heavy drapery. The single slit and the tiny amount of light passing through left her shielding her face. She tried to roll away but her body refused to respond to her commands.

"Be still," a deep, familiar voice whispered near her ear.

"Kabril?" Rayna asked, twisting around and suffering the fate of such a choice almost instantly. Pain shot through her and she cringed.

Kabril put his hand to her cheek and cupped it gently. "*Ta'konima*, I beg of you to rest. The doctor has given you something to help you sleep."

"My arms are heavy and I'm mad at you," she blurted out.

The corners of his lips twitched. "I know. It will pass, as will the pain. I can only hope your anger with me subsides as well, Rayna. If I could take your pain from you, I would. My power does not extend to that point."

Her brow knit as his words trickled through the recesses of her mind. "Power?" She drew in a shallow breath. "Wings? They had wings, Kabril. Huge wings that came right out of their backs. They could fly." She closed her eyes as a dull throb began in her head. "They said you were a king and that you had wings, too."

She waited for Kabril to laugh. He didn't. Instead, he simply watched her through cautious golden eyes. Rayna's gaze darted around the room. She'd been in Kabril's bedroom once before, to help him pack for the trip. This was not his room. This room was grand with vaulted ceilings and lamps suspended from chains. The oversized four-post bed they lay in was carved from dark cherry-colored wood. The Mediterranean blue, plush coverlet engulfed her and matched the silken gown she now wore. Her heated gaze flashed back to him and locked on the tawny expanse of his chest.

Suddenly, her mouth was very dry.

"W-where are we and why are we in bed *together*?"

"Excuse me, my lord," a feminine voice said, causing Rayna to sit up faster than her aching body allowed.

She swayed and Kabril was there, steadying her with his powerful arms. "Rest, Rayna."

Ignoring Kabril, Rayna focused on the female in the doorway. The woman held a tray of what looked to be fruits and a decanter of something. Her long blonde hair fell in waves to her slender waist. As much as Rayna didn't want to be jealous, she was.

The woman inclined her head and offered a non-threatening smile. "My lord," her attention went to Kabril, "Iorgos ordered food be sent up. Your brother worries because you have not eaten since..." The woman averted her gaze. "Since...erm..."

"Since the queen arrived?" Kabril supplied, a teasing note in his voice.

Rayna had thought the blonde was gut wrenching enough. Hearing there was a queen to go along with the king left her feeling as if she'd been struck with a bat. She looked up and shook her head. "Waking up and finding myself in my boring country house would be great right about now. Really, I'm full up on winged macho men. I'd like to go back to simple, sexy bird doctors. Ones who may be odd at times but don't have stacked blondes showing up to feed them grapes."

"Set the tray down and leave us," Kabril said.

The woman did as she was instructed. Rayna rubbed the back of her neck and let out a soft laugh. "Am I crazy? Be honest."

"Rayna, your sanity is not in question." He ran his fingers down the back of her arm making a shiver ripple through her. When he reached her hand, Kabril laced his fingers through hers, the move intimate. He brought their joined hands to his lips and planted a chaste kiss on hers. "What I wish to know is if you can accept me as I am?"

"You're not an avian vet, are you?" she asked, already knowing the answer but needing to hear the truth from him.

"To your people, I know more of birds than they could ever hope to." Kabril lifted her hand and spread her fingers wide, kissing the tip of each one. "But, alas, I am not."

She wanted to yell at him for lying to her but the feel of his full lips trailing over her skin was too distracting. He made his way up her arm, slow and steady. When he reached her shoulder, Kabril nipped lightly at her skin, catching the strap of the gown she wore. He dragged it down before returning to kiss his way up her shoulder, towards her neck.

Kabril knew Rayna needed her rest but the taste of her skin was too tempting to resist. He thought she'd shriek in fear of him after he learned she knew he was not human. Once the castle doctors had informed him she would indeed recover, Kabril had set out to learn what had happened from the sources. By the time Kabril reached Humbert, Sachin had already beaten the man within inches of his life. Kabril didn't question Sachin on the matter. If his friend felt the need to take such measures, they were clearly called for.

Lazar was slow to recover and in his fevered state revealed snippets of the conversation he'd held with Rayna. Kabril had wanted to be the one to tell Rayna all his secrets, not have her learn by way of kidnapping at the hands of his enemy. The minute Lazar regained full consciousness he would be tortured for his role in the attack on Rayna. There was little point in inflicting pain on a man who was not aware of the goings on around him.

Pushing thoughts of torture from his head, Kabril concentrated on the bounty before him. His mate. His soon-to-be wife. Rayna stared at him with questioning eyes and he wanted to kiss the doubt from them. He'd sensed her unease with the serving wench and didn't need to search far inside himself for the reasons behind her mood. She was jealous. It was foolish considering he'd never given the wench a second look much less bedded her, but the comfort from knowing Rayna cared if he did left his heart swelling and his lips sealed.

He moved his hand across Rayna and managed to ease her to the bed. Sliding over her, Kabril tried and failed to control his breathing. Her hair fanned out around her as she stared up at him with wide eyes. His senses were keen and he picked up on the beating of her heart. As much as he wanted to take her, ram his cock into her depths and claim her for his own, Kabril knew she needed to fully recover. "Sleep," he whispered, going to plant a kiss on her forehead.

Rayna tilted her head and caught his lips with hers. She thrust her tongue into his mouth, causing Kabril's chivalry to crumble. His cock hardened at an alarming rate and he rubbed his body against hers. The need to join with her was great. He drew air through his flaring nostrils, behaving more like a rutting bull than the king of hawks. He pressed his distended flesh to Rayna's mound and it only took a second before he felt the proof of her arousal.

"You are wet, *ta'konima,*" he whispered between kisses.

Rayna pushed on his chest. "And you are rude. Get off me. Now."

Her spunk only added to her allure. He nodded, making no effort to bend to her wishes. Instead, he feathered his tongue over her bottom lip and relished the shiver that moved through her.

Rayna's foot made its way up the back of his leg before she wrapped her legs around his waist. The feel of her countering his movements was too much. Kabril gave in to the desire to go further. He'd already had a small sampling near the river and could scarcely await more.

He settled between her legs, a reminder that she wore nothing under the sleeping gown he'd had her put in. His own sleeping pants pulled taut as his cock fought for freedom, the promise of paradise close.

Rayna raked her fingernails down his back hard enough to cause his skin to welt but not hard enough to draw blood. The shifter in him could smell even small traces of blood.

She returned his kisses, searching his mouth with her tongue and no doubt finding it welcoming. Rayna arched against him, leaving his cock rubbing against her wet slit. Moisture soaked through his pants and the scent of her arousal pushed him over the edge of restraint.

Growling, Kabril ran a hand into the back of Rayna's hair and tugged, forcing her head back so he could devour her neck—smothering it with heated kisses. He moved downwards and planted kisses on the swell of her breast. Kabril pulled the other strap of her gown, freeing her glorious globes in the process. He took a pink-tipped nipple into his mouth and sucked evenly. Rayna's moans spurred him onward. He crushed her breasts, cupping them with his hands while he coated them in kisses.

"So sweet. Like ripe berries." He licked a line around her erect nipple, staring up at the rapture on her face.

Her mouth fell open and a cry broke free. "Kabril. Please."

Working his hands down her body, Kabril continued to vary kisses and licks on her nipples. He kneaded her thighs, all the while fighting an internal battle to keep from coming as he inched the gown upwards. He dipped his head, laying kisses low on her stomach. As he neared the thin thatch of well-maintained hair on her mound, Rayna lightly ground her body against him. "Patience, *ta'konima*."

He spread her drenched folds and eyed the prize. Her rosy clit was swollen with lust. Kabril drew it into his mouth mindful to be gentle and flicked his tongue back and forth. Rayna's entire body tightened and he had to seize hold of her hips to keep her from moving up and off the bed.

She cried out, laced her fingers in his hair and held firm, riding his mouth. He lapped cream from her slit while taking one hand and stimulating her clit. He found a steady rhythm and chuckled into her pussy as she began murmuring a mix of curses, pleas and threats.

"Dammit, Kabril. Uh, more. There." She thrust her hips upwards. "There. Oh, yes!"

Rayna came with a start and Kabril continued to work her clit, swirling his tongue and lapping her juices. Her cream was every bit as sweet as she was. Unable to resist her any longer, Kabril moved up and over her. He supported his weight with one arm as he freed his cock from its confines with his other hand.

He nudged her entrance with his cock head and locked gazes with her. "Rayna Vogel, do you accept me—all of me from now until the end of time?"

The look Rayna leveled on him was scorching. Purring, she cupped his face and Kabril anxiously awaited her answer. In order for his claim to be official and for Rayna to be the queen in the eyes of his people, she had to accept all of him—his magik included.

A lone tear made its way down her smooth cheek and Kabril felt as if his heart had shattered. Assuming she was rejecting him as her mate, he went to move away. Rayna held steady to his face.

"Kabril?"

"Y-es." He cleared the emotions lodged in this throat. "Yes?"

"Does your skin itch too, when you're not able to shift forms for a long period of time?"

The question caught him off guard. Stunned, he nodded.

She traced a path down his neck and to his shoulders. More tears escaped their watery prison and Kabril had to look away to avoid weeping himself.

"I never meant to cause you pain."

"Rayna?" He wiped her cheek. "What do you mean?"

Her voice shook. "You didn't...change...because of me. Did you?"

Kabril moved slightly, causing the head of his cock to press into her hot core. Fire shot through his lower body and the fierce need to lay claim to what was his was almost debilitating. "Rayna, please. I beg of you. Do you accept me—all of me from now until the end of time?"

She stared up through lust-filled eyes. "Show me, Kabril."

His body felt as if it were going to burst. "Speak not in riddles, *ta'konima*. Though I may be a king, I am still but a man."

The slow, sexy smile that slid over her face eased his tension a bit. "I want to see your wings, Kabril."

My wings?

At any other time he would have attempted to reason with her, make sure she was ready to see him shift forms, but his resolve was weak. He let go, allowing feathers to emerge on his upper shoulders first and then his shoulder blades. One barely there pinch later and his wings unfurled. A blanket of brown, white and gold enveloped them as Kabril extended his wings out and around them.

Rayna squealed and touched one of his wings tentatively, as if she was afraid she would cause him pain. Her touch had the exact opposite effect. Pleasure shot straight through his body, settling in his cock each time she touched his wings. He bit his cheek, trying to focus on anything other than the fact he was close to paradise. "R-Rayna," he ground out. "Do you accept me—all of me from now until the end of time?"

"Yes, Kabril. Yes."

With that, he surged forward, sinking his cock into her silken depths and relishing the feel of his mate's body encasing his own. Her pussy held him to her. She was tight. Made just for him.

The base of his spine tingled and Kabril knew additional feathers were forming on his back. He also knew his magik was rising, preparing to share itself with her, granting her the ability to live as long as him.

"Uh, Kabril," Rayna panted as he began to slide in and out of her. She clung to him, countering his thrusts and rubbing her body against his. Her pussy clenched around his cock as Rayna tipped her head back. "I'm coming. Kabril, yes!"

Liquid warmth made their already glorious merging even better. His magik picked then to rise, circling them with static-charged energy. Rayna continued to come, paying no mind to the power around her. For Kabril the moment was momentous. Never before had he shared his magik with another. Doing so during the act of coupling forever bound Rayna to his heart and his soul. She was now, in the eyes of his people, his wife, his mate, his queen.

He exploded, rooting himself deep within her core as his cock twitched, jetting forth seed. Kabril's entire body shook from the force of it all. The intensity was unlike anything he'd ever experienced. His cock remained hard, even after his seed was spent.

Wrapping his arms around Rayna, Kabril captured her mouth with his as he used his extended wings to lift them from their current position. Rayna yelped and held tight to him.

Chuckling, Kabril slid his hands down and cupped her ass. "Ride me, *ta'konima.*"

She glanced down, looking uneasy.

"Worry not. My power helps in keeping us afloat. We will not fall."

Rayna nodded, biting her lower lip and driving him mad with desire. She began to move her hips slowly at first, before working into a faster rhythm. When she varied her movements, moving up and down on him, Kabril seized hold of her and started impaling her on his cock.

Cries, moans and animalistic grunts broke free of them both. The smell of sex filled the air and Kabril's magik still buzzed around them. The moment was perfect and worth waiting four hundred cycles for.

Rayna's pussy milked his cock as her legs tightened around him. He knew she was coming and wanted to join her. He pumped feverously into her, savoring the feel of his mate. His sac drew up a second before he expelled his seed, filling her with all he had to offer.

"*Ta'konima,*" he whispered, nuzzling his face into the crook of her neck and planting kisses there.

A sultry laugh bubbled up from her. "Mmm, tell me what *ta'konima* means."

"It means my love in my language. *Ta'konima* from a man to a woman and *to'konimo* from a woman to a man." He kissed her again and she stiffened. "Rayna?"

"You love me?" The question, while so innocent, nearly broke him.

How could she not know what he felt for her? How could she not see what he'd done?

Because you have not told her and she knows not your ways.

"Yes, Rayna. I love you. I have loved you since you took me to see your Henry. Each day I fought the urge to lay claim to you." He expelled a long, tired breath. "I could wait no longer."

"Lay claim to me?"

He eased them back onto the bed and withdrew from Rayna. "What happened between us means, in the eyes of my people, you are my mate. Umm, my wife. I know it is not the same for humans. Sachin explained their customs to me, but what transpired, the sharing of my magik and our bodies, makes you queen to my people, Rayna."

Kabril waited for her to explode in anger. When tears arrived, he wasn't sure what to do. "Rayna, are you in pain?" Guilt consumed him. "I was selfish, taking you when you were not yet fully recovered."

"Shhh." She pressed her hand to his mouth. "I love you too, Kabril."

For a moment Kabril felt as if he had been struck senseless. The sound of his heart pounding filled his ears and his breathing increased. "You love me as well? You are not vexed by my..."

"Shut up with the vexing and kiss me, king." She pulled him to her.

Kabril laughed as he drew his wings back into his body, leaving no trace of them behind. He rolled, putting Rayna on top of him so he could stare up at her beauty. "I will cease my blathering if you commence with the games." He wagged his brows and Rayna blushed.

"The games, huh?" She raked her nails down his chest lightly. "Mmm, I think I can come up with a few things, *to'konimo.*"

Chapter Six

Rayna moved down the seemingly endless stone corridor in search of Kabril. She'd woken to an empty bed and needed to see him. Recessed portions of the wall held sconces. A candle burned bright in each one. A navy-blue runner ran the length of the hall, keeping her bare feet from padding against stone.

The moment Rayna spotted a curved staircase she quickened her pace, bounding down them at a speed she shouldn't have. She tried and failed to come to a stop at the bottom. Instead she slid on a slick, cold floor and crashed shoulder first into the wall.

The sound of Sachin's voice caught her attention, making her ignore the pain shooting through her arm. His voice was faint but unmistakable.

"My lord, mayhap he speaks the truth."

"He lies!" Kabril shouted, his voice so deep and dangerous that it vibrated around her. "The knave spouts venom from his lips with his deceit. My queen would never rush to the aid of my enemy."

Aid of the enemy? His queen?

The sound of something cracking grabbed her attention. She followed the noise and tripped over the edge of a heavy wooden bench. Rayna put her arms out, in hopes of catching herself and ended up grabbing hold of a wall sconce. It turned, lever-like, and the stone wall nearest her opened, revealing a dark staircase.

Sachin's voice became clearer. "My lord, ask the queen."

This time it sounded as if something snapped. The noise was followed by a painful cry and Rayna recognized the voice immediately—

122

Lazar. She ran down the steep steps and when she came to the end she covered her mouth, unable to believe the sight before her.

Kabril cracked a whip and it bit at Lazar's exposed chest. Lazar's wrists were bound above his head as he hung, suspended from iron chains. Blood trickled down him as his chest heaved. Rayna's gaze traveled the length of the large room. A cornucopia of torture devices lined it. With her mouth agape, she stared at Kabril.

His black hair clung to his sweat-soaked face. The feral look in his eyes made her take a step back as he grit his teeth, his attention still solely on Lazar. "You dared to harm my mate. To take her from me and leave her for dead. For this, you shall suffer my wrath." He drew the whip back again and Rayna dashed forward, putting her body between Kabril's and Lazar's.

Sachin was suddenly before her, shielding her with his massive body. "My lady!"

"S-Sachin?" she asked, her voice barely there. "Don't let him hurt Lazar."

"Go," Lazar whispered.

Sachin stepped to the side and Rayna faced Kabril head on. His golden gaze was still burning with rage. The veins in his neck stood out noticeably.

Rayna put a hand on her hip and glared right back at him. "If you're going to shout orders at me or try to hit me with that whip I'll have you know that I'll..."

Suddenly, Kabril dropped the whip and backed away, the fire draining from his eyes. "Hit you? Rayna, I would never raise my hand to you. Never."

"But you'd beat a helpless man? One who tried to keep me safe from his own people?"

Kabril grimaced and tipped his head. Sachin took hold of her shoulder. "Explain."

"Lazar took me from the campsite but when he found out Kabril had done nothing but lie to me for months, he decided I'd been through enough. Plus, I don't think he agreed with what they had in store for me. He was going to take me home when the other Falco Per-e-something or others arrived."

Sachin bit his lower lip. "*Falco Peregrinus?*"

"Right." She nodded, adding, "He killed one of his own men to keep me from being hurt and I think he would have done the same to Humbert if I wouldn't have infected his wound with soil from Earth. He'd been suffering from the effects already and it was too much for him. He fell into the water and I went in after him." Rayna blushed. "After I kicked Humbert where it counts."

"Where it counts?" Sachin asked.

She centered her gaze on his groin and he winced. "Yeah, it worked so don't knock it."

Kabril stood, listening to his mate talk of how Lazar came to her aid. Guilt for having allowed her to be taken to begin with settled over him. Seeing the shame in Rayna's blue eyes as she shielded the Falco with her body didn't help matters any. He was king, it shouldn't make a difference what anyone thought of him but it did. He cared what light Rayna viewed him in.

Sachin tipped his head. "My lord, permission to remove the prisoner's restraints?"

He nodded.

Rayna crossed her arms under her breasts, causing them to thrust forward. "Prisoner? How about a guest? I like the sound of that better."

"Rayna, you cannot possibly think to—" The stern look upon her beautiful face silenced him.

She tapped a finger against her arm. "I'm still mad at you for lying to me, Kabril. Don't think you're going to get on my good side beating Lazar to a bloody pulp. Let him down, clean him up and see to his wounds. He needs a doctor and something to eat, not to be interrogated by you."

Sachin opened his mouth to say something and Rayna shot him a nasty look. "One word from you and I'll make you eat my famous chicken divan."

Gulping, Sachin put his hands up, signaling defeat. Kabril's stomach churned at the thought of eating chicken anything. His long-time friend thrust him towards his mate. "For the love of the gods, see to your woman before she truly does clip our wings."

"Your woman?" Rayna quirked a brow as she stared at Kabril.

He gave into the smile wanting to come and went to one knee as Sachin had told him human males did in situations such as this. He took Rayna's hand in his and stared up into her blue eyes. "Rayna, you will marry me the way humans do."

Sachin cleared his throat and Lazar laughed under his breath. Kabril thought hard about Sachin's instructions and realized he'd commanded Rayna instead of asking her. He decided to try again. "Uh, umm, Rayna, would you do me the honor of being my ball and chain?"

It was Rayna's turn to laugh, and laugh she did, tipping her head back and covering her mouth with both hands. "Ball and chain? Heaven help me. My man thinks that's a compliment."

"Be my chick?" he asked, hopeful he got it right.

Rayna laughed harder.

"My sexy significant other?"

She closed the distance between them, snorting softly and shaking her head. He went to try another only to find her pressing her fingers to his lips. "Shhh, Kabril. Yes, I'll be your wife the way humans do it, too."

His heart soared. He swept her off her feet and rushed towards the staircase. The need to get her back to their chambers and make sweet love to her was too powerful to resist. The Oracle had chosen well for him. Rayna truly was his perfect match.

Epilogue

Earth, three and a half months later...

Kabril slid his arms around his wife and held her close, running his hands over her low, swollen abdomen. The life they'd created grew within her. Every moment since its conception seemed like a miracle to him, to Rayna and to the people of Accipitridae. Already the somber moods had lifted and the people rejoiced once more. A festival was in the works, the first in many years. It was to honor their union and the coming of their child. At least that is what the people claimed. Kabril suspected they were looking for a reason to celebrate after so many cycles of dwelling on the negative.

The threat of war was still imminent. Relations with the *Falco Peregrinus* were still nonexistent. Lazar's presence in the castle sparked controversy at first but he was beginning to grow on everyone, including Kabril. Sachin insisted the Falco could be useful for establishing relations with the *Falco Peregrinus* in the future. Lazar seemed to think he would never be welcomed back by his own kind. Kabril tended to side with him on the matter. Lazar was always welcome in Kabril's kingdom.

The wind picked up, causing orange and yellow leaves to scatter about. Rayna sighed and leaned back into his embrace. "It's so beautiful, Kabril. I'm going to miss it."

He kissed her temple. "*Ta'konima*—my love, I have told you time and time again that you do not have to sell your grandmother's home."

She nodded. "I know, but we don't need it. You're keeping the one down the lane on the off chance one of your men wants to visit and we live in Accipitridae." She glanced over her shoulder at him. "Your castle sleeps about a hundred people or better so I don't think we need this as a guest house."

"It holds sentimental value to you, Rayna." He rocked her gently, drawing in her sweet scent.

"I'll make new memories with you, Kabril. You're my family now."

He cringed, not wanting to broach the subject he needed to. "Speaking of family. You met my brother Iorgos."

Rayna arched a dark brow. "Yes and I still think you're too hard on him. But I don't think that's what you're getting at. What's up?"

"Word came of my other brothers arriving soon to welcome you to the family."

She licked her lips and grinned. "Are you going to tell me how many brothers you have finally?"

Kabril stiffened. "I have eight brothers. Two were born minutes behind me. There are two sets of twins, one includes Iorgos. Then, there is Thrandr, he was a single birth."

One. Two. Three. He mentally counted down until Rayna's temper flared.

"You have how many sets of what?" Rayna spun around in his arms, her eyes wide in disbelief.

"There is more," he said, against his better judgment. "For our kind, multiple births have nothing to do with the female. Apparently, male shifters, of our kind, release a chemical in our sperm which encourages a high fertility rate. The chemical has been absent for some time as it is tied to our magik."

Rayna clutched his arms, her fingernails digging into his skin. "Are you trying to tell me there is a good chance I have more than one baby growing inside me?"

A sheepish smile swept over him. "Yes."

"And this is coming up this late in the game why?" she asked, tapping her foot.

"I love you."

Rayna batted her lashes and let out a soft sigh. "I love you too but if you don't start telling me important things up front, you're going to be sleeping in the birdhouse."

He cringed and she laughed. "Ah, my queen, you have my word, you know now all of my secrets."

About the Author

Mandy M. Roth grew up fascinated by creatures that go bump in the night. From the very beginning, she showed signs of creativity. At age five, she had her first piece of artwork published. Writing came into play early in her life as well. Over the years, the two mediums merged and led her to work in marketing. Combining her creativity with her passion for horror has left her banging on the keyboard into the wee hours of the night. Mandy lives with her husband and three children on the shores of Lake Erie, where she is currently starting work on her Master's Degree.

To learn more about Mandy, please visit www.mandyroth.com or send an email to mandy@mandyroth.com. For latest news about Mandy's newest releases subscribe to her announcement list in Yahoo! groups. http://groups.yahoo.com/subscribe/Mandy_M_Roth.

Firebird

Jaycee Clark

Dedication

This is for my girlfriends who know their minds and aren't afraid to tell you, me or anyone else exactly what they're thinking.

Prologue

Laru Mountains

The forest was silent. The quiet too oppressive to be normal. Silently humming, she settled into the carriage next to her mother. Her brother sat across from them talking softly to their father who smiled at her then frowned.

"It's too quiet," Cyzarine said, her soft voice carrying on the cold air between them. She reached up to shove the gold velvet curtain aside, but her mother grabbed her hand and smiled. Yet her mother's smile didn't reach her blue eyes as it normally did.

No one in the carriage spoke. They were traveling for her to visit with her betrothed, whom she'd only met once before. Thinking of the arrogant Rourik made her frown. Cyzarine was a princess, her parents the last of mated fabled firebirds. Their kingdom in Western Russia had been in the throes of civil war.

A shrill cry rent the air followed by the long howl of a wolf. She knew the sound...lycans.

The howl was joined by another and then another. This was the sound of their enemy, a warning, a promise...

Their father looked out the carriage, then thumped on the roof. "Derik, do not stop the coach, keep going."

But even as her father gave that command, the carriage pulled to a stop, the horses stomping the ground. The night swirled between sleeping and awaking around them.

She glanced out the window, but her mother pushed her back. "No, stay still."

They heard it again, the lone cry of a wolf, followed by others— from one side, then the other.

"They're around us, Papa," her older brother, Gavril, said.

She checked quickly out the window.

Her father shared a narrow gaze and slight frown with their mother before he smiled at them both and climbed out. Her mother remained in with them for just a moment, then told them to stay and climbed out as well.

Cyzarine looked at her brother, only a year older than she. "What's wrong?" she whispered.

"Shh." He peeked out the window of the other side. His eyes went dark, as they did when he wanted to see, to look beyond what was seen by mere mortals. He startled and his face went white. "We need to get out. We must get out now," he whispered. Grabbing her hand, he opened the carriage door on the side opposite their parents and pulled her out.

"Gavril? What's going on?" She tried to tug her hand free, but her legs sank into the snow up to her knees. She wasn't wearing her boots.

The wind picked up and Gavril jerked her along behind him. "Run, Cyzarine. No matter what happens, you must run!" He picked up speed and she stumbled along behind him.

"What's..." She glanced behind them, surprised to see they'd gone so far from the carriage.

But from here she heard the howl again, the snarl.

A low cry rent the air and she saw a burst of flames, a fire of blue, green and bright red.

Her mother...

She tried to stop, but Gavril urged her on. She could hear him whispering.

They were running to the west, the tall trees spearing up and blocking their path.

For the first time since they'd started their journey, she wished they'd reached her betrothed's home. He was strong. She knew that. Had seen it.

Again she glanced back over her shoulder, not realizing they had climbed up an embankment. "Gavril," she panted.

"Come on, Cyzarine." He jerked her harder and she almost fell, but still she looked over her shoulder.

Below, she saw them.

The wolves, white and grey, some black, closing in a half circle around her parents, who weren't flying away. They'd shifted into firebirds, their feathers brilliant, luminous, but they didn't rise.

"Why won't they fly?" she whispered.

Gavril turned and saw them. "Oh no. They think we're in the carriage," he whispered.

She opened her mouth to yell. Gavril slammed his hand over her mouth. "No. Hush. Come, Cyzarine. Hurry."

But she stood rooted to the spot. Their parents' wings flapped, snow rising from the motion, the red of their feathers like blood against the snow.

"We need the falcons," he whispered. Then he jerked her around. "Call him, Cyzarine. Call your falcons."

She frowned. "I don't have any."

One wolf leapt and snapped at their mother.

Cyzarine shook her head. No. No! Mama!

"Call them!" He grabbed her shoulders. "Now! Rourik, your betrothed. He's a falcon, their leader. Call him. You must!"

She glanced back over her shoulder and thought of the young man she hadn't liked very much. *"Rourik, I need you. Help us."*

"Come on, Reen! We can't just stand here." Gavril pulled her behind him, both of them running and falling in the snow.

"We should shift," she panted.

He shook his head. "I can shift faster than you. You haven't mastered it yet. I'm not leaving you." He pulled her up again when she stumbled in the snow. "Hurry, Reen. Hurry."

She could hear the wolves baying closer.

Rourik! Rourik! Please, we need the falcons!

Something slammed into them from the side. Flames burst all around them as the cold snow covered her face. She felt Gavril beside her one moment, then he was thrown away.

Growls and snarls filled the air.

"*Run, Cyzarine. Run!*" She glanced down the hill and saw feathers littered the pristine snow, saw the wolves jerking apart the body of a bird. "No!" She screamed.

Cyzarine stumbled to her feet, the dagger her mother had given her pressed against her side. It was a gift from her betrothed. She hadn't wanted it. Hadn't wanted...

Please come! Help!

Something bit ice cold into her shoulder and she screamed, whirling and falling into the snow.

"Wait for our leader, he likes them young," a voice said.

She wrenched her dagger free. Blood ran down her arm to drip from her fingers, making her grip slip on the dagger handle.

"I'll be careful." From the shadow of the trees a force knocked her again to the ground. She could smell the wet wolf and yelled, stabbing at it with the dagger in her hand.

Cyzarine whimpered. *Where are you! Help! Please!*

The wolf whined, whimpered and lashed out at her. Claws raked across her chest and she could only hiss a breath out.

Cries, high pitched and warning, screamed through the air.

Cyzarine's vision wavered and she turned her head. The snow was so cold. A rock pressed against her back and she could see down the hill. The carriage was now on its side. The wolves circling it, looking up the hill.

Need to fly...to shift... But she couldn't. The wound on her shoulder blazed through her to merge with the pain in her chest. Her breath puffed out into the cold air.

Scuffles and growls then a scream to her right made her look. A wolf ripped into her brother's throat.

Cyzarine could only blink.

Then shadows arrowed down, swooping, screaming. She knew that sound.

Falcons...

Something grabbed her, wind rushed against her skin as she felt herself lifted.

So cold...

The world disappeared around her.

Chapter One

Present day, 20 years later

He studied his prey through the glass wall into the room beyond. A white cheetah paced one way, then the other, in front of the glass.

From here he couldn't hear the growl, but he knew she was growling at him. Knew she had learned the Collector liked to watch her.

After all, he'd told her he loved to watch her, had shown her, taught her what he liked and what he didn't.

She was beauty.

She was precious.

She was his.

From her side, the large wall window looked like a wall of mirrors. He'd had it specially made. The previous occupant, an albino panther, had lasted almost a year before she died. Well, she wouldn't have died if it hadn't been her time.

He sat in the velvet chair against the brick wall and pressed the intercom button. He inhaled and wished he could rid the converted warehouse of its lingering factory scent of oil and machinery. Even after he'd completely remodeled the old building, updating, taking special care for all the things he needed, it still often smelled of peasant workers.

A low growl filled the air. He smiled even as he reached over to the cherry-wood side table and poured himself a snifter of vodka. He sniffed at the warm slide of it down the back of his throat. So many loved the flavored vodkas, as old as Russia itself, but he was a purist. He hated additives.

Which was why he only went for the perfect, for the rare.

Nribo, his current find, was perfect. She was fast, so damn fast. He'd seen her in a nightclub in Nairobi. And he'd known, known how rare she was, how special.

How she would be his.

"Are you hungry, lovely?" he asked, as he sipped his drink and watched her.

In human form, she was tall, lithe, her muscles tight and ready for battle. Fucking her had been a wondrous thing. She'd fought him like the cat she was.

But, in the end, she was no match for him. He was, after all, the demon who guarded treasures. His own personal gift was to find said treasures.

All part of the job, in his book. Or maybe it was more he was enjoying the fringe benefits. He smiled. "Lovely, pacing like that will wear you out," he told her.

As he knew it would, the comment didn't please her. She hissed, growled and leapt at the glass, her claws scarring the surface.

He chuckled. "Still so feisty. There's no way out." He stood and straightened his silk shirt. "You've scratched my mirror, that wasn't very nice. I guess you'll just have to wait for your food. But don't worry, when you get weak," he said, dropping his voice right against the intercom, "I'll come revive you."

The white cheetah roared.

He smiled and clicked the intercom off, then killed the lights in her room. Let her sit hungry in the dark. He'd know when to go to her, when to use her, when to appreciate her.

He petted the golden jaguar beside him, the metal precious beneath his touch. He glanced around his chamber, at all his special statues. Jaguars, tigers, lions, birds of prey, wolves, even a few vamps and gifted, rare humans...

His pretties, his treasures… Just to show her what happened to those who didn't appreciate his attentions, he pressed another button and one of her walls faded from dark to be lit behind—revealing one of his favorite rooms.

The room was lined with furs, tusks, claws, feathers, headdresses—whatever his fancy. Before he'd discovered his golden touch, he had liked to keep something from those whom he had to dispose. He loved to show his prize catches off to the new finds, who often needed a bit of incentive to do as they were told. Barbaric, yes—

The loud roar, turned to a mewl.

—but effective nonetheless.

She might be easier to break than he first thought. Wait until she saw what he planned to do to her. Now, he no longer skinned his pretties. That process had been messy and, though fun at first, quickly lost its appeal. The treasure he found, the golden athame, was ancient, cursed and blessed. It held great power, which was why he guarded it. It also took life and gave riches. Or in his case—a quick and rather simple way of keeping his rare beauties.

He'd decided to *turn* them. Now they were perfect for him, large as life, jeweled eyes, and…treasures of wealth. Again he ran his hand down his last pretty. What had her name been? Oh yes, Trish. He patted the golden head and turned down the hallway.

For now, he needed to check on his other pretties. He rubbed his hands. He had a new one to play with.

Chapter Two

Russia

Reen wiped the blood out of her eye and limped up the stone steps. She really hated this job sometimes. Her black boots rarely felt this heavy. The doors at the top of the steps opened into the grand foyer. The mansion looked like any other in Europe, except it was still a functioning castle. Not merely a museum for retirees and backpackers to tour through, this castle had a purpose. It wasn't just any castle, this one was special—a defense like castles of old.

It was headquarters for the Hunters.

The Hunters tracked supernaturals that had become problematic. In this day and age of decadence, where the supernaturals were both worshipped and ignored by mortals, they often became bored. No longer was the world their playground. Now sciences wanted them for research, men and women alike wanted them for the simple fact of novelty and other supernaturals felt merely displaced. Displaced. She snorted. Supernaturals with identity crises gave rise to the new super shrinks—a new breed of psychiatrists. Whether or not she agreed with therapy for the confused supers, was irrelevant.

Cyzarine knew some people needed such help. Her? She'd rather eat her leather boots. Vamps, weres, the fae, all were trying to figure out how they fit into the new order of the world quickly outstripping itself of humanity.

Powers shifting and vying for attention left vacuums for greed, corruption and crime.

That's where the Hunters came into play. The supernaturals still needed balances, checks and in most cases, retribution.

She was a Hunter. Though more specifically, she didn't just hunt the criminals, as many Hunters did, she eliminated the problems.

She was an assassin.

She was no different than many of her kind before her—a firebird could destroy. She merely cashed in on her genetic legend.

Petrov, the guard, nodded to her as she passed him, her trench coat hiding the weapons she used.

She shoved through the waiting area, completely ignoring Valerie at the outer desk in front of Erik's office.

The doors were shut, but she also ignored the unspoken rule to wait until invited into the inner sanctum of her boss. Opening it, she saw someone stood in the shadows in the corner, smelled the spice of his cologne, gave him a quick glance, and then ignored him as well. She had only one man in her sights.

"Erik."

"Reen." He looked at her from behind his desk with a raised brow. "I'm busy."

"You call me in off a job, have your boys pick me up and expect me to wait prettily?" She shook her head and walked to the desk, tossing down the amulet she was supposed to have retrieved, which of course, she had. "Target is taken care of."

Erik was a vampire, ancient, as the office rumors went. She knew for a fact the whispers weren't just rumors. Though she'd never actually come out and asked the man how old he was. Some things were better left alone.

He looked at it for a moment, then turned completely from the window behind his desk to pick up the dull necklace. The stone glimmered faintly as if whispering secrets, and the gold beckoned to be polished.

Cyzarine merely waited. Erik brushed the stone and then the chain with his thumb. He was dressed as he always was. Black. Black shirt, black pants, black shoes. She often gave him a hard time. Every chance she got, she gifted him some bright tie, scarf or pair of gloves. He'd yet to wear any of them. Not that she cared either way, right now she was pissed.

"I should shove that up your ass," she said, again wiping the blood from her eye. She pressed her fingers to the wound in her scalp still trickling blood over her forehead and down her ear.

His gaze narrowed on her. "I should lock you in the infirmary."

She blew out a breath and strode to the windows, looking out on the cold winter landscape. She hated the winter. Hated the snow, and here in Grubsretep there was plenty.

"I'll be fine."

Someone cleared their throat and she was reminded of the other person in the room. Without looking at him, she turned from the window and strode towards the door, saying over her shoulder, "I get one day off, then you can give me my next assignment."

"Actually, I can't do that."

She stopped halfway to the door.

"Reen, sit down."

Her eyes narrowed on his and for the first time, since storming in, she took a deep breath and tried to read the situation.

Erik was calm, but then he generally always was. He was however, frowning, the lines around his mouth and across his forehead deeper than normal.

Something warned her she might not like what was coming.

"I want to introduce you to someone." He motioned to the other occupant of the room.

Reen waited as the man stepped from the shadows. He was tall, taller than she, but then many were as she was average in height. Where her hair was black, his was blond, almost white. Her eyes had a golden hue to them that many had often commented on. Including Erik.

This man, with his pale hair, had dark, almost black eyes. She had no idea if the color was dark brown or dark blue, they were just extremely dark. His body was long, not lean, but not overly muscular, reminding her of a runner. He had muscles, she could see them through the tight pale blue shirt he wore.

His face was altogether different. One might expect with his coloring and build that he'd have a refined face, one of beauty, of the classical statues she'd seen in Greece and Rome on her journeys there. But his jaw was too square, his brow too deep, making his eyes appear even darker. His nose was ridged, giving him a birdlike appearance almost. Bird, she almost snorted. He sure as hell wasn't a sparrow.

He merely raised a brow. Or she assumed he did, as his brows were as pale as his hair.

He offered a hand. "Saker."

Saker. It meant falcon. Falcon. A cold, hard twist rolled inside her. She took a deep breath and merely looked at the long-fingered hand, the sinews of the wrist, noted the scars on the back, across the knuckles.

Without taking it, she looked back up to his face and said, "Reen."

The man arched a brow and lowered his hand. "We worked a case together a few months back."

"Did we?" She didn't remember him, or didn't think she did.

He smiled slowly. "Yeah, we did."

She tilted her head. "Did we get the bad guy?"

"Yes, we did." His gaze stayed locked on hers.

A tingle of awareness swirled down her spine. She frowned.

Erik cleared his throat. "Now that the introductions are out of the way..."

She glanced at Erik and shook her pounding head. "Luv, what have you cooked up now?"

He glared at her. Erik rarely glared at anyone. Reen wondered what she'd done to aggravate him. Then again, she normally did very little.

Without another word, Reen sat in the chair. Her head hurt, her arm throbbed where one of the target's guards had caught her with a knife toss.

She rolled her shoulder, leaned her head back and closed her eyes. Still applying pressure to the wound on the side of her scalp—thanks to the target and his sword—she merely said, "Get on with it, Erik. You obviously worry I won't like it or you'd have already spit it out, then."

She could sense it, hostility in the air. And it wasn't hers.

Still she didn't open her eyes. Instead, she shoved the pain away and thought of light. Light a pale pink, tinged in blue. Light soothed her, the colors of twilight calmed her more than anything.

With her eyes closed she could smell Saker even more, outdoors and...something dark. Saker. Now that she thought about it, maybe she did remember him. He was with the undercover team. Or was he? She *had* heard about him. Saker and Company did freelance work. Mercenary. He was some sort of bird shifter—falcons.

She had no use for falcons. Anger swirled through her, but she pushed it aside. Falcons—in her opinion—were very unreliable.

Erik cleared his throat again. "We've got a problem," he said finally.

"Usually do," she muttered.

He sighed. She knew the sound of Erik's sighs. The way so much emotion could be in one little sound. Anger, frustration, resignation. His was currently a mixture of all three.

"Luv, just spit it out."

"Would you stop calling him that?" the other man asked.

She slowly opened her eyes to see Saker looking at her from across the small sitting area. He did not sit. He was leaning against the chair, his arms crossed. His voice was even timbred, deeper than she would have thought.

"Why?" she asked.

He opened his mouth, then snapped it shut, and turned a look onto Erik. If she hadn't been watching, she would have missed it. But Saker's eyes turned from black to a dark green glow.

She glanced to Erik, whose eyes hadn't changed. As always he was calm, or appeared so.

"Look, we might have worked together before. But you obviously didn't leave an impression on me. I don't know who you are, but I *do know* that Erik and I go way back. I can call him luv, Erik or dickhead if I so choose, none of which you have any say in. And I really need to get going if that's all."

What the hell was going on?

"Sit down," Saker said, not looking at her.

She walked to him and poked him in the chest until he looked at her, her own power, so recently used, still close to the surface. She felt the heat tingle along her fingers. "I don't know who you think you are, Saker, but—"

Those glowing green eyes swung back to her and stilled.

Something in them made her pause...

"Reen," Erik said on a sigh, "please sit down. We've got a serious problem and we all have to work together. You're not the only one pulled off an assignment. Higher ups than me have asked that you two work together."

It was her turn to cock a brow. "What do you mean, higher than you? You mean *she* asked for the two of us," she motioned between her and Saker, "to work together on some problem?"

Erik took a deep breath, nodded and raked a hand through his hair. "Yes. In a manner of speaking."

She rolled her eyes. "Erik, cut through. What's the bloody problem?"

"The higher up's daughter. She's missing. And Navalovich's pulled in all the best. That's you two."

"I said, no, Erik," Saker said.

She glanced to the man and shook her head. Very few told Erik no. Whatever history he and Erik had, she didn't care.

Erik's words sunk in. "Oleana is missing?"

Oleana was Navalovich's daughter. Alexandra Navalovich, founder of the Hunters and very quiet about her role as their supporter with the governments. The reason for her secrecy, she had a family and didn't want them harmed.

"Who?" she asked.

"We think she might be the latest target of a person only known as the Treasure Collector. It's possible and we're investigating every possibility."

Treasure Collector?

"I said no, Erik," Saker repeated.

Her mind was already sifting through what she knew of the Treasure Collector, which wasn't much.

"Isn't he also known simply as the Collector? Missing rare shifters or something?" She thought she remembered reading something about him in one of the files.

"Saker," Erik warned.

"No."

She turned on Saker. "Fine. You said no. There's the fucking door."

Leana. Her mind crashed through with memories of her friend. They'd met at the training academy as young girls and had always been close. The cat shifter, a white tiger. Rare even as supernaturals went, Leana had a lot of power. Her mother was also one, but Reen had no idea about Leana's father.

"How do we know it's the Collector?" Maybe they were wrong.

Erik sighed and waited until she looked at him. "He's a blot on the books. People want him. They want the man found. He's elusive as smoke or has been in the past. But there are too many women shifters, rare descendants, who have vanished from similar circumstances. No bodies are found, but missing is missing. And someone is taking them."

"And you don't believe in coincidences."

He only arched a brow.

"When?" she asked, pacing.

"Three days ago."

"And Navalovich is just now getting to this?" Anger swirled in her, her fingers tingling even more.

"Now, Reen. Leana is as old as you. She's a grown woman, with her own life. It was just when she didn't show up for a meeting with her mother that Navalovich started looking. And then she realized and pieced things together."

Reen shook her head. "Three days? Do you have any idea what could have happened in three days?"

"Which is why I jerked you off the job you were currently on."

"You could have said that to begin with."

She paced away, forgetting about the wound on her head, and walked the length of his office.

"We have discovered that the Treasure Collector is a collector of the worst kind."

"Of anything specific?" Saker shifted his weight.

Erik sighed. "Women. Girls. He likes female shifters. The rarer the better. We think he took or had her taken because...well, Oleana is one of seven registered Siberian tiger shifters. Before her, there's a missing file on both a cheetah and a jaguar from early summer. The cheetah just went missing this fall."

A collector.

"When did you learn this?" she asked. She glanced over her shoulder and noticed that Saker was glaring into the fireplace, watching the flames dance.

Pissed at the rude man, either because he rubbed her wrong, or just because he was of the useless Falcon order, she let her power flow over her and into the fire. It leapt out at him and licked his hand.

He slowly turned and cocked a brow at her.

Arrogant.

One corner of his mouth lifted on a grin.

"We've traced him to a club in Grubsretep."

"Which club?"

He didn't answer her.

"Which club?" she asked again, pulling her attention from Saker to Erik.

Erik rubbed his forehead. "Bindings." He shrugged. "We think. From previous reports on him, he seems to hop from club to club. We're not certain who he is. He might be a worker in these places, a patron, or an owner. So we're now investigating."

"And how many other shifting women disappearances have been labeled as his?"

"Not certain again. Could be as few as half a dozen, or worst, more than three dozen."

She could only stare at him. "Three dozen?"

Again, he shrugged. "This is in the last twenty years. Frankly there's been little known of him, so he's never been a priority until now. People go missing. Some get killed, some vanish because they want to, Reen. But going with what intel is learning now of a man collecting rare breeds of shifters as a...hobby—for lack of a better word—it looks like he can be accredited several disappearances and possibly several deaths as well, probably his earlier works."

She could only stare at him. "A serial? Is he human? Supernatural? Shifter? Vamp? Do we even know?"

He sighed and fell into his chair behind his desk. "Now that we have a place to start, and with this latest development, we're setting up a team. Undercover all the way."

She noticed he didn't answer her questions. Then his words registered. Undercover team. "Good, when?"

He glanced for a minute towards Saker, then locked his gaze back on her. "As soon as we get everything in place."

Blood ran down her forehead again and she wiped it away with a curse.

Erik frowned. "How much blood have you lost?"

She glanced at her shoulder, noted her pants were stiff with it where she'd constantly wiped her hand, her collar where it had dripped from her head. "I don't know, does it matter?"

Saker cursed.

"What's the plan?" She ignored the man.

Erik cleared his throat. "From the orders I received, we're to go in—"

"We?" she asked.

He nodded and looked at the file on his desk. "Yes, we. You and I posing as a couple and he," he said, motioning to Saker, "as your bodyguard."

"Like hell," Saker all but snarled.

Chapter Three

Saker tried to calm the emotions raging through him. But he knew he was doing a piss poor job of it. Damn it.

He looked again at her. Reen.

Cyzarine.

Once upon a time... He'd been known as a prince, and she'd been his.

No matter that he hadn't wanted her, hadn't answered her when she'd called to him years ago.

Never mind that the bind between them had been broken by his own father.

Now he was standing here. He'd worked with her, though from a distance, on another case a few months ago, which had led him to question his father.

Alive. She was alive and all but vibrating with life, even as he knew she dealt death as quickly and efficiently as an adder.

...you obviously didn't leave an impression...

A muscle ticked in his jaw and he was pissed at the fact he couldn't do a damn thing about it.

Technically he had no claim on her. Hell, he'd been told she was dead. Had spent half his life blaming himself for a youth's idiotic mistake.

He looked at her over his shoulder. Long and lithe, dressed in black tight enough nothing was left to the imagination, she was breathtaking and he couldn't help but admire her. She was beautiful.

Her skin reminded him of moonlight for some reason. The line of her jaw was a bit more square than most women he knew, but the fate's knew that tilt of stubborn chin only mirrored her hardheadedness. Sleek black hair hit just beneath that stubborn chin. Her lips were wide and full, and already he'd had too many thoughts of what he could do with her mouth. Straight nose. Her eyes—he remembered those eyes the most. They sat beneath dark, delicate brows that winged over wicked eyes framed by thick dark lashes. Tilted at the corners, like a cat's, her eyes held a strange golden hue he remembered, that had haunted his dreams and nightmares for years.

He remembered a child. A young girl who hadn't liked him, a spoiled princess who could have cared less who he was.

He remembered her scream of terror even as he'd lain with another woman. But he'd shrugged it off, just a moment, just for a second, instead of going to her.

It had cost him the throne. Not only had his father answered her call, but he'd severed the bind and disinherited Saker.

Fine.

And she lived.

He took another breath, watched as she ignored him yet again and walked to Erik. Erik, a death caller, a nightwalker, a living dead. A fucking vamp.

Saker studied her even as she draped an arm around Erik's neck and whispered in his ear, though Saker had no trouble hearing. "We're going to be a couple? How fun. It's been awhile since we got to play that role. Want a bite?"

"Reen," Erik tried, his eyes turning an iridescent purple.

Saker knew Erik knew *who* he was, probably knew that they were—or had been—mated.

Saker still wanted to rip his fucking heart out.

He had no right to lay a claim on her, but he couldn't help it. She was...

So damn alive.

Erik shook his head and reached for her arm, drawing it down. She merely smiled at him and kissed him on the mouth, traced Erik's lips with her own, with her tongue. She reached, swiped at her still bleeding head and offered her bloody finger to Erik.

Saker was across the room quicker than he realized.

"What is your problem? Don't like taking orders from women?" She stepped away from Erik, running her hand down over his chest as if straightening his shirt. The act seemed more intimate to Saker than the damn kiss.

"Depends on the woman and orders."

She rolled her eyes and swayed, blinking. "Damn."

Erik reached for her, but Saker already had her arm. They both held her. "I think maybe you should sit down. How much blood did you—" He saw then the dried blood coating her collar, noted it on her pants and realized he hadn't noticed before because of the color of her clothing.

"You should be in the infirmary."

"So he said." She motioned to Erik. "Hate the smell of blood," she muttered and slumped.

They both had hold of her and, for just a moment, she hung suspended between them.

Erik, a muscle twitching in his jaw, pulled her towards him. Saker didn't let her go.

"She doesn't know you," Erik said, his voice gruff. "And if she did, she'd probably kill you."

Saker took a deep breath and hearing the truth, let go.

Erik lifted her and laid her on the couch. "She hates the smell of blood. And do you know why, Saker?" he asked, brushing the dark black hair away from the side of her head to see the wound. "Do you?" He looked over his shoulder, his eyes still glowing.

Saker didn't care. "No. Strange to hate the smell of something she's so good at."

Erik growled, and Saker saw the fangs peeking from his friend's mouth. "She was supposed to have been a queen, you stupid fool."

"I know that. And she was supposed to have been *mine.*"

Erik merely turned around and muttered under his breath. "She has no idea who you are. I can tell you this. She hates falcons. Thinks they're useless. Doesn't care for them. Or their kind. *Your* kind. Can't imagine why she'd have that prejudice."

"I didn't kill her parents," Saker snarled, leaning over her.

Erik slashed out with his hand and shoved him back. "No, but you sure as hell weren't there for her either. If not for your father, she'd be dead. And where were you, I wonder? Little late to stake your claim now."

Though the man was right, he couldn't give up. Couldn't just hand her over now that he knew who she was. "I'll go to Navalovich."

Erik shrugged. "Go, I don't care. You think she's going to take your side on this while her daughter's life is at stake?" Erik cursed. "Bastard got her deep." With that he picked her up and carried her out of the room. Saker started to follow them, but decided against it.

He listened as they left, cursing and then made his own decision. He knew his father, knew the man had been angry, and damned if the king wouldn't have known all these years that Cyzarine lived. Saker wasn't surprised his father had broken their bond, and he even understood the why behind it. Hell, he'd have done the same thing if a son of his hadn't lived up to his obligations. Now, however, he wondered if there was anything he could do to change it all.

Without a doubt. One thing he knew. He wanted Reen and he had to have her.

Chapter Four

Erik watched her as Dr. Johnson looked her over. "This is deep. If she'd been mortal, it'd have killed her. A hair's breadth deeper and he'd have split her skull."

Erik crossed his arms over his chest and leaned against the wall. He was tired of this job. But such was life, or his life.

He kept looking to the door. He knew Saker was still here, but at least he wasn't in the room. Erik looked back at Reen and wondered what to do. He'd always respected Saker, at least what he'd heard of him. He knew Reen and Saker had previously worked on the same task force, though Saker was undercover, a few months ago.

Erik assumed, from Reen's reaction, she had no idea of the previous partnership. He knew for certain the woman had no clue who Saker really was. Once she did? He sighed and rubbed his face.

There wasn't a woman he respected more. He'd been in love with her since she first started her work for the Hunters. When they became lovers, he thought it might become more. But it took less than a month to realize that may never happen. Reen was the most guarded being he'd ever encountered, including himself. He knew her past, knew what happened to her. She was willing to share her body, even pieces of herself and her soul.

But he knew it would be a miracle if she ever gave herself completely.

So he'd do what he'd always done. He'd be here for her. It's what he'd do regardless of how he felt for her. Saker might not like it, but Erik really didn't give a damn. Saker hadn't held her when she woke screaming from nightmares. Hadn't calmed her when the past threatened to pull her under. Watched her when her job, the scent of blood, became too much and she shut down for days at a time.

Saker could kiss Erik's ass.

Reen stirred. "Damn," she whispered.

"You're staying here tonight."

"Like hell." Her voice was thready. "No time. Besides, I know Doc will give me some delicious meds that will have me back by tomorrow."

Erik walked to her bedside and leaned down until his nose was inches from hers. "That may be. But you're staying tonight or I'll tell Navalovich you're in no shape for this job. You want to be part of it, you stay here."

Her golden eyes flashed at him, but he saw past the anger, saw the childhood fear. He brushed her hair away from the bandage and sighed. "I know you hate these places, Reen. Did I mention, I'm staying tonight?"

She opened her mouth, but he leaned down and lightly kissed her. She didn't shy away from him as she once did. "Don't argue with me. You know in the end I'll win."

Reen shook her head. "I can't stay here, Erik. She's out there. And he's got her. I've got to do research, I've got to..."

Erik had been distracting her, while Dr. Johnson prepared a syringe. He injected it into her before she could knock it away. The balding doc, a lycan, quickly stepped back. "Not too often I manage to sneak up on her."

"Ass. I'm not... I'm going to..." Her eyes slowly slid shut.

Erik huffed out a breath and brushed the dark strands of hair off her pale forehead. Her blood wafted up to him and, like always, he fought the urge to lean in and taste.

He kept brushing her hair back from her face, softly, listening to her breathe. She would be pissed, but if he didn't sedate her to keep her here, she'd be out and straining against her limits. She was needed at top form and he'd make certain she stayed there, even if she didn't like his methods.

The doctor left them alone and Erik sighed, leaning close to press a kiss to her forehead. "Get some rest, sweetheart."

"I don't like you kissing her." The growling whisper came from the doorway.

Erik didn't need to turn around to know that Saker stood there. Saker, Rourik, whatever he went by these days. Rourik was heir to the Falcon throne. Saker was a mercenary, a bodyguard, one of the elite who did whatever necessary to get the job done he was hired to do.

Erik pulled the white blanket up and tucked it around her. Motioning to the other man, they walked out. He didn't miss the way Saker's eyes began to glow when they rested for any length of time on Reen.

They didn't talk as they walked down the hallway, up the two flights of stairs back to Erik's office.

"I don't want her part of this," Saker said again.

"It doesn't matter what you want. These are troubled times, Saker, she'll do what she's ordered to do whether you like it or not. Regardless of whether I like it or not. And if you knew her at all, you'd know the easiest way to get on Cyzarine's shit list is to tell her what she can and can't do." He poured them both a shot of vodka from the chilled bottle he kept in the fridge. "But go ahead and order her. It'll be entertaining at the very least." Handing one to the other man, he motioned for them to sit at the small table in front of the window. He sipped and looked out the fog-edged window. The air outside was cold not surprising as this time of year it was still chilled. Spring was breaking slowly over the frozen land. The daylight just now beginning to come back. Probably another reason he was tired. With endless nights, he didn't have to worry about limiting his sunlight exposure. "She's not a frightened child anymore," he said, still looking out at the frozen landscape.

Saker said nothing and Erik finally looked at him.

"You had your chance to save her. You chose to lay with another woman instead. Even your father doesn't think you deserve her." He leaned up and stared the man down, letting his own power rise. "Your inactions almost cost her her life once, I won't allow your sudden change of heart to compromise her again."

Saker took a deep breath and looked at a man he respected and might have considered a friend once upon a time. Instead he was angry. Angry that this vamp with the violet eyes had more of Cyzarine than he'd ever had.

"What is she really to you?" Erik asked. "She's not your mate. You can't go before Navalovich with that as your reasoning. If the binding had never been broken, you might have a leg to stand on." He shrugged and Saker wanted to wipe the smirk off his face. "As it is, you'd sound like a spoiled child who tossed his toy away only to decide later he wanted it back."

"She's not a damn toy."

Erik swirled the clear liquid in his glass, grinned down into his drink before sipping it. "Indeed. I couldn't agree more. If you follow orders in this mission, you might just learn something. Not only about her, but yourself." He leaned close again. "I'll warn you now. You start to cause problems and I'll go directly to Navalovich and tell her we can't work with you. We've got a limited time here, so shove your issues aside as the rest of us are doing and get the damn job done."

Saker took a sip of his own drink. "I always get the job done. If I didn't, I wouldn't be here."

Erik saluted him with the glass. "True. Use that same meterstick to measure Reen's ability to get her job done. She's the best." He finished his drink and smiled, amusement swirling the violet in his eyes. "Probably better than you. Look, I'll let you pursue her all you want. Away from the job. If she wants you, I'll not do anything to stop it from happening."

Saker could only stare at the man, both pissed and relieved.

"But," Erik continued, his eyes again going violet, "you hurt her again, I'll rip you to shreds then turn you into a vamp." He smiled and flicked his tongue over his fangs.

Saker took a deep breath to calm the anger and his own power surging up through him. He nodded. "You'll step back?"

Erik's smile wasn't amused. "If she really loved me, we wouldn't be discussing this, would we?"

Chapter Five

The club—Dark Fantasies—raved. Music, from hidden speakers, beat through the melee. Bodies slithered and twirled together. The scent of sex and booze filled the air. This club, like Bindings, like the others they'd visited, all smelled the same, all felt the same.

On the stage both men and women danced against poles, in cages, and chained to each other.

Places like this made Reen twitchy. She didn't want to be here. It was the darkness blanketing such places that made her uneasy. She liked the light. It was as if all the light, all the good, had been sucked out by evil.

Not that she thought everybody gyrating, headbanging, or boozing in the joint was intent on causing misery and horror. Far from it. Most here were young, bored, and just wanted to have fun.

Most were doing just that.

This was the fourth club they'd been to in three days.

"I wish we hadn't come here," Erik told her. His dark hair was slicked back and caught at his nape.

She ran a hand down his partially unbuttoned, purple silk shirt. In her four-inch-heel platform boots, laced up to her thighs, she almost looked him in the eye. Her leather corset clung to her, her arms bare and her skirt, just shy of grazing the tops of her boots, was black and leather as well. She wore a collar, attached to a chain that her "husband" held.

Behind him stood Saker. That man had done nothing but watch her since they started this three days ago. He hadn't said a word to her, but instead, just studied her, making her skin...not crawl...hum. That was the only way to describe it. When he looked at her, his eyes just short of shifting, an electric charge hummed along her skin, slid underneath and swirled through her blood, called to her.

The techno beat slowed, the music more of a chant. Erik leaned in and kissed her on the mouth, hard and fast. She felt Saker's gaze boring into her, felt the soft hum charge until a current seemed to zing through her. After three days, the feelings no longer shocked her, yet she wasn't exactly comfortable with them. It was as if something sharpened inside her so she was even more aware of him, caught herself watching him from beneath her lashes when he wasn't looking. The man popped into her head at odd moments. She pushed back from Erik and smiled up at him as she knew she was supposed to do. He ran a thumb over her collar and leaned close to whisper, "Sorry about the cover. But that's these clubs for you."

She leaned into him, wrapped her arms around his waist. "Don't worry about it. You know I'll do whatever I have to, to find Oleana."

Erik fisted his hand in her hair and pulled her head back, looking into her eyes. "That's what I'm afraid of. No stupid stunts, Reen. I mean it."

"I don't plan on pulling any stunts. I want to get her out of this alive."

Erik took the chain and led them to a table. There, he leaned down and whispered in her ear, "You know he loves the rare."

"And I'm as rare as they come. One of the last of a dying race," she said, turning to look up at him. "Worried, darling?"

He narrowed his gaze at her and jerked his head to Saker. "Watch her."

"Always."

Saker stood just to the side of her, dressed in a tight black shirt, and black pants. A jacket did the job of hiding his gun. She took a deep breath and could smell the dark, outdoors scent of him. Her blood settled into a low hum. Since they'd gone to two clubs like this last night and the night before that and another calmer, more tame club earlier, Erik had been acting as weird as Saker. Both watched over her as if at any moment she might disappear.

She hoped she did. She wanted this bastard. After reading the file on him, she knew that even if caught, he wouldn't give up what he would perceive as his greatest treasures. It wasn't as if he sold the girls on the underground market. He didn't deal.

He collected.

The men thought if they had him, they'd get him to talk.

Reen knew otherwise.

This man was accomplished, established, had perfected his *art*. So she'd draw him out.

She let her power tingle through her skin and wave out over the crowd. Nothing huge, nothing more than if she were excited, angered, or hell—turned on.

Which, around Saker, she seemed to be a lot the last three days. Something about him seemed familiar, called to her, aroused her.

Saker put his hand on her shoulder. "Don't."

She looked up at him from beneath her lashes. "Aww. Worried about me?"

The hand on her shoulder tightened, then he leaned down, whispering in her ear as Erik had earlier. Though she was playing Erik's wife, his whispers didn't send shivers down her spine as Saker's did.

"You're going to gain his attention if he's here," he all but growled, the air warm on her ear, his lips soft on the outer edge.

"That's the point," she whispered back. Licking her lips, she watched him. Sure enough his gaze dropped to her mouth and followed her movements. Tempting fate, she reached out and ran a short, trimmed nail down his arm, feeling the muscles bunch beneath. "Want to dance?"

His gaze rose back to her, his eyes swirling green. She'd gotten to him. Reen smiled.

He took her hand and jerked her to her feet, the chain dangled between them. He picked it up, ran it between his fingers. "You like this?"

She hated it, but she smiled again and licked her lips. "I like a bit of danger."

"Careful, or you might get a hell of a lot more than you bargained for."

He didn't move them towards the dance floor, just stood there staring at her.

80C3

Kladovik watched the gyrating bodies from his loft above the club. She was here.

He knew exactly who she was.

Cyzarine—Reen—a Hunter. An *assassin*, no doubt looking for her dear friend, Oleana.

Well, if she wanted to see her, he could definitely arrange it. After all, he wanted to get to know dear Cyzarine more. Much, much more.

He smiled at the men with her. He knew all about them. When he'd heard of her, he'd run a search and found all he needed to know.

She was a firebird. The rarest of the rare.

He only wished she were white. Bright white feathers that could flame and destroy or bring luck.

She would be his new lucky find.

He smiled to himself and watched as one of the men she was with spoke to her beside the table, his hand going to the chain and the collar around her neck. Was she into both men? He knew they all worked together. He had ways of finding things out. But past the job, did she do both?

He'd wondered. Trios were nothing new around here, nor were same-sex partners. None of them mattered to him.

All he cared about was the Firebird.

Normally, he searched for treasures and when he found them, he took them. Rarely did they all but land in his lap. Tempt him, know he was looking and searching for them.

This was a refreshing new twist. Did they, did *she* know whom she taunted?

A demon?

Guardian of treasures? He chuckled. Poor stupid fools.

He pressed an intercom button and waited. A female voice came on. "Yes?"

"Natasha, I want the woman who's sitting at table four. Make certain you give her enough. And the men as well."

A pause. "Yes, sir. What specifically do you want me to give them? One of the men just placed an order of drinks."

He thought about it for a moment. He wanted the men to be relaxed, not on guard. He knew supernaturals. Knew they were most vulnerable when they'd spent a lot of power. Short of getting into a fight, the best way to relieve energy was sex.

He might even get to see how well his newest treasure performed. How passionate she could be.

He smiled. "Make sure they get a performance drink. I want to watch her bind with a mate." Whichever one it was. And it wouldn't matter. She'd be so lustful after her drink, anyone would do. If she caused a fight, and distracted her two bodyguards, he'd move then. Otherwise, he'd wait... And watch...

Then take...

Chapter Six

Saker pulled her closer, keeping enough slack in the chain on her collar that he didn't jerk her this way or that.

Her body moved against his, taunted him. He glanced around and noticed others jostling around them on their way to the dance floor.

A woman in the cage screamed, drawing his attention. But it was hardly a scream of pain. One of faked pleasure. A man holding a dildo was with her.

Saker hated these places. He'd worked in enough of them. It wasn't that he detested being here, so much as he couldn't stand the thought that Reen was here.

He was still trying to wrap his mind around the fact she was... A what? An assassin.

He'd known, but knowing and accepting when every instinct in him was growling for him to protect, were two very different things.

She sure as hell didn't look like an assassin in her current dress. She looked like a fuck-girl. Or what he thought of as fuck-girls. She screamed sex, of submissiveness. Which was what they'd all planned on.

All but him.

She was *his*. The more time he spent with her, the more he couldn't get her out of his damn mind.

He knew her smell—woman, exotic, strong. It was a dark and tempting scent that wrapped around him every time he was around her. Her pulse, just there, beat quickly where her neck joined her collar. He ran a thumb over the pounding skin, pale as moonlight and soft as silk. The ends of her hair skimmed the back of his knuckles. He tucked a strand behind her ear and looked back at her slanted, amber eyes. "You really shouldn't be here."

A slow smile lifted her lush lips, painted scarlet red. "You just want me all to yourself," she whispered, her voice husky and full of promise.

He narrowed his gaze at her. "What game are you playing?"

Her tongue slowly licked her bottom lip.

Saker wanted her.

Plain and simple.

Erik cleared his throat. "Drinks are here." He passed them around, along with a warning look at Saker, until Saker finally let the chain slide between his fingers.

Erik reached over and snagged the end of the links.

Reen's laughter danced out, as sensual as the woman herself. She picked up her drink and took a sip, then drained it.

Saker raised his brow. "Thirsty?"

She eyed his drink then challenged, "You chicken? I thought all you warrior types could hold your own."

"Reen," Erik warned.

She turned and offered him a smile. "Come on, Erik. It's not even alcoholic, I'm just giving the ass a hard time."

Erik's gaze shifted from her to Saker. Saker downed his own drink.

Erik shook his head, and sipped his, frowning, then set it aside as he sat in his chair. "We should mingle."

"You mean I get to wander around all by my little lonesome? And here I thought I was your slave for the evening." She leaned over, her corset-plumped breasts right in Erik's face.

Saker reached out to jerk her back, but then fisted his hand.

The mission... He didn't want her flirting with the damn vamp.

He gritted his teeth as she ran her fingers through Erik's dark hair.

The club pulsed around them.

She took a deep breath, closed her eyes and straightened. "I want to dance."

The music, still slow, deep, dark, floated over the room. The lights flickered off and on.

Erik's hand held the chain, but Saker snatched it from the other man. "Fine, let's dance and see what we can learn." To seem as if he didn't have a care in the world, he added, "Place is probably a waste of time just like the last." He held the chain and led her to the dance floor. It was crowded and they made their way through the melee of bodies closer to the stage where there was a bit more room.

The dark music seemed to move through his body, swirl around his head. He shook his head and took a deep breath, but all he smelled was her.

Cyzarine's scent. Dark and promising.

An image of them wrapped and tangled together flashed in his mind.

It seemed to come alive, manifest itself.

His cock grew, pressed against his black pants. He pulled her closer, looking only at her eyes.

She moved against him, her thighs brushed his, then her groin, her hips, her trim waist, her breasts.

A wave of liquid desire brushed and moved against him.

She sucked in a breath, her amber eyes glowing gold at the edges.

The music beat against the air. Something buzzed through his system.

Her desire wrapped him in a tight fist and he shook his head again. But all he could think about was her, her body, sinking deep and hard into her. Her arousal wafted between them and he jerked her closer, insinuated one thigh between her boots, pressed and pulled until she straddled him.

The music filled his head, thoughts of fucking her slammed into him, twisted the desire tighter and harder inside him until that was all that he could think of. All he could focus on.

She raised her arms, and her breasts, pushing against the edge of the black corset, threatened to pop free. He leaned her back over his arm and bit down at the sight of her areoles, then her nipples, a pale dusky pink. Saker could no more stop himself than his next breath, even as some inner voice blared a warning in his head.

He could feel her power, her lust brush against his.

Her eyes were shut, but he didn't care. He kissed the top slope of one pale breast, then moved to the other, quickly licking and laving the sensitive peaks.

She grasped his skull, her fingers raking through his hair. "Saker," she said, an edge of plea to it.

He pressed his thigh higher, harder against her and could feel the heat from her core. She was already wet.

He growled and jerked her up, chest to breast to him. Her mouth devoured him, her tongue feasting and dueling with his.

"I want you," she muttered between kisses, "I want you now."

Some sane part of his brain knew this wasn't right, but he couldn't stop. Couldn't keep from raising her skirt.

"Please..."

"Just a minute, baby," he told her, glancing to their right and the small stage. He turned them, grabbed her ass and set her on the edge of the dark stage. Blue lights rained down on them.

He didn't care.

The music thrummed against his skull. And only one thought burst through.

Take her.

Take her.

Take her.

He grabbed the scrap of silk between her legs and ripped it away, and shoved it into his pocket.

Her eyes were golden pools of light, vague, yet as bright as topaz.

"You're mine," he growled.

In some part of her mind Reen knew this wasn't...right. It was what she wanted, what she needed, what she *had to have*. But something didn't seem right.

All she could smell was him—dark forests, deep secrets. Images of them wrapped together, of Saker thrusting into her filled her mind.

She couldn't think beyond him, beyond her want of him.

Her breasts were still caught above the edge of the corset, every rake of his clothed chest against her nipples made her gasp, made her want.

Then he ripped her thong away and her body pulsed.

She knew she couldn't shift. Couldn't let her power fully free. But the need to was almost overwhelming.

It had never been like this before.

Lights started to swirl around them, but she couldn't think about that, couldn't concentrate.

"Now, Saker, for God's sake. Now!"

His cool fingers parted her, jerked a moan from her throat as they grazed over her pulsing flesh, wet and slick with her own needs. His fingers slid deep and she arched against him, even as his thumb pressed her sensitive peak.

"More. I need more."

"And you'll get it."

"Move! Move!" A voice yelled, but she didn't care.

She could feel him poised there, hot and hard, just there at the edge of her opening.

"Reen! What the hell are you doing?" someone shouted.

Reen grabbed Saker's ass and arched against him, jerking him into her.

She cried out and the air exploded around them. "Damn it! Stop!" the voice yelled again.

But she couldn't, simply couldn't. Saker groaned above her and she could only stare at his eyes. The air around them glowed, shimmered and shifted, and muffled everything, the music, the yells, the people.

All she saw was Saker, his black eyes glowing green, a muscle ticking in his clenched jaw. All she heard was his breath, faster and panting, his growls and groans, her own.

Then he reached down and flicked his finger over her clit and she shattered, screaming out her release as Saker yelled his own and thrust again into her one final time. Sparks rained down on them and for a moment everything seemed to still, to calm, to comfort.

"Fucking A!" the voice yelled, then Saker was jerked from her. Her brain couldn't get around anything.

The room seemed to spin around her.

"What the fuck are you doing, you stupid son of a bitch?" Roars and curses filled the air, pressed in on her.

Something's very wrong...

She couldn't stop, couldn't grasp...

Someone lifted her from behind. "Come, my pretty, let's get you out of here."

A prick bit the side of her neck and she moaned as fire burned beneath her skin.

"No," she mumbled.

Reen felt herself lifted, tried to turn and see who it was, but didn't have the energy, couldn't...

Stop...

The world went black.

Chapter Seven

Erik slammed his fist against Saker's jaw, snapping the other man's head back. Saker's eyes glowed green.

"You sneaky bastard," Erik snarled, his own power charging over him.

Patrons had made a semicircle around them.

Saker shook his head, and swiped out at Erik. "She's mine!"

"Not any more." Rage roared through him. Erik had no idea what the hell had happened, but one minute he was weaving through the crowd, up on the catwalk. Then an energy, pure sex charged across the club, aroused the air and thrust against him.

He'd looked over, across the converted warehouse to see a couple on the edge of the stage.

Fury had lit inside him like this only a few times before. Saker and Reen. The air glowed around them, as it only did with true mates. For long seconds, then moments, Erik couldn't get to them.

Saker and Reen.

Reen...

She'd been fucking a *falcon* on a stage before a club full of people.

Warning screamed through him.

But it had been as if a barrier kept them from everyone else.

Until, finally, Erik, enraged, had gotten through then jerked the sonofabitch around. "How *dare* you."

"I dare because she's *mine*," Saker stated, his eyes still glowing, his power too close to the surface.

Erik growled, felt the sharp edge of his fangs against his tongue and wanted to suck the bastard dry.

He glanced to the stage.

The empty stage.

He froze.

Saker slammed into his jaw, and Erik didn't even try to fight the man off. Instead he tamped down on his own rage, to focus.

He shoved Saker away. "She's gone," he rasped.

The fury in the other man still hummed in the air, but Saker stopped, lowered his raised arm and turned to look.

"No. No!" Saker let out a cry, high-pitched and shrill. The call of the falcons.

Fuck. Erik said into the microphone hidden in his sleeve, "Flame is missing. Repeat Flame is missing. Report. Search the outer perimeter of the building."

Saker shoved people out of the way, and leapt back onto the stage, his own team members pulling out of the crowd and surrounding him. One man, Gregori, Erik recognized. Gregori had left the royal palace with the young dethroned prince years ago and had remained loyal ever since.

"Perimeter is clear, sir," a voice said in his ear.

Damn it. Damn it. Damn it!

Saker whirled and across the expanse of the space, Erik knew that whatever their differences, they would work together to find the woman they both loved.

ഇൽ

He carried her through the underground passage. The club's music beat through the floor, the pulse hard and pressing against his nerves. He knew he needed to get back or they might suspect him.

Not that they would find him. And if they did, chances were they wouldn't find his pretties.

They'd looked before and no one had found them. Not when they were still alive, and not when he'd turned them into his.

The tunnel, dripping wet from overhead pipes, the old bricks slick from years of mold and slime, turned sharply to his left. He glanced over his shoulder and smiled.

He looked down into her face.

Perfection...

A firebird? He smiled and leaned down, sniffing, pulling her scent deep within his lungs.

He'd have fun with this one. She was passionate. He now knew that.

Kladovik frowned. The lights. He'd seen the lights shimmer and dance as this pretty mated with, not the one she arrived with, but with the bodyguard. He'd seen lights like that before.

The Mating Glow, many called it.

So who was her mystery man? Or had it simply been his little additives and incantation?

Kladovik shrugged. It hardly mattered. Those looking for her would be all over the club.

The darkness enveloped them as he quickly carried her. He slung her over his shoulder and climbed the ladder, shouldering the manhole lid out of the way. At the top, he scanned the deserted area.

Empty.

Three blocks away.

He quickly climbed out and deposited her in the waiting limo he'd called. The driver was a lower demon trying to climb through his powers and ranks. Still had a lot to learn, but he was eager to prove his worth. There weren't any better.

Kladovik didn't question the younger demon's loyalty.

"Take her to her new home. Put her in the third room." He straightened, then secured her hands and as a last precaution, hung an amulet around her neck. He muttered a binding curse and pressed it to her chest.

Her legs were long. He ran a hand down her torso and felt his dick harden. "It won't be long now, pretty." He nodded to the driver and slammed the door, slapping the roof of the car.

With that, he closed his eyes and concentrated on his office. He hated transporting, especially when he had so much to do later and knew it would drain his energy.

High screeches faintly traveled on the air. He frowned, wondering what they were.

Transporting. His own phobia. It was like claustrophobia. For seconds it felt as if something or someone were pressing all the air from his lungs, pressing the world down on him, pressing.

With a faint pop, he took a deep breath, and found himself inside his office. He quickly straightened his tie and picked up his cologne, and splashed some on his hands. One of the security monitors showed two males—her males—pass his own guards. He clicked the monitor to another channel, this one surveilling the dance floor, and quickly used his power to erase the clip where he'd taken his latest pretty. He held the bottle of cologne and waited. Just as his door burst open, he let it tip, dumping the overpowering scent all over him.

He scrunched his nose and cursed. Then shook his hands off and picked up a towel from the nearby sink. "Gentlemen, may I help you?"

They both stood glaring at him, the blond, his eyes as cold and hard as the rarest of emeralds, the other, dark-haired with violet eyes. Supernaturals.

He merely wiped his hands off and then sat behind his desk, pulling out a cigar from his humidor. He waved to his guards who came limping into the doorway. "It's all right, Vladimir."

The guard muttered something beneath his breath, but the two men ignored it.

"Now, how can I help you?"

"A woman is missing," the violet-eyed vamp all but snarled. "As the owner of this club, we demand your cooperation."

Kladovik raised a brow. "A woman? Is there a specific one you're referring to?" He swept his arm out. "I assure you, we can probably find you another."

The blond only raised his head and sniffed, his eyes glowing. Then his gaze fell to the bottle of cologne.

Hell.

"Where is she?" the blond asked.

He looked at the men, then at the tip of his cigar. He clipped the end and lit the best Cuba had to offer. "Who is she?"

Neither answered.

Kladovik inhaled and blew the smoke out into the air. "I don't appreciate people coming into my place and fighting, disrupting my dancers, causing problems." He motioned with his cigar towards the blond and stood. "I do have to commend you on your performance. It's not too often we get such an authentic..." he smirked and thought for a moment, then shrugged, "...blatant display of pleasure for the sake of entertainment." He motioned to the sidebar. "Drinks, gentlemen?"

The black-haired man flew across the room, his fangs extended, even as his hand wrapped around Kladovik's neck. He took a deep breath, then leaned in and took another deep inhale. The violet eyes lit with rage and the hand around his neck tightened, the vamp's fangs clear and threatening. Yet another first.

They knew.

"Where the hell is she?" the vamp asked in a low, icy voice.

Deciding now was the time, Kladovik only smiled, blew out the stream of smoke into the vamp's face and then, transported. The crushing sensation and reemergence wasn't as smooth as he'd have liked. He literally popped into the limo.

Sighing, he leaned back and looked at the woman draped in the seat next to him. He ran a hand over her short dark hair and then chuckled. Plans changed. He wouldn't try to dissuade them of his involvement. He'd thought he could. Thought he'd cover her scent by his cologne. But they—the Hunters—had clearly smelled her on him, or the vamp had. Who was the other man? The mate? He shook off the worry. In hindsight he realized perhaps he should not have returned to his office. Then again, maybe it wouldn't have mattered. This upped the challenge of eluding the authorities. Supernatural authorities were not as lenient as mortal ones. No, the punishment was swift and severe.

A trickle of worry slithered through him, but he shrugged it off and studied her. The perfect angle of her wide cheek bones, the lush lips...

This would be more fun.

A little more danger.

He laughed and ran his finger over the bridge of her nose. "We're going to have fun, you and I."

Chapter Eight

Saker paced the office. He didn't want to be here. He wanted to be out there looking. Searching.

She was his.

His head hurt like a son of a bitch. When he found the bastard behind this...and he would... *"Otmudohat',"* he cursed.

Erik nodded. "We will."

He stopped at the window. He had his best combing the city. He'd even sent an emissary to his father to let him know what had happened.

And what the hell had happened?

He couldn't remember. Not really. He remembered dancing. He remembered her scent, dark and promising. Seduction.

But there'd been no seduction.

He'd fucked his mate on a stage in front of a room full of people.

Erik simply stood against the wall. Other vamps and shifters were scouring the city looking for Reen.

Cyzarine.

An image of her wrapped around him, her breasts his for the taking, as he plunged into her, her cry filling his ears, burst into his mind.

He had to find her.

Had to...

"I can't believe I'm so stupid. So selfish," the woman said yet again.

No one answered her. The leader of the Hunters was currently not acting like a leader but as one who had lost a loved one.

"I love Reen as a daughter. Both my girls. What was I thinking, Erik? You tried to talk me out of it. You tried."

Erik shoved away from the wall. "What do you think Reen would have done if we hadn't involved her?"

She wiped her eyes yet again, her hair as blonde as Saker's. Her eyes as blue as folded snow. "She'd have gone out on her own. That's what I kept thinking. I knew, knew she wouldn't stop. But I never thought. Never stopped to think that maybe, that she could be..."

She raised watery eyes to Erik and shook her head. "I'm turning this all over to you, Erik. I can't think. I can't... I'm too close. I don't want this job anymore. I have two sons. I can't..."

Saker cleared his throat. "We're going to find Reen. We'll find your daughter as well."

Those eyes swung back to him and whatever softness, vulnerability, he might have glimpsed in them was gone in a blink. They glittered.

"What I want to know, Saker, is how the hell you managed to accomplish what you did."

He sighed and raked a hand through his hair. "I don't know."

She snorted. "I do. You wanted her, you had her and damn the consequences. Just like always." She sat heavily in the large maroon leather chair. "So many mistakes. So much to fix. So little time. Why do I feel like we have so little time?"

"I still want to know what the hell he was thinking," Erik growled.

"Jealous, blood sucker?" Saker taunted. He was spoiling to finish what they started.

Erik stared at him, his anger to the point that his eyes still had the look to them they'd gained at the club. Those iridescent, violet eyes had yet to return to normal. His fangs still shone in the lights.

"My only concern has ever and always been Reen and what is best for her. Unlike some, I put my own needs behind those."

Saker shrugged. "Well, if you hadn't. She might be yours now."

Erik growled.

Saker stood still waiting, just waiting.

"Boys," Navalovich admonished. "We don't have time for this. Either Reen and Saker were honestly meant to be together and no amount of bond breaking or separation would keep them apart, or they won't be and the...binding..." she said, frowning at Saker, "...won't matter."

"It matters," he said, softly, surprised.

She only raised a brow. "Saker, you had your chance with her and, if memory serves, you decided she and her power were not worth your or your people's time."

He looked back out the window and wondered when Gregori would return. Would his father know anything? A sliver of unease sharpened along his nerves. His father. The king would not be happy about this last turn of events—well, Cyzarine missing, obviously, but also Saker's bonding with his past mate.

He sighed and rubbed his face. An image rose again in his mind.

A dark place, fear...a shimmer of hope.

He frowned and closed his eyes. What the hell.

Again, but this time sharper.

The room was dark. A golden circle with spokes wheeling out from the center. A faint breeze. The scent of...

"Kladovik."

The cologne.

"We know he has her, tell us something we don't know," Erik shot off.

Instead of meeting the taunt he concentrated. *Please, please, please.* He had to find her. Had to...

A darkened window. And still that scent of sandalwood and—sulfur?—teased his senses.

A shuffle of something. The sense that the room was large, the ceilings tall. He tried to see more, to get more of an image, but then blackness shuttered down, and fear slithered through him.

Until he opened his eyes.

It wasn't his fear.

It was hers.

She was scared.

Chapter Nine

Reen tried to focus, tried to understand what was going on. But she couldn't grasp her thoughts. Couldn't really see. She felt as if she were tilting one way then the other. As if she were rocking.

Rocking?

Was she on a ship?

She didn't care for ships. Opening her eyes, she tried to concentrate on what was around her. Instead, blackness pressed down on her eyes. She tried to move, but couldn't. Her hands were behind her, her fingers tingling.

Bound.

She moved her feet and relief flooded through her at the fact her legs were at least mobile.

Where was she? What the hell had happened?

What did she remember?

Think.

Think.

Think.

The last thing she remembered was...was...

Dancing.

With Saker. His dark black eyes glaring down at her, a muscle ticking in his jaw...

The music pumped through the air. She remembered...

Wanting him.

No, *needing* him.

An image of them entwined, his arm muscles tight and corded on either side of her as he pumped into her rose into her mind.

No.

No.

She did *not* fuck a man on a stage in a room full of people.

Did she?

Pain beat in her head. She rubbed it and realized she was lying on soft, silky sheets.

What was she doing at the club in the first place?

The Collector.

Her heartbeat slammed in her chest.

The Collector.

She needed to stay calm. The worst thing, she wouldn't get out of this. Best thing, she could at least free Oleana.

She closed her mind to all but her friend. She'd tried the exercise for days, but had gotten nothing but disjointed images. It was something they'd learned at the Academy.

Focus and you'll find your target. Or the victim. Link with one, you might find the other. Find more.

If she could do that, maybe she could link her mind with Saker.

She froze. Saker?

No, Erik. She'd meant Erik.

No. Saker.

The lights, shimmering, dancing. The mating glow.

No. No. Hellfire! Could it be? For a moment, all she could think about was those stupid lights, periwinkle and pink shimmering around them as they'd—damn—bonded.

She was bound to *Saker.*

She was *bound* to a fucking falcon!

Reen sat up, glad for the hundred plus crunches she did religiously. How? How the hell could she be so...so...so...

She closed her eyes as the room spun.

She'd been mated to a falcon once before, but she hadn't really remembered Rourik. All she remembered about him was...

Was...

She frowned and tried to recall the young man she'd only met once who had acted as if she was beneath him.

But who was he? What color was his hair? His eyes? She tried to recall.

White-blond hair that had brushed the top of his collar.

Anger and confusion slithered around her stomach. Blond hair. And that arrogant tilt of his lips. How could she forget?

No. It couldn't be. He *wouldn't*. He *wasn't*.

Saker. She'd mated with Saker. Rourik had been her betrothed. Just because they had the same smirk and hair and *saker* meant falcon didn't mean they were the same.

Maybe they just knew each other, or something.

White-blond hair.

She closed her eyes. "I'm an idiot."

Saker.

Forget it. She slammed down the walls in her mind, anger beating back the fear. She had a mission to do, and she'd do it if it killed her. She'd kick his ass later, whoever he was.

Her muscles limber and stretched, she worked her body until she sat on her hands and slowly wiggled through the loop her arms made. It wasn't easy. It had been years since she'd done that stunt.

Panting, she nibbled at her bindings, pissed that her knife was missing from her thigh.

Who took it?

The Collector? Who the hell was the bastard? Had he watched her all evening? Was he a patron? Or did he work at the club?

Taking a deep breath, she imagined Oleana in her mind. Imagined her friend laughing.

But as usual, it seemed to take too long to connect to her friend.

And then the images were in black and white. Black and white, the room strangely dark, but lit. As if seeing at night.

Then Reen knew...

Oleana was shifted.

Knowing that, and rebuking herself for not realizing it sooner, she focused, and tried to find her friend the albino tiger.

Pain pulsed through her body.

Tired...so tired...

There was only a partial view of the room. From low. The rug was expensive. The far wall, a classical painting hung, the gilded frame, seemingly heavy. The chairs had been shredded.

Come on, come on, look around. Tell me where you are...

"Reen... Go... Leave. Don't come here. He'll keep you. Hurt you..."

"Hurts so bad. I hurt."

Waves of intense pain crashed through her body.

Reen gritted her teeth, tears pricking her eyes. "Hang on. Please, hang on, Leana."

"I just wish he'd kill me already, Reen. Tell Mom I love her."

"No. No. Hang on. You hang on. I can't lose you."

She wouldn't lose another person she loved. She'd lost everyone else.

Reen worked on the ties that bound her wrists. Leather. Why couldn't the bastard have used rope or tape? Hell, even fishing twine. But no, he'd used leather and she couldn't get it.

"Where are you?"

She stopped, listened. The only sound was her panting breath. She looked around the darkened room and wondered where she was.

Again she looked up.

"Cyzarine, where are you?"

She ignored the voice and carefully stood, the pain in her head a dull throb now. She walked towards the window, but stopped when she realized something was in her way. It was so dark she could barely see.

The faint light from the window told her where the window was located. But the rest was completely black.

She tried to move again and ran into a slim something. Shoving with her toe, she knew it was connected to the floor. She felt out in front of her, followed the smooth metal rod from in front of her up as far as she could reach. Then she ran her hands down until she met the hardwood floor.

Her heart fluttered in her chest.

She moved a few feet to her right and felt another one. And another one. Every foot there was a bar that ran up higher than she could reach. She made her way slowly around the entire room. Or what she could of it. She realized then that the bed was in the center. The window was beyond her reach. And every two feet or so, there was a horizontal bar. What the hell.

Then she knew.

A cage...

She trembled, shivered and sat on the floor, pulling her knees to her chest.

No. No. No.

No cages.

Everyone knew that firebirds couldn't be caged.

They weakened.

They died.

I hurt...

Chapter Ten

Kladovik stood in the hallway and listened. He smiled. He could hear her, shuffling about inside. Trying to get away? Trying to learn where she was?

Wouldn't she just love his surprise for her? He made certain all his pretties had the best accommodations, perfectly suited for each one's particular needs.

In the case of most felines, he found dungeons, damp and dank often did the trick. For lycans, he preferred light, lots and lots of light. Avians—well, for them, cages for many. Sometimes mere separation from their mates. Clipped wings also worked wonders.

He smiled and popped his knuckles.

This was going to be such fun. He'd never had a firebird before. He glanced over his shoulder to the golden eagle screaming for all eternity. She'd been beautiful in both forms. A solid white eagle, but he'd clipped her wings and she couldn't fly away.

She'd never flown away.

And neither would his firebird.

Reen. Cyzarine? From the fabled massacre in the Laru woods? Royalty on top of rarity.

He stopped in front of a tall mirror that hung from his high ceiling almost to the floor. He pressed the button hidden in the frame and waited. The mirror went dark, then lit from behind. And he could see her.

Sitting in the dark.

He took a deep breath and even through the wall could smell her fear. There was just something about knowing a beautiful woman was afraid. Not just worried, but *afraid,* bone deep fear. It was even a headier feeling to know that he caused that fear.

When the fear turned to terror...

He took another deep breath and watched her. She shoved a dark strand of hair behind her small ear.

"Untied ourself did we?" he asked, rubbing his jaw. "Can't say I'm surprised. Not surprised at all."

She would be more of a fighter, a survivor than the others. She was trained after all. Her history proved she was a survivor.

Of course the last one had been as well, but then he knew they could all be broken.

He pressed the intercom button. "I hope you've found your new accommodations to your liking."

He grinned as she stood and whirled, looking one way, then the other, then up. Her darted looks, her panted breath...

He chuckled. "Don't worry, I'll be back."

"Who are you?" she asked, her voice low, but still he caught the tremble.

"Aw, anxious for a meeting? I'm honored, I am." He leaned up and whispered against the microphone. "Don't worry, my pretty, I'll be back and we'll get to know each other a whole lot better."

"Not in this lifetime," she hissed.

He smiled and let go of the button, and watched her for a minute more. This would be fun. But he also knew, he would have to hurry. Yet he didn't *want* to rush. He wanted to enjoy. Necessity or pleasure?

He frowned at the knowledge he couldn't take his time as he wanted to, as he'd like to, as he *deserved* to. She was one of the rarest of the rare.

This time, though, he'd have to hurry. Sadly, he didn't have months or weeks. He'd be lucky to have days with this one.

The best things should never be rushed.

However, he didn't see a choice.

The Hunters were after him.

⁪⁫

Erik watched Saker pace, the conference room had been turned into a working hub of activity. Photographs had been pinned to the board. Women, so many women. The left side was reserved for those they knew were victims of the Collector. The right side of the board was possible victims.

Rare women who simply vanished. Mostly from either clubs or very exclusive parties.

No recent bodies had ever been found. So what the hell did the bastard do with them?

"I don't get why no one has ever found a trace of these women," Gregori, Saker's man, muttered.

"He keeps them," Saker said.

"The Collector." Erik nodded. "You're right. He wouldn't go to the trouble to find his treasures if he simply planned on throwing them away when he was done. That would be ordinary. He's different."

Saker pointed to the board. "They're different. All shifters, for the most part. Though these two are humans, sensitives and gifted, but still humans. Talent and rarity."

Erik nodded. The door opened and Navalovich strode in, dark circles under her red-rimmed eyes and her clothing rumpled.

Erik assumed they all looked that way. The incessant tick of some inner clock spurred him on. They had no idea where to even look.

"We checked all his properties?" Saker asked again.

"The answer hasn't changed." They'd searched all the clubs, calling in all constables, local enforcers, state enforcers, even feeling their underground systems. Nothing. At least not yet. There were two warehouses that had been listed as developing properties in Moscow and Amsterdam. But they'd yielded nothing.

"You both smelled sulfur on him. I'm assuming we're checking to see if he's a demon or of a sect? Where are we on that information?" Navalovich asked.

"The local demon council is investigating and said they'll send a liaison to speak with us," Erik answered.

Damn it, he couldn't really feel Reen. He could sense her, vague wisps of fear, of worry, of rage.

But he couldn't get a lock on her.

Not like Saker—damn the man.

Since they'd bonded at the club, Erik could feel his small stake on her fading and there wasn't a thing he could do to stop it.

Swallowing past his own jealousy and anger, he stared at her picture on the board. "Can you feel her?" he asked Saker.

Saker gave one nod. "He's locked her in a cage."

Which would weaken her. "He's not stupid."

Saker turned and looked at him, the dark black eyes glowing green. "Oh, he's stupid. He dared to touch her."

Erik tilted his head and studied the other man. "When this is all over and we have her back..."

"She's mine."

"Even if she doesn't want that? She might be pissed at the way things played out."

Saker didn't look away. "I'm not letting her go again." He strode out the door. Gregori looking after him.

"The king laughed his ass off until he realized she was missing and taken by a very evil man." Gregori, a respected formal general of the royal Sokul Guard, nodded to Erik. "The king's offered his services in whatever way they are needed. As we speak, his best are scouring the city to find her."

Erik hoped to hell someone did before the Collector made Reen a permanent part of his collection.

Chapter Eleven

Reen sat between a nightstand and one of the bars on the cage. Air still flowed around her. She tried to see past the cage, but night vision was never a strong point. She could see great distances in scorching light, blinding snow-white light, but darkness...

She shivered. She hated the dark, hated not having her back against a wall.

She felt exposed. She tried again to connect with Leana, but hadn't made a solid connection, not like before. Either her friend was blocking, or...

No, she wouldn't go there. Oleana was alive. Alive. She had to be. If Leana were dead, she'd know it, sense it, feel it.

It wasn't that she felt—nothing.

She simply couldn't connect.

She did, however, feel others pushing against her walls. Saker? Erik?

She had a feeling it might be both. But Saker's attempts were stronger, harder, more intense and her head was already aching. Now the pain pulsed through it in a wave. She closed her eyes and tried to meditate, calm her racing heart.

This—the cage, the fear—was nothing but the Collector's sick and twisted mind games and damn it if she wasn't letting him get the upper hand. The more emotion she wasted, the less power she'd have.

Already, she could feel her power waning. It was the fact she was locked in a cage.

Not just any cage. Only a special cage, one cursed and custom designed, could do this. He'd obviously seen her before tonight. He'd been waiting on her. She wondered when and where she'd first come across his notice. At least she was closer to Leana.

The man knew his victims, what made them tick, what they feared, what sapped their strength.

Behind her closed lids, she imagined her pale pink and blue light. Light that had shimmered around her and her mate.

A sliver of anger shot through her mind, but she tamped it down. She'd kick his ass later. Right now, she wasn't about to let pride get in the way of getting the hell out of here.

What happened to the others? Were they all trapped here?

No, they were dead or kept somehow.

So much trouble and planning into what? *For* what?

Again, pain shot through her head from blocking. She concentrated on the sounds, concentrated on the window.

Then she opened her mind.

Images and feelings shouted against her mind. She took a deep breath and tried to understand, tried to focus...

"Saker? Saker? Where are you?"

Shock, like lightning, bolted down her spine.

"Where are you?"

"I don't know. With him...the Collector. I don't know where. It's quiet, I can't hear traffic noises. It's dark..."

"Can you get out of the cage, Cyzarine?"

Even from here, she could feel the worry, fear and rage in his thoughts.

It had never been this sharp, this intense with anyone. Not even when she and Oleana had constantly practiced at connecting with each other. Not when she and Erik were lovers. With Saker, it was so...easy.

"Reen, what do you see out of the window?"

She opened her eyes and left the connection in her mind open. *"I don't know...it's dark, not as dark as the room."* She stared at the window and saw something fly by. She frowned and focused on it.

A click from the other direction made her gasp. She looked to the doorway and saw the silhouette of a man. He flicked his wrist out and the room flooded with lights.

"Stay with me, Cyzarine. Keep your eyes open and look at him. I need to see him..."

It's weird, having someone else in your mind with you. She shoved the thought aside as the man spoke and she tried to blink, adjusting her eyes to the light.

He stood on the other side of the cage. He looked...

Normal. He wasn't what she'd call second-glance handsome, let alone gorgeous. His hazel eyes were round, and deeply set, his face angular, his mouth thin. His hair was dark and wavy, cut close to his head on the sides, but longer on top. The suit was expensive, the shirt silk. A ring on his hand.

She focused on the ring, her vision narrowing as if she first viewed it down a tunnel, then as if she'd zoomed in with a camera.

A demon's skull and a treasure chest.

Almost like the human pirates.

But this was different. She knew it.

"What is your name?" she asked, looking back up at him, shielding her eyes.

He slowly walked around the cage, which she now saw was enormous and bolted in the ground. The cement ground. The ceiling...there was no ceiling here. Here there was only the bare metal trusses—a warehouse.

She closed her eyes and listened more carefully, focused on the window, focus....

Focus...

The lap of water... Softly...

Water? She opened her eyes and watched as he walked the perimeter of the cage. A golden cage. His hand negligently trailed from one bar to the next as he walked closer and closer to where she sat.

Carefully, she moved away from the edge of the cage.

"What do you want?" she asked.

He smiled. "I rather thought that was obvious, *moyo zolotse.*"

She held his stare, seeing past the hazel eyes to the blackness that lurked just beneath. "Who are you?"

He grinned even more and she could see how many might fall for his charm. "I apologize for not introducing myself earlier." He bowed at the waist. "I'm Kladovik."

Kladovik? "That's not an alias?"

He waved his ringed hand. "No. I've used them in the past, but figured why?"

Kladovik...

Then it clicked. "A guardian demon." She shook her head. So simple.

He raised a brow. "I prefer dark spirit." He tsked. "Demon leaves such a negative connotation, don't you think?"

"I couldn't possibly imagine where anyone would get that idea," she muttered.

He stopped in front of her and she pressed herself back against the bed. For just a moment, he let his charming shield drop and she could see the monster beneath, with the dark bruising, scaled skin and black empty eyes. "You and I are going to have lots and lots and lots of fun." He licked his lips.

Inside, she shuddered. Instead, she crossed her arms and knew he couldn't get her without coming inside. "Really? And how are we going to do that? You coming in here?"

He narrowed his gaze at her. "My dear, I've been at this a lot longer than you. Trust me, I'll get in..." He smiled and it held no amusement. "When you least expect it. It's much more fun this way. Leaves you on edge." He grinned. "That's more arousing."

She let her own power rise up, an ancient power of fire and vengeance. "Hide behind darkness, do you? Poor thing. Maybe one day you'll be man enough, or would that be demon enough, to face an adversary straight on."

His nostrils flared.

"Stop baiting him, damn it!"

She slammed the walls back up between her and Saker.

೮೦ಆ

"Damn that woman. Do we have anything yet?" he snarled to the room at large.

A guardian demon. Their analysts knew they were dealing with a treasure keeper.

Apparently this particular one was even wanted by his own kind. Treasure keepers were entrusted with secrets, with artifacts. They also guarded power.

Though their responsibilities were great, their power wasn't, lest they lust for that which they guarded.

"Right in front of our faces all this time. Where is he?" Navalovich asked, pacing from one window to the other.

Saker hadn't told her what else he'd felt from Reen. The pain that had coursed through her—not her own, but that of Oleana's.

Anxiety prickled down his back and he rubbed his neck. He looked at Gregori, still pissed. The other man only shrugged. "Look, at least your father is helping as best he can."

"He just didn't lock the binding in, bless it or make it official."

Gregori merely stared at him, then asked, "Did you really expect him to?"

"It could help damn it. I'd have a stronger connection to her."

Gregori shrugged. "You know your father."

"Yeah, I know my father."

He cursed and strode from the room. Water lapping. He'd heard the water lapping. With their location here in Grubsretep, he knew it would be on the docks. And there were numerous warehouses down in that district. Outside, he called the falcons. He'd find her. If it was the last thing he ever did.

With or without his father's blessing, she was his and it was bloody time everyone knew that. Regardless of what they may or may not think.

Erik stood beside him. "You wouldn't be hoping to rescue her all by yourself, would you?"

Saker, tired and angry, snarled, lashing out at the other man. "Worried she'd love me?"

Erik stared at him, let his eyes glow. "You endanger her going off half-cocked."

Saker took a deep breath. "She's mine. I'm going to find her. Then I'll let you know. Surely your people can find me."

"I'm going with you," Erik said.

Saker laughed. "You learn to fly, dead man?"

With that, he shrilled out a cry again and falcons swooped down from building tops to circle around his head. Muttering in his father's tongue, he closed his eyes and shifted seamlessly. One moment he was standing in the alley behind the Hunter's headquarters, the next he was flying, higher and higher, his guards around him, more coming.

They were larger than normal falcons, larger than any eagle. Their kind was almost extinct and only whispered of in legends.

He opened his mind, his eyes sharper, the landscape in black and white as he soared over buildings, towards the quay.

Again her fear and loathing slithered over him.

He flexed talons that could lift a grown human and crush his bones between their sharpness.

That's just what he planned to do to one Kladovik, after he ripped the bastard's eyes out.

Chapter Twelve

Erik watched the circle of falcons, some small and normal. The others, larger than any other bird, swooped, dove and then aligned, a military fleet, searching.

They needed to do damage control.

Some human would be shooting at them in no time. He needed just one more problem.

He had a meeting with a liaison from the demon council. They needed to strip this bastard of his power.

Damn. Rubbing his head, he tried again to catch the elusive feel of Reen, but knew it was useless. She was blocking and Saker's connection to her was too strong.

Cursing fate, he strode back into the building. He hoped like hell they wouldn't be too late.

Once inside, he met with the liaison who confirmed the council's information that Kladovik was the man, or demon—Erik figured monster covered it—they were looking for.

"We have a team moving in, but for the safety of the women that might still be alive, we want him stripped of his powers," Erik told the man.

The council leader lifted one corner of her mouth. "That's currently being taken care of. I've a feeling by the time your team arrives, he'll be as human as the next person on the street."

໖⊃໖

She watched his dark form circle the cage.

"Do you know what I want to do with you?"

She ignored him. He kept walking one way, then the other, his ring clinking on the metal bars. Knowing it was a scare tactic, a way to weaken her, to play with her mind, helped.

"I want to fuck you. I love sliding between the legs of women like you. Strong women, women who are used to being in control." A click and hiss as he struck a match and lit a candle beside the cage, then another and another until she saw the candles were on a large candelabrum.

"Women who hate to answer to any man." He stopped and dipped his chin, smiling at her, his eyes locked on her from beneath his lashes. "I love to wear women like you down, until you're broken."

He laughed.

Reen shuddered.

"What are you scared of, Reen? Or should I call you Cyzarine?" He took a deep breath. "Are you scared of wolves?"

She froze, her lungs not moving even as her heart slammed against her chest.

"You are." He smiled, his eyes glittering. "Poor, poor Reen. Such a fake you are. Dealing out death, when in reality you're terrified of it."

She shook her head. "I'm not scared of death."

He tilted his head. "You're scared of wolves."

She didn't answer, saw no reason to. But he knew. She hated wolves, hated their smell, their sounds, just...them.

She knew all lycans were not dangerous, were not out to rid the world of good. But the scars of childhood were deep and no matter how many lycans she met, she was never comfortable around them.

He pressed a button on a remote he pulled from his pocket. A pale light lit one corner and she saw the shape of a wolf.

She scrambled up and onto the bed.

His laughter reminded her of things that slithered in the night. "Oh this is fun. It's too bad I don't have a lively one." One corner of his mouth lifted with a hint of evil amusement. "Not to say I don't have any *alive*. I do, but as of yet, none are in any condition to fight you." He studied her again with his hazel eyes which seemed to go more silver the longer he stared at her. "Such a lovely you are. It would be a shame to have you shredded. I could offer to let one of my pretties go if she would kill you."

She didn't utter a sound. The man liked to pause.

"There comes a time when I reduce you all to simply surviving." He looked at his fingers, picked at a nail. "You'd do anything, anything if you thought there was a hope of getting away."

Her heart thundered against her ears and she realized she was playing into his hands. Doing exactly what he wanted her to. Become afraid, see him as the controller, the monster, the giver and taker.

She closed her eyes and concentrated on calming her breaths. She'd need her energy to defeat him, not let him sap her by baiting her emotions.

For the first time she realized an amulet hung from around her neck. It wasn't hers. She didn't open her eyes, didn't look at him. She reached up and ripped it off.

"While you're meditating, you should know that I won't let you go. I never let any of my treasures go. They're all mine. Permanently. For me to play with, admire...pet."

She opened her eyes and glared at him, this time she let her mind open, let her power flow over and through her.

She didn't shift very often. Too many feared and revered what she was. A legend of great wealth and destruction.

His eyes widened, and he panted.

She kept her eyes on him and chanted words she'd learned as a child at the monastery, of protection, of guidance, of courage.

This time, she felt the pain of shifting, of her bones realigning, of her sight changing, becoming sharper and clearer.

She flapped her wings, the spread too large for the cage.

Wind arose and stirred the air, the dust from the floor.

He smiled and stepped back, clapping.

Fire leapt from his right to his left, circling, closing in.

It's my turn, you bastard, she thought.

"*Cyzarine,*" Saker shouted in her mind. "*Wait for me, damn it. You wait.*"

"*No. I waited for you before. I won't again.*" Even as she thought it, she wanted to pull it back. She wanted him here. Needed him here.

With that she let loose all the power she normally kept contained, normally didn't call forth.

Fire burst up in every direction, except the inside of the cage. The heat was fierce.

Still she heard his laughter, his damn clapping. "More! More! Yes!"

She stopped and took a deep breath.

"That was just lovely. Do it again," he whispered right beside her.

She whirled, thinking he was inside the cage, but found him still standing on the other side of the cage.

As if reading her mind, he said, "I could get inside if I wanted to." He smiled. "But I don't want to, not yet. Not yet, pretty, pretty Cyzarine. I do things in my own time, otherwise it ruins the entire experience." He took a deep breath. "God, I don't know if you're more beautiful as a woman taking on her enemies or as a firebird. Look at your feathers..."

She shivered, drained. Oh hell. What was she going to do?

"*Maybe I do need you,*" she thought, swallowing her pride.

౮౧౪

Her feathers all but glowed. It was as if they themselves were shifting flames. Reds, golds, bright hot blues... Shifted and shimmered on wings of gold.

She tilted her head and looked at him. She was perched atop the table he'd set to one side, not too close to the edge of the cage.

There was also a swing hanging from the top center of the cage. He wondered if she'd use it.

"You just wasted so much power. Power that you can't replenish in a cage, can you?" He leaned in through the bars and blew her a kiss. Then he pressed the button again and let all the lights flood the room.

She turned her head, the gold plumes atop softly shifting with her movements. He watched her eyes. Those golden eyes taking in what she saw...

The statues.

"My treasures," he said and walked to the nearest one, running a hand down the spiked spine of the werewolf. He loved that he'd ended her as her hackles had risen. "Isn't she beautiful? Her name is Coral. I found her in Ireland. Working in a dreary pub, singing with a *ceili* band." He brushed his hand over the head, the mouth open in a golden snarl. "Now she's mine. Mine to keep. She's one of my favorites."

He looked back at the firebird. A real, live firebird.

"I wonder how many have ever actually *seen* you?" He walked closer to the cage. "Such passion, heat and darkness." He bent over and thought he heard a screech from outside the window. He picked up the golden down shed when she'd shifted. He glanced to the window and then turned back to her. He ran the feather beneath his nose and sniffed, smelled the acrid scent of smoke, but also one of *her*. "Do your feathers really bring luck?" He ran the feather over his mouth. "I think I'll have to make you shift back into a human. I want to play with the discarded feather. With you. See what excites you."

Already blood flowed hot and thick through his veins, swirled down his spine and tightened his gut, flooding his groin.

The window crashed open. Shrill cries screeched across the air.

He whirled, ready to face the enemy. But even as he threw up his own shield and tried to transport himself into the cage, he knew something was wrong.

He couldn't...

His hands felt heavy.

What...

He only had a moment before birds, larger than the firebird, bulleted into the room, shrieks and cries filling the air.

"No!" Again, he tried to shield with a binding curse, a blocking spell, but nothing happened.

The familiar tingle didn't flow through his hands.

The birds all screeched around him.

From the cage, the firebird called long and sad, pleading, yet anger laced the sound.

Kladovik turned to look at her, holding the feather.

Wings flapped before him and he raised an arm to ward off the birds, but the talons still sank into his skin. He felt the bones of his arm break, felt the skin on his face rip, then pain pierced his eyes and he saw nothing.

He screamed.

His treasures.

Firebirds...luck...

Heat engulfed him, as the talons crushed his chest.

Then he felt nothing at all.

Chapter Thirteen

Reen stood in her shower, letting the water wash away the nightmare of the last several hours.

It could have been worse, she knew that. Knew it with every fiber of her being. But still evil chilled her blood, scraped her raw nerves.

Oleana and three other shifters were in the hospital. Oleana had been moved from Intensive Care to a regular room.

One, a cougar, had been released after a round of antibiotics. The other two, a lioness and lynx, were still unconscious. The lynx probably wouldn't make it. They had no idea who those two women were.

She knew they'd matched and would continue to match the statues with missing women who went years back from all over the globe. The most recent being the gilded form of a cheetah. Forensics matched the cat to a missing woman from Nairobi.

So many families would finally find peace, even as the hope was taken away. Families Kladovik ripped apart because he wanted more.

Because he was greedy.

Simply because he wanted and could and did.

She sat on the tiled floor, the tiles warm as the hot water beat down on her. Her arms were bruised, the wrists abraded and purple where they'd been bound. The bindings had popped when she shifted. As had the shoulder that she'd hurt on her previous assignment.

She was now officially on leave.

Water poured over her and dripped off her nose. She was tired. Tired of everything.

And scared.

She didn't want a commitment from or to anyone.

But damn if she wasn't tired of being alone.

Alone.

Saker. He'd killed Kladovik, simply came through the window, ripped the man's eyes out and then crushed him with his talons. Wicked talons.

She couldn't push it all aside anymore. Everything seemed to shut down with the blackness of death and violence.

Blood...

The room had been filled with the scent of blood, with the scent of fire.

Kladovik had been right. She hadn't had the energy to shift back. The power to shift had drained her. She remembered seeing the body drop, seeing the flames getting closer to the body. Saker had shifted from a falcon to himself and grabbed the small golden feather from Kladovik's bloody hand. "That's mine."

That's mine...

She remembered that. Vaguely remembered her body being lifted, the cold air rushing against her face and body as if she'd been flown through the air.

Like she had as a child.

But this time, he'd come. This time, it had been him.

What did it mean? She had no idea and she was too tired to think about it all. She just wanted some sleep.

One thing that wouldn't leave her alone. For just a moment, just a second after they'd mated, and again when he'd carried her through the air, before she'd lost consciousness—she'd felt peace like she hadn't since that fateful day long ago.

Peace...

Hope.

He slipped through her door, surprised and pissed it was so easy to get to her. He'd stationed one of his men below on the stairs, another on the roof. No one was getting to her tonight.

No one, but him.

He could hear the shower running.

For a moment, he stopped.

Her apartment was a reflection of the woman. The furniture was simple and functional. Nothing flashy or expensive. The electronic surveillance equipment on the table was top of the line. The walls were bare. No television. He rounded the corner.

The wooden floors echoed faintly with his steps.

Her room was as neat and tidy as a long standing member of the military. Her bed covers tight and tucked.

He grinned and wondered if she was ever relaxed, ever messy?

Her closet door was shut, all the drawers of her chest closed.

There didn't seem to be a single line of dust anywhere.

He wanted to learn more about her. Learn who she was. Learn what she liked and didn't.

Saker cursed himself for his own stupidity, but the past couldn't be changed. He had no idea what the hell the future would hold for them, but he wanted to find out.

Saker stripped and silently let himself into the bathroom.

Steam rose around the door of the shower, filled the top of the room and fogged the mirror.

He stood just outside the door for a moment.

"Reen?"

A huddled form on the floor shifted, stood and whirled, kicking out the door.

He barely sidestepped it before it crashed into him. Instead he caught it and stood staring at her as she glared at him.

Her black, chin length hair was plastered to her face. Her body was wet and glistening, the scars and bruises standing out on her pale skin. He slowly raised his gaze to lock with hers, taking in every wet and dripping inch of her.

She didn't relax her stance. "I didn't invite you here." Her voice was low, throaty...tired.

He simply stepped in, crowded her back and shut the door behind him. Looking down at her, he brushed wet strands of hair behind her ears. "No, you didn't," he whispered.

She licked her lips and he caught the darkness shift in her eyes.

"What?" he asked, tilting her chin up. "Tell me."

She shook her head. "I don't care what you think of me," she muttered.

He raised a brow and leaned into her. "I've watched you for months, Cyzarine. Since that first assignment we were on together. You didn't even notice me. But I sure as hell noticed you."

She drew a deep breath even as she leaned back against the wall.

He ran a thumb back and forth over her lip, then down her chin. He followed her neck to trail a finger over her collar bone. "I'm sorry about the stage," he said, risking a glance back up into her eyes.

She watched him. "Are you?"

He trailed a path lower to circle her wet breasts. "The way it happened, the timing, yes." He looked back into her eyes. "But we would have made love sooner or later."

"That was sooner?" she asked, shifting closer to him, wrapping her arm around his neck.

Her tongue was hot against his neck. She pulled his earlobe between her teeth and he shivered.

He gripped her hips. "This is later. And I want to go slow..."

He hissed when her other hand reached between them and wrapped around his arousal.

"I don't want to go slow now. Slow is for later."

He turned and met her mouth. "I thought this was later."

Her lips tilted up. "That's for later later. This is for now later. I want hard, hot and fast. Like before."

She wrapped a leg around his waist. "I still hear him in my head, still see him." She kissed him, open mouthed and demanding. "Make me forget. On the stage, all I felt, all I saw, all I heard was you."

"You're mine," he said, lifting her. She shifted, slid down on him and locked her ankles in the small of his back.

Saker hissed.

She didn't answer him. He wondered if she ever would.

Her eyes locked with his and in them he saw...

Hope.

He rocked against her, slow and long. She might want it now, but they'd damn well do it his way.

"I'm going to make love to you over and over again, Cyzarine," he told her, holding her on him so she couldn't shift. "All you'll see," he said, thrusting into her, "will be me." Thrust. "All you'll hear will be my voice." Thrust. "All you'll feel is me."

She arched against him and moaned. "Saker."

He smiled as he lowered his mouth to hers. "You're mine whether you claim it or not."

He stared into her eyes.

"We'll see."

Damn stubborn woman.

The future with her wouldn't be dull, that was for sure.

He thrust home, playing her until they both flew, their orgasm ripping cries from both of them.

At least there was hope.

About the Author

To learn more about Jaycee Clark, please visit www.jayceeclark.com. Send an email to Jaycee at jaycee@jayceeclark.com or join her Yahoo! group to join in the fun with other readers as well as Jaycee! http://groups.yahoo.com/group/jayceesden/

Caged Desire

Sydney Somers

Dedication

To my husband. I'll never know how I got to be lucky enough to follow my dream *and* get the hero too. From the bottom of my heart, thank you for your unwavering support and love.

And to Jaycee, Mandy, Michelle, Shannon and my fabulous editor, Angie. Thanks for letting me be part of such a fantastic project.

Prologue

50 Years Ago

The moment Logan Callahan walked into the room he knew something was wrong. An eerie silence greeted him instead of a handful of voices. It was far too quiet. He had expected to find some of his clan members lingering about, but the mansion's library was dark and deserted.

Logan stepped farther into the room, trying to identify the unease slithering down his backbone. Both the clan and the mansion were well protected and no enemies could get within a mile without detection. He scanned the long shadows, his eyes almost as sharp now as they were in daylight.

Nothing stirred amid the immaculately kept stacks and shelves. Not even one of the servants who routinely looked after the area when clan members descended to converse or spend a day reading or studying. With the recent spiteful antics of his brother, Logan hadn't had time to sit back and relax with a book in a long while, something he would make time to remedy soon.

Logan couldn't pinpoint what made the hairs on the back of his neck rise. Nor did he know why no one else had arrived, considering he was late himself.

From the corner of his eye, he saw a shadow move.

His response was instantaneous. He shifted, using the ancient powers that coursed through his blood to take eagle form. Getting to higher ground would give him a better vantage point to determine the threat.

Twelve feet into the air, Logan knew he'd made a mistake. They'd been expecting him to shift, had counted on it.

A heavy net was thrown over him from the balcony above. The weighted ends tangled his wings and dragged him down. His heart pounded and anger at both his attacker and himself, for not taking more care, made him snap at the thickly corded netting. Even his talons were useless in stopping his descent.

Knowing he was at a disadvantage, he shifted back to human form. The net still slowed him down, giving those waiting beneath him time to attack.

Logan fought them off, satisfied when he heard more than one yelp, and another limb crunch as he lashed out.

There were too many of them. He came to that conclusion a heartbeat before he realized he knew his attackers. All of them.

His friends. Members of his clan.

Logan ceased his struggles, stunned by the familiar faces surrounding him. The harsh, resigned expressions were all it took to convince him this was no prank or accident. They had meant to go after him.

"What the hell is going on?"

Most glanced away, others glared back at him like he was a threatening predator caught in their territory.

Jack, his closest friend and clan leader, had the decency to look apologetic, but he didn't order the others to release their hold on Logan.

"I'm sorry, my friend. We have no choice."

"What are you talking about? No choice in what?"

"The prophecy."

"Prophecy..." Logan paused as he realized Jack had to be referring to one of the old scrolls some of the elders had been working on deciphering since they'd been found a few years ago. Scrolls far older than even Logan's four hundred years.

He tried to jerk his arms free. "How does the prophecy explain this?"

Jack's silence spoke for itself, though Logan couldn't believe for a minute that his best friend could think *he* could be the traitor an elder clan member had prophesied about hundreds of years before.

"I demand to see the scroll, this proof you must believe exists to take such action."

"Expose the back of his shoulder."

Logan's head snapped up at the sound of his brother's voice.

Dominic stepped past those crowded around him. His severe features looked more cruel tonight, his light hair and pale face a ghostly contrast to Logan's own dark hair and tanned complexion.

No doubt his twin brother was enjoying this, if he hadn't orchestrated it himself. Logan wouldn't put it past him, shared blood or not.

Someone yanked his jacket down and ripped his shirt. They wanted to see his tattoo. Why?

Jack moved closer to see for himself. His shoulders slumped.

Logan held his friend's gaze. "If my brother told you this means something—"

"You have your proof," Dominic interrupted.

"The hell they do." Logan lunged for his brother, but the others kept him restrained.

Jack moved back to the edge of the crowd.

Again, Logan tried to pull free. "Whatever he told you—"

Logan didn't get to finish his thought. Someone struck him from behind and pain ricocheted through his skull. He slumped at their feet, fighting to stay conscious through the pain and the nausea curdling his stomach.

"I will not kill him," Logan heard Jack say. "You may not hesitate to condemn your own brother to death, but I will not be so reckless."

"But the prophecy," Dominic insisted.

"The council and I have made our decision."

Logan felt himself slipping under, but not before he heard Jack's last weary command. "Bring in the cage."

Chapter One

"You're not going to let me get a punch in are you?"

Eve grinned at her assistant, Abbey. "Nope. Not unless you don't want to improve." Swinging around, Eve kicked out.

Abbey dodged to the side, dropped into a crouch, and at the same time slashed her leg in a wide arc.

Eve was a second too slow to respond and staggered back on one foot as the other was knocked out from under her. She recovered in enough time to catch Abbey as she launched herself at Eve. With a half-turn, she tossed Abbey behind her. Even before her friend hit the gym mat, Eve knew she put too much strength behind the move.

She darted across the mat and knelt next to Abbey's motionless body.

Abbey cracked one eye open. "*That* is definitely going to leave a bruise."

Eve grimaced as Abbey sat up. "Sorry." She held out a hand and pulled Abbey to her feet.

Rolling her shoulders, Abbey bent to retrieve her water bottle at the edge of the mat. "I'm the one who should know better than to let a vamp be my training partner."

A year ago, Eve had hired Abbey on Kyle's recommendation. Eve made it a point *not* to follow her closest friend's advice very often. It tended to go right to his head. This time, though, she had made the right decision. Abbey's family had been employed by a number of vampires over the years, so when Eve realized she could use a hand with the more tedious side of her writing career, Abbey was the perfect choice. While she slept during the day, Abbey looked after everything from some line editing and playing the go-between for her and her editor, to answering mail from those who wrote in about Eve's suspense books.

Abbey stretched. "Well, I'm calling it a day."

Eve caught the towel Abbey whipped at her and sank down on the gym mat. Putting in the athletics room had been another one of Kyle's suggestions. With Abbey's training lately, the room was actually seeing some regular use. Eve preferred to get her exercise by feeding in the rougher parts of town, more than willing to tangle with her prey first.

"Your instructor should be impressed. You've improved a lot over the last few weeks."

"And I've got the scars to prove it," Abbey joked. "I left notes and a to-do list on your desk."

Eve feigned a lopsided grin of enthusiasm. "Oh goody."

"And you should do something fun tonight. Take a few hours off."

"Wasn't this fun?" She didn't even come close to sounding insulted. Maybe if she wasn't smiling.

Abbey propped a hand on her hip. "I mean something that involves leaving the house *without* your laptop."

"I leave the house every night." Hard not to, having to live on blood and all. She couldn't stomach cold stuff.

"I'm not talking about feeding. Go see a movie or something."

Eve stretched her legs. "Go home and shower already."

Abbey rolled her eyes. "See you tomorrow night." She paused at the door. "I almost forgot. Kyle had something delivered from South America."

"No doubt another trinket he dug up." Eve had wanted to go along with him on his latest treasure hunt. The trips never failed to be a good time. Unfortunately, she had switched her deadlines around too much already and didn't have any room left to juggle.

"Must be some trinket. It's in a huge crate."

"Really?" Eve followed Abbey along the upstairs hall and down the winding staircase that looked over the foyer. The staircase had been one of the focal points she'd fallen in love with when she bought the house nearly ten years ago. Along with the fact it sat on the edge of town and guaranteed the privacy she sought.

Eve frowned at the large wooden crate in the middle of the foyer. It wasn't typical for Kyle to ship anything home ahead of him unless it was something small. The crate was a little taller than she was.

"How did you forget to tell me about this?"

A flush crept up Abbey's cheeks. "You've only been up an hour and I got a little excited thinking I might finally take you down."

"Better luck next time." Eve circled the crate. There wasn't anything written on the outside to hint at its contents.

"Hey, I almost had you."

"Almost doesn't count," Eve said absently, her attention completely focused on the object in front of her. What was in there?

Abbey snorted. "Must have cost a pretty penny to ship this sucker back. It took three guys to get it in here. Almost didn't fit through the double doors. The paperwork is on your desk." Abbey swung her bag over her shoulder. "Have a good night."

"You too."

The door closed quietly behind her, leaving Eve alone with the mystery crate. She wasn't big on surprises, preferring to see what was coming at all times. Kyle knew that and seldom went to much trouble to conceal what he was sending. Most times he even called to let her know something was being delivered. He liked to joke that Eve might decide to snack on the delivery guys if she didn't know ahead of time. Not one for random snacking on the innocent—as Kyle liked to call it— even the idea of it put Eve off almost as much as the crate sitting in the middle of her foyer.

Figuring the paperwork would be the best place to start, she headed back upstairs, again wondering why Kyle hadn't called about the crate. That wasn't like him.

The one page Abbey signed off on told Eve nothing about the contents. She could only assume Kyle had bribed customs officials not to label the crate or make note on the documentation.

Odd.

After a fast shower and a quick change into a plain olive green T-shirt and beige pants, she tugged her long red hair into a loose bun and returned downstairs. Once more, she circled the box, trying to imagine what could be inside.

Eve turned around with the intention of going to the garage in search of something to open it with, and spotted a crowbar and hammer on the table near the door. Abbey didn't miss a trick.

With no noticeable opening, Eve picked one end and went to work, jamming the flat head of the crowbar beneath a wood slat in the frame. It took a few forceful jiggles to get a corner loose. Had she still been human, it would likely have taken an hour to get into it. For her it only took a few minutes.

Grabbing the top corners, she tugged it down so one side of the crate lay at her feet. Eve took a step closer, puzzled by the sight of the metal bars.

A cage?

Light slashed across the lower half of the cage, not that she needed it to see exactly what was inside the dark crate.

Eve blinked and took another step closer, her eyes locked on the large feathered creature inside. More than three feet tall, the dark bird of prey perched on a horizontal bar a few inches from the bottom of the cage. Thick, sharp-looking black talons that could easily sever an artery gripped the bar.

For a moment Eve thought the creature was stuffed. Now that would be just like Kyle, to send her a big mystery gift and have it turn out to be some tacky knick-knack. Albeit, an oversized knick-knack.

Golden eyes followed her movement as she leaned forward, the assessing gaze zeroing in on her the same way she did when she found an appropriate subject for her nightly feeding.

Vampire or not, cage with thick bars or not, Eve backed up. The damn thing was definitely alive.

Why in the world had Kyle sent her this?

Taking her chances, she gripped the bars and pulled hard. The cage was heavy, but without too much trouble—and without the bird making a move for her fingers—she dragged it free of the crate. With every step around the cage, her curiosity grew, her eyes never straying from the creature that turned its head to follow her.

Was this some late April Fool's present? Seeing as Kyle had once sent her a snake as a joke, she wouldn't put it past him. He could be sitting in some South American bar right now, laughing his ass off as he pictured her reaction to his gift.

Inside the cage the eagle—which was her best guess—inched down the horizontal bar, its talons curling tighter. She wouldn't have thought birds this large existed anymore. Obviously rare. Which made it all the more strange Kyle sent it to her in the first place.

The creature's golden eyes surveyed her carefully, as though it sized her up the same way she assessed a potential threat.

"You're certainly beautiful, aren't you?" Eve whispered.

The eagle squawked at her.

Still puzzled, Eve moved until she was just shy of touching the bars. She could quickly back away if need be, but she couldn't stop from getting as close a look at the large bird as she could.

How long had it been in transport? Had anyone fed it? A few small skeletons littered the cage floor, but told her nothing about how old they might be. She didn't want to give much thought to what a bird this size would eat. Somehow she doubted field mice would come close to putting a dent in this creature's appetite.

At the thought of food, her own hunger pulsed fiercely inside her. First, she'd try to get in touch with Kyle then she could hunt. There was a blood supply here, but she preferred to keep that for the rare nights she couldn't tear herself away from her latest book.

With one more curious look at the eagle, she turned towards the kitchen. Kyle might not be anywhere near a tower capable of carrying a cell call, but she had to try. As she punched in the numbers on her cordless phone, she found herself moving back to the foyer.

The eagle followed her movements, but didn't appear nervous. Maybe he was used to seeing people.

As expected Kyle didn't pick up. Eve gave the feathered animal another once-over, still unable to figure out what Kyle had been thinking, and then crossed to the front door. Once she took care of the thunderous need surfacing within her, she'd decide what to do about the eagle.

Logan watched the woman dim the lights before letting herself out the front door. The sound of it closing echoed in the front hall.

Who was she? She had looked surprised to see the contents of the crate he'd been shipped in. Did she know the man who had found him in the rotting hole Dominic and the rest of his clan had banished him to more than fifty years ago?

Overhearing the present date after he was found a few days ago shocked him. At the beginning of his imprisonment he kept track of the days, but eventually that became harder to handle than simply not knowing.

An invisible fist clawed his insides at the thought of how they had locked him away because of a prophecy, one he was more certain than ever involved Dominic, not Logan. But upon discovering the contents of the encrypted scroll, Dominic had no doubt feared he himself would be banished and had taken steps to ensure that didn't happen.

And so Logan spent the last half a century buried in some abandoned temple in South America, barely surviving on the occasional creature unfortunate enough to get within striking distance. Immortal or not, he still needed to feed to live and only in eagle form could he manage that. He was far stronger than the average mortal but he'd been unable to free himself from the cage with only his hands.

But then someone had stumbled along and found the temple. Logan hadn't cared who the man was that arranged to have him shipped back to the U.S. He had bided his time, waiting for the most opportune moment to try to get free of the cage. One way or another he'd find a way out, familiarize himself with the changes fifty years had brought about, and then he would track down his brother.

Logan wasn't sure how much time had passed before the front door opened and the woman again stood in front of his prison, studying him. The smell of blood teased his senses and he shifted in place, the animal within reacting to the scent. He looked her over, but saw no sign of injury.

Like before, Logan found his attention drawn to her extraordinary blue eyes.

She wasn't mortal.

The realization spun through him, unexpected, but intriguing. He had wondered when she opened the crate with far more ease and speed than he would have expected. Still, it left him speculating on whether or not her immortality had anything to do with how he wound up with her.

Logan tilted his head to the side, watching the woman brush a few red curls that fell from their clip over her shoulder. He was glad to be in eagle form. As a man the sight of her, the soft, warm scent that was distinctly feminine, would have been damn painful to bear after being far from the opposite sex for so long.

The woman inched closer. She tried not to show she feared him. Not that he blamed her. His talons could easily tear through her flesh.

Her eyes widened when he hopped off the bar and moved towards the bars. She stayed rooted in place, her lush lips parted, her expression curious before a frown brought two sculpted brows together.

What he wouldn't give to know what was going through her head.

The woman sighed thoughtfully and headed up the curving staircase to the upper level. Would she be gone for long? After decades with only himself for company, anyone close—even if they were on the opposite side of the cage—kept him from being alone.

Resigned to continue his imprisonment for a while longer, Logan paid closer attention to his surroundings.

His heart pounded. How had he missed noticing that she left the crowbar on a nearby table? A table he could surely reach if he shifted back to human form.

Logan glanced towards the stairs, listened intently for any sign of approaching movement. Had she gone to bed? He stared at the crowbar, at his ticket out of the damn cage. With a practiced skill, he fluidly transformed, cringing at the ripple of pain that ran down his spine. Along with the change, his senses shifted, no longer quite as sharp, a disadvantage he was willing to work with to get free.

Rising from the crouched position, Logan crept to the far side of the cage closest to the table. The bars seemed to press in on him and he gritted back the panic that wanted to surface. Fifty years in a cage and still his human side found it hard to handle.

The crowbar was less than four feet away. Giving the stairs one more glance, he then turned his attention back to the table. Arm outstretched, his fingers just brushed the end. Logan pushed his shoulder as tight to the bars as he could manage.

Almost...

The tool slipped over his fingers and fell to the floor with a dull clang.

Logan froze. No immediate sound came from above. Could she have heard it, or was she too far away in the house? He didn't move for a long minute. Each strained breath whispered out in a mix of adrenaline and relief.

He finally bent and reached through the bars and came up short at the sight of two feminine bare feet that suddenly filled the space between him and freedom.

Chapter Two

Eve didn't move, didn't so much as blink. The sight of the very naked man crouched in the cage pushed her once useful heart into a full gallop. She also didn't need to further examine the cage to know the eagle wasn't in there with him.

Where had it gone? And how had a man wound up in there instead? Eve cocked her head, her heightened senses immediately picking up on the most obvious fact

He wasn't fully human.

A shifter of some kind? A handful of times over the centuries she had heard of immortals capable of shifting between human and animal form, but this was the first time she had ever come across someone like that. If indeed that's what he was.

In the same moment, Eve realized the man hadn't moved, his arm still outstretched through the bars. Her eyes followed the muscular slope of his shoulder, down his arm to where the crowbar lay only a couple inches from his fingers.

Reacting instinctively, Eve kicked the bar across the floor, far out of reach. Until she knew what he was, she certainly wasn't helping him out of the cage.

What almost sounded like a sigh escaped from the man's lips. He pushed up to his full height, but was forced to duck a few inches. That put him a few inches over six feet since the cage was about that tall. Tangled black hair fell just past his shoulders and the same piercing amber eyes as the eagle stared back at her.

Eve shook her head and took a step closer, reassured by the bars. If he could get out on his own, he wouldn't have needed the crowbar.

His unreadable gaze skimmed over her face and then down the front of her. His eyes lingered on her breasts a heartbeat longer than anywhere else before returning to her face to hold her stare.

A little unnerved, she shifted in place, ridiculously aware of the fact he was naked, only a few feet away, and...aroused? She couldn't stop her gaze from dipping down past the powerful shoulders, his smooth chest and lower to—

The man in the cage angled away from her, giving Eve a rather enticing view of his behind. Most of his skin was covered in a thin layer of dust of some kind but not for a minute did it detract from the impressive masculinity of him. A strange looking tattoo marked the back of his right shoulder, and she moved closer to get a better look at it.

The man turned back around. He gripped the bars, a hint of an amused smile touching his full lips.

Almost politely he said, "I want out."

Eve blinked, both at the fact that he'd spoken to her and the raw gravelly sound of his voice.

Her lack of response brought his brows together. "Let me out." Firmer this time, there wasn't anything threatening in his tone, but the primal edge to his expression told her just how dangerously serious he was.

Eve shook her head. A cage that held a bird no more than an hour ago, now housed a man, a very attractive, very naked man. She had a few questions that were going to be answered before she even thought of opening that door.

His hands tightened on the bars, the only sign he didn't like her answer.

"How did you get in there?" If he was an immortal of some kind, then maybe someone had a good reason for locking him up.

The man didn't respond.

"What are you?" she asked. "You're not human, not even mortal, are you?"

He frowned, but made no attempt to answer her question.

"If you won't talk, why should I let you out?"

"Please." The sincerity in that one softly spoken word caught her in the chest and his golden eyes implored her to help him.

She couldn't. Not yet. Not until she knew more about him, hell anything about him would do. Without another word, she turned on her heel and strode away. She needed to talk to Kyle.

"Wait," he called out, the sandpaper voice echoing in the foyer.

Eve glanced back over her shoulder and tried not to be swayed by the vulnerable picture he made with nothing between him and her but the bars. Whatever had he done to make anyone imprison him?

She tilted her head to the side. "Yes?"

He hesitated, lowered his eyes. "Could I have a drink of water? Please."

Again that one word sank under her skin in a warm wave. There was almost an arrogant edge to the plea, like he hated to have to ask her for anything. But it was the unvoiced need, a desperation that got to her.

Eve nodded and left him. While she was in the kitchen, she tried calling Kyle again with no results. Not even his voice mail picked up. Had Kyle known the creature in the cage was capable of shifting to human form? Was that part of his joke?

She grabbed a bottle of water from the fridge and at the last minute dialed Abbey's cell number. Abbey didn't answer either. When her voice mail kicked in, Eve spouted off, "There's a naked man in the cage that was delivered and I have no clue what to do with him."

Instantly she regretted saying anything at all, and quickly added, "That would make an interesting story idea, don't you think? Not my usual style, but you just never know." Before she rambled any further, she told Abbey she'd see her tomorrow and disconnected. The cover up was lame but Abbey was used to Eve bouncing plot ideas off her and hopefully wouldn't think twice about the odd call.

Eve found the man in the same position she'd left him. He looked curiously at the bottle she carried, then slowly reached through the cage.

Normally, she wouldn't have hesitated to near any man, fully confident she could take care of herself if she had to. But not knowing exactly who she was dealing with left her more cautious than usual. She closed the short distance between them and held out the bottle. Their fingers brushed and her gaze shot to his as a shiver curled up her spine.

His eyes darkened and he wrapped his hand around her wrist.

She started to jerk free.

"Thank you." He slowly released his hold on her and angled away from her.

Eve curbed the impulse to take another two steps to the side to see if he had turned away to hide an erection.

He drained the bottle of water and handed it back through the bars. "Could I have more?"

"Yes."

She returned to the kitchen, grabbed the water and then headed up the back stairs and down the hall to the guest room Kyle used when he visited. From the few clothes he left there, Eve picked out a pair of drawstring track pants and a T-shirt. With the clothes and water bottle tucked under her arm, Eve used the front stairs.

The second she started the descent, she could feel him watching her. Eve made a conscious effort to sift through his thoughts.

Nothing. Not even a hint of emotion radiated from his mind. In her two hundred and fifty-one years of being a vampire only the strongest of her kind could keep their thoughts so closely shielded.

The man arched a brow. Had he felt her trying to read his thoughts?

She kept her attention on the bars as she held out the clothes and quickly stepped back before he could touch her. She didn't know anything about the man in the cage, so it was wise to avoid physically touching him when her body responded to even the briefest contact.

Eve chalked that up to the fact that it had been months since she let any man into her bed.

"What's your name?"

"Logan," he answered easily, then drank the second bottle down in one long gulp. He closed his eyes, drew in a deep breath before starting to dress.

Crossing her arms, Eve turned away while he pulled the pants on.

"And your name is," he gently prompted.

"Eve."

The corner of his mouth hitched up in a half smile, and her pulse jumped. That was the thing with being a vampire. While those bodily functions no longer kept her alive in the same way they used to, the smallest reaction was magnified.

And she was definitely reacting to him.

Logan leaned forward as though to impart something important. "I would like out of here, Eve."

Her stomach tugged at the sound of her name on his lips. Still, she shook her head. "I don't think that's a good idea."

He held out the empty bottle, his face blank instead of annoyed like she would have expected.

Eve reached for the bottle.

Moving quickly, he snared her wrist and hauled her to the cage.

Even her own incredible strength couldn't break the hold he used to keep her pressed close to the bars. Though firm, his grip didn't hurt her. His piercing amber eyes darkened as he searched her face, pausing again on her mouth.

"You have nothing to fear from me," he promised. And to prove it, he eased his grip, but didn't release her completely.

She could have pulled away, but his next words rooted her in place.

"I promise not to hurt you, vampire."

Eve's eyes flared, and Logan smiled, his guess having been correct.

So the woman was another immortal, like himself. Only a handful of times since his birth had he come across one of her kind and none of those encounters left him with any great love for the night-walkers. Most were too heartless. Was this woman any different? Given she had brought him clothes and something to drink showed she was capable of some compassion. But did it run deep enough she would let him out?

Logan waited for the soft woman, tucked in the arms he'd stretched through the bars, to pull away.

"How did you know?"

"I can smell blood that is not your own."

Her brows drew together.

"And I guessed," he added.

"Good guess." She still didn't back away from him. The warmth from her skin seeped into his veins. His brother and clan might have left him in a warm climate, but being alone like that for so long left him so cold inside, he wondered if he'd ever be truly warm again.

Eve continued to hold his gaze, and an all too familiar need sparked to life inside him. Was she a woman who would arch and moan beneath his touch, or being a vampire, was her passion as cold as her lifeless heart?

Her lips parted questioningly, as if she could read his thoughts. Logan smiled, knowing she couldn't. She finally backed out of his arms. The loss of contact he'd gone so long without, even shared with a stranger, squeezed his chest. Not only that, but the determined glint that flared in her eyes told him she was going to be stubborn about this.

"Who put you in the cage?"

Logan sighed. She wasn't going to move an inch to open the door without some kind of response. Everything about her body, from one hand propped on her hip to the lift of her chin, said as much.

"My brother."

"Why?" She didn't even pretend to look convinced.

"We don't get along."

"He hates you so much he locked you in a cage and dumped you in the middle of nowhere?"

"Yes."

She glanced to where she had kicked the crowbar.

"I have no reason to hurt you, Eve."

Indecision crossed her face. "Unless there is another reason you were locked up and are lying."

He crossed his arms. "I'm not."

"Convince me."

"How?"

She shrugged. "As cute as you are, I'm not lifting a finger to help release you until I'm sure you're not dangerous."

"So you're afraid of me."

"No."

Logan almost believed her. Vampires were notoriously strong, but since he knew what he was dealing with, and she didn't, he couldn't really blame her for hesitating. But understanding that wasn't getting him out of the cage.

"I give you my word not to harm you."

"I don't know you, so your word—"

"Is all I have left. I've been locked away with nothing. My brother deserves my wrath, not you."

She took a step towards him and then stopped.

"Please, Eve. You've only been kind to me. I have no wish to make you regret that."

For the third time that night, he watched her nibble on the inside of her cheek. A good sign, he hoped.

She turned away from him and his hopes sank. Near the stairs, she changed direction and retrieved the crowbar. Brilliant blue eyes drilled into his. "You had better be honorable."

"Completely," he assured her.

With a "we'll see" look, she jammed the edge of the bar next to the locking mechanism. Logan reached through and gripped the end of the bar and pulled hard along with her.

The lock snapped and Logan smiled at how easy his brother had ultimately made his escape. His clan obviously hadn't counted on anyone stumbling across him or they would have taken more extreme measures.

Eve stood back and held the door open as though she fully expected to be wrong about him.

Logan picked up the T-shirt she gave him to wear, but didn't put it on as he took his first step out of the cage in decades. He closed his eyes and reached his arms out to the side to test that it truly was no trick or illusion. His fingertips met with empty air. Logan smiled wider.

He was finally free.

Chapter Three

"How long were you in there?" Eve asked.

"Fifty years."

Eve gaped. "Fifty years?" Alone in a cage.

Logan took another step and his knees buckled.

Eve was at his side, supporting the little weight he allowed himself to lean on her.

"Weaker than I thought." The sexy half grin brought her own smile to her lips.

"Let's just go as far as the living room then."

He nodded, but made no attempt to take a step. The arm across her back felt strong, warming her skin straight through her shirt. Being pressed so close to him felt far too intimate for strangers. She tried to think of how long it had been since any man other than Kyle or Brett was this close to her, but Logan's proximity made it difficult to concentrate on anything beyond this moment.

Eve kept her gaze focused on the floor, but could feel him watching her intently. Those amber eyes of his cut right through her, and being so close, she didn't trust him not to be able to pick up on just how much her senses spun by the physical contact alone.

Logan's fingers tightened on her side, each step brushing them a little bit closer to her breast. By the time they reached the living room, he was actually holding most of his own weight, but didn't relinquish the hold on her until she nodded for him to sit on the couch.

"Thank you."

He really needed to stop saying that. The poetic, rusty tone of his voice played havoc with her insides.

The wall mounted plasma TV clicked on and music blared from the surround system as a video played on MTV.

Logan jolted, his eyes going wide at the unexpected sound. He leaned forward, frowning. Eve spotted the remote control tucked into the cushion behind him. She reached down to grab it and Logan turned abruptly, bringing their faces close. Very close.

"What are you doing?"

She forced her attention from his full lips to his eyes. "Getting the remote."

He arched a brow, but whether it was because he didn't believe her, or because he didn't know what a remote control was, Eve couldn't say.

His lips turned up at the corner. "Are you done?"

"You need to lean forward again." Eve couldn't keep her eyes from straying to his mouth. The longer she spent around him, the more aware she became of him.

"It's been a long time..." Logan trailed off.

"Since..." she prompted, trying to get a grip.

He pushed a wayward lock of hair behind her ear. Her cheek warmed under the feathery brush of his finger. Her eyes nearly drifted shut at the seductively tender gesture.

A loud rumble echoed in his stomach.

Eve straightened, using the remote to turn the volume down on the TV. "You're hungry," she guessed.

"It's been a few days since the last—"

She held up her hand. "If it was an animal, I don't want to know the specifics."

Logan laughed. "This coming from a vampire who lives on human blood."

"Yeah well, I prefer my food not to come with fur, scales, or a tail."

"Then you're missing out," he teased.

The more he talked the less rough his voice became, and the more Eve relaxed. She just couldn't decide if that was a good thing or not.

"So what do you feel like eating?"

"You cook?"

Nothing on his face gave him away, but Eve got the distinct impression he was amused by the possibility.

"I happen to like cooking."

"So you eat the food you make?"

"Sometimes, but it's never really satisfying. I cook for my assistant Abbey more than anyone. It's therapeutic."

Logan frowned. "Therapeutic?"

"Cooking helps me work through my issues."

He looked even more confused.

"I'm a writer," she explained, "and sometimes when I get stuck, I cook until a solution comes to me."

"I see."

Eve turned towards the kitchen then paused. What if he was just waiting for her to leave the room before he took off? Maybe he really had been locked away for a reason and couldn't wait to get back to whatever unpleasant things landed him in the cage in the first place. A guilty man would run the first chance he got. But was he as innocent as he proclaimed, or had he manipulated her from the start?

The doubt must have shown on her face.

"I'm not going anywhere, Eve."

Eve hesitated, wanting to believe him. With no other choice but to trust him, she finally nodded. "I'll just be right through here if you need anything." She moved back to the couch and handed him the remote. "And this button lets you change the channel."

He glanced at the TV. "No dial?"

Smiling, she shook her head. "Surf away. Forget I said that," Eve added when he gave her a puzzled look.

Alone in the kitchen, she planted her hands on the counter and closed her eyes. Not in a hundred years would she have expected her night to turn out like this. A man who could shift into eagle form locked in a cage. She shook her head at what it must have been like to spend hour after hour, day after day, alone and imprisoned.

Eve opened the fridge to take stock of the food on hand. Spotting the bacon, she smiled and pulled it out along with a carton of eggs, some sausage and cheese, then dug through the pantry until she found a box of pancake mix.

All too easily the rest of the world fell away as she set the bacon and sausage to fry and whipped the eggs up for an omelette. At one time the smell of cooking would have made her stomach rumble as loud as Logan's had. Things were different now, and the enjoyment from regular food was the one thing she missed the most about not being human.

She was so focused on cooking she didn't hear Logan approach until he was only a couple feet away. The man was certainly light on his feet.

"It smells good."

Eve grinned. "Hope you've got lots of room."

"I'm sure I'll manage."

Turning away from him, she retrieved another bottle of water from the fridge and handed it to him.

He opened his mouth.

"Don't thank me again. Please." One more low, gravelly response and she might moan aloud. His voice reminded her of a couple of her favorite raspy-voiced singers, ones who made you want to close your eyes and listen to them all night long.

Eve kept her back to him as she finished cooking. She glanced at the clock but knew she still had a few hours until sunrise. What would she do with him while she slept?

A splatter of grease sprayed her hand and she jerked back, finding it as annoying as ever that while so few things could actually kill her, her pain receptors made a very mild burn hurt like hell. Her skin healed the surface of the minor injury with barely an effort, but the nerve endings underneath still pulsed like she had plunged her hand straight into the grease.

She turned on the faucet. The cool water would do nothing to ease the pain that would pass in another minute, but it gave her something to do.

"You burned yourself?" Logan stepped up beside her. He drew her hand from under the water and studied it. "Where?"

"It's fine."

"Where?" he repeated patiently.

Eve rolled her eyes. "Just below my thumb." Already the pain was subsiding and she became all too aware of the gentle hold he had on her hand.

Logan blew a soft cooling breath over her skin.

Eve barely checked the urge to close her eyes as she felt the whisper of air all the way to her toes.

"Are you tired?"

Okay, so she had closed her eyes after all and opened them to find Logan closer, a sexy smile curving his lips. His heated stare bored into hers as he brought her hand up to his mouth. One slow sweep of his lips and it was all she could do to keep the needy sigh trapped firmly between her lips.

Logan eased towards her, bringing her body in full contact with his naked chest. Part of her fiercely wanted to kiss him—undeniably the sex-starved part of her—but the other remained hesitant, guarded. She didn't know him, but that didn't stop her getting caught up in the attraction. Didn't stop her from wanting more than a kiss.

Logan slipped an arm around her waist, and lowered his mouth—

"What was up with that voice mail you left me?" Abbey skidded to a surprised stop. "Oh."

Logan let his arm fall back to his side as Eve stepped away from him.

The blonde, who inched backward as though she could undo the interruption by retreating, had very bad timing.

A few hours ago kissing a woman was the farthest thing from his mind. A few seconds ago nothing seemed more important than tasting

Eve's lush mouth for himself. To be released from his cage was fortunate, to be a breath away from discovering if the vampire's kiss would meet the expectation his mind built up since he laid eyes on her, was as close to paradise as he'd come to in a long, long time.

"Sorry," the blonde said, almost to the doorway. "Really, really sorry." She jerked her thumb over her shoulder. "I'm gonna go. Just...pretend I wasn't here." With an apologetic smile, she spun on her heel and left.

"Abbey." Eve called out in a voice caught somewhere between relief and disappointment.

"Go," Logan said when she appeared unsure about leaving him.

The woman clearly had some trust issues, but considering his brother and best friend's betrayal, Logan supposed he did too.

Alone in the kitchen, the smell of the food Eve prepared overwhelmed him, and his stomach growled. It took him a minute to figure out how to press the button to turn the burner off on the strange looking stove. All around the kitchen were numerous gadgets, some of which he couldn't begin to guess the function of. To an immortal fifty years wasn't a very long time, but if the unfamiliar surroundings in Eve's home were any indication, there would be a few things to get used to.

As he sat at the table, having dug through the cupboards for a plate and loaded it up, Logan could hear Eve and Abbey talking. The hushed conversation prevented him from making out the words, but the other woman's laugh reassured him Abbey wasn't trying to convince Eve to make him leave.

Unless Eve was uncomfortable, he was in no rush to go anywhere. Until he became accustomed to all the changes the world and technology had seen while he was "away" it would be foolish to confront Dominic. Far better to bide his time a bit and try to learn what his clan and brother had been up to for the last fifty years.

"How is it?" Eve walked back into the kitchen.

Logan devoured the last piece of bacon. "Wonderful. You're a very good cook."

She took away his plate and empty water bottle, and grabbed him another one from the fridge. He started to thank her, then remembered the odd look on her face when she cut him off the last time.

He took another long drink, wondering if this damn thirst would ever go away. From the corner of his eye he watched her fill the stainless steel sink with water and bubbles.

Logan stood and crossed to where she deposited the few dishes. "You're odd for a vampire, you know that?"

A captivating grin stole across her lips. "Oh, and how many vampires have you known?"

"A few."

"Friends or enemies?"

"Neither."

She opened a drawer and pulled out a dishcloth. "Since you know a whole lot more about my kind, how about you tell me something about you?"

"What would you like to know?"

"What are you exactly?"

He tipped his head forward, another grin coming easily to his lips. "So you think there is more to me than just the handsome and charming man in front of you?"

Eve's smile widened, and his stomach tightened. She was beautiful to begin with, but the smile made her stunning.

"Seriously," she prompted. "Beyond that you can change into an eagle, I know nothing. Is it a spell of some kind that allows you to shift?" Skepticism lurked behind the question.

"Sort of."

"You like being vague on purpose, don't you?"

Logan took the damp cloth from her and started on the dishes. "The elders of my clan date back to the days when the Greek gods weren't just considered mythical."

Her mouth dropped open. "You're a god?" Her tone matched that of a doubtful child who just pulled the beard off a department store Santa.

"Half god would be closer to the truth. A very long time ago eagles were the messengers of the gods. There was a mortal, very loyal to Zeus, and as a gift the man was rewarded with immortality and the ability to change into the form of a creature Zeus so admired. After a time the man returned to Zeus because he was lonely and wanted a mate who could share both the earth and the sky with him. Zeus not only granted his request, but gave each member of both the couple's loyal families the same gift, just asking for their commitment of help whenever he should need them."

"And those original family members are your elders?"

"Some of them."

She let that sink in, then asked, "And how old are you?"

"Four hundred and fifty-four." Logan finished the last dish and set it on the rack. He let the drain out of the sink, the swirling water reminding him how long it had been since he last enjoyed a bath or shower. Staying clean had been easier in eagle form, and right now the thought of a shower sounded too damn good to ignore.

"Would you mind if—"

"You'd probably like a—"

They exchanged smiles. "A shower then?" Eve suggested.

At his nod she led the way up the back stairs. Even his surroundings faded to the back of his mind as he studied the tempting curve of Eve's ass. The black pants were a snug fit, and all Logan could think about was slowly working her pants down to find out if the sweet curves were as smooth to the touch as he imagined.

Eve paused on the stairs. Logan was too busy staring at her behind to notice right away and barely avoided a collision that would have sent them tumbling.

"Were you just checking out my butt, eagle eyes?"

Logan laughed. "If you mean staring, then yes, I was."

She continued up the stairs. "And how does it stack up to the other vampires you know?"

"If you're fishing for whether or not I've ever been with a vampire, the answer is no. But I do find the prospect very appealing."

237

Eve stopped at the top of the stairs, and Logan waited for her to turn around.

She didn't. "I was actually just wondering if you thought I had a nice ass, but that will do."

Logan heard the smile in her voice and followed her down the hall.

"Bathroom is in here. Towels are in the closet next to the window." She started into the bathroom, but changed her mind and turned back around.

He didn't give her an inch as she drew in a deep breath, obviously not having realized he followed so close. His eyes drifted past the smooth porcelain skin, the few freckles dusted over each cheek, and lower to the soft swell of her cleavage.

"If you need anything else..." She trailed off, her gaze locked on his.

Logan propped a hand against the doorjamb. "I think I'll be fine."

"Good," she breathed.

The sweet scent of roses that Logan identified as Eve's tantalized his senses.

"You're blocking the door," she pointed out, her voice only a notch above a whisper and as sultry as a siren's.

"Am I?" Logan reached out and smoothed his finger down her cheekbone to her jaw.

The next soft sigh to pass her lips ignited a buried craving to do more than touch her face.

"Eve?" His heart pounded through his chest, his insides hot and hard.

She nibbled on the inside of her cheek again. "Yeah?"

"I want to kiss you. Badly." He leaned in.

She planted a hand against his chest. Logan watched the war wage in her eyes before she shook her head. "I'll be down the hall in my office if you need anything."

It crossed his mind to block her exit more fully when she tried to slip past him, but he let her go. For now.

Logan lost track of time as he made no rush to shower quickly, savoring the hot water that sluiced down his body. By the time he finished, the room was a soft cloud of steam. Staring at his reflection in the mirror for the first time in fifty years wasn't full of surprises. The only thing that changed was his hair and not much at that. He dug through the vanity drawers, frowning over more than a few things he would have to ask Eve about later.

When he couldn't find what he was looking for, he wrapped a thick towel around his waist and went looking for Eve. He found her seated in front of a small screen, a flat typewriter of some kind beneath her fingers, but she wasn't typing. She stared out into space.

Eve swiveled her chair around just as he opened his mouth. It was the barely veiled hungry expression on her face that stalled his request on his tongue. The burning gaze she trailed over him left no mistake that she felt the same attraction he did.

He swallowed against the longing that rose up in him sharp and swift. "Scissors?"

She blinked. "What?"

"Do you have a pair of scissors?"

She stood and crossed to another desk, opened a long drawer, and then handed him a black-handled pair.

He stared down at them. "Could you...cut my hair?"

"You want me to cut your hair?"

"If I say yes, are you going to echo me again?"

The sensual curve of her mouth stirred the growing lust swirling through his gut.

"Just a bit," he clarified.

Hesitant, she finally nodded and followed him back to the bathroom.

Eve gestured to the chair she pulled from the corner. She held out her hand for the scissors. "If you're sure?"

"I am." He slid into the chair, and bit down when she pushed her fingers through his damp hair. She lightly worked them through before she used the comb. He closed his eyes as she went to work, savoring the small connection to her for as long as it lasted. The time passed all too quickly as his mind took the soft glide of her fingers over his scalp and imagined them sliding over his naked skin.

"I haven't cut anyone's hair in a long time. What do you think?"

Logan opened his eyes, found she'd taken a few inches off, bringing his black hair closer to jaw length. He met her gaze in the mirror. "Perfect."

She came around front to inspect her work, and once more tunneled her fingers through the front of his hair.

He caught her hand and pulled her down to his lap. He gave her three seconds to get away from him, three seconds to be sure she wanted to kiss him. Then he lowered his mouth to hers, sweeping across her lush mouth.

Logan moaned at the taste of her, more so when her lips yielded to him completely. He deepened the kiss with one slow stroke of his tongue after another.

She curled her arms around his neck and shifted in his lap so she straddled him. The action rocked her center against his already hard cock.

He growled softly, holding her close. She started to pull back, then her eyes drifted shut.

He nipped the corner of her mouth. "Did you want to say something?"

Eve dragged her teeth along the edge of his jaw. "Yeah, don't stop."

Chapter Four

Logan cupped her chin and coaxed her mouth back to his. With bone melting precision he slowly skimmed over her lips. Each soft pass made Eve's body clench until she trembled. He made no attempt to hurry, but savored each gentle nip and hot stroke as though kissing her could last for centuries.

Eve moaned into his mouth, the feverish ache deep in her sex pulsing stronger. His hand slid under the hem of her shirt and splayed across her lower back. She leaned into him, seeking more of the warmth that radiated off him. He threaded his fingers into her hair, holding her steady as he left her mouth, searing a hot path from her jaw and down her throat.

At the same time, his other hand moved under her shirt and up her side. His thumb brushed the side of her breast. Eve couldn't decide which ache she needed him to soothe first, her hardening nipples, or between her legs. She shifted on his lap, rubbing against the steel arousal nestled close.

He groaned and gripped her hips, tugging her harder against him.

"Oh." Her breathless response followed the electrified contact.

Logan offered up a decadent grin. "More?"

With a shaky nod, Eve waited for exactly that.

He pushed her shirt up and palmed one full breast. She arched her back, lifting it higher. Logan gently rolled the tight peak back and forth between his thumb and finger. Then he leaned forward to catch her whimper with his mouth. Almost as though he moved in perfect sync, his tongue slid over hers as his fingers plucked her nipple.

The sensation deep in her core coiled into a fiery tangle of need, and when he bent his head and first laved, then sucked her nipple between his lips, Eve cried out.

For endless seconds he repeated the same deliciously thorough torture on each breast before he trailed his hand lower. He rested his palm on the inside of her thigh. His haunting amber gaze raked over her face, asking without words if things should stop.

Eve placed her hand over his, and guided it between her legs. It had been too long since she felt such potent hunger for anything other than blood.

A soft growl worked up Logan's throat as he pressed his hand against her sex. She rocked into his palm, desperate for more pressure there. She had no doubt he knew it and deliberately traced her cleft through her pants with a feather-light touch meant to drive her wild.

Again, he closed his mouth over a nipple, sucking harder this time. Eve whimpered and ground against him.

"Stand up," he coaxed.

She did and closed her eyes when his fingers dipped past her waist and massaged her skin with lazy circles. He unbuttoned the top fastening and tugged the zipper down, his eyes never leaving hers.

In the back of her mind she registered the phone ringing and heard the answering machine down the hall in her office click on.

Logan stood and reached around, sliding his hand inside the back of her pants and down over her bare ass. He pulled her flush against him, his arousal nudging her belly with the sweetest friction.

Static filled words filtered through the sensual fog, and Eve tensed as she recognized Kyle's voice. No matter how badly she had wanted to talk to him earlier, she might have ignored this call if not for the edge of concern that laced the few words she could make out.

Logan didn't protest when she eased away from him and then sprinted down the hall. Her hand closed over the phone, but the click that echoed over the machine said he'd already hung up. Eve hit the playback button.

"An important call?" Logan guessed coming up behind her. He slipped his arms around her waist, the affectionate gesture flooding her body with a different kind of warmth, but one just as strong as when he touched her seconds ago.

Eve tensed as Kyle's voice replayed through the machine. With so much interference on the line, she could only make out the words cage, careful, and be there soon.

Perplexed, she played the message again, but got nothing more from the message the second time. She immediately dialed his cell number, not really surprised but still concerned when he didn't pick up.

"A good friend of yours?" Logan asked. He withdrew from her and scanned the room.

"Yes." She caught the flicker in his eyes before he went back to looking around, and added, "Just friends."

He nodded, a sheepish grin pulling at the corners of his mouth.

"He's the one who...sent you here."

Logan frowned. "Why here?"

"That's what I've been wondering since I spotted the crate. He didn't know about you did he?"

"That I was anything other than an eagle? No."

Kyle's message made no sense. Was he warning her to be careful or telling her he needed to be careful. And that made even less sense. Once more she tried his cell and hung up with a stab of her finger moments later.

Why wasn't he answering? Either way he was on his way back. Soon she'd find out what was going on.

From the corner of her eye she watched Logan pick up her PDA. He peered intently at the small screen when he accidentally turned it on. No matter what Kyle was trying to tell her, she knew he couldn't have been warning her about Logan. If Kyle hadn't known about him, then there couldn't have been any ulterior motives for delivering it to her place.

"I have a lot to catch up on, don't I?" Logan asked with a mix of excitement and wariness.

"You can stay here as long as you need to."

243

Eve hadn't realized she'd made up her mind to let him stay until the words left her mouth.

He blinked, as if equally surprised by her offer. A slow smile eased over his lips. "Thank you. I don't think it will take too long to learn what I need to confront my brother on an even playing field."

"Will he try to kill you?"

He shrugged. "Probably."

She started to tell him not to go, not to face his brother, but it wasn't her place to deny him justice for being locked away.

"Is your brother a prominent person?"

"Why do you ask?"

"Here," she moved to the computer, "you can Google him."

Logan laughed. "What?"

"It's a search engine." She glanced over her shoulder and caught the curious look on his face.

"It's a computer," she explained as she clicked to open the web browser. "And the internet is one big source of information."

"I can find information about my brother on this?" He sounded as skeptical as she had before she let him out of the cage.

For the next few minutes she went through the basics, right down to how to use the mouse, letting him experiment with it. He caught on quicker than she expected, his grin widening with every awkward stroke of a key.

She offered to help him, but he declined. Eve figured his insistence on doing it alone had to do with not wanting to tell her anything further about his brother and their feud.

"I need to sleep soon," she added before leaving him to play on the net.

He turned the chair around, not looking as out of place as she would have imagined a stranger in a towel would be in her office.

He took her wrist and drew her down. "Good night," he whispered then slid his lips over hers.

Slow and sweet, he coaxed her tense muscles into complete meltdown. Just when she wanted to sink deeper into the kiss, he pulled back. Regret flashed in his eyes as he released her arm. "I'll be sure not to disturb you until sunset."

"I can still talk if you need anything though, so just knock on my door and I'll hear you. And help yourself to whatever you want in the kitchen."

"I will."

"Good." Without a good reason to keep standing there when he obviously wanted to start researching, she said, "Night, Logan." By the time she reached the door she could hear the slow pound of keys.

Inside her room she made sure the shutters and fail—safes for the bedroom's only window were working. She perched on the edge of her bed with her laptop. There would be no work tonight. Not with the sexy shapeshifting stranger in the house. Just to be on the safe side she keyed in the automatic lock on her side of the door. As much as she wanted to trust him when he promised no harm would come to her, she hadn't lived this long by being careless. It was always better to be safe than sorry.

So then why did it feel like she was locking him out of more than just her room?

ဆဝ03

Logan sat in the chair across from Eve's bed. After three days she'd left her door unlocked, and he hadn't been able to resist a peek at her. When he had entered, she opened her eyes and gave him a sleepy smile and then drifted back to sleep. But not too deeply, he suspected.

She had actually goaded him into sparring with her in her impressive home gym. While he was pretty agile, she moved fast and with a sharp precision that bespoke years of training. Logan was confident if he dove at the bed, she'd probably have him pinned before the blankets even settled back into place.

Now that he thought about it, that didn't sound like such a bad idea. He could all too easily imagine peeling the sheet down to reveal one luscious inch of her after another. Her bare shoulders peeked out from the top of the sheet, and his cock twitched at the thought of her sleeping naked.

In three days he hadn't made a single move to finish what he'd started the first night. He wasn't staying much longer, couldn't risk leading Dominic here. And as much as his body craved her, somehow his conscience temporarily overrode his lust. There was much to settle with his brother before he could even hope to satisfy his growing need to drown in the woman in the bed opposite him.

If she had at least initiated something, had given him any indication that whatever he could offer her now was fine, he'd already be in bed with her. But she hadn't. In fact, she went out of her way not to touch him whenever possible. He wondered if it had to do with the call from her friend his first night in the house.

Eve stirred under the covers. Logan took one more minute before she woke to study the beautiful face relaxed in sleep. He wanted to kiss the soft splash of freckles across her nose, then her cheeks and her mouth.

Her brilliant blue eyes opened. A dreamy grin curved her lips.

His heart kicked up at the sexy, vulnerable picture she made lying there, and he dug his fingers into the chair to keep himself in place.

"How long have you been sitting there?"

"An hour."

The sheet slipped lower when she lifted her arms over her head in a feline stretch. He ran his gaze over the smooth flesh to the top of one breast. His new pants grew tight across the seam of his zipper.

"How's the research coming?" She propped herself up on her elbows.

"Not so good," he lied. At this point the less she knew about his clan the safer she was. Once things were settled he could tell her without fear that her freeing him would bring her pain.

"How long have you been a vampire?"

Eve laughed. "I thought we covered that."

"No, you told me a woman never divulges that information. That's not an actual answer."

"Sure it is."

"Women who will forever look to be in their twenties don't get the same liberties." He waited to see if she would change the subject again.

Eve sighed. "Two hundred and fifty one."

The age, while it didn't surprise him, reminded him how very little he knew about vampires. He knew they fed on blood, slept during the day, weren't fond of ingesting garlic and could read people's thoughts.

"Where do you come from...vampires?" he added. "How did you come to be?"

Her answer surprised him. "No one really knows."

Logan frowned. "How can no one know their origins?"

Eve shrugged.

"It doesn't bother you not to know your roots?"

Her gaze darkened. "I'm more than familiar with my roots."

The veiled pain he heard in her voice was indication enough she wasn't speaking of the vampire race, but her own roots. He took a guess. "You were turned against your will."

Eve sat up, looked ready to rise, then remembered she wasn't wearing anything under the sheet.

Logan moved to the edge of the bed. "Tell me."

She glanced away and he sat in patient silence until she was ready to tell him.

"My husband betrayed me."

"You were married?" He shouldn't have been surprised.

"Once. It wasn't a love match by any stretch of the imagination. He had a friend who had been turned and the change twisted something inside of him. He came after my *husband*," she all but spat the word, "and my husband, smooth talker that he was, told his friend he should take me instead."

"So he changed you."

"Eventually, yes."

Eventually? Logan frowned as the implications of what she must have endured before that time sank in. A rush of anger swam through his belly. He clenched a fist. "Are they both dead?"

Eve gave him a half smile. "My creator still lives, but my husband, he was betrayed himself and died in front of me before I was turned."

"And all this time you've never found another one worthy of you?" One Logan didn't want to choke for his cowardice.

"No. I have never wanted to bond myself to another forever."

"Vampires bond forever?"

She nodded. "It's hard not to drink from each other while we make love, and when two vampires do that it joins their life forces."

Logan was bizarrely pleased she hadn't found a mate. "I still don't understand how no vampire knows about your history."

"I've had two hundred and fifty years to accept it. There are two minds, those who believe that our true origins are purposely kept secret from all but a few—"

"To what end?"

"Who can say? Power is knowledge. Perhaps they know something they don't wish to share. The other mindset is that there are no real origins and vampires just...are."

Eve shifted in bed, clearly indecisive about whether or not she should get up or ask him to leave.

Before he could think the action through, he leaned forward and grasped the sheet. Their eyes locked, and Logan gently tugged the thin cover down.

She made no move to stop it. The sheet slid over her flesh in one smooth wave. His eyes were instantly riveted to the pale, full breasts, naked for him. Under his gaze, the rosy tips hardened.

Logan reached out, filled his palm with one breast and drew the pad of his thumb over her nipple. He hadn't meant to start anything. Or hadn't he? He'd known coming here would tempt him. He moved closer and bent his head to close his lips over the rock hard peak. Her soft whimper made him suck harder.

Eve tunneled her hands through his hair, holding him to her. Logan moved to the other breast, curling his tongue around her, then pulling her deeper into his mouth.

Her back arched, and Logan pulled her down in the bed so she was again flat on her back. He slanted his mouth over hers, and groaned when she swept her tongue across his.

The taste of her licked through his veins, twisted his stomach and made his already hard cock, ache. He tipped her chin up, kissed her again then moved to her jaw and down.

"I don't want to stop this time." He nipped the side of her throat. "I want to taste every inch, stroke every curve," he trailed a finger over her breast and nipple. "And I don't want to stop until I've made you scream for me." He sealed his lips over the peak again and sucked hard.

Eve moaned, her body bowing up to his mouth. "Who said you had to stop?"

He searched her face. "I'll have to leave soon."

Only a brief flicker of disappointment dimmed her eyes before she blinked it away. "I know."

He smiled, the look in her eyes giving him a reason to come back to better get to know the vampire who had proved to be the most intriguing woman he'd met in centuries.

Eve cupped his face and brought him down to meet her mouth. This time the kiss was hungry, passionate and he felt it all the way down his spine.

She nipped then teased her tongue over his bottom lop. "And I don't care if the house burns down around us. Don't stop touching me."

Chapter Five

Logan's sexy grin confirmed that following her gut was the right decision. She wanted him, craved his touch. The desperate need simmering under her skin felt way too good to stop. And he'd be leaving. She knew when she told him he could stay as long as he needed, he wouldn't take her up on it for long.

He might never return and if she didn't let this moment happen now, she knew she'd regret it later. She'd rather have the memory of one scorching night in Logan's arms than spend a century wondering how he would look poised above her and locked deep inside her.

Her core throbbed, the images in her mind jacking her internal temperature a hundred degrees.

Logan sat up and peeled the sheet all the way down her body. Only for a second did she feel exposed, then enjoyed how every place his gaze touched warmed up.

He didn't touch her, but drank her in with those piercing amber eyes.

More comfortable now, Eve rolled to her side. "Maybe you didn't understand me when I said don't stop touching me."

Logan laughed, the sound rich and sexy. "It's been a while since I've done anything more than fantasize about a beautiful woman within my reach."

"Good thing this isn't a fantasy." She sat up long enough to drag his shirt over his head, then tugged him down on top of her.

The warm weight of his body, strong and potent, did incredible things to her stomach.

Logan nipped her bottom lip and kissed her deeply. She wrapped her arms around his neck, anchoring him to her. The silky stroke of his tongue flamed the fire blazing inside her.

She cradled him between her thighs, and he rocked against her. The hard press of his cock made her wish she'd stripped off more than just his shirt. Instead, each roll of his hips tormented her. She wanted to feel every inch of him sink into her, hard and fast, over and over and all he wanted to do was push his arousal against her sex with light teasing arches.

Logan drew back and moved down her, trailing hot kisses in his wake. His cupped her breast, her nipples tight and hard. She arched up, brought them closer to his mouth. He captured one between his lips and rewarded her with a series of slow, wet tugs.

Eve cried out, urgency snaking through her blood. She strained beneath him, her core stretched taut and aching. She needed his hand there, fingers caressing her towards the release that hovered. But instead of sliding his fingers inside her, he positioned himself between her bent knees and slid his palms under her ass.

Logan bent his head and flicked his tongue over her clit in a lazy swirl. Her whimper turned into a deep-throated moan as he laved the tight knot before he sealed his mouth over it and sucked. He barely kept her on the bed, and when he drew back to trace her damp slit with his fingers, she went out of her mind. The coiled threads deep in her womb quivered at the breaking point.

He slid a thick finger inside her. Two slow, easy glides and he added another.

"Logan." Her breathless plea got trapped between their mouths as he reared up and caught her lips. He continued one wicked pump of his fingers after another, faster now.

Beneath the sheer carnal craving, a new hunger wove through her system. She hadn't yet fed and the pleasure of Logan's touch brought a fresh desire thundering to the surface. Her eyes were drawn to the strong curve of his neck and the vein that pulsed there.

No. She couldn't. Not this time.

A flicker in his eyes told her he knew exactly what she was thinking, studying his throat so intently. Not looking concerned about it, he smiled and brushed her clit with his thumb. One need fought with the other for control, but Logan made up her mind for her when he slowly parted her slick cleft with one delicate caress after another before filling her once more.

Eve lifted her hips, riding his hand with every thrust. Another quick circle over her sensitive clit and Eve burst apart. Her nerve endings melted together in a hazy, satisfied fog.

Logan stripped out of his pants, gripped her hips and drove between her thighs. Wild now, he didn't seek to draw out the torture but buried his cock inside her again and again.

"Eve." Logan closed his eyes, his jaw clenched. "You feel too good." He pulled back and rocked back in. "Too tight. Damn..."

He pushed her legs over his arms, changing the angle. Now he stroked the sensitive bundle of nerves deep in her sex and her inner muscles squeezed around him, fighting to keep him from withdrawing each time.

"If you keep doing that—" He leaned down, his mouth hungry as he kissed her like a man drunk on tasting her.

She swayed up to meet the next thrust and cried out, her orgasm breaking. Eve clung to him, heard his deep, satisfied growl as he came.

Logan hovered over her and dropped a soft kiss on her mouth before he rolled over and stretched out beside her. How easy it was to curl up against him, feel his heart pounding under her ear. Again Eve felt the bone deep craving for blood, but she pushed it down, not willing to sacrifice the overwhelming rightness of the moment for anything.

She closed her eyes and enjoyed the soft circles he drew on her arm. "Did you sleep much today?" Since he'd been here, he'd been keeping the same hours she did, but tonight he looked more tired.

"Some."

She tipped her face up. "It's because of the cage, isn't it?"

"Fifty years is longer than it seems, and when I close my eyes..."

"It's hard to remember you're not in there anymore."

Logan nodded. "But I am free of it. Thanks to you." He brushed a kiss across her forehead.

"Kyle was the one who found you."

"But you didn't have to let me out." He cupped her face. "Did I thank you for that?"

Another smile tugged at her lips. She'd been smiling a lot over the last few days actually. "You did. But I never tire of hearing it."

"Is that so?"

Something flashed in his eyes, and before she could interpret the look, he rolled over and pinned her to the bed. "Allow me to be very clear then." He slowly dragged his lips over hers. "Thank..." His tongue slid inside her mouth to tangle with hers for endless seconds. "You." He drew back. "I mean that. Truly."

And she believed him. Never did she recall anyone looking so sincere as Logan did right now. Eve lifted a hand to bring him back down, and froze.

Something wasn't right.

Logan didn't make a sound when she sat up, head cocked. She knew the house, knew every sound it made, every echo that drifted from any open window. She was on her feet and halfway to the door when she realized someone else was in the house with them.

Someone who didn't belong.

It was the soft flap that alarmed Logan the most. He feared they would track him here, to Eve. And somehow they had. Was his brother here too? Or had he remained behind to keep himself protected? How many had he sent to Eve's home?

Naked and annoyed, she looked ready to face whoever was in the house exactly as she was.

He grabbed her arm before she could get another foot away from him. "Get dressed and get out of here."

"This is my house." Determined eyes dared him to argue that point again. "I'm not going anywhere."

"They're here for me."

"No one is taking you anywhere."

Logan almost smiled. It wasn't fair that he was just getting to know her, getting to know this world and already the time for confrontation had come. It was what he wanted, just not now, not like this. Not with Eve so close. He didn't want to see anything happen to her.

She moved quickly to her closet and dressed. Logan yanked his own clothes back on, listening for any sign they had moved to the upper floor yet. He had to get her out of here. If she wouldn't go on her own then he'd take her. Dominic would use her if he thought it would hurt Logan, and he refused to let that happen.

Eve's head snapped up and he knew she heard someone moving up the back stairs, the same as he did. She flattened herself to the wall next to the door and when the stupid fool of a clansman entered the bedroom as though he belonged there, Eve beat Logan to him. She threw him against the wall, stunning the man. His clansman had been too busy staring at Logan in the middle of the room to pay attention to her. And even if he had, he might not have realized right away what she was.

Before the man could shift, Logan struck him, knocking him sideways. He grabbed Eve's hand and they raced from her bedroom and towards the back stairs. At least five of them were in the house and three were near the foyer.

"Back door," he whispered.

She shook her head. "The unwanted guests are leaving."

"No. They could hurt you."

"I'm just as strong, and maybe even faster."

"But they can shift and I know the sight of my talons made you uncomfortable. Let's not be stupid here."

He was relieved when she didn't try to drag him in the opposite direction, towards trouble. Even as they crept downstairs, he could see the wheels spinning behind her eyes. She didn't want to leave them in her home and he didn't want her confronting them.

Logan heard the running footsteps headed in their direction as they hit the bottom stair. Two burst through the kitchen door. One he definitely recognized. His brother's friend, Mitchell.

"The council wants to talk to you." Mitchell made no move to grab them, his hard gray gaze pinning them in place.

"Your council can go to hell." Eve glared at the two men, clearly not intimidated by them. Every second he found something to admire about her even though at this moment he wished she wouldn't provoke them.

Logan stayed close to her. "You can tell my brother his plan failed. He can no longer pass me off as the traitor from the prophecy. And I'll make sure everyone knows the real truth."

Mitchell frowned, but didn't appear swayed by Logan's plan.

Eve took that moment and snatched the closest frying pan off the middle island and biffed it at the two men. The man next to Mitchell didn't respond fast enough and took a direct hit to the chest.

Logan didn't wait for them to retaliate, but snared Eve's hand and hauled her to the back door. The others pounded down the back stairs.

Outside Eve finally gave up on going back in and led the way to the garage. The side door was open and she locked it behind them after they slipped inside. She snatched a set of keys off the hook by the door.

"Get in."

He stared at the car, having only seen such vehicles on the television he spent much of the time watching while Eve slept. With no time to spare he slid into the passenger seat of the white Ford Mustang. He remembered this one from a commercial with a buxom blonde behind the wheel, her breasts pouring out the top of her tight white shirt, as she flirted her way out of a speeding ticket.

Eve punched the button to open the garage door and she managed to back the car out in a peal of rubber on asphalt before the first eagle speared across his peripheral vision.

"How fast does this thing go?"

"Faster than they can fly."

"You remember that part when I mentioned we're all half-gods, right?"

Eve laughed. She swung the car around and dragged the stick in between them into another gear. The car shot forward. "They might stick close for a while..."

More eagles shot past them.

"Damn you guys are big." She jerked the wheel to the side, hit the release for the security gate out front and narrowly scraped through the opening gates without taking paint off the car.

"This is like something out of one of my books you know. Minus the eagles." Though she said it with amusement, he could hear the underlying tension in her voice.

"I'm sorry you got caught up in this."

"I'm not." She shot him a reassuring smile. "But they sure as hell had bad timing."

The last of the pursuing eagles faded into the background. How had they found him? Were they somehow able to track his shipment? Or had Eve's friend told them? His brother could be persuasive when he wanted to be. And that could explain why Kyle still hadn't arrived. Dominic might have caught up with him and detained him, but Logan didn't share that theory with Eve.

"I hope Kyle is okay." She glanced at him, looking for confirmation.

Logan didn't say anything. It was all too possible his clansmen were holding on to him. He doubted they would be crazy about holding another immortal. In many ways the vampires Logan had come across kept to themselves, but he had heard a handful of stories about them supporting each other when needed, especially when some of their keepers, hunters of some kind, decided to control the vampire population in a way that broke the few rules Eve outlined to him the other night. Their hunters could only interfere with vampires when they turned too many humans, preyed on the innocent, or threatened to expose their kind. A cross between human and vampire, the hunters had been around as long as vampires from what Eve said.

As much as he was at odds with his clan for locking him away, Logan had no wish to see bloodshed. No one had any way of knowing what holding a vampire could bring about. Maybe nothing, maybe more trouble.

"Open the glove box for me?"

Logan followed her gaze and released the lock on the drop down compartment.

"Hand me the cell phone."

It took him a minute to identify the folded silver case as the *cell phone*. It wasn't the same as the one he saw in her house, nor did it look exactly like some of the ones he'd seen on television. People of this age certainly appreciated diversity in their toys.

He handed it to her. "Calling the police?" He couldn't see the vampire contacting the authorities over something that would be impossible to explain.

Eve shook her head. Skillfully dividing her attention between the phone and the road, Eve flicked it open and keyed in a number.

"Damn, voice mail." Eve frowned then spoke into the phone. "Abbey, steer clear of my place for a few days. I ran into a little complication with some of Logan's *friends*. I'll call you soon."

Logan had enjoyed having someone to talk to off and on during the last couple of days while Eve slept. Even being out of the cage, he still found himself seeking out any distraction that would make him feel less alone. After the last half-century, he was eager to spend time with anyone other than himself.

He glanced over at Eve. "Where are we going?"

Eve drove them deeper into the city. "Someplace safe."

Someplace turned out to be an apartment over a small, run-down bar that looked like the primary patrons were bikers. The second Eve strode through the door, Logan felt a dozen pair of eyes zero in on them, on her.

She ignored them all and breezed to the bar. "Is Brett around?"

The skinny redhead behind the bar shook his head. "On a date."

"Really?"

"She's a hot one too." The guy held his hands out in front of him. "Tits like a—"

"Do not make me jump the bar," Eve warned.

The man grinned as though he expected her response, and then bent down to search for something under the counter. He held out a pair of keys. "The place is yours for as long as you need it. I assume that's why you're here."

Eve leaned over the bar and planted a kiss on the bartender's face. "Thanks."

The man actually sent Logan a smug look. The only thing that stopped Logan from addressing it was the strong grip Eve had on him. She led him through the crowded bar, down a hall and outside to the back alley and a set of metal stairs they climbed.

Inside the above apartment, she shut the door behind them. "Tell me everything. Why did they lock you up? You said it was your brother who did it. Why?"

Logan barely registered the apartment's comfortable furnishings. "Who's Brett?"

"Just a friend. Stop avoiding the question."

Logan merely arched a brow.

Eve rolled her eyes. "He and Kyle are good friends. They found me not long after I was changed and both have a fondness for playing big brother. Satisfied? Now, your brother...locked you away..." She trailed off meaningfully.

"Because of a prophecy."

"About what?"

"A member of my clan who will threaten our kind's existence."

"And they think you're the one," she said hesitantly.

He tugged his shirt off and showed her the tattoo. "I think this has something to do with it."

She brushed her fingers over it, her touch gentle. Gentle to the point it dipped under his skin and skated through his blood. "How does this fit into the prophecy?"

"I don't know exactly, only that when the others of my clan saw it, it was what condemned me." Before the next line of logical thinking could cross her mind, he added, "And before you ask if maybe they know something I don't about the significance of my tattoo, then you need to know my brother has the same one."

Eve frowned. "You both got the same tattoo?"

He shook his head. "We were born with them."

"Is that a common thing for your clan or family, to be born with such a mark?"

"No."

"And you think it's your brother the clan should be worried about. But don't they know he has the same one?"

Logan nodded. "They should, but my brother was sick often when we were kids and the sun was hard on him, so he seldom went anywhere without his clothes on. I never got the chance to remind them. But I'm sure he must have told them something else to convince them I was the one who should be locked away."

"They won't lock you away again." The vow touched him far more than he wanted it to, even as ridiculous as it was for her to think she could stop members of his clan if they caught up with them.

Logan drew her close and kissed her, the gesture the only way he could tell her how much he appreciated her being there. He rested his forehead against hers. "I need to face my brother."

"Not tonight."

"Eve," he began.

She shook her head. "You walk out that door and I'm right on your heels."

"This is not your fight."

"They made it mine when they walked into my house."

His palms framed her face. "I don't want you involved."

A steely determination filled her eyes. "Then you shouldn't have asked me to let you out of that cage."

Chapter Six

At the sound of footsteps on the outside stairs, Eve tensed. How could they have been followed? She made a move for the door, only to have Logan bring her to a stop.

"Eve?"

Relief pitched through her.

Kyle.

Reassured by her smile, Logan let her go.

She opened the door and Kyle grinned at her. "I was hoping I'd find you here. You okay?" He swept his gaze head to foot, then his gray eyes landed on Logan.

He moved around her to stand protectively between her and Logan as she shut the door. "Is he one of them?" Kyle asked.

"You've come across them then?"

"Not until two days ago. I knew something was up when I called you. I was actually followed and got a bad vibe. I didn't know at first it was because of him."

Eve moved closer to Logan. "I've been trying to get in contact with you since then."

"I ditched my phone. I think some of his people were using it to track me."

Logan crossed his arms. "How do you know they didn't follow you here?"

"I was careful."

Logan didn't appear convinced. He glanced at Eve. "We shouldn't stay here."

Eve knew Kyle would never knowingly bring trouble to her door. He would have been careful, but if he knew even less about Logan's clan than she did, there was no telling if he'd been successful.

Right now she didn't want them getting close to Logan. The thought of them forcing him back into that cage made her gut clench. Only this time he might not get so lucky as to have someone like Kyle stumble across him. If they even bothered with a cage the next time. She had no idea what his kind were capable of if they truly believed he was a serious threat to them.

"Maybe we should go. Abbey's family has a summer place not too far from here. It would do for now." There were more than enough hours of darkness left to ensure they arrived well before sunrise.

"We should stay put." Something about the firm insistence in Kyle's voice concerned her.

She searched his face. "What's going on?"

He frowned, but it fell short of convincing. "What do you mean?"

Her stomach bottomed out. "What did you do, Kyle?"

"Eve..." Guilt plagued his features before he turned away from her.

"You cut a deal with them, didn't you?" Logan didn't sound surprised.

Kyle straightened, his finger pointed accusingly. "I won't have her caught up in your feud."

"They're coming for him, aren't they?" She didn't need the confirmation reflected on Kyle's tight expression. She reached out for Logan. "We need to go."

He tensed, his gaze already on the door. "Too late." He turned to Kyle. No animosity showed on his face. "Get her out of here."

Kyle had the decency to look uncertain before he started to push her towards the stairs leading to the loft's rooftop exit.

Eve shoved him back. "No." She didn't know who she was more furious with, Kyle for making a deal with Logan's clan or Logan because he continued to try to keep her out of something she had a stake in now. Logan had edged under her skin and she wasn't about to tuck tail and run. If his clan wanted him, then she planned to stay right there and fight them every step of the way.

"Now's not the time to argue about this. These people mean business, Eve."

She glared at Kyle. "I'll deal with you later. If you want to go, there's the door." She stood opposite Logan. "How can you challenge your brother if they take you with them?"

His silence spoke for itself. If they took Logan before he could confront his brother without him expecting it, Logan wouldn't get the opportunity he needed.

"I'm staying."

Angry now, Logan gripped her arm and propelled her to the stairs. "You're not."

Three sets of feet started down the steps above them at the same time the side door crashed open.

More than ten shifters blocked the exits.

Eve knew she could take a couple of them down, but had serious doubts the three of them would get through all of Logan's clan members. Not when she suspected they were each as strong as Logan.

She offered a faint smile in face of the circumstances. "Maybe I should have just locked myself in the cage with you."

"Ah, but such a dynamic creature such as yourself shouldn't be locked away, but enjoyed to the fullest."

Eve stared at the blond-haired man who strolled through the door like he owned the room and everyone in it. The facial similarities between the newcomer and Logan made it apparent the two were related. Logan's brother, she assumed.

"The question now is," he continued. "What do I do with you before I take care of my brother for good?"

∞⋈

Eve prowled the inside of the basement room they'd locked her in. A few minutes ago she'd heard the low grunts of pain from another room close by and knew Dominic was hurting Logan. Fury turned her blood cold, but made her no more capable of getting out. The solid metal door had already taken a few good shoves and kicks and left her nothing but more frustrated and hurting.

"I screwed up, huh?" Kyle sat on the floor, his eyes closed, his dark head back against the wall.

"Do I have to answer that?"

"How could I know you had a thing for the guy?"

"I don't know what I feel."

"But you like him."

Eve nodded, but didn't look at her friend. She knew he had only been thinking of her and keeping her safe. But reassuring him of that fact didn't seem as important as how quiet things were.

What had they done to Logan?

"I was hoping he was still in the cage when I agreed to tell them where to find him. They promised they wouldn't hurt you."

She snorted. "Good thing they lived up to their word."

"They'll let us go."

"If they were leaving us out of it, they wouldn't have brought us here." Here being some old building in the run-down part of town. But what they planned to do with them was the next question. She'd known the odds weren't good when they were escorted from the apartment. She doubted that many were going to come through the room's only exit the next time and didn't plan on being as cooperative.

"What are you thinking?"

"How much I want to hurt Dominic."

"How do you know that the prophecy he's talking about isn't true?"

She arched a brow. "Because Logan was never anything but good to me while Dominic locked me in here. That makes it pretty clear in my book." Aside from the fact that looking into Dominic's pale blue eyes gave her the creeps, and few beings on the earth ever reduced her to being creeped out. She wrote gritty suspense novels thanks to her vivid imagination, not to mention the real life scary things she'd encountered so far in her lifetime. And none of that compared to the chilling look Dominic gave her hours ago.

"Sorry, Eve. I should never have sent the eagle to you in the first place."

"Why did you anyway?" Since pacing wasn't getting her anywhere, she sat down next to Kyle. Her friend looked tired and probably hadn't fed. She hadn't either and could feel the need gnawing at her insides. It was only her fear of what was happening to Logan that kept the hunger from consuming her.

"I figured you'd be the only one brave enough to go near it until I could get back home and decide what to do about it."

"How long until sunup you think?" Already she could feel herself growing tired. She might have been able to fight it off more effectively if she'd fed recently. Plenty of times before she'd gone a night without feeding, but never two. She should have gone out and fed the night before. Instead she and Logan had stayed in and watched movies until sunrise.

"A couple hours maybe."

Footsteps echoed in the hall and Eve bolted to her feet. She didn't, however, make it to the door before it swung inward.

Dominic stepped through, his hand up, and black talons where the tips of his fingers should have been. He'd been ready for her to attack.

He tipped his head. "Tell me, how long does it take for a vampire to bleed out?"

∞

Weak, Logan jerked at the chains holding him to the floor. Where was Eve? He hadn't been worried about her too much until his brother walked out of the room, leaving him alone with a guard to make sure he didn't shift to escape his bonds. The room wasn't large enough that shifting would have done him much good to begin with, but Dominic obviously didn't want to chance it.

He didn't trust Dominic not to hurt her, especially not after he spent the last couple of hours taunting Logan with his plans for the vampire. Logan doubted Dominic realized how capable Eve was. Hell, even her determination to stick by him when he insisted she stay out of it, didn't fail to impress Logan. He was torn between hoping she didn't lash out and provoke his brother, and wanting to see the stunned look on Dominic's face when she did.

He wiped at the trickle of blood dripping into his eye. He didn't hurt as much as he let on to Dominic. Letting his brother think he was still weak from being locked up could only work to his advantage, although at the moment he didn't have much of one. He might not have been up to his usual strength before Dominic cornered them, but he was pretty close. Close enough to take his brother down if given an opportunity. But his brother wasn't stupid and surrounded himself with clansmen who would foolishly try to protect Dominic.

He didn't know who was more stupid, his clansmen for blindly following Dominic, who already voiced designs on challenging Jack for leadership of their clan, or himself for not making a move the minute he found out where his brother was. He'd known the first night Eve showed him how to use the Internet. Discovering his brother was living no farther away than a couple states surprised Logan, and should have been the push he needed to face him. Instead he'd chosen to stay with Eve for a few days, and because of it she was here, somewhere, at his brother's mercy.

The door opened and Dominic shoved Eve inside.

Logan's gut clenched at the sight of her. At first relieved to see her unharmed, Logan's relief quickly faded. Icy apprehension dripped down his spine at the dark expression on Dominic's face.

Dominic pushed her again and Eve tripped forward. She caught herself and then whirled around on Dominic. His brother slashed out, the shifted talons cutting into her arm.

She cried out, cradling her injured arm to her chest.

Logan jerked on the chains, wanting to tear his brother apart for touching her.

"If you lay one more finger on her—"

Dominic cut off his warning with a vicious laugh. "You'll what?" He circled Logan. "I don't think you're in any position to make demands, traitor."

"The only one who has betrayed this clan is you."

Dominic smirked. "If that's the truth, then why were you the one imprisoned?" His brother turned back to Eve. "Didn't he tell you?"

"I don't believe you." Her bored tone only served to infuriate Dominic.

His brother glanced at Logan, then swung back, his open palm cracking across Eve's cheek.

She flinched and staggered back a step, but didn't whimper.

Bastard. Logan tore at the chains, anger driving his pulse to a thunderous roar that drummed in his head.

"I don't think he liked that." Dominic sneered at him, then reached for Eve again.

She dodged him, and when he tried to grab her a third time, she dropped into a crouch and swung her leg out, knocking Dominic off his feet.

Fear for Eve and a desperation to get her out of there, surged through Logan. Her fierce gaze locked on his and she lunged for him, grabbing the chains holding him to the wall. Together they pulled hard, but it wasn't enough.

Logan saw Dominic coming and maneuvered his body between his brother and Eve, taking the hard swing to his face. Pain snapped up his jaw, blurring his vision for a moment.

Eve went on the offense, but some of Dominic's men filled the space between them, ready to block any move she made.

Logan glared at his brother. "Eve, don't. The more you play with him, the more he enjoys it."

The twisted smile that Dominic shot Eve greased Logan's stomach. His brother was far from through with her, and Logan couldn't do a damn thing about it.

Feeling brave again, Dominic stepped around his bodyguards. "I do love a woman who likes to play games. I know all kinds I'd like to show you."

Eve cocked her head. "The whole intimidation tactic doesn't really do it for me. I write about more sadistic bastards than you for a living."

"Ah yes, you're a fiction author." Dominic ventured closer to Eve.

Logan bristled with every stalking step.

"The one difference though is that they aren't real." He raised his hand, waving his shifted talons tauntingly. "And I am."

Eve didn't even blink. "Fuck you."

"Bitch," Dominic snarled and launched himself at her.

"Playtime's over," another voice boomed from the doorway.

A mix of anger and relief flooded Logan.

Jack.

Looking every bit the leader he was, his oldest friend strode into the middle of the room. All eyes were riveted on the black-haired warrior who looked as though he'd dropped straight down from Olympus as their ancestors had.

At this point it didn't matter if they put him back in the cage or not, as long as Logan knew Eve was safe from his brother. Whatever feelings were left between him and Jack, he knew his friend wouldn't let her be used by Dominic.

Dominic glared at the intrusion. "I've got everything under control."

"I can see that," Jack said without looking at Dominic. His friend's gaze swung from Eve to Logan. What almost looked like guilt crossed the clan leader's face. "You didn't clear any of this with the council."

"I had to move quickly before he fled."

"If he was planning on running, do you think he would have stayed with the vampire for even this long?"

Dominic shrugged, but Logan recognized the animosity humming under his brother's cool exterior. "He was too weak to get far yet."

Jack noticed the blood on the floor. "And what were you doing with her?"

"The bitch attacked me."

"She defended herself." Logan's voice rang through the room.

Eve stood beside him, her bleeding arm ignored. She raised her chin, her piercing blue gaze locked on Jack. "And I'll attack you too if you take one step in Logan's direction."

A hint of a smile touched Jack's lips. "You always had a thing for the stubborn ones."

Confused by the tone in Jack's voice, Logan frowned.

"The council already made their decision," Dominic reminded Jack. "He was banished, and he will go back in the cage."

"Over my dead—"

Eve was just close enough he could slap his hand over her mouth, cutting off the serious warning. "Not helping."

The gesture earned him a frosty look.

"The council did make their decision. But there are customs that predate such decisions." Jack looked pointedly at Logan, reminding him that although Logan hadn't been given the chance earlier, he could defend himself now.

Logan straightened. With Eve having already helped loosen the chains, a good strong pull ripped the locking hook from the basement wall.

He looked at Jack. "I call upon my right to challenge a clan member."

"On what grounds?" Dominic sputtered, not liking the turn of events.

Logan almost grinned. "Betrayal."

"Granted." Jack stood back, taking Eve with him, who immediately jerked free.

"It's fine," Logan said, without taking his eyes off his brother.

Dominic launched himself at Logan.

Logan anticipated his brother's impulsiveness. They'd been fighting since they were children and his brother had never learned to watch his opponent and wait for the right opening, always expecting the first strike would give him the upper hand.

Today was no different. It was no wonder Dominic surrounded himself with clansmen. Even he must have recognized his own weakness.

Logan turned as his brother came at him, pitching Dominic over his shoulder. His brother's talons raked his shoulder, and Logan hissed. He pressed his hand to the searing wound.

Dominic smirked.

Taking his brother's lead, Logan shifted enough so his brother no longer had the edge, and his own talons were exposed.

Confidence drained from Dominic's face and he glanced at Jack.

Logan slowly shook his head. "He can't help you."

"You were banished," Dominic snapped at Logan.

"What did you tell them to convince them of my guilt?" Logan circled, waiting for an opening.

"The evidence spoke for itself." Dominic's voice wavered.

"Evidence that has recently been discredited by the council." Jack's announcement earned the desired reaction.

Dominic glowered. "Impossible."

From the corner of his eye, Logan saw Jack shrug. "Not really. Not when Logan's 'attempt' to divide the clan proved to be a fabrication and your present plans to challenge my authority were exposed."

"Lies," Dominic snarled. He lunged at Logan and caught him in the ribs with his fist. Eve made a move, but Jack caught her.

Dominic moved in again, and this time Logan moved out of his path, throwing the length of chain dangling from his wrist around his brother and taking him to the floor. Before Dominic could throw him off, Logan pressed the edge of his talon under his brother's chin.

They were immune from death by a number of things, but not each other. One clip of his jugular and it would be over.

"Did you betray me?" Logan demanded.

His brother was too much of a coward to deny it and risk death, and they both knew it. "Yes."

"Were you plotting against the clan?"

Dominic hesitated, and Logan nicked his flesh with the tip of his talon. "Were you plotting against the clan?"

"Yes," Dominic hissed.

Logan lifted his head and met Jack's gaze. "Bring in the cage."

ഇൗങ്ങ

"How's your arm?"

Eve's tentative smile loosened some of the tension in his chest. "How's yours?"

Both their wounds were bandaged, but already the healing had begun. Jack had taken away Dominic to be tried before the council. Before he left, he had apologized to Logan for not doing more sooner and promised that he'd spent at least half the time Logan had been locked away trying to find a way to expose Dominic. His brother had recently fouled up in confessing to the wrong person his plans to challenge Jack. Although challenges were allowed, Dominic boasted of his plan to partially poison Jack before he made the challenge.

After making arrangements to meet when Logan was ready, Jack and the rest of the clansmen left. With the sun up, Eve and Kyle couldn't go anywhere, and Kyle had already disappeared into one of the building's other rooms to sleep.

He and Eve retreated to a room that held a few pieces of furniture, among them a couch that looked passable enough to sleep on.

Eve gave him a tired smile. "You don't have to stay."

"I'm not leaving you here."

She closed her eyes, her brows drawn tight.

"What's wrong?" He closed the distance between them, catching her chin in his palm.

"Nothing."

She was lying, and she looked far too pale. "When did you feed last?"

"Night before last. I'll be fine. Just weak when I wake up."

"How weak?" He didn't like the way she refused to meet his gaze.

"It's fine."

He didn't believe her. "Does it hurt when you go too long?"

Eve moved away from him. "Can we just go to sleep?"

Well, there was his answer.

Logan stepped up next to her. "Use me."

Eve merely laughed at the suggestion. "I'm going to sleep now."

Logan gently gripped her elbow and brought her back to face him. "Why not? You're weak."

"And I'm not about to just drink from you."

He quirked a brow. "Afraid I might taste bad?"

"Let's drop it, okay?"

Unfortunately he recognized the stubborn streak in her, but after recalling the way her eyes had lingered just under his jaw hours ago... He wasn't worried she would take too much. He was strong enough he could get her off him if he had to. A little blood loss would be quick enough to recover from. After what he put her through tonight, he owed her.

And if he was being completely honest with himself, he wondered what it would feel like to have her drink from him.

Eve had her back to him when he walked up and slid his arms around her waist, drawing her back against his chest.

"Exactly how tired are you?" He trailed his mouth down the side of her neck, both relieved and turned on when a soft sigh escaped her lips.

"I'm open to a couple possibilities."

Logan slid his hands under her shirt and filled his palms with her breasts, softly dragging his thumbs over the nipples that peaked beneath his touch. "I was hoping you'd say that."

He unsnapped the front button on her pants and then eased them down her hips. Already hard, he pressed his cock against her, quickly losing himself in his own need. Their one time together hadn't been anywhere close to satisfying the fathomless craving he had for her.

Logan worked her pants all the way down, keeping her back to him. She arched against him, encouraging the slow trail of his fingers down over her smooth belly and to the soft curls between her legs. He stroked down the middle, parting her folds to find her clit, then purposely bypassed it to tease her opening.

She trembled in his arms, from a hunger for blood or for him, he didn't know. Lust zipped along his nerves and coiled into a ferocious need to take her. This was supposed to be about her, coaxing her to feed from him the only way he knew might tempt her. But with her lower body naked and tucked so provocatively against his, his own needs were roaring to the surface.

He dipped and swirled around her clit with one hand and used the other to cup her breast, rubbing and tugging one hard peak until Eve moaned.

In only a few lazy caresses, she was damp and ready for him.

Eve turned in his arms and tugged impatiently at his zipper. Fueled by the desire raging in her eyes, Logan pushed her hands away and stripped them down himself. He brought his fingers back to her sex, slipping two fingers inside her. She moaned and locked her hands on his shoulders as he withdrew and then pushed them back in.

"How hungry are you, Eve?"

Through glazed eyes she searched his face, catching onto him. She shook her head, but didn't pull away from him. "I won't do it, Logan."

He gently outlined the slick knot between her legs, then pumped inside her once more. "Don't fight it, Eve. Give in. Take from me. I want you to."

She shoved at his chest, but not hard enough to get away from him. "No."

Lifting her, Logan turned and perched her on the edge of the table against the wall. He bent his head and trapped a nipple between his lips, drawing it into his mouth. Over and over, he worked his fingers deep in her sex, feeling the silky heat clamp around him each time.

His cock ached with an insatiable need to be inside her, thrusting hard. "You don't really want me to stop, do you, Eve?"

"You don't understand, don't know what you're asking me to do." Her breathless explanation did nothing to sway him.

Logan pressed his mouth to her throat, scraping with his teeth. "I know exactly what I'm doing." He edged her thighs apart, half expecting her to stop him. The uncertain restraint on her face was nothing he couldn't overcome.

He gripped her ass and lifted her up, bringing her just a bit higher, then sank his cock fully inside her.

Eve groaned and sought out his mouth, her tongue hot and slick as it slid over his. Her panted breaths drove him crazy, and he rocked against her, one slow thrust after another. Then faster.

Logan saw her carnal gaze dart to his throat and this time he leaned forward as he stroked the head of his cock against the ribbed muscles deep within her.

She licked and sucked at the tender flesh beneath his jaw. Lost in the mindless rhythm of plunging into her, he pressed his throat more fully against her mouth, and shivered when she dragged her teeth over it.

He could feel release steamrolling closer and lifted her into his arms. Bracketing her between him and the wall, he used the leverage to drive into her harder.

Eve cried out and just as he came, her teeth pierced his throat. The sharp pain was quickly replaced by an erotic sensation that stormed through him, dropping him far over the edge.

The stinging returned for a moment as she drew back, not drinking from him as much as he expected.

She dropped her head on his shoulder. "Wow," she mumbled.

"Exactly." He carried her over to the couch and lay down with her.

"You were being underhanded there."

"You can make me pay for it later."

She smiled at him, the same smile that reached in and kick-started his heart. "Oh, I intend to."

He tipped her chin up for a long kiss. "I can't wait."

"You do realize my punishment will involve locking you away at my place until I tire of you." Eve snuggled against him, and he couldn't recall ever wanting a woman to be so close to him before.

"I guess I'll have to tell Jack I'm going to be preoccupied for a while then."

"A very long while. Is that going to be a problem?"

"No objections here." He brought his mouth down over hers. "As long as you cook for me, I'll be your permanent love slave."

"Love slave, huh? And you'll do anything I ask?"

He grinned. "I'm at your beck and call."

Her blue eyes glittered with anticipation. "You're gonna regret such a promise."

He smoothed her hair back from her face. The urge to kiss her into eternity filled every inch of his soul. "Somehow I doubt that."

About the Author

To learn more about Sydney Somers, please visit www.sydneysomers.com. Send an email to Sydney at sydney@sydneysomers.com or join her Yahoo! Newsletter to keep up to date on Sydney's upcoming releases, contest info and sneak peeks at what she's working on now. http://groups.yahoo.com/group/flirtingwithpassionnewsletter.

Seize the Hunter

Michelle M. Pillow

Dedication

To my fans. Thank you for your constant support. And to the wonderful authors—Jaycee, Mandy, Sydney and Shannon—who it has been my great pleasure and honor to work with on this anthology.

Chapter One

Princess Ari of the planet Falconia disliked the warriors who flew in the Falcoan Army, but none punctured her thoughts like Commander Rurik of the Fifth. She hated him and his smug, self-confident attitude. He'd thought himself so superior when they were children—swooping down to knock her on her ass so that her new gown would get covered in muck, or overtaking her in games because of his naturally enhanced stamina and strength—and all because he was born a falcon shifter. His kind was rare and given the utmost consideration, as they were destined to lead the armies that guarded her home planet from outsiders. All other warriors turned after birth, their powers enhanced by choice, not fate. Rurik was a falcon by destiny and it made him impossibly arrogant to deal with. He'd grown up training at her home in the palace and constantly around to torment her.

And now he was coming back.

Well, she had news for him. She was no longer the awkward, gangly girl he'd known. She'd gone through puberty late, very late, but her powers had come to her, as they did all non-shifting Falconians. She'd been sixteen seasons, nearly twenty-four years old according to the calendar they observed from the Old Way, and her father had begun to worry that she'd never bloom. Too bad Rurik had been deployed to his post merely days before it happened. She would've loved to prove him wrong about her.

It didn't matter. Now she was a powerful, envied princess, and soon she'd be queen. With her mother gone, she was the sole female of power on their planet. She controlled the armies. She controlled Rurik.

And, with the evening's coronation ceremony well upon her, she'd control the entire planet. Her father would step aside, for men did not rule as well as women. Falconian males' blood ran too hot.

That is why Rurik was coming back. All commanders were to be in attendance, for tonight was the shifting of power. But first, there was another ceremony—one that took place this very afternoon. Today she would drink from the sacred Chalice and awake next to the man who was to be their future king, her husband, her mate, her eternal lover. And it couldn't come too soon, as far as she was concerned.

Whereas normal women of their society could take as many lovers as they pleased, she was held to a higher standard. Until she married, she was allowed three semi-lovers with whom all pleasures of the flesh were allowed but one—the final claiming of her heart. If things got too close, she was obligated to end it. In a life that kept her in front of the eyes of all, she longed for someone to hold her in the night, to look at her with eyes not judging but seeing. She wanted the comfort and safety of a man who would not leave her.

Her first lover, a traveler and diplomat who visited them soon after her powers had come to her all those years ago, had been to spite Rurik. He'd been an *enfem*, a slender, pale man who spoke and acted as far from a hot-blooded warrior as possible without being an actual woman. She still cursed that wasted pick. Whereas he did hold her, he also cried most of the night speaking of his feelings. Falconian women were stronger than he was. The second man she thought she could someday love, until she realized that lust and love were two different things. The third was a practical choice, if not her best one. He'd been an older man, a trainer who instructed more than participated.

Ari looked at her reflection in the still water that made up one wall of her bedroom. She could touch the wetness, but magic kept it from caving in on her and soaking her. It was a good thing too. Her hair had taken three skilled hairdressers four hours to do. The waist-length red locks were twisted around strands of wire to keep it in place and then bent around her head to fashion an intricately beautiful crown. It towered above her, five hand spans high in the front and tapered down to a half span in the back.

Her gown was of the finest weave, held into place with a thick metal band that wrapped around her chest and back, leaving her tanned shoulders bare. The band was bent to fit her body perfectly, molding along the top of each breast to keep the flowing material that hung from it from falling down. The royal dark-red material moved with her, clinging and releasing her curves with each step as if it were air.

Holding her arms to the side, she waited as her attendants slipped silver coils onto her arms. They wound around from shoulder to wrist, decorated with the shiny black stones found only in the dark depths of Falconia's lucid waters. A matching stone hung from the chain that dangled from her hair, down the part in the middle of her head.

Black makeup outlined her large blue eyes, made all the more noticeable by a dark red stripe that stretched from temple to temple, encircled both eyes and crossed over the bridge of her nose. The red matched the color on her lips.

Turning, she looked to the mating bed that had been prepared in the center of the room. The Chalice never chose poorly or with cruel intentions. It was neutral and often its choice led to happiness for both parties. At least, it gave a happy start. What the two people did with the mating given them was up to the couple and there had been those who ruined a good thing.

Unlike the peasants who could draw a circle in dirt to form the mating circle, her bed was that of a princess. It was high up on a raised platform, so high she couldn't see the top of it from her place on the floor. Above it, the water wall curved with the true ceiling, giving her a reflection of thick gold and red pillows encircling the edges and an abundance of silk to lie upon. Sweet herbs were scattered on the floor around it. So strong was the ancient spell, no one could cross the herbs and reach the bed. Only the Chalice's magic could break through the boundary, carrying her and her husband inside. She knew that even if she were inside, none could see her. All they would see was the view she saw now...a reflection of an empty bed.

Inside the herbal circle, it would be as dark as deep space. The magical boundary around the edge would keep them from falling as she and her mate consummated what was to be. Whether they shared names before was up to them. Some married couples did, others didn't. Ari had decided to let the male's actions guide hers. Clearly, since it was her marriage ceremony, he would know who she was.

"Princess?" Vara, her best friend and head attendant spoke quietly, signifying that they were done and it was time.

In all there were ten attendants, all daughters from noble families. Vara was a cousin, as was her younger sister Petra. Should Ari die, Vara would take the throne. Some thought Ari foolish for keeping Vara as a close and trusted friend, but she wasn't scared. Vara would never hurt her. Their bond was too close for that. Besides, Ari knew Vara's deepest secret. She longed to be in the armies, flying into battle. Politics were too tame for her. Someday, Ari hoped to give Vara a chance at her dream, though she hadn't told her cousin as much.

Petra was just a child—the youngest attendant honored because she was family. Maura, Aurelie, Thora, and Lena came from the different providences around the queendom. She knew them from childhood and thought well enough of them to honor them.

Lucia, Adria, Jael and Clarinda were all from a neighboring castle. Their dark skin was a beautiful brown, enhanced by the beauty of their big, round, brown and green eyes. Their father, Lord Viceious, was Supreme General to all the armies and a man Ari had dealt with on many occasions. Their being honored as attendants was merely politics. She had no close connection to the four girls.

The women had been unusually quiet, as was tradition, giving her time to contemplate whatever it was she should have been contemplating on this day. Unfortunately, Commander Rurik was the thing that kept popping into her head. She knew it was because she'd heard his name that morning, whispered in girlish excitement. A maid had seen him arrive with his men, swooping down from the skies to land within the palace walls.

"I am ready," Ari stated, lifting her chin. With a small wave, she parted the liquid along the water wall, creating an archway. "Join the others in the hall. Vara will walk with me."

The attendants rushed from the room through the new door, leaving Ari alone with Vara.

"You're distracted." Vara threaded her arm through Ari's. Her cousin was a slender woman, but had the skill of the best warriors when it came to using a talon glove. With it, she could be deadly. Looks really were deceiving. Vara's purple gaze, wavy brown hair and dark brown complexion were the envy of many women.

"Yea." Ari nodded. "Rurik is here."

"Ah, I remember him. He's the one you gave a blood oath to avenge yourself against." Vara gave a small laugh. "Is that what you're doing on your Mating Day? You're plotting revenge for childish hurts?"

"Childish?" Ari gasped. "You call wanting a little vengeance for being knocked off a platform into a bed of dung in my coronation dress on the day I was crowned as a princess a small affair? It's permanently recorded in the Book of Ari as historical fact. I can't erase that. Only three moons ago I saw it again when I was flipping through my life."

"Ah, perhaps not."

"Or when he slipped that love note under my pillow, making me believe that Mikael wanted to marry me? I made an ass out of myself in front of the whole palace."

"Mikael is still very sexy. I don't blame you for being mad about that."

"He still looks at me as if I might try and kiss him again," Ari mumbled.

"You did embarrass him by doing it in front of the other flyers," Vara said. She pulled Ari's arm, urging her to walk through the door in the water wall. A long hallway stretched before them, angling toward the ground, leading directly to the hall. Since her chambers were set high above the ground without support from underneath, the door in the great hall was the only way in or out—unless you were a falcon shifter, in which case you could fly up to a window. "Did you ever discover for certain whom the note was from?"

"Nae. I cannot prove it, but I'm sure it was a prank. Rurik is the only man who'd have the nerve to do such a thing. He didn't deny it." Even now, remembering the simple, horribly unpoetic words, she felt a twinge in her heart.

"That's mean," Vara whispered needlessly.

"I'll show Commander Rurik that I am no one to be trifled with." Ari smiled at her cousin. Yea, she would show him and when the supreme power to rule was hers, she'd make sure he and his legion of men were shipped to the other side of the planet. He would spend his days protecting Falconia's marshes from outside invasions.

ꙮ

Commander Rurik smiled as he entered the palace's great hall in the center eye of the castle. They called it the "center eye" because the castle looked like the stylized shape of an eye when they flew over it. Two curved walls formed the battlements along the outside. Yards and gardens were where the whites would normally be and in the iris was the main palace tower.

It was strange being back in the palace after so many years away. He'd grown up there, as did the other natural born falcon shifters. They had been treated like royalty, given the best education, trained to be lethal warriors and yet held apart by what they were. Being natural born gave them one place in Falconia's society—the life of a commander. Other warriors chose to fly in the armies; the pure bloods were born to do it.

He would be expected to marry a woman with little money and power. His position afforded him any comfort and it would honor his name to elevate a woman who had little, and help to support her family, but he wasn't allowed to marry a nobleman's daughter—not with his bloodline. He never fully understood how he could be so revered, so trusted to protect lives, and yet so undesired as a son because of his falcon birth. Honor kept the commanders from rebelling, and they never thought of taking over the planet, though they easily could.

The pure falcons had ruled before and they'd nearly lost the planet due to their rash actions. After, it became acknowledged that women would lead, not hot-blooded men. And since pure falcons were the most hot-blooded of all, it wasn't smart to let them reproduce with nobles of power. The fear ran deep that the actions of the past would be repeated. Besides, none could argue that the women did not do a superior job in making decisions and managing politics. Half of politics was dinner parties and hosting dignitaries anyway. Kings made for excellent bodyguards to their women, not to mention they raised the children, training them to defend themselves. Since Falconian men had naturally more physical energy, it only made sense that they would tend to the children.

The hall was filled, so packed with people that they spilled over into the courtyard outside. Rurik felt someone grab his arm. It was a light pull and he automatically smiled, expecting to see a female beside him. He wasn't disappointed.

"Let me be your guest tonight, Commander," the petite blonde said, pursing her lips. She was dressed like the middle class, in a long tunic gown of light green. The sleeves tightly fitted to her wrists with decorative buttons up the side and the rounded neck of the gown revealed a pleasing amount of cleavage. The bodice hugged her curves before flaring into a skirt at the lower hip.

"No, I want to be your guest, Commander," another woman said, a pout in her tone. He looked at his other arm, seeing a dark-haired temptress dressed very much like the lighter one, only in blue. Only commanders, nobles and guests of honor would be seated in the hall, with others only as room permitted.

He wasn't surprised they knew his position, for the two long, dark wings were hard to miss. Unlike the non-military Falconians, the warriors had wings. Pure born had them since birth, others grew them in time with the help of magic when they took their vow into the army. But, unlike the others, natural wings were darker and longer, reaching nearly to the ground when laid flat against the back.

The blonde put her hand on his chest, twining her fingers in the laces that held his tunic shirt together, which was more like a long jacket. The laces crossed down the front, from neck to waist, only to hang open at his legs so as not to hinder movement. The delicate silver and blue material was of the finest quality. As the woman's fingers traced the laces down to his waist, his cock stirred in response, pressing against the tight black breeches he wore underneath.

"I'd do almost anything to see Princess Ari's Mating Day," the blonde said, batting her lashes with obvious meaning.

Rurik suppressed a frown as he thought of Ari. She'd been a stuck up child and rumor had it she'd turned into an even more pretentious adult. Over the years, her true nature had been more than apparent. She'd signed the order to send his men on some of the worst missions. It was as if she wanted him dead and all because he had a little crush on her when they were children. Sure, he'd teased her, but mostly because he wanted her to loosen up.

Well, they weren't children anymore and he'd outgrown Princess Ari. Now he was an acclaimed warrior of the Fifth and if his keen sense of smell was any indication, these two women were definitely interested in helping him pass his time at the palace.

Lifting his arms, he hugged both women to his sides. "Now, ladies, don't fight. You can both be my guest. There is plenty of room on my lap for the two of you."

The women giggled. Rurik lifted his gaze briefly to the high throne in the middle of the hall, to where Princess Ari would drink from the Chalice. Let the princess have her mate, and blessed wings save the man chosen to it.

Already the hall was filled. Soon it would be time for the ceremony. Drinks were set out in goblets along the lower tables. Seeing some of his men in the back, he could tell they were already far into their cups by the way they moved and laughed. Rurik led the women alongside him toward the table.

"May the poor sod be whisked away on blessed wings, far from this palace and the arms of the princess," said Lleu, his second-in-command. The others laughed at the toast.

"Likely she'll dagger him in her bed tonight," Ivor added. The warrior was missing an eye, thanks to Ari's command to go into battle against the Medical Mafia who tried to set up posts in their marshes. It wasn't that any of them were afraid of fighting the mafia, but at the time they'd been exhausted from defending the skies against pirates. It wasn't bad, except Terrick, Commander of the Fourth, later told them his men had been without a thing to do for months. Ari seemed to have it in for them.

"Only if it was a man from the Fifth," Rurik said, holding the two women to his side. "She does like to see our blood run, doesn't she?"

"Oh, have you been hurt in battle, Commander?" the blonde asked.

"See now, my most pretty feather, the commander merely floats in the sky as we warriors do all the work," Ivor said. He pointed meaningfully at the blue eye patch that covered the empty socket. "If it's stories of battle you'd like, then come sit by me. I've got many wounds that could use a female's gentle touch."

The women giggled.

"Get your own." Rurik laughed, taking a seat. With a swoop of his arms, he hauled both women onto his knees. "These two are my guests."

"Then you'd better take a drink, doves." Lleu slid a couple goblets in front of them, "Because I'm told the commander only looks cute after a few dozen goblets."

Rurik laughed at the good-natured ribbing as Lleu handed him a goblet as well, taking it off a nearby table.

"Hey, that's mine!" a burly warrior with long blond hair yelled.

"Go squawk to someone who cares," Lleu answered, just as surly.

Rurik closed his eyes, ignoring the men as the blonde kissed his ear. The darker woman reached down so that her hand rested against his inner thigh, her fingers tapping lightly as she took a long drink of the stout liquor. His cock filled in response and he squirmed in his seat. Looking up at the empty throne, he thought that the ceremony couldn't come fast enough. He wasn't looking forward to seeing Ari again and the sooner he could get out of her hall the better. And the sooner she was mated, the sooner he could forget all about her by burying himself in the two willing beauties before him.

Chapter Two

Ari held her head up as she walked under the archway into the hall. She had waited in the hallway leading from her bedchambers until her father could escort her.

The red stone of the palace had been adorned with the long purple flowering vines found in the prairies outside the battlements. They were strung in garlands along the tall ceilings and archways. Regal music sounded, announcing her arrival, as she walked down an aisle formed between the tables. Noble families and esteemed warriors filled the many tables around the center platform. All of them were well-dressed, though some more wealthily adorned than the others. At her appearance, those gathered in the packed hall stood in respect, though they didn't stop talking amongst themselves. It was an old tradition, one carried on for millenniums, supposedly long before her people had come to inhabit Falconia.

In the crowd, she was able to pick out a few of the better-suited males to be her husband. Sure, she had no real final say in the match, but usually the wishes of the bride were magically taken into consideration. The peasants rarely had trouble in mating to the men they loved. But, being as she was royalty, her future would not be so certain. If she had her choice, she would pick Lord Cyril of Karvof's son, Lynus. He was a little young, but very sexy and his father was a great nobleman with a lot of land close to the palace. Lynus smiled at her as she passed and she let the corner of her mouth lift in response. It wasn't love, but a prudent choice.

Suddenly, a round of feminine laughter caught her attention. It was just a little louder than the rest of the voices. She looked forward, but couldn't see who was making the noise. The music continued. When she looked at her father, so finely dressed in his dark green robes, her smile widened. He led her to the steps that wound around the edge of the platform. Circling around it, they climbed to the top. From the vantage point, she was better able to see the crowd. They were seated first as she waited before them. Slowly, she drew her gaze to the side, where the feminine laughter was coming from.

"Rurik," she whispered in surprise. She'd have recognized him anywhere. His chin-length dark brown hair was longer in the back, shorter in the front. The bangs framed his piercing black eyes. Ari had forgotten how much his eyes had disturbed her when they were younger.

"Ari?" her father asked. "Did you speak?"

"Nae," she answered, shaking her head. She forced her eyes away from Rurik, only to find them drawn back to him. Seven seasons had passed, nearly twelve years. How much time had changed things, and how little it did as well. It took all of Ari's willpower to continue to smile at the gathered crowd. He was much bigger than she remembered, with a harder edge to his features. But that was not all that had changed.

Her jaw tightened in irritation. Rurik had two women on his lap and they were indecently rubbing themselves against him. A pang of irritation shot through her at the sight. Not that she wanted Rurik or anything, she assured herself. It was just rude of him to act in such a way in her hall, on this day. Ari refused to notice a few of the other men who also sat with amorous women—some of whom were her honored attendants.

Rurik's eyes met hers and he stopped moving his hand on the dark-haired woman's back. Ari recognized the woman. She was the daughter of the palace baker and had already given herself to many of the men in the palace, including Ari's father in recent years if rumors held true. She looked at the king, wondering if he was jealous. He didn't even notice the woman.

Seeing movement at her side, she saw the Chalice attendant coming up the stairs. The music stopped and the hall quieted. The young girl wore a white robe with a dark green and yellow stripe down the front. Her red hair hung loose about her shoulders, nearly touching the floor.

Without a word, she held up the Chalice. Ari's fingers shook as she reached out. Hesitant, she took it. Feelings of hope and fear warred inside her. She'd managed to stay calm until this moment, but now her body shook from head to toe. She didn't want to drink and in a moment of panic she almost threw the Chalice to the ground in refusal. She looked at Lynus, wondering if she'd wake up next to him. Then, as she brought the cup to her lips and tasted the first sip of the magical pink liquid, her gaze darted to the side. Rurik's eyes were on her, steadily staring at her like everyone else's.

The liquid was unlike any she'd ever tasted, somewhat like punch and liquor and tingling herbs all in one. It slid thickly down her throat and she coughed lightly, forcing herself to drink it all. A buzzing started in her ears as she drew the Chalice down from her mouth. She'd heard the sensations described, but feeling them was something else altogether. Her hands went numb and she looked down in time to see them become transparent. The Chalice dropped and the young girl leaned over to catch it. Suddenly, a bright white light bombarded her and she heard droplets of rain seconds before the world went black.

Rurik bit the inside of his lip, his gut clenched as he watched Ari lift the Chalice to her lips. Even from across the hall he could see that her eyes hadn't changed in their blue intensity. She saw him, he had no doubt, but she didn't smile, didn't show that she recognized him.

Part of him wanted to watch her, the beauty of her face, the soft curves of her body as she moved beneath the clinging material. The years had been kind to her, maybe too kind for they'd made her a gorgeous woman. He'd heard people speak of her beauty, but in his mind she was always the young girl, awkward and without power. He'd been attracted to her then, but now, now she was a woman and attraction didn't even begin to cover what he felt.

The two women kissed his neck, but he didn't feel them, not really. Their hands were on his thighs, but in his mind he only wanted one person and neither of them was she. His hands trembled, and he longed to wipe the makeup from her face, longed to run his fingers through her loosened hair.

Ari drew the Chalice down from her mouth, her eyes wide as she looked down. The Chalice dropped from her hand and he felt a strange tingling in his stomach, an almost nauseous sensation. Jealousy? Regret? Anger? A shiver worked over his spine and he couldn't move.

"You're cold as ice." The blonde pulled away from him. "Commander, what is it?"

"He's freezing," the dark haired temptress added.

"Commander?" Ivor and Lleu said simultaneously.

Rurik opened his mouth to say he was fine, but a rush of air hit him, filling his lungs and knocking the breath from him, followed by a blinding light. He couldn't see a thing as the noises of the hall disappeared into the pounding sound of warriors' feet running over a battlefield seconds before they took to flight.

Then, suddenly, darkness replaced the light, a heavy, disorienting contrast. Soft cushioning pressed into his hands and knees and he realized he was bent over on a soft mattress. Something warm was by his leg and he reached over blindly to feel what it was.

"It's done," a woman whispered. There was relief in her tone. "I can't believe it's finally done."

His fingers ran over a leg, buried within a gown. It didn't take long to ascertain it belonged to the woman.

Nae, not just a woman. It belonged to...

"Ari?" he whispered.

Rurik drew his hand away as if burnt. Jerking back, he spread his wings slightly. They bumped an invisible boundary. He reached for it, feeling the air like a thick wall encircling them and keeping him trapped with the princess.

"Yea," Ari said. Her tone had deepened into an almost sultry, vixen's tone.

"Princess Ari?" he said, more to himself than to her.

"Yea, are you well, Lord?" she asked. "Did the transition take you by surprise? What is your name? Who has the Chalice chosen for me?"

"I can't believe this. It's a mistake."

"The only way it's a mistake, Lord, is if you are..." the woman paused, "...a pure blood."

Rurik froze and started to lower his naturally deep tone an octave more, but then stopped himself. He didn't expect Ari to remember his voice. "No taste for pure bloods?"

"What? Um, nae, it's just they can't rule."

His gut tightened. The way she said it, so knowingly, so finally, as if it were fact. His kind had ruled without problem until the end.

Rurik didn't know what came over him, but he was suddenly aroused with passion like he'd never known before. It was a mixture of desire, anger, the need to conquer once and for all. He didn't stop to think as he reached for her leg. Ari tensed beneath his hand, moaning softly. He could sense the need in her, the swift rush of passion at his touch. She was not immune to him.

When they were younger, he'd wanted to touch her so badly. He'd dreamt of her, masturbated to her, was tortured when she thought his love note to her was from another. How could he not lie about it though, when she'd laughed in his face at the thought of it being from him?

All the feelings he'd suppressed as a young man came surging forth and he had to touch her, had to show her he wasn't the same person. Rurik had to show himself. He would make her respond to his touch, make her moan, make her fall in love before she ever saw his face and then...

He couldn't think beyond that part in his plan. The bed was soft, the area dark. Concentrating, he tried to see, using his naturally superior vision to pierce the darkness. It didn't work. He couldn't see through the magical barrier the Chalice created.

Running his hand down to her ankle, he pushed up the thin material of her gown. Even now he could picture her, standing by the throne, in the seductive, clinging gown, her long hair an impossible mess of twists to form a crown. He would've much rather seen the long red length down about her shoulders.

She was naked beneath the gown and he lightly caressed his way up her leg, her thigh, her hip. The texture of her skin was like a dream. This couldn't be happening. Ari's breathing audibly deepened and the sweet smell she emitted made his insides tense.

"Hold." She sounded insecure. "A moment. Hold."

"You're beautiful, Ari." Rurik didn't stop. He couldn't. "When will we ever get another chance for this day? Let it happen. Let your mind think what it will."

Lightly, he kissed her hip, trailing his lips along her flesh. There was a bittersweet pleasure when she gasped. Would she be so willing, so passionate if she knew it was his lips that kissed her? Rurik hesitated, warring with himself. This was destined. The Chalice's magic brought him to her, gave her to him. But what if magic had gotten it wrong this time? What if the potion had been tainted?

Then this would be his only chance to have Ari. Years had passed and he'd thought he was over her, but obviously that wasn't the case. Being a warrior, he knew how to take what he wanted. Rurik would not, could not back down.

Leaning back, he ripped her gown open along the front. The metal band around her body would be too hard to take off as it was bent to the shape of her chest and back. Tossing the material to the side, he closed his eyes, picturing her naked body before him.

Ari made small noises similar to prey cornered by the hunter. Her legs were restless. As he leaned over, she reached to touch his chest. He stiffened, worried she might explore him and find the wings along his back. They'd give his position away and she'd know he was a warrior and that a mistake had been made.

Stretching his wings back, he was careful not to lean too far forward as he kept his shoulders out of reach. Lifting her leg, he brought her ankle to his lips, kissing a hot, wet trail along her calf. Ari pulled on his shirt, tugging at the laces over his chest. When she couldn't work them free, but instead merely loosened them, she reached lower to his breeches.

Rurik dropped her leg, angling his body between her thighs. Pulling her down so her legs were bent over his, he caressed her hips and stomach, rubbing in slow circles up toward her glorious breasts. They were soft, pliable mounds in his palms, so big they overflowed in his hands. The gown she wore had hid their true size from him and he relished the discovery of her large nipples. The erect peaks begged for his lips, but he held back, fearful she might discover his wings if he leaned forward.

Her fingers skimmed over his clothed arousal, the touch so hesitant yet unyielding that his cock couldn't help but fill to the point of explosion. By law, he knew she had only three lovers at most to minimize the risk of jealousy over her position, so it was possible she was nervous.

When she didn't free his erection, he reached for his own waistband and unfastened it. He pushed his breeches down just far enough to free his cock for action. Her fingers glanced over the turgid flesh and he nearly came.

Rurik grabbed her wrists, holding her arms to her sides as he finally leaned down. Worshiping her with his tongue and mouth, he licked and kissed her stomach and breasts, moaning softly just to taste her. Ari wiggled beneath him, her body so warm and eager. Not letting go of her arms as he dragged his tongue down to the apex of her thighs, he moaned louder as he tasted the sweet cream of her pussy.

"Ah," she gasped. Rurik closed his mouth around her sex, licking and nibbling along her folds, only to suck her clit. "Oh!"

When the sound of her voice turned into incoherent pleas and her body was thrusting in rhythm to his tongue, he knew it was time. Crawling on top of her, he slid her arms up, keeping her hands from exploring.

Leaning over, he pressed his mouth to hers. She jolted in surprise and he used the chance to kiss her deeply. Her hands slipped from under his hold, reaching up to capture his neck. She kept him to her mouth as he spread her legs wider in invitation. In all his wildest dreams, he never imagined that Ari would be in his bed.

He hesitated, feeling a wave of guilt. The uncertainty was as unfamiliar to him as losing and he didn't know what to do. Rurik started to pull back. With a few words, he could drive her away forever. She wasn't his. He knew that. They came from different worlds, were born into different worlds. She was born to rule, he was born to fight.

"Nae," she whispered. "Stay."

Ari ran her hand down to his cock, rubbing it as she drew the tip forward to her sex. She offered her body to him, so sweet, so soft. He was powerless against her. She seized a part of him, a part that she'd always held, a part that kept him from all others throughout the many years. Rurik hadn't wanted to admit it his whole life. Once, he'd dared to hope, but he now knew how foolish hope was.

Once, he thought, taking what she offered. He thrust forward, sliding in her cream as he pried her body open to his. The tight feel of her squeezed him and he groaned in pleasure. His wings beat slowly, as he thrust, their subtle yet strong movement propelling him steadily in and out.

He couldn't take it. She jerked, tensing as she came. Grunting, he joined her in the blissful surrender of release, letting his seed spill within her, claiming her as his, marking her. Without thought, he collapsed forward, sure he'd never felt so scared or so happy in all his life. He tried to cling to the moment, knowing that it couldn't last, no matter how badly he wanted it to.

Chapter Three

Ari couldn't believe how blessed she was. Her body sung with the intensity with which she came. The pleasure she'd given herself in the silent hours were nothing compared to the feel of live, confident flesh. The Chalice had indeed chosen wisely for her. Her mate was strong and fit. By his girth, she knew that it wasn't Lynus, or Ger, or any number of the men she'd considered over the last year. Nae, this nobleman was most likely a stranger to her. His voice held a trace of the familiar, but she couldn't place it.

She stretched her arms, feeling her loose hair about her shoulders. The crown had disappeared when she was brought to the bed. All that hard work for just a few moments in the hall. Such was the life of a ruler. She could spend hours getting ready for a ceremony that only lasted a few minutes.

Her heart pounded with the knowledge of what she'd done. She'd had sex with a man and didn't even know his name. Nae, not just a man, her mate. It was right that she was with him. The Chalice would not choose wrong for her. She had faith in that.

Ari didn't like how he held her hands down during sex, but maybe he was nervous. Perhaps he had a scar he didn't want her to feel, or maybe he wasn't the best looking of men. It didn't matter. With a body that moved like his did, she could well get past an ugly face. Things like faces didn't matter to her. All she cared about was that he was kind and faithful and of a good noble family.

Lightly, she ran her hands over his shoulders, curious to know more about him. He was breathing hard and she smiled in giddy pleasure. "Mm, the Chalice chose..." Just then, her hand struck a protrusion along his back.

What...? A wing?

Jerking back, she pushed at his chest to get him off her. "What are you? A soldier?"

Suddenly, light flickered. Ari screamed in protest, knowing that light would reveal them to the world as a married couple. She blinked as her eyes adjusted. Dark eyes met hers.

Nae, it can't be...

"Rurik?" she squeaked.

"Princess." Rurik tilted his head. His clothing was still on, only slightly disheveled. Though he looked directly at her, she couldn't read his closed expression.

Ari sprang into action, backing away from him. This was one man she didn't want to be in closed quarters with, let alone in the mating bed—*her* mating bed! She would've fallen, but the magical boundary held her up. Her back pressed against air.

"It's been awhile," he said.

"How...? What do you want with me? Why did you do this?" She couldn't get far enough away from him.

His eyes traveled down her body and he looked amused. How could he look amused? Ari wanted to cry. He was mocking her. She could see it in the familiar smirk on his face. His body might have changed but that look was the same. It mocked her. He'd always mocked her.

"I didn't do anything," he assured her, looking very pleased with himself, "that you didn't beg to have done to you."

"I hate you," she whispered, for lack of anything better to say. "You haven't changed at all, have you? You're just a mean—"

"And yet you lay naked before me, like an offering ready to be fucked again."

Ari glanced down in horror, scrambling to pull the ripped pieces of her gown together to hide her body. "You haven't changed, have you?"

"Neither have you."

"Commander Rurik, leader of the great Fifth." She shook her head, still pressed against the invisible barrier. He knelt before her, just as handsome as she remembered him being. "How dare you—*ah!*"

The barrier gave way and she fell backward off the bed. Screaming, she flailed briefly in the air. Rurik's hand wrapped around her wrist, catching her. She bumped along the bed's hard side.

Suddenly, a stunted pounding started from below. Horrified, Ari looked down. Beneath her, a crowd stood tapping their feet in applause. Thankfully, she was turned toward the bed and her torn gown was hidden from view.

"That was fast," she heard someone comment from behind. "The mating went well. I've never seen a couple come out so quickly."

"Pull me up," Ari whispered.

"What?" Rurik asked, smiling down at her.

"We'll bring a ladder, princess," someone offered. "No need to come down that way."

"Pull me up," she hissed, glaring at Rurik. "Now."

"Ask nicely," he grinned, holding her as if he could let her hang there all day without straining himself.

"Please," she said through gritted teeth. Something about this situation reminded her all too well of her childhood. Would the man never cease to embarrass her publicly?

Slowly, he pulled her up onto the bed, barely breaking a sweat. When she was safe, she jerked her arm away from him. It was a little too soon and she nearly tumbled over the side again. This time, she caught herself, swatting at his hand as he tried to grab her.

"You haven't changed. Even as a child you had to torment me," she hissed. "This is just like that time you knocked wet cement on my head."

"We were using them in training. You shouldn't have been on the field," he protested, just like when they were younger.

"You didn't have to aim it at me," she ground out. Then, holding up her hands, she said, "There's no point in this. It's a mistake. We both know it's a mistake. We can't be mated. You're a soldier and soldiers can't rule. My true mate will be king."

"So soon you forget?" His grin was sinfully wicked and she shivered at his meaning. The last thing she needed was a reminder of her wanton behavior. "The Chalice chose me."

"Come down, Ari," her father called. "Join the celebration."

Ari looked over, seeing the ladder.

"I can fly us," he offered. "It'll be faster."

"Nae," she said, too quickly. The idea of his hands touching her made her skin tingle. She needed time to sort this out. "I'll climb."

His intense eyes bore into hers for a moment and she had to look away first. He didn't say another word. Rurik's arms didn't move as his wings stretched to the side. They flapped, lifting his body up. He'd fixed his breeches when she wasn't looking and before she could speak, he was over the side, gliding to the floor.

"Oh," she sighed, shaking horribly. She was all too aware of the water wall arching overhead. They might not have heard her below, but they could see. She took a deep breath and then another. It would seem time had not changed much. Rurik could still thoroughly disarm her.

"Ari?" her father called. "Do you seek assistance?"

"Nae," she yelled back. Tugging at the annoying coils fitted to her arms, she took them off. "I'm coming."

ജാ

"Ari, I know it's strange to be mated to the commander, but the Chalice's magic has ultimate authority over our laws," the king said. Ari couldn't look at her father's eyes as she sat on a low, armless couch. They were in her father's chambers, near the library. Her father's belongings were being moved to a private room on the other end of the royal courtyard. By nightfall, this section of the palace would belong to her, as the new queen.

How could he agree to this? To Rurik? Ari shook her head in denial. "But he's a warrior, a pure shifter."

"Yea," the king agreed, nodding. "And pure bloods did rule the land at one time."

"And look where that brought us!" she argued. "We almost lost the planet to a bunch of overgrown, warmongering slugs."

"Gryger looked at the laws. There were none made saying pure bloods couldn't rule. It was just agreed that they shouldn't for a time and left at that. No one ever thought to look, because for the last several centuries the question never came up. However, he did come across a prophecy stating that one day, after the sins of the past could be forgotten, a pure blood would take the throne, combining the planet's strengths. Perhaps the time has come for them to reclaim part of the throne. Commander Rurik will make you a fine mate, and you will still have ultimate power over the planet."

"We both know Falconian prophecy is just a way for old men to ramble about what could happen and look smart." Ari shook her head. "Four thousand years ago they said a fiery ship would fall from the sky and alien men would steal away the daughters of noblemen."

"It could happen," the king protested.

"And yet it hasn't and we still have the law banning noblewomen from walking alone at night because of such nonsense."

"Ari," her father sighed heavily. "You must resign yourself to your fate. You chose to walk the path of the Chalice. You did not have to drink. If you would have poured the liquid on the floor, you would've remained unmated for the rest of your days. You knew the risk and you accepted it."

"Right," she drawled. "I'm sure everyone would have loved that. There goes our family line, right onto the floor with the magic."

"It was your choice, whatever reasons you used to make it."

Ari frowned.

"Now, why don't you get dressed." Her father motioned toward the long tunic she wore. It was plain and white and not at all fitting for a princess about to become queen. "The hall is probably far into their cups and I'd like to pass this crown to you so that I may join them."

༚ः༚

Ari paced her chambers, doing her best not to look at the high bed. It did no good, for she couldn't stop her gaze from following the water wall up toward the ceiling, to where the site of her most unmentionable shame was reflected back to her.

Holy Comet, she'd wanted him. She still wanted him.

"Ari?" Vara spoke softly, her purple gaze shining with concern. Her friend held her coronation gown. It was much more concealing than the mating dress with the metal band.

"I was thinking about him, that's why the Chalice chose him," Ari said. "I'm being punished because I wanted revenge."

"It doesn't work like that and you know it." Vara laid the dark-red dress down on a low couch and joined Ari by the water wall. "The Chalice doesn't make mistakes."

"It did this time," Ari exclaimed.

"I'll admit it's strange." Vara sighed. "You should've seen the crowd when you two disappeared. First you, then suddenly those two women who were on..." Vara's eyes rounded in horror and she covered her mouth.

"On Rurik's lap," Ari finished dryly.

"It just means he's virile," Vara offered.

"Great." Ari shook her head. "Not only am I mated to a commander who mocks me, he'll be sleeping with everything that comes within wingspan of him."

"Rurik isn't like that. He's not one of those. If anything, he does have honor. There isn't so much a blemish on his reputation."

"But why him?" Ari whispered. Taking her friend's hands, she held them tight.

"What aren't you telling me?"

"When we were younger and I thought Mikael gave me that love note."

"Yes?"

Ari took a deep breath. "You remember I told you how Rurik delivered it, or saw it, or I can't remember exactly how it happened that he was there when I discovered it because I was in such shock, but at first I thought it was from him. You know how I laugh when I'm nervous? Well I laughed because I thought it was from him. I wanted it to be. But, he was just so mean about it and that's when he told me it was from Mikael and I..."

"You never forgave him," Vara finished.

"He was always so mean to me," Ari said, her shoulders slumping by small degrees.

"And you hated him for it because you liked him."

Ari didn't want to delve into it. She should've never started this conversation.

"That would explain why you've pined for him over the years. And why the Fifth gets all the dangerous missions."

"Nae, I don't—" Ari began, ready to deny that she sent Rurik and his men out on all the dangerous assignments. "Oh, blessed stars, I do, don't I?"

Vara nodded. "Half the noble court believes you want to have him killed."

"And the other half?" she asked, cringing.

"Think you want to have him maimed." Vara laughed softly. "That's why all the young boys pretend to be in the Fifth."

Ari rolled her eyes heavenward and gave a small laugh.

"So, now that we're talking about it, why do you send his men on the most dangerous missions?" Vara touched her shoulder, forcing Ari to look at her.

"The night before he flew out," Ari closed her eyes, remembering, "I heard him say he wanted nothing more than to have a long career filled with dangerous missions."

"I see." Vara grinned knowingly.

"What?" Ari lifted her hand. "Nae, never mind, I don't want to hear it. So, tell me, what happened in the hall. The two women did what?"

"Oh, yea, they screamed as they were both dropped on their asses. The crowd exploded into a frenzy when they discovered one of the soldiers had been chosen. Really, what could they do about it? Though, Lord Cyril did demand a reading of the laws and strangely Gryger was able to produce the book with little effort."

"What do you mean, strange?"

"He turned right to a prophecy that said—"

"Let me guess," Ari interrupted. "One day, after the sins of the past could be forgotten, a pure blood would once again take the throne, combining the planet's strengths."

"Yea, that is it." Vara nodded. "And that this day was the day that the prophecy said it would happen. When Lord Cyril heard that, he couldn't deny the validity of the marriage. In his irritation, he grabbed Lynus and together they left the palace."

Ari giggled. Then, as what her friend said sunk in, she scowled. "What did you say? My father and Gryger knew that today this would happen?"

"Appeared that way to me."

Ari crossed over to her gown and sat on it. "How could they not have warned me that I was to mate with Rurik? Do you think they told him?"

"I doubt it. The prophecy didn't say who would be picked, only that a pure blood would become king. And your father didn't tell you because he's not allowed to influence the mating decision. It is something you need to come to on your own, for your own reasons."

"You want to know my reason, Vara?" Ari gave a self-depreciating snort. "I wanted sex."

Vara laughed. "That's a good enough reason for me."

"Not just sex, but companionship. I told my father it was because I was duty bound to carry on the family name by having children, but the truth is I want to be held at night. I'm tired of being alone. I want a husband I can fall asleep with at night and wake up next to in the morning."

"And Rurik can't be that person? Ari, have you looked at him? He's gorgeous, he's built like a walking god and he can fly. Can you imagine being in the arms of a soldier?" Vara giggled, kneeling by Ari's legs so as not to sit on the coronation gown. Taking Ari's hands, she said, "What more could you ask for in your bed?"

"He's not the holding kind," Ari said. "People who... Men like him... He's a soldier."

"Haven't you ever wondered what it would be like to have sex with a man who could fly? Hovering above the ground as they take you?"

"You should take a lover," Ari said.

"I haven't met any men who appreciate me and I won't settle." Vara shrugged.

"I should have poured it on the floor," Ari moaned, wanting nothing more than to hide.

"You should get dressed and face Rurik like an adult. You have grown up, chances are, he has too."

Chapter Four

Ari stared wide-eyed, stunned to silence as Rurik's bold fingers pressed between her thighs. Even through the thick red material of her coronation gown she could feel him rubbing along her slit, stirring her passions even as she fought to keep them at bay. The dress was a beautiful tunic gown with a dark red overskirt above a light cream underskirt. It fitted tight to her waist, held together by thick corded ribbons that crossed under her breasts, holding them up. Her breasts were covered with a soft cream material that matched her underskirt. Suddenly, she wished she had a little more protection against the onslaught of Rurik's hands.

Oh yea, she thought sarcastically as she witnessed the childish taunting in his eyes, *he's really matured.*

"If you don't mind," she hissed, wiggling to be free. It didn't work. Her movements only caused his hand to rub all the harder. "I have a crown to accept."

"I'm surprised you didn't try and have the mating dissolved," he said, not letting her go. He had somehow snuck into her bedchambers. Her guess was he flew through a window in the shape of a falcon before making himself known. How long had he been there? Watching her dress? Hearing her conversation with Vara?

Nervously, she laughed. "I am a princess. I hold true to my word, Commander. I chose to drink from the Chalice and in doing so I have accepted the fate that is laid out for me."

"Huh, I thought it was because there was no defense. What, with the prophecy."

Her lips tightened in irritation.

Rurik laughed. His voice lowered and his wings spread to the side as he leaned over to press his face close to hers. "Or was it because you liked it when I touched you?"

"I don't..." She couldn't finish the sentence. His fingers felt too deliciously wicked against her pussy and he was nibbling at her ear. "Mm."

"What was that, princess?" He kissed her neck. His wings came forward, their dark feathers looming forward to block out light.

"I..." she tried again, only to rock her hips forward into his hand. She felt safe next to his large body. All thoughts of duty and coronation left her as he continued his assault on her neck. He still wore the same clothes as before and she ran her hands over the front of his tunic shirt, pulling at the laces.

"You felt me when I came inside you, didn't you?" His soft whisper was hot against her ear. "You feel my claim even now."

"Why are you doing this, Rurik? We both know you have no wish to be mated to me. Why aren't you trying to get out of it?" Ari bit her lip to keep from crying out. His fingers curled upward, making for an even deeper caress along her clit.

"Why else? For the power. Maybe now you will quit trying to have me and my men killed."

"What?" she gasped. He pulled back, his hand still intimately wicked along her sex, working her toward release through her clothing. His dark eyes pierced her with their intensity. "I nev-er, *oh.*"

"What was that, princess?" he demanded, keeping her trapped to his will.

"I said I never tried to have you killed." She couldn't think. Ari desperately wished he'd lift her skirts and take her as he had on the bed. His touch made it hard to concentrate, and yet she got the strange feeling that this was punishment as much as it was pleasure.

"I have scars on my body that beg to differ," he growled. "As do the bodies of my men."

Ari got a wicked flash of naked warriors in her mind, their hard, muscled bodies scarred. And in the forefront was Rurik, with his wings spread wide from his naked back.

"I didn't..." She tried to reason with him, but it was too hard to concentrate. Ari grabbed onto his shoulders, moaning softly as she rocked into his hand, completely accepting his touch.

"You did," he growled. "And I plan on making sure you grovel for my forgiveness by bathing and kissing each and every one of my scars. Then, you're going to kneel before me and ask me nicely to forgive you as you wrap your sweet lips around my cock."

"I am to be queen. I don't kneel and I don't beg, not to anyone, not even a king."

"You'll do it, Ari, and you'll be thankful that I don't make you grovel in public. Too many times has death touched us, too many times by your will."

Her climax was close. "Nae. I won't...grovel."

Suddenly, Rurik pulled back, denying her his touch. She gasped as the pleasure stopped and she was suspended in the torturous moment before release. Her hands shook and she thought of continuing on her own, but pride kept her hands away. Rurik was staring at her as she let her gaze roam over his body. His cock was hard, but he didn't act as if it affected him as he stood, arms crossed in displeasure.

"You'll grovel, princess, trust me on that point." He smiled, a deliciously wicked look as he licked his lips. "You'd better hurry. The hall is waiting to crown their new queen."

With that, he walked away, leaving her aroused and confused. What was that all about? Why did he stop? When she was alone, Ari suppressed a groan and reached between her thighs to replace where his hand had been. She rocked her hips, trying to end her own torment. Her body jerked, but it wasn't the same, it wasn't the intense orgasm promised with Rurik's touch and it left her angry and disappointed.

ഇൗൽ

Walking away was the hardest thing he'd ever done, but Rurik knew he had to leave her to think. He'd heard her talking with her cousin, Vara, about the past. To know she laughed at his note out of nervousness and not spite did something to him. But the note was only one thing in a trail of many childhood injuries they'd inflicted on each other.

His cock ached for release and he knew that if he'd wanted, he could've pressed his mate against the wall and taken his pleasure in her sweet, wet pussy. Holy stars, her breasts looked good, pressed up by the tight corset of her bodice. This dress did nothing to hide the large, full shape of the mounds. It was all he could do not to turn around and rip the cream linen open so that they might spill out for his pleasure, while still being held high by the tight bodice.

But he couldn't. The way he saw it, there was only one way to find happiness with the lot the Chalice had drawn for them. He had to show her that he was a commander. That he could respect her, just as he could be trusted to lead her. All their lives, she'd acted better than him, been told she was better than him. Over the years, it was her decisions that controlled his life. Well, it was time for the tables to turn. He would teach her to grovel so that she could walk beside him as an equal. Rurik would show her how much she wanted him, would make her admit to those desires. He'd long ago admitted to his.

ജരു

The crowd tapped their feet in applause for the longest of time, happily receiving Rurik as their king and as her chosen mate. She'd expected more of an uprising, but it appeared the people were really ready to forget and forgive the unfortunate incidences that took the pure bloods from rule. Could it be the prophecy was right? Were they more than just ramblings of old men? She would make a point of studying what the prophecies said a little more closely after she took her official rule.

Falconian ceremonies were simple and her father had only to take his crown and place it on her head for it to be over. There were no words, as the symbolic passing of the crown was enough to convey what was happening, just as her drinking from the goblet had been enough to seal her fate to Rurik.

Ari was all too aware of her new mate next to her, his taller height towering above her. She waited as Rurik was given a smaller crown. Suddenly, his wings spread wide and the hall went crazy with excitement, pounding their feet and cheering for their new king.

Show off, she thought. Her body was still tense from her almost climaxing and she resented Rurik for starting something he didn't finish. After the ceremony, music was played and couples took to dancing as well as drinking. Ari was amazed to see her father amongst the other nobles, acting more carefree than she'd ever seen him. She didn't dance, but instead sat on her throne watching.

"Do you wish to join them?" Rurik asked from her side. His voice was deceptively soft and she stiffened to hear the niceness of his tone.

Blinking, she looked at him. "Nae. It isn't done."

"According to...?"

She opened her mouth to speak, but the truth was, she didn't know. It really wasn't written in law that she couldn't dance or do any number of things, it was just traditionally how it was done.

"I propose, my queen..." Rurik began. The title still jarred her slightly, though she'd been prepared to accept it.

"Yes?" she breathed, unable to form a solid word.

"I propose that it's time to let a little more blood into the rule," he said.

"What do you mean?" Ari wrinkled her brow in confusion, studying him.

"When my kind was banished, it was thought that women, who had more control over their passionate blood, should rule for a time. They have and your family has done a good job of it. But the throne lacks passion. Perhaps it's time to let some of the fun back into ruling Falconia. Our people were never meant to be passionless, Ari. Our ancestors ran from passion because of what it brought. Perhaps it's time to reclaim some of it."

"So you're saying...?" she asked, thoroughly intrigued by what he suggested.

"I'm saying, let us join our people and dance. There is no shame in a queen enjoying her life. Come, let us flush that perfect complexion of yours and make you break a sweat."

"I, ah, sweat," she protested, even as she allowed him to touch her hand. "I exercise."

"Dance with me," he insisted. "Let us start this reign with blood in its veins."

Ari was too stunned by the prospect to protest as he pulled her to her feet. The hall suddenly lost some of its buzz as he led her along the stairwell that wound down the platform to the floor. She was well aware of the eyes on her.

"Rurik," she pulled at her hand, trying to stop him, "a queen doesn't..."

"A queen *hasn't* in a long time," he corrected. "Do you really want to live your ancestors' lives? Or would you rather live the life of Queen Ari and her hot-blooded king?"

There was something intimate and accepting to the way he linked their names together and she would've agreed to almost anything at the moment. He led her down to the hall. The musicians had stopped, looking unsure.

"Play something lively," Rurik yelled, as if commanding all those around him. "The new queen wishes to dance with her people."

Ari's stomach tensed and she expected a riot of outrage. Instead, no one seemed to care that it wasn't done in the past. They cheered, several reaching out to pat her on the back in welcome. Rurik grinned, pulling her close as a lively beat started over the hall. She felt the definition of his tight muscles against her body, pressing to her breasts, which suddenly felt heavy and achy against him.

Soon she was swept into a whirl of turns and spins. Rurik led her skipping along the floor in one direction, only to spin her around and lead her in the other with his chest to her back. She'd seen the dance performed several times, but had never done it herself—well not any place where she could be seen and never with a partner.

Rurik was a wonderful dancer, lifting and leading her around the floor so that it looked as if she'd been dancing for years. Ari laughed, feeling carefree, reveling in the hard pumping blood in her veins. Rurik was right. This was exactly the kind of thing her rule needed. Suddenly, the burden of being in charge lifted and she felt as carefree as a peasant.

"It's crowded," Ari said after several songs had passed in lively dancing. He kept her close, going so far as to lift her feet off the floor to keep time with the music. "And hot."

Rurik danced her past a table and grabbed an unused goblet set up at the end. Slowly, he handed it to her. Ari swallowed the stout liquor, gulping it down. It wasn't the same kind she was served as royalty. There was a heady flavor to it. Rurik took the goblet when she finished and set it down, before grabbing another and offering it to her. Ari drank that one down as well. She hadn't eaten too much and the instant effects of the strong drink in her blood were easy to feel.

"Fifth," Rurik yelled. "Into dance formation."

Ari tensed in surprise at the barking order, her eyes round as she tried to pull away from Rurik. He held her tight, grinning widely.

"Hold on, my queen," he said, before leaping up into the air over the crowd. Ari gasped, clutching onto his shirt. As he spun her, she realized he'd merely moved her out of the crowd to give them more room to dance.

"But my skirt," she protested, wondering if people would see her naked body beneath if they looked up.

"We'll be spinning too fast," he assured her. Several of his men had gone up into the air at his yelled command and she saw the stunned expression of the other women as they were flown around the room in the dance.

Below them the crowd cheered, blurring with the sound of the music. Ari's head spun from the liquor and she laid it on his shoulder as he twirled her around. Closing her eyes, she held on, feeling the subtle movements of his body. It was arousing, yet frightful, to be under his complete control. Ari couldn't fly and if he were to let go, she'd fall.

311

"I'm curious," Rurik said.

She didn't lift her head. Unbidden, the deliciously erotic movements of his body against hers began stirring her passions once more. Wicked thoughts entered her mind, so arousingly wicked that she didn't want to stop and think. Vara had mentioned the idea of having sex while in flight and she could see how exotic and wonderful such an idea could be.

If they were alone, she would've forgotten who he was and would've demanded he have sex with her right where they were. Good thing the crowd was there to keep her at bay. His earlier words entered her head, words about wanting her to humble herself before him. Where did that man go? That impossible, controlling man? The Rurik who held her didn't remind her of him. Nae, this Rurik was almost sweet, gentle, fun. This wasn't the man who demanded she grovel, or the boy who teased her mercilessly as a child.

Her breathing deepened. Would it be so bad to explore the scars on his body? He might think he was punishing her, but it would give her ample time to explore his naked form. She did want to see him naked. Her fingers kneaded against his shoulders and she wished she could remove the shirt off his muscular chest. Every inch of him was solid and firm, just as a warrior commander should be. The breeze around them stirred with the wings of Rurik and his men, but the commander's wings moved with such light grace that she felt as if she were floating on air.

When he shifted, his body would become compact as his shape molded into the form of a true falcon. She'd seen the men shift in the past, for they often entered the palace and left it in such a way. It allowed them to fly faster and more efficiently over long distances. But she'd never seen a naked pure blood before. When they shifted, the fibers from their clothing were absorbed into the body so they'd have clothes when they un-shifted.

Ari held him tighter, very aware of how her breasts rubbed against him. Her nipples ached for his attention and moisture gathered within her thighs, readying her body for his claim. The feelings felt too wonderful to fight, though she knew she should grasp onto whatever dignity she could.

"I'm curious," he repeated. Ari had no idea how much time had passed since he'd last spoke.

"Yea?" she answered.

"What are your powers, my queen?" he asked. "Word was spread that you got them, but none have seen what they are besides a select few."

Ari laughed, but didn't answer him. "Don't you worry. They are great."

"Show me," he said.

"Nae," she answered, not wanting to take her mind off the feel of him pressed against her. She just wanted to enjoy the moment. "I just want to dance."

"Then tell me what they are," he said.

"I can control water." It was an oversimplification of all she could do, but she didn't want to get into all the little nuances of her gift. She could snake it through a room, or make it dance, or create a wall that never fell. She could call upon the ocean to give her its jewels if she wanted—though she never would because it would take jobs away from some of the sailors.

"Will you show me later?" he asked.

"Perhaps." She lifted her head. "If you beg me to."

"How soon you forget, but it is you who must beg me." As if to punctuate his meaning, he adjusted his hips, letting her feel the full length of his erection. He was as aroused as she. Ari tried to wiggle away from the prominent erection, but being as they were in the air, there was no place for her to go but down. "Are you ready to retire, my feather?"

"Not with you," she quipped, trying to think straight, trying to remind herself that she disliked him.

Rurik frowned, his wings working furiously as he turned them around in faster circles.

"Hold," she protested. "Please, you're making me dizzy."

Suddenly, he stopped spinning. Before she could catch her breath, he beat his wings hard against the air, sending them speeding over the hall toward the entrance to her princess chambers.

Chapter Five

"You didn't mind my touch earlier."

Ari blinked, surprised at his abrupt words as he set her down on the mattress of the mating bed. She'd barely had time to part the water to let them through without getting wet, as they sped into the chambers. Looking down over the edge, she knew she couldn't easily get down without help. Her belongings had already been moved during the coronation and the room seemed empty.

"Whose idiotic idea was the high bed anyway?" she mumbled.

"When the pure bloods ruled, they were not an issue," he said. "They were to protect the royal family against invaders."

"For a warrior, you're pretty smart," she said.

"You know, feather, that might be the first compliment I've ever gotten from you." He reached for her, touching her face in a gentle caress.

Ari's head was a little fuzzy from the drinking and dancing. Already her flesh stung with the pleasure of his touch. She wanted him. There was no denying it. The bed reminded her of how they'd come together, in the dark, his hands pinning her down. She wanted to explore him, to see him, to watch his face as he entered her body.

Slowly, she reached for his waist and gently set to work on the laces. Tugging on them, she pulled them free, slowly revealing his stomach and chest. The backs of her hands glided over his taut flesh. Once she'd finished, she crawled to his back and set to work on the laces beneath his wings.

Rurik pulled the shirt over his head and tossed it aside, only to sit back on his knees. Ari stared at his dark, beautiful wings. They protruded out of his back, held to the side by strong muscles. Running her hands over the soft feathers, she shivered. Then, finding the tanned flesh of his back, she touched a long scar that ran down along his spine. He'd wanted her to bathe him and she did, leaning forward to lick the scar as she dragged her mouth over him. Rurik tensed, his wings spreading wider as her mouth neared the back of his neck. Smaller scars puckered his skin and she sprinkled hot, wet kisses over them.

She called the water from the wall, urging a tiny strand to form and heat so it would be warm. Like a liquid snake it slithered through the air. Rurik gasped as she controlled it easily with her mind, making it glance over his chest to where she couldn't see. It didn't matter. If she wanted it to touch his nipples, it would, such was her power over it.

When she'd made her way kissing and licking his back and arms, she slowly moved to stand before him. The water had left small trails over his chest. She urged the water to form a hand. With it, she cupped his face and bid him to stand before her. He did and she instantly leaned in to kiss his chest, teasing the scar she found with her tongue. The water trail held still as she lightly sucked a hard, wet nipple between her puckered lips.

Rurik's hands found her arms and he began pulling at her gown to undress her. Her shoes were gone, but she didn't remember taking them off. She pulled back only long enough to lift the gown over her head and toss it aside. Her long hair tickled her back as she pressed her body against his. The heat of him instantly made her nipples into hard beacons. She moaned, wiggling her hips as his hands glided over her naked ass. He pulled her cheeks, spreading her from behind ever so slightly as he massaged in hard, perfect circles.

Trembling, she reached for his cock, stroking it several times through his tight breeches. It wasn't enough. She needed to feel the turgid flesh in her palms. Eagerly she tugged at his waistband. Rurik kicked off his boots, before helping her push his pants down from his hips. Soon he was standing gloriously naked before her, his cock thick and long and ready.

Moaning, she kneeled, kissing each and every scar she saw, bathing them with her tongue. His sinewy flesh was salty-sweet and so very addictive. She ran her hands over his tight ass, squeezing and caressing every hot, hard inch of it before moving over his large thighs.

She drew the water snake forward, heating it before urging the liquid to wrap around his cock. It shaped over him like a cocoon, ringing around his shaft and balls. Rurik gasped, thrusting lightly in the air. It was a gorgeous sight, seeing his beautiful body straining with passion. She made the water rush around him, fast and vibrating. Ari's breath deepened at the erotic show and she urged the water back against the sensitive flesh between his thighs, buried behind his balls. She'd used water for pleasuring herself many times, urging it between her thighs. Hot moisture gathered in her slick folds, both from her body and the water. The liquid did not enter her, but instead vibrated and rushed over her clit in waves.

Grabbing his hips, she let the water part over his cock to make way for her mouth. She concentrated the liquid on her body and his balls, as she licked the thick tip of him.

"Ah-ah," he gasped, as she sucked him between her lips.

Since he was wet from the water his cock slid easily into her mouth. Her nipples ached for attention and she made the water caress her there as well. The more aroused she became the harder and faster she sucked him, rolling her tongue over his thick shaft, trying to fit him deep.

She moaned, reaching to grab his wet balls in her hand through the vibrating water. Rurik's fingers buried themselves in her hair and he jerked his seed hard into her mouth. She drank him down, sucking on him for more.

With a groan, he pulled her off. The water retracted back toward the wall, all except the stream along her clit. She closed her eyes, reaching for her own breasts.

"Let me," he said, breathlessly. Rurik had her on her back before she could stop the water from behind. It squished against the bed, wetting the sheets. She let go, only to discover how much better his mouth felt against her pussy. Warm hands cupped her chest, playing with her nipples. "I love your breasts."

Keeping one hand on her chest, he drew the other to her sex. His mouth did wonderful things to her clit as he audibly drank her cream. Suddenly, a thick finger thrust up into her and she tensed in pleasure as Rurik took her with his hand and mouth. He knew just how to touch her and it wasn't long before she was coming, crying out his name and begging him not to stop what he was doing. When the tremors subsided, Rurik collapsed alongside her trembling body.

ಬಂ

Ari wasn't sure when it happened, but somehow she'd fallen into a blissful sleep. When she awoke, it was to find Rurik beside her, his body aroused and pressed along her back. He was kissing her neck and ear.

"I want to be inside you," he whispered. "I want to feel the tight silk of your sex wrapped around me."

She opened her mouth to speak, but suddenly a shout from below stopped her.

"My queen, my king!"

Ari reached around for something to hide her body with, automatically forcing the water arch down so it didn't reflect her body to whoever was below.

"Ari?" the person called again and she realized it was Vara.

"Vara?" Ari asked, leaning over the side. She must've left the door open in Rurik's flight to get her into his bed.

"Ari, it's Lord Cyril. He says he found a way to end your mating to a pure blood. He's here with his son, trying to lay claim to the throne."

Rurik tensed behind her. Ari blinked, suddenly feeling sick to her stomach. She looked at her mate, her heart squeezing in her chest at the idea of losing him. But what would he choose? He was a warrior. Could he be happy in a queendom at her side? Or did he long for the open air and freedom of being a commander with his men? Would he choose her? Would he leave her if he had the choice?

"Rurik," she whispered, not knowing what else to say. Did she confess to him, let him know how she felt, that she wanted him, had always wanted him?

"Duty calls, my queen," he said, his words clipped. Then, louder, he yelled, "We'll be right down. Please wait outside."

"Yea, king," Vara answered respectfully.

Not knowing what to do, Ari looked around. Weakly, she said, "My dress."

He had his breeches already pulled on and was working on his boots. "I'll fly us down. Come here."

Ari wrapped her arms around his neck at his bidding and he glided them toward the floor.

"One day and already someone challenges the throne," he said wryly as he set her down.

Ari wanted to say something to him, wanted to ask him if he could possibly be happy as her king, but the words wouldn't come. She opened her mouth, but she felt like a young, tongue-tied girl and all the insecurities that came with such an age rushed over her.

"Did you want to say something?" His eyes narrowed. He looked like the hunter. Would the hunter be happy out of the hunt, or would he resent her for keeping him?

She knew her answer. A man like Rurik wouldn't want to be caged, even if the bars were gilded. She'd felt the freedom of his arms, but knew that was only a dance, one moment out of a lifetime of serving her people. She looked at his wings, knowing they'd only remind them both of what he had to give up against his will.

"You're free," she whispered, leaning to pick up her undergown. She slipped it over her head, trembling.

"What are you saying?"

"You're free, Rurik. This is your chance to get out of this. No repercussions will come of it. In fact, Lord Viceious will be stepping down soon as Supreme General. The job will be yours if you want it. As

Commander of the Fifth, you and your men have more than earned the honor. None will protest."

"You mean you'll be free," he said, a severe frown crossing his face.

"The life of a queen is hardly freeing." She pulled her gown over her head, before working her hair out of the back.

Walking to the water wall, she looked at her reflection. Her cheeks were flushed with sleep and her hair was a mess. Running her fingers through the locks, she sighed. It was no use. She needed a brush and her belongings were elsewhere in the palace. Regardless, she did the best she could with it before turning back to him.

"Your motives in this are hardly pure. You wish to buy me off with your offer of Supreme General, don't you?"

Ari swallowed nervously, avoiding his eyes. It wasn't a complete lie, though she wouldn't have used the phrase "buy him off". True, as Supreme General he would come to the palace and be her liaison to the troops. The offer was selfish of her. She wanted him close. Now that their bodies had joined, she knew she needed more of him. If it was decided that she remain unmarried or even in the unlikely occurrence that she took another husband, she knew in her heart that she'd take Rurik back into her bed—scandal or not.

"You haven't changed, have you? You're still the spoiled little princess who is too good for us soldiers." His wings stretched, his whole form tense with anger.

"What?" she gasped, ready to defend herself.

"Don't bother, my queen." The words were tight. "You've made your point." Then, stepping closer, he growled, "But just remember, this pure blood's hands were all over your body and you begged for me to touch you."

Ari blinked in confusion. Why would she ever want to deny it?

Rurik's body shifted. His eyes narrowed and his nose and mouth molded into a beak. Feathers sprouted over his body and his wings beat against the air. Soon he hovered in the air before her, his body compacted into a large bird of prey. With a fierce speed, he turned and flew out of the chambers toward the hall. She was still staring after him, long after he was gone.

ℰℭℬ

Rurik was livid. Did their time together mean nothing? Was she so ready to throw him back at the first chance that presented itself? Oh, and offering him the position of Supreme General. That was a nice touch. It was the highest honor for a man like him. Or, it had been until he'd become king.

Coming to the hall, he instantly saw Lord Cyril and his simpering son, Lynus. It was no secret that Ari spent time with the young man. He hadn't wanted to listen to rumors, but her name was spoken and he couldn't help but hear whatever was said about her.

Swooping past the nobleman's head, he glided up toward the throne. He didn't bother to shift as he perched on the back of the high chair. It was early in the morning and he realized they'd slept all night in each other's arms. What was odd was he never lost track of time like that. Ari just did something to him. She always had.

If she would just want him as he wanted her. If she would but ask him, he'd lay down his life. But she didn't seem to want his heart or his life. Nae, but she'd wanted his sex badly enough. It was a bittersweet victory.

The former king was seated close to Lord Cyril. The royal librarian was with them, leaning over an old, weathered piece of parchment. Rurik turned his head, listening to them speak. Their tones were low, but he could make out their words easily enough.

"See, there, it says 'in a time that the deeds of the pure bloods can be forgiven,'" Cyril said. "Well, that's simple. I for one don't forgive them. And, if a noble house cannot forgive the deeds, then surely there are others who feel the same."

"It doesn't specifically say 'forgiven by the house of Cyril of Karvof,'" the old king argued. If he'd been able to, Rurik would've smiled. The old king had always shown him favor, even as a child. He'd taken him under his wing, so to speak, and taught him to be a man. "I think Commander Rurik to be a fine choice. Besides, the magic of the Chalice should not be challenged."

"Should not, not cannot," Cyril argued. "I say it's been tampered with. Something was wrong with the magic. The old wizard was sick. There has to be an explanation."

"And let me guess," the old king mused. "You propose we set aside this decision for what? To pave the way for your son Lynus?"

"Queen Ari had shown great favor for my son and Lynus would make a fine king." Cyril didn't miss a beat. "He's noble of birth and temperament. He's politically minded. He has already met with many of the dignitaries that come to the planet."

"And I say Rurik can meet those dignitaries and whatever graces you think him to be lacking can be learned." The old king shook his head.

"Forgive me, old highness," Cyril sneered, "but the decision and translation of these scrolls are no longer yours. They are the queen's. We'll see who she picks—some barbaric commander or my son, a true king."

Rurik squawked in anger at the slight. Diving down from his post, he swiped past Lord Cyril's head and grabbed a talon full of his hair. With a mighty pull, he yanked it out and flew out of reach.

The old king laughed. "I think someone doesn't like being called barbaric, Cyril."

Cyril growled in outrage, rubbing his head. "My point exactly. Barbaric!"

Chapter Six

"What is this?" Ari appeared, her voice calmly coming over the barren hall. "What reason have you to interrupt my morning, and so early at that?"

Even disheveled, she kept her chin up, doing her best to look regal.

Seventy-five percent of being royalty was in the attitude. Walking slowly, as if she hadn't a care in the world, she made her way up to her throne. She'd found her crown on the floor along with Rurik's. They must have lost them the night before in his wild flight toward the bed, but she hadn't realized it until she found them in the hall.

As she came up the circular stairs, her eyes landed on the falcon perched on the back of the king's chair. She shivered, automatically knowing it was Rurik. She would've recognized those eyes anywhere, shifted or not.

"My queen," Cyril said, bowing. His son was behind him and they were joined by her father and Gryger, the librarian.

"Lord Cyril," she said, nodding at him to speak. She stared down her nose at him. Inside, she shook violently. She didn't want to let Rurik out of their mating, but he'd left too fast and she hadn't had time to ask him what he wanted.

"May I be blunt?" Cyril asked.

Ari nodded. "Please, do."

"Though a great soldier, Commander Rurik is hardly a man fit to be king. He's a pure blood, and as we all know and accept, that comes with a certain amount of," Cyril paused, rubbing his head, "hot-blooded temperament."

"Yea," Ari agreed. Her stomach tensed. That's one of the things she liked about him—his hot-bloodedness. Her thighs tingled and moisture gathered in her sex as she thought of just how wild he could be. Damn Lord Cyril for interrupting what had promised to be a very enjoyable morning! A little harshly, she demanded, "And?"

"It is my feeling that we don't have to accept the Chalice's decision. I have proof," he pulled a folded parchment from his jacket and held it up, "that the Chalice's magic has been overturned in the past and a marriage dissolved to the agreement of both parties."

"Give me that," Gryger demanded. The normally mild-mannered librarian unfolded the parchment and began reading to himself. "But, this is your great-great-grandfather's..."

"Yea, it is, but it proves that marriages can still be dissolved happily," Cyril interrupted.

"I know this case. The wife died within the year," Gryger said. "The dissolvement wasn't recognized by all."

"Completely unrelated. She was happy before she died." Cyril took the parchment back and stuck it into his pocket.

"The king—" Cyril began.

"Gentlemen, I do not have patience for this," Ari said. "Your point please, Lord Cyril."

Looking pleased with himself, he said, "I propose you dissolve your marriage to Commander Rurik by royal decree and choose for yourself a proper husband of noble birth."

Ari looked at her father. "Are you aware, Lord Cyril, that my father was a farmer and not of noble birth when the Chalice chose him for my mother?"

"What? I..." Cyril looked around, stunned.

"And you propose to insult my father?" she asked.

"Nae, nae," Cyril insisted. "I meant no disrespect to the old king."

"Lord Cyril," Ari stood.

"Yea?"

"Leave," Ari commanded.

"Excuse me?" The nobleman looked around the empty hall.

Ari felt a stirring by her side and paused to see Rurik standing beside her. His clothing looked impossibly perfect and she assumed that was partly due to the shifting.

"I don't want you..." she started to speak, hesitating before looking up into Rurik's eyes. When he was in falcon form it had been easier for her to ignore that he was there, right beside her as she tried to say what she needed to. But now, seeing him, she knew what she had to say was for her mate's ears, not Lord Cyril's. She didn't care about Cyril or his politics. She didn't want Lynus for a mate. She only wanted Rurik and it was time she told him, flat out, what she felt. If he rejected her, then at least she would know she tried. He looked away. Her heart beat wildly. She had to say it. "I don't want you to leave, Rurik."

His hot gaze turned back to hers, his eyes narrow slits as he studied her. "What did you say?"

"I don't want you to leave me. Please, don't leave me to rule alone," she whispered, stepping closer to him. "I want... I want y..."

"Ari?" He started to lift his hand. It hovered by her cheek before falling away, not touching her.

"I want you to be king, I mean my king. I want you to be my king. I've tried, but I can't think of a single thing to entice you into wanting the job. It's not battles and I know you wanted to be in battle, but... Stay anyway. Rule with me." Ari's whole body trembled and she wasn't sure whether to laugh or cry. Why didn't he speak? She so wanted him to speak and yet at the same time she was terrified by what he might say. "Bring blood to the throne."

"You wish for blood?" He laughed softly, a small smile curling the side of his mouth for a brief second, so brief she wondered if it was just hopeful wishing on her part.

"Nae, yea, I mean your blood, pure blood. I mean," she took a deep breath, "love me."

He took a step closer, tilting his head to the side. "Did you just say...?"

She nodded. "Yea. Love me, Rurik."

"As my queen?" he asked, his expression guarded as if he was purposefully misunderstanding her.

"As my mate," she said, only to backtrack. "Unless... Yea, as a queen."

Finally, he touched her and she felt her entire being freeze in wonder at his touch. Leaning forward, he shook his head. Her heart dropped. "Foolish little feather, don't you know? I've loved you since we were children."

Ari gasped. "You're just saying that. You could barely stand me as a child."

"Then why did I write that note for you?"

"You? That note was from you?" She gasped in surprise. "But, you said..."

"I remember what I said, but you laughed at it. What else could I do?" His fingers ran over her cheek. "Why do you wish for me to love you, Ari? You have people to love you as a queen. I need to hear you say it."

"Because I love you, Rurik. I always have. I'm sorry I laughed at your note. I was stupid, nervous, a young stupid nervous girl and I—"

His crushing lips cut her off as he seared her mouth with his, delving his tongue to conquer and explore her depths. Ari moaned, grabbing onto his arms for support as her knees buckled beneath her.

"Ah, Ari?"

She ignored the voice.

"Ari?"

Again, she ignored it. Rurik's kiss felt so right. Her body stirred to his.

"Daughter!" her father yelled, finally getting her attention. She blinked, turning to look at him in stunned surprise. "You want to finish..." He motioned to a red-faced Lord Cyril.

"I was finished," Ari glared down at the man.

"But..." Lord Cyril stared at her, his mouth working but no sound coming out.

"I said get out," Ari ordered.

"You heard my queen," Rurik barked. Instantly the man rushed from the hall.

Ari laughed. "I should be upset that he didn't listen to me when I commanded it."

"Don't worry," Rurik said. "I'll teach you to scare people."

"Mm." She wrinkled her nose before leaning forward for his kisses once more. Rurik loved her. The knowledge poured over her, giving her more pleasure than she ever dreamt possible. "No need. You can scare them for me."

He stepped forward, walking her with him toward the edge, but she wasn't scared. Looking deep into his eyes, she trusted him with more than her life. She trusted him with her heart.

"I love you," she said. "I've wanted to say that for a long time."

"I love you," he answered, leaning as if to kiss her.

She pulled back. "Fly us to our royal chambers this time, okay?"

He nodded, laughing softly as he turned directions and walked her the other way.

"Come on, Gryger," her father said. "Let's leave these two alone."

"Where would you like to go, highness?"

"Old highness," the old king corrected. "I'm thinking to the country. There has to be a woman or two out there that doesn't know I was king."

Ari giggled, not taking her eyes off Rurik. He leapt, hooking a leg around hers to hold her close as he carried her through the air toward their new room.

Rurik landed by a low canopied bed. She smiled, glad that it was closer to the floor than the mating platform had been in her old chambers. Paintings of Falconian men hovering above their women as they took to the sky decorated the top panels of the room. The deep colors were brilliant in their rich tones. Dark wood from the black trees that grew in the nearby forest was used to carve the canopy and matching panels along the wall. Some of the panels would lead to secret rooms within the palace but she wasn't sure which ones. The wood was polished to a black gleam, reflecting the soft light that came from the high palace windows. An archway led to a similar dressing room.

The air smelled sweet and welcoming, having been scented by the palace servants. Soft material met her hands as he laid her down in the bed. The coverlet was new, as was the rest of the bedding.

"I'm sorry for all that was done between us," she said.

"As am I, but we were children." Rurik kissed the corner of her mouth and moaned softly. He ran his hand over her side to touch a breast through the material of her dress. "And you have grown into a fine woman, Ari."

She giggled in pleasure. "And you make a very fine figure of a king, Rurik."

He kissed her again, this time deep and long. His tongue edged along her lips, begging entrance into her mouth. She sighed, taking him in as his fingers explored her body. She wanted him and it wasn't long before she was aroused and wiggling for more.

"What about those women on your lap? Are you sorry for them?" Ari asked, breathing deeply. She closed her eyes as he pulled at her skirt.

"What women?" he groaned, kissing her neck.

"At the mating... Oh, that feels really nice." She parted her thighs, allowing his fingers access to her slick folds. His thumb pressed into her clit, rubbing in small circles.

"There are no other women but you, Ari," he said.

Ari laughed. "That's the perfect answer."

"It's also very true."

Rurik continued to kiss her neck as he worked his hand against her sex. Ari grabbed onto his shoulders, pulling at his shirt but unable to get it off.

"Undress for me," she ordered, eager to see and feel him once more.

He quickly obeyed. She watched him, squirming restlessly on the bed. As he reached for his pants, she hurriedly pulled at her own gown. Naked, she tossed the dress aside and lay back down. He was glorious, with his dark hair and eyes, his impressive wings spread out behind him. With a wickedly playful gleam in his eyes, he reached behind him and pulled out a feather. Angling it toward her, he grinned as he brought it to her leg. The light tickling caress made her jolt as it worked its way up her inner thigh. He stroked it over her sex to circle her breasts in tantalizingly flawless sweeps across the nipples.

She touched his naked thigh, loving the feel of his flesh on her palm. He was hot, firm yet smooth. Lids lowered over her eyes as she looked at him—strong muscles forming the perfect man. Ari fisted her hand over his shaft, stroking the hard length. Rurik dropped the feather on her chest and instantly drew his hand down to her pussy.

Ari licked her lips and wiggled lower on the bed. Opening her mouth, she angled it toward his cock. Rurik gasped as he got her meaning, but didn't hesitate as he came above her, straddling her head with his thighs. His thick shaft was close to her mouth and she eagerly drew it to her lips, darting her tongue out over the tip to lightly lick him.

With a small sound of pleasure escaping her, she spread her thighs wide. Rurik latched onto her clit, sucking vigorously as he made love to her with his mouth. His tight body flexed above her but he was careful not to smother her with his weight as he rocked his hips back and forth, urging her to take the tip more fully into her mouth.

She kissed him gently, twirling her tongue around the ridge, before sucking him deeper. His groans became louder. She pulled back, using her hands to guide him where she wanted him as she nibbled her teeth up and down the sides before latching onto him once more.

Her mind warred with itself, torn between the pleasure of his lips and concentrating on giving as good as she got. He was too large to take comfortably in her mouth, so she used her hands to help stroke the extra length.

Rurik jerked. Ari gasped as he flipped her over, taking her with him as he maneuvered onto his back. The position made it a little easier to breathe and move. He kept her flush to his mouth even as he rocked his hips up toward hers. It was empowering, giving and receiving gratification at the same time.

He grabbed her hips, moving her body against him. Rurik moaned, softly begging her to stop before he exploded in her mouth. Ari greedily refused to let up, wanting to taste all of him. Her lips rolled faster, sucking harder.

"Ari," he growled, pushing her hips up and away. She fell over to the side and he was over her before she could catch her breath. His tight body pressed her into the soft mattress.

Spreading her legs, he brought his cock to the apex of her thighs, nudging her open wider with his hips. Rurik closed his eyes and groaned as he thrust forward, burying his cock deep inside her in one confident push. She cried out at the tight fit, the sound joined by his muffled groans.

Rurik smoothed his face between her breasts, massaging both mounds enthusiastically as he began to rock back and forth inside her. He played with her nipples, as if fascinated by them, rubbing at the hard peaks only to take them deep into his sucking mouth.

Ari drew her legs up along his sides, allowing for deeper thrusts. It felt good, the way he moved his hips, working them along hers, thrusting within her as he continued to drown her breasts in kisses.

Rurik pulled back, leaning up on his hands as the pace quickened. He kept moving, hooking his arms beneath her legs to pull them over his shoulders. Closing his eyes tight, it was as if he was savoring each stroke of their flesh.

The man definitely knew how to move and each rhythmic push was punctuated by the graceful flap of his wings as he propelled himself forward.

"Yea, oh, yea," she moaned, arching up into him for more. "Just like that. Yea. Yea!"

Ari tensed, her body building into a climax. He didn't stop thrusting as he reached for the pearl hidden in her slick folds. Her body jerked, tensing on its own accord as she was taken over by the force of her release. Rurik's fingers continued to stimulate her, even as her clit became so sensitive she thought she'd explode if he kept touching her there.

He slowed his pace and she came down for the briefest of seconds, before he was building her right back up again. It hit her hard, just as good as the first. She tensed, crying out his name in pure ecstasy. "Rurik!"

Suddenly, he grunted, stiffening as he came deep inside her. Ari's body went numb and her limbs fell to the side. Rurik fell next to her, breathing as heavily as she. Her heart hammered in her chest. Weakly, she wrapped her arms around him, holding him close, liking the feel of his body next to hers. He was safe and she felt small and protected next to her commander mate.

"I can't feel my body," she whispered.

Rurik chuckled in manly satisfaction, running his hand lightly over her hip. As the back of his hand glanced near her sex, she jerked in sensitivity. "It feels just fine to me, my queen."

"Mm," she moaned. Even now her body tried to stir him to passion. "Are you going to regret living here at the palace, away from the battlefield?"

"I like the freedom of fighting," he admitted, "but I love you, Ari. Wherever you are, that is my place."

"But what if you come to regret palace life?"

"Then you'll have to make sure it stays interesting." He kissed her shoulder, as he rested his hand against the mound of her sex. Lightly, he wiggled his fingers, tapping them against her slit.

"I'm sure I can come up with something," she teased, mimicking his movements by moving her hand to rest along his inner thigh, right below his shaft. "I know the decision is officially mine, but I'd like to defer the placement of your men to you. I'd like for you to pick your successor."

His eyes met hers and he looked so proud she couldn't help but kiss him.

"Thank you," he said, nodding once.

"There is something I want you to do, since we're on the subject of soldiers," Ari said.

"What's that?"

"My cousin. I'd like for her to join the Fifth."

"Her?" Rurik repeated in obvious surprise.

"Vara, my cousin," Ari said.

"A woman in the Fifth? It hasn't been done in a long time."

"So? It's been a while since a pure blood has been on the throne. I think it's time we shook this planet up." Ari smiled.

"When you look at me like that, how can I refuse? It'll be my last standing order with the men. Vara will get her chance, but she'll have to prove herself just like any other soldier."

Ari nodded in pleasure. "Oh, she will. I've seen her fight."

"Now, enough talk of battles, unless you'd like to discuss this soldier right here." Rurik grabbed her hand and slid it up his thigh to his shaft. He kept his hand around hers, moving it up and down over the growing length. It hardened in her hand and he groaned in satisfaction.

"So many wasted years," she mused. "If only we hadn't been so stubborn. We might have come together sooner."

Rurik rolled onto his back, lifting her so she sat on his stomach. He rubbed her thighs. "Nothing could come of us before. I think fate knew that."

"Why's that? Why would fate deny us the last years?"

"I had to make myself worthy to be your king and you had to prove to yourself and your people that you could rule. If we would've gotten together back then, it would've made these long years harder to bear. Carrying the faint hope that we might some day be was hard enough. If I'd have known you'd be mine, I would've died from the agony of waiting."

She smiled as she leaned over to kiss him. "For a soldier, you've got a most romantic view of things. I like it."

"For a queen, you've got..." He stopped, grinning.

"What?" she laughed. "Can't think of anything?"

"...the most amazing breasts I've ever seen," he finished, pulling her forward so his face was buried between the large mounds. Taking them in hand, he smothered his face. "Mm, I *murphm memm. I murphm mu oo.*"

Ari laughed, understanding him perfectly. "I love you, too, Rurik. I love you, too."

About the Author

To learn more about Michelle M Pillow or her other titles, please visit her website at www.michellepillow.com. Send an email to Michelle at michelle_pillow@yahoo.com or join her Yahoo! Group to learn of upcoming and current releases!

http://groups.yahoo.com/group/michellempillow/join

GREAT cheap fUN

Discover eBooks!

THE FASTEST WAY TO GET THE HOTTEST NAMES

Get your favorite authors on your favorite reader, long before they're out in print! Ebooks from Samhain go wherever you go, and work with whatever you carry—Palm, PDF, Mobi, and more.

Samhain Publishing ltd

WWW.SAMHAINPUBLISHING.COM